TYING THE KNOT

A Marie Jenner Mystery

E.C. Bell

THE MARIE JENNER SERIES

Mom —
Hope the wait was worth it !

TYING
THE KNOT

A Marie Jenner
Mystery

E.C. Bell

E.C. Bell

TYCHE BOOKS LTD.

Tying the Knot
Copyright © 2021 E.C. Bell

Published by Tyche Books Ltd.
Calgary, Alberta, Canada
www.TycheBooks.com

Cover Design by Indigo Chick Designs
Interior Layout by Ryah Deines
Editorial by Rhonda Parrish

First Tyche Books Ltd Edition 2021
Print ISBN: 978-1-989407-25-7
Ebook ISBN: 978-1-989407-26-4

Author photograph: Ryan Parker
PK Photography

This book was funded in part by a grant from the Alberta Media Fund.

Government

To Mom and Margarita, and everyone else waiting for this book.
Sorry it took so long.
Blame the pandemic. I am.

JIMMY:
WHAT HAPPENS IN VEGAS
DIES IN VEGAS

MY LAST NIGHT in Vegas I won big, and I felt invincible.

I called Rita as soon as I settled in Room 214 and invited her over. She wasn't happy about me being at the Dunes, but eventually she agreed to help me celebrate.

The rest, as they say, was history.

Rita brought a bottle of champagne with her. Champagne wasn't really my thing, but she insisted. So I said, "What the hell," and she opened it. Then, we screwed.

Was it the best sex of my life? It was all right. It had been a long night, and I wasn't a kid anymore. But it was decent. Decent enough, anyhow.

After, I could hear her rustling around as I fell asleep. She was gathering her clothes, and I kept thinking I should say something to her. Tell her how great it had been. Maybe invite her to stay. Maybe invite her go to breakfast with me to the IHOP, like when we'd first met. But I couldn't move. As she opened the door, I tried to claw my way out of the darkness that seemed to have me by the throat. I must've made a noise, because she looked over her shoulder at me, silhouetted by the hallway light spilling through the open door.

"I'm sorry, Jimmy," she said. "I did like you. You have to know

1

that." And then she was gone, and the door slid shut. I still couldn't move, and before the darkness took me, I felt afraid. But it was nothing compared to how I felt when I woke up the next morning, dead.

GLADYS, THE HOUSEKEEPER who had cleaned the rooms in the Diamond of the Dunes Tower for as long as I'd been coming to the place, walked in and stared at my body, which had fallen half out of the bed.

I'd expected her to scream and throw her hands over her face, because she knew me from before, but she didn't. She stared for a long moment, then sighed and shuffled out of the room without touching a thing.

Then Victor Tupilo came into the room, and I shuddered when I saw him, because seeing him meant that something had gone horribly wrong and things had to be cleaned up.

The only thing horribly wrong in that room was me.

"Where are the cops?" I muttered.

Of course, he didn't answer. Just called someone, and said, "Room 214. Complete clean. Leave the body."

He listened for a moment, his face tight. "That's what I said," he snarled. "The body stays. I have enough to explain without Jimmy Motherfucking Lavall disappearing out of my hotel. Just get it done."

And then he left, because he wasn't one to get his hands dirty when there was a problem. He paid people for that.

They showed up and cleaned the place. Took the champagne and glasses off the side table and wiped everything down. Even changed the sheets on the bed before they tucked my body in, all nice and cosy. Wrapped everything up and disappeared.

Then the cops came. And the coroner. Lots of talking, and at the end of it all, they'd decided I was a heart attack before they packaged my body up and hustled it out. Then Gladys came back and cleaned the room, again. She cleaned that room from top to bottom, as if there was some way she could get the smell of me dying out of it. And then she was gone, and I was alone.

IN THE MONTHS that followed, people wandered in and out of the room, sleeping and burping and farting and screwing their way through their holidays in Sin City.

That was fun to watch for about a minute, and then I just wanted to be left alone. I didn't want to think about anything anymore. I just wanted to sit and stare out the window at the Vegas skyline and pretend I was still alive—that I was just waiting for Rita to come back so we could go down to the IHOP and talk about how we're going to spend the rest of our lives together.

That had been my plan when I'd called her that last night. She and I were going to celebrate and then have one last meal before we left town, so we could spend the rest of our lives together. Preferably somewhere warm. It wasn't going to be Edmonton. That was all I knew for sure.

That obviously hadn't happened, but I pretended it was going to. I waited for Rita to return so we could spend the rest of our lives together right until the moment Crystal Desmoines walked into the room and everything changed.

CRYSTAL WAS DOING research for a book about ghosts and had convinced someone downstairs to let her into the room just for a minute, to take some pictures. Gladys unlocked the door and then stood stoically waiting as Crystal pulled her old-fashioned camera from her sequined backpack. Apparently, this room had a few deaths attached to it. Two suicides, and me.

She looked at me, pop-eyed.

"Holy shit," I said. "You can see me, can't you?"

She hustled Gladys out and then asked who I was. I could see the disappointment on her face when I told her. It changed to something close to panic when I told her she had to help me get out of the hotel.

"No way," she said. "I'm not taking you anywhere. You're dead. You're going to stay put."

She turned to the door, and I realized she was going to leave. That was when I panicked and grabbed her by the arm.

"I'm not staying here," I said. "I have to find Rita, and you're going to help me."

I clung to her like a tick to a dog as she unsuccessfully tried to get free. I imagine we looked kind of funny, but there was nothing funny about my situation. I wasn't letting her leave. Not without me.

She finally gave up and stomped out of the room, and out of the hotel, with me in tow. I felt thin, stretched, as we left the hotel proper and the valet brought up a big white van with the words "Crystal's Ghost Tours" scrawled on the side in purple and pink. The air conditioner blew nothing but hot air and the stink of dirty feet as she squealed east on Flamingo Road and away from the Strip.

"You have to let me go sometime," she said.

"Not until you help me find Rita," I said.

"What if this Rita person isn't here anymore?" she said. "Lots of people move away, you know."

"I know," I said. "But she'll be here. She wouldn't leave. Not without me. We had a plan. We were going to live, you know, happily ever after."

"Hmm," she said, noncommittally. "Didn't you die last year?"

"Yep," I said.

"But you still think she'll be here, waiting for you," she continued.

"She wouldn't leave without me," I said, stubbornly. Stupidly.

"But you're dead," she said.

"I know!" I yelled. "She wouldn't leave!"

"All right, all right," she said, obviously trying to calm me down. "I'll help you find her. But first, I have to go home and give Rambo his pill."

"Rambo?" I asked.

"One of my cats," she said. "He has furballs something terrible. He needs a pill."

"*One* of your cats?" I asked. "How many do you have?"

"Right now? Twelve," she replied. "Miss Prissy Pants had a litter, so my apartment's pretty full. Hope you like cats."

I didn't answer, because I didn't like cats at all, but if I was going to find out what happened to Rita, it looked like I'd have to put up with them for a while, at least.

But Jesus. I'd attached myself to a cat lady.

IN THE DAYS that followed, Crystal was as good as her word. She searched for and found all the Rita Sullivans who lived in the Las Vegas area, and we visited them. All but one.

"I'll go back," she said, after we'd gone to the dingy little apartment house where the last Rita lived, but hadn't found anyone there. "Let's go home."

We'd settled into a strange sort of domesticity since she'd

rescued me from the Dunes. During the day she'd leave the television on for me and the cats. I got caught up on all things daytime television, which nearly drove me crazy, but the cats seemed to like it.

In the evenings, she came home, fed the cats, and then prepared for the ghost tours she ran. I went with her once, but didn't see any ghosts and soon tired of the whole business.

"It's the way I pay the bills, Jimmy," she said. "Sorry you don't like it."

"You're not trying hard enough to find Rita," I mumbled, staring out the window at the bright neon lights of the Strip glowing off in the distance. "I bet Jim could."

"Who is Jim?" Crystal asked.

"My nephew," I replied, reluctantly. "He worked with me, at home."

She blinked. "Where's home?"

When I told her, she dove to her computer, and in a few minutes, she had a website up.

"Is this it?" she asked.

I looked at the computer screen and gasped. It was the front door of my office. The frosted glass door with "Jimmy Lavall Detective Agency" etched into it. I'd paid a ton for that glass, back when I thought I was going to take over the world.

"Well, look at that," I said. "He kept the place open."

She pressed a button, the screen changed, and there was the phone number to my old office. Beneath it was another number for after office hours. Beneath that was a link to a website simply called "Marie Jenner."

"Don't call him," I said. "It won't do any good."

Crystal frowned at me. "Don't you think he'd want to know that your spirit is trapped here?"

"He won't care," I said, and shook my head. "He and I—we were on the outs for a long time. He will have moved on."

My guess was he had probably been relieved when I'd died. Things hadn't been good between us for a long time, and when I'd left for Vegas that last time, he hadn't even been speaking to me.

I hadn't been planning on going back to Edmonton, or to him. This trip was supposed to have been the last. I'd had plans, and none of them involved that small, cold city, or my nephew.

"Just let it go," I said, but she ignored me and pressed the "Marie Jenner" link on the website. When it opened, she whistled.

"You might be right about him not wanting to know that your spirit is trapped here," she said. "But I bet Marie Jenner will. It looks like your nephew found himself a psychic, too." She smiled crookedly, then clicked back to the page with the phone numbers, and picked up her cell.

"Time for your nephew to get involved," she said, and before I could stop her—as if I actually could—she'd dialled Jim's number.

I QUIT TALKING to her after that, but here's the thing. I never left her apartment. I waited for Jim to show up, because even if we had been on the outs, he was good at his job. Our job. And I thought that maybe, just maybe, he'd be able to do what Crystal couldn't.

Maybe he could locate Rita and find out why she never came back.

STAGE ONE

THE CON

MARIE:
OUR HOLIDAY AND WHAT CAME AFTER

THE WATER WAS cold, the night sky was dark, and I was afraid. I could hear James splashing around somewhere behind me and tried to turn, but the stupid wedding dress I was wearing was soaked with seawater, and with every move I made, it threatened to pull me under the waves.

"Where are you?" I grunted, fighting to keep my head above water. Something touched my arm. I screamed and flailed away from the shark or whatever it was. I was pretty sure I was doing everything wrong, but I couldn't stop myself. I was food for whatever was in the ocean with me, and this was what food acted like.

"James!" I screamed. "Something's got me! Help!"

"It's me," James said, next to me. "I'm here. Take my arm."

I turned, and my head briefly went underwater again. I came up choking and reached wildly for him. Acting like food again. Stupid, drowning food.

He took my arm and steadied me. "You have to get that dress off," he said. He sounded so matter-of-fact that, for a minute, I felt calm too. "Turn around."

I turned, thrashing my legs frantically to keep my head above water. I could feel him tugging at the back of the dress. Trying to undo those stupid little buttons that he didn't realize were fake.

"There's a zipper," I said. My teeth were chattering so hard I

9

could barely speak. "It's just a zipper."

"Thank God," he muttered, and fumbled with the zipper hidden beneath the myriad of teeny buttons. It seemed to take forever, but then I felt the dress loosen, and I was free. Well, mostly free. The straps clung to my shoulders, and I couldn't get them loose.

"Help," I said again, under the water again. Choking again, but I didn't have the strength to push my head up past the waves.

James tried to work the straps free, and I felt another choking wave of terror when they briefly pinned my arms to my sides. He wrenched at them, pulling me deeper under the water until finally, finally, my arms were free, and I was able to pull myself to the surface and gasp in air.

"Kick it off, if you can," he said. He was gasping nearly as hard as I was, and I started to fear not just for my own safety, but for his as well. So, I tried to comply. I really did, but I couldn't feel my feet anymore.

I fought the fear and the cold, and pulled at the dress, fighting the sodden material until finally, finally, I was able to kick free. I bobbed up and took another deep breath. And then, for the first time in what felt like forever, I felt like maybe I was going to live.

"You looked amazing in that dress," James said. "I kinda wished we could have taken it home."

"I'm glad it's gone," I said. "I just wish I'd been wearing more, underneath. I'm freezing."

"Give me your hand," James said.

I reached out and he grabbed my hand in his. It shook me that I could barely feel his fingers as they tightened around mine.

"We're going to float," he said. "On our backs. Together. Just until we get our strength back. That sound good to you?"

"Like otters," I mumbled, but pushed my head back and felt my feet float up until I was nearly horizontal. "Like otters, when they sleep."

"Sure," James said. "Sure, whatever. Just don't let go of my hand, all right?"

"Just like the otters," I mumbled again. I hooked my arm through his, and interlocked my fingers with his, and stared up at the sky. The sun was finally beginning to break over the horizon, and the waves and wreckage were painted with pink and gold from the sunrise.

"It's kind of pretty, isn't it?" I said.

"I guess," he replied.

We both jerked when we heard another explosion off to our left. Light and heat washed over me as I tried to pull myself vertical so I could see, but James grabbed me and held me close to him as waves caused by the explosion buffeted us.

"It was the yacht," he said. "My guess, the fuel finally caught."

"So they aren't going to save us," I said.

"They were never going to save us," James said gently. "They wanted us dead."

I saw a faint light floating toward us from the direction of the burning yacht, and sighed. "Uncle Jimmy's here."

"Aren't we ever going to get rid of him?" James asked.

"Guess he's still not ready to go," I replied. My teeth were chattering so hard I could barely understand my own words.

Through the cold of the water, I could feel something colder touching my shoulder. I knew it was James's dead uncle Jimmy.

"Nope, not ready yet," he said, pretty matter-of-factly for someone floating somewhere off the Californian coast next to the burning pieces of what had once been a really expensive yacht. "Gotta make sure you're both going to make it, first."

"Always thinking of us, aren't you, Jimmy," I muttered.

"Always," he said. "You know that."

"He says he's always thinking of us," I said.

James grunted out a humourless chuckle. "It would probably be safer for us if he didn't."

A random wave splashed over his face, and he choked, grabbing my arm convulsively and momentarily pulling me under. Then he broke the surface, took a breath, and relaxed, and I floated back to the surface beside him.

"You all right?" I asked.

"I'm all right," he replied, then shook his head. "I sure wish we hadn't decided to come to Vegas, though. Know what I mean?"

"I know exactly what you mean," I said.

Another explosion from the yacht, and more heat and light poured over us. The waves picked up again, and we clung to each other like—well, like two otters who were on the verge of drowning.

"This has been a really weird holiday," James said as we were buffeted by the waves.

"The weirdest," I replied.

"I'm with you," dead uncle Jimmy said. "And I'm dead, for Christ's sake."

He almost made me laugh. Almost. But I couldn't. Nothing was funny.

Nothing at all.

MARIE:
WE ARE GOING ON A HOLIDAY.
AN ACTUAL HOLIDAY

72 Hours Before . . .

THREE DAYS AFTER James Lavall received the phone call from Crystal Desmoines, a psychic in Las Vegas, we were there. In actual Las Vegas.

I thought Edmonton was hot in August, but it was nothing like the heat that slapped me across the face when we stepped out of the McMarran International Airport and took the shuttle to the Rental Car Centre to pick up our car. And it was only 9:30 in the morning.

As soon as we were in the car, we turned the air conditioning on full to keep from melting to a couple of puddles of goo.

"How hot do you think it is?" I gasped, pulling at the neck of my tee shirt in a vain effort to let anything resembling cool air touch my skin. All I wanted to do was change out of my jeans and into a pair of shorts. I hadn't packed enough shorts.

James looked down at the dash. "This says one hundred four," he said. "So, it's around forty degrees. Are you okay?"

"I'm fine," I said. "Just hot. And hungry. How long until we get to our hotel? Speaking of which, don't you think it's time you told me where we're staying?"

James had made all the arrangements for the trip. Told me not to worry about anything. He'd handle it all. And I'd been happy to let him do it. I'd had enough on my plate, trying to find out everything I could about Crystal Desmoines, the psychic who'd let us know that Jimmy Lavall's spirit had not left Las Vegas with his body when it had been shipped back to Edmonton for burial. Something had happened to hold his spirit to the place where he'd died. And Crystal Desmoines was the one who'd found him there.

She wasn't thrilled about it and wanted us to do something—anything—to make Jimmy leave. That was why we were there. To help Jimmy move on to the next plane of existence.

From my research, it looked like Crystal really was a psychic, or at the very least was sensitive enough to feel the spirits of the dead around her. And it looked like she had quite the little enterprise built around the dead. She ran ghost tours all over Vegas and had a storefront business where she read tea leaves and the like. And she was writing a book tentatively entitled *Ghosts I Have Known*. From what I'd researched, it looked like that book would be about a thousand pages long, because Vegas—and Clark County—had the highest death rate of any place in the United States, and had held that dubious honour for many years.

That had kind of taken the shine off the idea of going to Las Vegas for a little holiday, to be honest. I try to stay away from places where people had recently died, so I don't get all caught up in their afterlife drama, and it looked like that would be a very hard thing to do in Vegas.

But—and this is a big but—Las Vegas had always been on my bucket list. One of those places I wanted to see before I shuffled off to whatever afterlife there was waiting for me. So, I decided I just didn't care how many potential dead there were wandering around trying to figure out how to move on. I was going to go and see Sin City.

And now, I was.

James set the GPS for the Dunes Hotel, and I looked at him.

"We're going to stay at the hotel where your uncle died?" I asked. "Really?"

"Well, at first I thought about the Oasis," he said. "But I figured you wouldn't like that too much."

The Oasis Motel was a grungy little dive on Crystal's "Super

Supreme" ghost tour, and its only claim to fame was the fact that a couple of people had died in the same room. One of them had been a TV star once.

"You're hilarious," I said. "So, the Dunes it is."

I gawked out the window as we drove out of the airport on the Connection Road to East Tropicana Avenue. I could see the hotels of the Strip looming before us and tried to keep the loopy grin off my face. I was actually seeing Las Vegas!

"Are we going to see the sign?" I asked.

"The what?" The traffic was bad, and James really had to concentrate.

"That 'Welcome to Fabulous Las Vegas' sign," I said. "Are we going to see it?"

"Not yet," he replied. "We'll get there, though. Don't worry."

Then we were on the Strip. The actual Vegas Strip. I "oohed" and "aahed", snapping a flurry of blurry pictures with my phone.

He pulled into the Dunes Resort. It wasn't as flashy and fancy as some of the other hotels we'd driven past, but it was one of the original grand hotels in Vegas and definitely good enough. I snapped pictures furiously as we drove up to the 180-foot tall pylon sign, with the onion dome shape on the top of it, and "Dunes" scrawled across it in gold. "That won an award," I said. "Did I tell you?"

"No," James said.

"Yeah," I said. "I did a little research on it."

He laughed. "I knew that," he said.

Actually, I'd done a lot of research on it, because the Dunes had a seriously colourful history. It opened on May 23, 1955, with a serious Arabian Nights vibe, right from the beginning. It did all right and was expanded to a full resort, with a golf course and a huge swimming pool and everything. Then, it fell out of favour and began to lose money hand over fist. It looked like that was the end of the Dunes. In 1993, it was slated for demolition, and another hotel, the Bellagio, was supposed to be built on its spot.

The Bellagio was going to be even bigger and better than the Dunes, and the artist's rendering of the fountain that was going to stand at the entrance of the hotel looked like it would have been amazing. But funding for the Bellagio fell through, and all work stopped.

Then funding for the Dunes magically appeared, and the

massive renovations started, and the Dunes was once again a jewel in the crown that was the Vegas Strip.

And we were there.

He drove under the huge canopy that sheltered the entrance of the Dunes from the merciless Nevada sun. A fountain was set at the parking lot end of the canopy, and I took a few more pictures. It was beautiful.

I followed him out of the car, and even though we were in the shade of the canopy, the heat hit me hard. It was even hotter than it had been at the airport, if that was possible. I could smell flowers. Looked around, and to either side of the entrance were low bushes covered in tiny white flowers. Whatever they were, they smelled nice.

A Jeep covered in balloons with a "Just Married" sign duct-taped to the front grill pulled up behind us, and a young woman in a wildly poofy wedding dress jumped out, dragging her entourage behind her like a bouquet of flowers wilting in the heat. She smiled and pointed at the fountain.

"It's picture time!" she said, and posed for a second as though she expected me to start taking photographs.

"Congratulations," I said.

"Third time's the charm. Right?" She grinned up at the man who had been trying to convince the valets that the Jeep could be left right where they'd abandoned it, because they were only there for a minute. Really. Her newest husband, I suspected. He looked as wilted and tired as the rest of the entourage who had poured from the car. I was actually pretty impressed with the number of people who had been inside. It was like a wedding clown car.

"Hurry up," the bride said. "I want this done before it gets much hotter. Then, we're going on the roller coaster."

I mentally wished groom number three good luck, and turned to James.

"What now?"

"Let's get settled," he said. "And then, we'll go see Crystal."

Cool.

WE DROPPED THE rental car off with the valet and got the keys for our room on the sixth floor.

"Can you remember what room your uncle died in?" I asked as we waited in a small crowd at the bank of elevators. A couple of people glanced at us, looking fairly aghast, and I wished I hadn't said anything.

"Room 214," James replied. "According to Crystal."

The crowd around us backed away, and I guessed that people didn't want to hear about someone dying here. Even though it was the truth.

The elevator opened and two men walked out. They pushed past us like we weren't even there, and I glared at them, trying to think of a truly cutting remark to make. But I stopped, because there was something familiar about one of the guys. At least I thought there was.

Seeing people out of context sometimes made it very hard to connect the dots, memory-wise, but I was certain I'd seen him somewhere before. Not recently, but when I opened my mouth to say something to them, James gently placed his hand on my arm like he could read my mind.

"Not now," he said.

So I shut my mouth and watched the men walk past. They were dressed in suits, and I blinked when I realized I could see the outline of a gun under the armpit of one of them.

Who the heck were these guys?

"Do we know them?" I asked as James and I stepped into the elevator.

"Not now," he said again, and pressed the button to close the doors. And as they slid closed, I saw the guy I thought I recognized glance back at the elevator, and us.

He looked back. At us.

I turned to James. "Who was that?"

"That was Ric Svensen," James said, his voice like ice.

"Ric Svensen?" I said. I didn't recognize the name.

"Sylvia Worth told me his full name," James said. "You probably remember him as R."

It took me a minute to connect the dots, even after all that. Then it hit me. R worked for Ambrose Welch, a drug dealer, in Edmonton. "Are you sure?"

"I've never been more sure of anything in my life," he said.

"What's he doing here?" A stupid question, and I knew it.

"No clue. But I'm going to find out."

The thought of having to deal with Ambrose Welch's men again made my blood run cold. He was the closest thing to a sociopath I'd ever had to deal with, and even though he was still in jail awaiting trial, I had the feeling that his reach was long.

"We should stay as far away from those guys as we can," I said. "They're dangerous."

"We'll have to be careful then," James said, and pressed the button for the second floor.

"Be careful?" I squeaked. "Be careful? That doesn't sound like staying completely out of his way. Which is what we have to do. Right?"

"Don't worry," he said. "We won't do anything to attract his attention. Promise."

That still didn't sound like anything close to staying away from the guy. The door to the elevator opened and I followed James into the corridor. We didn't speak until we were in our room.

It was pretty darned fancy. A suite, more than a simple room, and we could see the Strip from the window.

"See?" James said. "I told you I'd get something nice."

I was still worried about the guy we'd seen on the main floor, but after I'd had a shower, I felt better. Las Vegas was big. Heck, the Dunes was big. We'd just have to avoid him and we'd be all right.

"Did you get hold of Crystal?" I asked James as I got dressed. "Where are we meeting her?"

"At her place," James said. "She's waiting for us there."

"And Jimmy's with her?" I asked.

"Yes." James's face closed. "I wonder what's holding him here."

I'd been wondering the same thing myself. It was funny, but in that mad dash to get ready for this trip, James and I hadn't really talked about his uncle. As a matter of fact, since we'd moved the last of Jimmy's belongings out of the ramshackle private investigator's office that James had inherited from his uncle and got the business running again, he hadn't spoken about his dead uncle much at all.

"Must be some unfinished business here," I said. "I mean, he came to Vegas a couple of times a year, didn't he? He must know people. Have connections. Did he ever talk to you about any of that?"

"No," James said flatly. "He never talked about Vegas at all."

"He must have told you something, James. Anything—any

information you'll be able to give me at all—will help me move him on. Please."

James shrugged "He'd been coming here forever. It was just a thing he did. You know?"

"I understand," I said. And, oddly, I did. My father would leave, sometimes for months at a time, and we never quizzed him about disappearing. Sometimes, it was better not to know.

But I needed information, if I was going to move his uncle on. And honestly? I was a bit nervous about meeting the man, even if he was dead. After all, he was going to be the first of James's relatives that I met, and that was kind of a big deal.

James hadn't told me much about his family, past the fact that his parents were dead and that he had no other relatives that he was close to. I hadn't pushed for his family history, because we'd had a busy year, what with all my dealing-with-the-dead drama. But still. He wouldn't talk about them at all.

I ran my brush through my damp hair and pulled it into a ponytail before it had time to curl. "Time for us to go," I said. "I can talk to your uncle, directly. He'll tell me what's holding him here."

"He was never very forthcoming," James replied, and stood. "So good luck with that."

Looked to me like not being forthcoming ran in the family. But I didn't say that. I didn't say anything.

We left the hotel without incident—meaning we didn't see Ric and his buddy—and after the valet brought the rental car to us, I watched James put Crystal Desmoines' address into the GPS.

"Here we go," he said, and then, we were on our way to meet Crystal and Jimmy.

Soon Jimmy and I would be face-to-dead-face, and even if James wasn't willing to tell me anything about his uncle, Dead Uncle Jimmy would tell me everything I needed to know. Then he'd move on quickly and quietly. And then, James and I would have our holiday in Sin City and it would all be wonderful.

That was the hope, anyhow.

JIMMY:
CLEANING UP THE CAT HOUSE TO
IMPRESS THE PSYCHIC

JAMES CALLED CRYSTAL at 10:30 in the morning, an ungodly time of the day as far as I was concerned, and when she hung up the phone, she flew into action.

"I wish you could help me clean this place," she groused as she shooed all the kittens into her bedroom in the back, and then frantically dusted everything in her living room in a vain effort to get rid of at least some of the cat hair.

"Well, that ain't going to happen," I said. "Ghost. Remember?"

"How could I forget?" she muttered.

She grabbed up all the *Bride* and *Wedding* magazines from the coffee table next to the cat-destroyed couch, and I hoped she'd put them all away, permanently. She spent so much time looking through those stupid magazines, like she thought a cat lady who could see ghosts ever had a chance of getting married. It made me sad. It really did.

But all she did was arrange them by date and then plop them back on the coffee table.

"Think I should vacuum?" she asked.

"Do what you want," I replied. "They're not my guests."

She glared at me and then scooped Rambo and Miss Prissy Pants up off the couch and deposited them in her bedroom with the kittens. Soon, she was vacuuming the hell out of the living room, and it did look a bit better when she finally stopped.

She put away the vacuum and then opened the door to her bedroom, smiling like some kind of an idiot as the cats all stampeded back out into the living room and immediately started depositing cat hair everywhere.

"You should probably leave all those things in the back," I said. "After all, aren't you trying to impress this Marie chick?"

She glared at me again. "She's the first real psychic I've ever met," she said. "I just want everything to look good. Why do you have such a problem with that?"

"I didn't want either of them here," I said shortly. "All you had to do was—"

"Find Rita," she snapped. "I know. I tried, Jimmy. You know I tried."

"Yeah, I know," I said. "But—"

"But nothing," she said. "You're going to work with Marie Jenner now. And your nephew. And I'm going to get back to my life."

She pointedly turned away from me and walked into the kitchen.

"You think they'll want sweet tea?" she called. "And maybe some cookies?" Before I could answer, she ran back into the living room, looking distraught.

"Do you think I should make cookies?" she asked. "You know, before they get here?"

"I think this place will be about a thousand degrees if you do that," I said. "So no, don't make cookies. Sweet tea will be enough."

"You're probably right," she said and smiled. Then she was back in the kitchen, rattling pots and pans in preparation for the arrival of my nephew, who I never thought I'd see again, and his business partner, Marie Jenner.

"I'll be in my office," I said, and headed for Crystal's bathroom, the only room in her apartment that wasn't continually overrun by cats. "Call me when you need me."

"Will do!" she carolled from the kitchen. "This is going to be so much fun!"

My nephew, and another psychic. Yeah. This was going to be tons of fun.

MARIE:
MEETING DEAD UNCLE JIMMY

WHEN I RESEARCHED Crystal Desmoines and found out she was running a booming little psychic business in Vegas, I expected to find her living in a nice house in the suburbs or something. But that was not where the GPS took us.

James pulled the vehicle into the parking lot of what looked like a rent-by-the-hour motel. We parked beside a swimming pool covered in algae blooms, with a couple of people asleep on deck chairs by it. It looked like they'd slept there all night.

"Are you sure this is the right place?" I asked.

"What were you expecting?" he asked.

"Something better than this," I replied.

We walked up the cheap carpet-covered stairs to the second floor and searched for Crystal's apartment.

"Why would she live here?" I asked.

"Maybe it's all she can afford," James replied.

"I thought she'd be doing better than me," I said. "After all, this is Vegas."

"Not everybody hits it big here, Marie," James said. "Come on."

Even though I had been looking forward to meeting Crystal, I was happy to see that James had decided to take the lead. After all, with Crystal came Jimmy and I wasn't sure how I was going to handle finally meeting one of his relatives—even if he was

23

dead. I looked down at my tee shirt and shorts, and wished that I'd thought enough to change into a dress or something. I looked like crap.

We walked up the stairs and through a door to an open hallway that looked down on the back alley. Through the doors I could hear TVs and music blaring, and from somewhere toward the back, a child cried.

"This is depressing as hell," I said.

He didn't answer me, just walked the hallway, looking for 204. Found it, and stood, staring at the scarred wooden door for a long moment.

"Want me to knock?" I asked, hoping he'd say no.

"I got it," he said, and rapped on the door twice. Hard.

We could hear noises behind the door, but no one answered.

"It's James Lavall," he said, and knocked again. "We have an appointment."

More noise, and I realized we were hearing cats meowing. Sounded like lots of them, and then a woman's voice.

"Move your little fuzzy asses," the voice said. "I gotta get the door."

"She's a cat woman," I whispered.

"Great," James said. Then the door burst open, and Crystal Desmoines stood, framed in the doorway.

She was about my age, I guessed, and small. She was dressed in a long skirt and a peasant blouse. She had a scarf wrapped around her head, and her dark hair spilled down her back. She smiled at both of us and then gasped.

"Grab him," she cried. "Dammit, grab him before he gets away!"

One of the cats had made a break for it and was loping down the hallway. James took off after it, with Crystal on his heels. I tried to blockade the door as the rest of the cats—mostly kittens— mewed and pushed to get out.

James made a grab for the cat who zigzagged away from him and then headed back the way he'd come. Crystal stepped out and neatly grabbed the big tabby as he tried to run by.

"Rambo," she said. "You know you're not supposed to be out here."

I half-expected the cat to fight for his freedom, but he simply wrapped his front paws around her neck and purred as she carried him back into the apartment. James followed, scooping up one of the kittens who'd managed to get past me.

"Sorry about that," Crystal said, and smiled. "He likes to pretend he belongs in the wild like his ancestors. He does not."

She snuggled the big tabby as she walked past me, pushing the rest of the kittens, who had almost managed to overrun me, back into the apartment.

"Hurry," she said. "Get in here and shut the door or they'll all escape."

I scurried through the door behind her. James followed and closed the door, then placed the kitten he'd been holding on the floor at his feet. The kitten scurried off to be with its siblings as Crystal set the big tabby on a table next to the closet. He jumped down and scuttled down the short hallway and disappeared. Finally, we were alone.

Crystal smiled at us. "I take it you are Jim," she said, and held out her hand to James.

"James," he replied. "My name is James." I noticed he did not take her proffered hand.

Her smile fell as she dropped her hand. Then she looked at me, and her smile returned. "You're Marie Jenner," she said. "Right?"

"Right," I said, and held out my hand.

She took it and shook it enthusiastically, until I was afraid she wasn't going to let it go. "I read about you," she said. "You're a little bit famous."

"Huh," I said, and pulled my hand from hers. "I didn't know that."

"Oh yeah," she said. "I saw the video. Amazing stuff."

She was talking about the video of me moving on a whole bunch of ghosts, on live TV. My fifteen minutes of fame.

"Yeah," I said. "Amazing."

"How did you make all those spirits move on, all at once?" she asked. "I can't even get one of them to get out of my space, for heaven's sake. And you moved a hundred—"

"One hundred and three, actually," I said. All right, maybe that was my ego talking, but moving on one hundred and three ghosts at the same time was kind of a big deal.

"That's incredible," she replied. Then she seemed to realize that we were all still crowded in the little entrance of her apartment.

"Sorry," she said, and walked past us, to a doorway on the right. "Come in. I imagine you want to talk to Jimmy."

James froze. "He's actually here?"

"Oh, he's definitely here," Crystal said. "Definitely."

I grabbed James's hand and pulled him with me into Crystal's living room. The room was crowded with a couch and three overstuffed chairs. All of them had at least one cat on them. A TV droned in the corner, but I didn't see a ghost anywhere.

"Where is he?" I asked.

"The bathroom," Crystal replied. "He's—nervous."

She pointed at a closed door crowded between two of the chairs on the far wall, then walked over to it, pounding on it as hard as James had knocked on her door moments before.

"Come on, Jimmy," she cried. "Your nephew is here. They're both here. Come out and talk to them, please."

"Not yet," came the muffled reply from behind the door. "Give me a minute, will you, woman?"

"He doesn't sound nervous," I muttered.

Crystal turned to us and shrugged. "He'll come out when he's ready," she said. "I have tea, if you like."

James shook his head. "We're here to see my uncle," he said. "So let's just get this show on the road, shall we?"

"You sound just like him," Crystal said, without smiling. "Isn't that cute?"

James didn't reply. Just walked to the bathroom door and pushed it. "We're here," he said as the door swung open. Then he looked at me.

"Can you see him?" he asked. "Is he really here?"

Jimmy the Dead walked out of the bathroom and stared at his nephew for a long moment. "I didn't think you'd show up," he said. "You always said you hated Vegas."

"Oh," I said. "Oh."

I don't know what I was expecting, but I never thought James's dead uncle would be in his underwear.

"What?" James asked.

"He's definitely here," I said.

"He's in his tighty-whities," Crystal tittered, and grinned at me. "You're embarrassed."

"Well," I said, looking anywhere but James's dead uncle. "I

thought—"

"I died in my sleep," Jimmy said, glaring at me. "At least I had underwear on, for Christ's sake." He turned to Crystal. "I thought she was some kind of expert."

"She is," Crystal replied. "She'll be able to help you. Right?" She turned to me, expectantly. "Right?"

"Right," I said.

I turned to James. "He died in bed," I said. "And—he doesn't have much on."

"Oh." James looked momentarily embarrassed. "Great way for you to meet my family, isn't it?"

"Well, he's dead," I said. "So, he doesn't really have that much control, wardrobe-wise."

I turned back to Dead Uncle Jimmy. "I'm Marie Jenner," I said. "I'm here to help you communicate with James, and then I'm going to help you move on to the next plane of existence. If you want."

"Move on to—what?" Jimmy asked, a sneer on his face. "If this is some life after death bullshit, I don't want to hear it." Then he frowned at me fiercely. "And don't roll your eyes at me, girl."

Oops. Hadn't realized I'd done that. I laughed, embarrassed. "Sorry."

"Tell him I want to talk to him," James stage-whispered.

"I think he knows," I said. "Just give me a second, all right, James?"

"James?" Jimmy said, and snorted. "When did he start calling himself James?"

"Let's focus," I said to Jimmy. "Just for a second. Please."

"All right," Jimmy said, and shrugged. "I guess I can do that."

"Focus?" James said at the same time, and then shook his head. "Sorry. I know the drill. I just can't believe he's here." He swallowed, hard, and I was afraid that he was going to cry. I'd only seen him cry once, and that was the day that he'd found out his uncle had died.

I didn't want to see that again.

"Just hold it together, James," I said. "I'll help you talk to him, but in a minute."

I turned back to Jimmy, who was staring at the agony on James's face. He swallowed, like he was choking up, too.

"I have a question for Jim," Dead Uncle Jimmy said.

I touched James's arm. "He has a question for you," I said, gently.

He sniffed and scrubbed his face with his hands. "What is it?"

"How's Bernadette?" Uncle Jimmy asked. "Please tell me you kept her."

I don't know what I'd been expecting Uncle Jimmy to ask, but it was definitely not that. "Bernadette?" I asked him. "Who's that?"

James answered before Jimmy could speak. "That was the name he used for the Volvo," he said.

Good grief. He hadn't seen his nephew in a year, and his first question was about the stupid car?

Then James shuddered. "It really *is* him, isn't it?"

"Of course, it's me," Jimmy said. "What? You can't believe what's right in front of you?"

"He can't see you," I said to Jimmy. "And just so you know, he kept the car. The car, the agency, the whole works. You'd be proud."

"I saw that," Jimmy said. "Crystal showed me the website. So, Jimmy Lavall's is still open for business."

"Yes, it is," I said. "It's making money and everything, isn't it, James?"

"Yeah," James said. "We're doing all right."

Uncle Jimmy looked at James for a second, then over at me. "He said 'we're'," he said. "So, you guys are business partners?"

"Sort of," I said. "I'm the receptionist."

"You're more than that," James said. "And you know it."

"Yeah," I said, and smiled at him. "I guess I am."

Dead Uncle Jimmy snorted. "So, not just work, huh?" he asked. "You two are together, aren't you? Like, together together?"

"He wants to know if we're dating," I said to James.

"Well, we are," James said, and put his arm around my waist. "So tell him."

"Now you know," I said to Jimmy, and smiled thinly. "You're the first of his family I've met."

Jimmy didn't smile back. "It's nice to meetcha."

"And it's nice to meet you," I replied. "Now why don't you tell us why you're here?"

"What do you mean, why I'm here," Jimmy said. "I died,

Crystal saved me, but now I'm stuck with her and her damned cats. Next stupid question."

I felt my oh-so-friendly smile snap off like I'd hit a light switch.

"What did he say?" James asked.

"He was rude," I said.

"To you?"

"Yes."

James snarled and looked around the room. "If you're not going to answer Marie's questions, I've got a few for you."

I shook my head, but neither the live nor the dead guy paid me any attention at all.

"Go ahead," Jimmy the Dead said. "Ask me your questions."

"Maybe you can wait with your questions until I know why—" I started, but James rode right over my words like I hadn't even spoken.

"What was your deal with Ambrose Welch?" he asked.

In a day filled to the brim with unexpected things, James had managed to surprise me with another. I glanced at Jimmy the Dead, and saw that he'd darkened to a grey smudge. Big reaction there.

"So, you know about Ambrose," he said.

"Why are you asking him about the drug dealer from Edmonton?" I asked.

"Because," James said, "my uncle was working with him. I just want to know what was going on."

"It's nothing to worry about," Jimmy the Dead said. "I just did a couple of jobs—"

"He said it was just a couple of jobs," I said.

"A couple of jobs?" James laughed raggedly. "How about fifteen in the two years before you died. Fifteen jobs, directly involved with Ambrose Welch. And you had me involved in a lot of them."

"All right, so I did some work for him," Jimmy the Dead said. "And you worked for me, so it follows that you worked for him too. But it was all above-board, Jim."

"He said it was all above-board," I said, and then frowned. "Why does he keep calling you Jim?"

"James," James said, and his voice had turned to ice. "Tell him I go by James now. And those jobs he did for Welch didn't look above-board at all."

"Well, they were legitimate," Jimmy the Dead said. His voice had taken on a nasty edge. "Just let it go, Jim. I wasn't doing anything illegal."

"He said he wasn't doing anything illegal," I said, then glanced at him. "James, you know this doesn't matter anymore."

"It matters to me," he said. "I need answers, Marie. Real answers."

"Well, he's getting nothing from me," Jimmy the Dead said gruffly. "I got nothing more to tell him about Ambrose Welch, or any other damned thing that was going on in Edmonton. You tell him that. Right now."

"I'm not telling him that," I said.

"What?" James said. "What did he say?"

"Nothing," I said, and glared at Jimmy the Dead. "He said nothing."

"But—" James started. I waved him to silence.

"Just give me a second, James. Please."

"Tell him there was nothing going on," Jimmy the Dead said. "Right now."

He'd dropped another lumen or two and was getting hard to see. He was lying through his teeth. "Just tell me the truth, Jimmy," I said.

Before Jimmy could answer, James jumped back into the conversation, with both angry feet.

"He's not going to tell me anything helpful, is he?" he said.

"He will," I replied. "Just let me talk to him. He'll come around." I swung my head in the ghost's direction. "Right? You'll tell him what he wants to know. Right?"

"I'm not telling that boy anything," Jimmy said. "In fact, it would probably be better if the two of you left. I'm happy here. Seriously."

"Generally, ghosts who are happy don't stick around," I said. "Happy equals moving on to the next plane of existence no fuss, no muss. Yet, here you are."

"I don't know what the hell you're talking about," Jimmy the Dead yelled. "I don't need him. And I don't need you. Why don't you both just get the hell out of here?"

Well, the conversation had taken a serious detour, and I wasn't sure how to get it back on track. I turned to James. "He thinks we should leave," I said. "He says he doesn't want us here.

That he's happy, right where he is."

"Well, you tell him to go screw himself," James said. "I need to know exactly what happened. Here and back home. He might be happy, but I'm not. Got that?"

Jimmy snarled and spat a gob of echo goo. It landed at James's feet, and one of the kittens ran over to play in it.

"I think he got it," I said.

"Good," James said. He turned and walked down the hallway and threw open the door. "I'm out of here," he said. "You deal with him."

"No!" Crystal cried. "No, you can't leave!" She turned to me. "He can't leave," she said plaintively. "Jimmy has to move on."

"Looks like that's not going to happen," Jimmy said. "He can get himself in a twist, now can't he? He's got to learn how to relax—"

I turned on Jimmy. "That's more than enough," I said. "Just shut up for a minute."

I was almost happy to see the shocked look on his face. My guess was, not too many people had told him to shut his mouth before.

Then, I looked at Crystal, who looked like she was about to burst into tears. "I'll go get him," I said.

"Thank you," she replied, and sniffled. "I can't do this much more. I just want to live my life. You know, I've only had one date since he moved in? Just one. A person can't live that way, with just a ghost and cats for company. You know?"

"I know," I replied. "I'll be back as quickly as I can."

I headed down the hallway to the open door, and heard Crystal scoop up kittens and call for Rambo as I walked through and slammed the door shut and scampered down the hallway to catch up with James.

JIMMY:
CRYSTAL, WE HAVE A PROBLEM

"WHAT THE HELL are you trying to prove?" Crystal yelled as soon as we were alone. "All you had to do was tell them about Rita. How you want to find Rita. Why didn't you do that?"

She was right, of course. But James was asking all those questions. Questions I didn't want to answer. I was dead, dammit! Why couldn't he have just left me alone. And the girl—Marie. Talking about me moving on, or whatever she'd said. I'd wanted to talk about exactly none of that.

"I don't know why you had to call him," I finally said. "I just wanted you to find Rita. That's all you had to do. Jim doesn't need to be here. You know that."

"That's not what you told me," she said. "Repeatedly."

Well, that was a little harsh. "You partied last night, didn't you?" I snapped. "You look hungover. Where'd you go?"

She didn't answer, and I glared at her. "You didn't go out partying, did you?" I felt an ugly spurt of anger, because I suspected that she had done just that.

"I didn't go out partying," she said. "Jesus, Jimmy, cut me some slack. I—I went out on a date."

"A date?" I asked, and frowned ferociously. "You didn't tell me. Why didn't you tell me?"

"Because it's none of your business, Jimmy." She sighed and shook her head. "I'm allowed to date, you know."

"I know," I muttered. She was starting to make me feel like crap, and I didn't handle that particular feeling very well.

"And you asked me to get your nephew down here," she continued. "Didn't you?"

"All I said was that he could probably find Rita," I yelled. "But hell, Crystal, we were doing okay. Weren't we? You probably could've figured out where she was on your own. Couldn't you?"

"No," she snapped. "He had to come here. You have to finally be done with this place. You need to leave, and I can't help you, Jimmy. You gotta know that."

She looked down at her chipped, black-painted nails. "Why won't you just answer him? You're dead, for heaven's sake. What's it going to hurt now?"

I blinked and turned away from her. If I told Jim even half of what was going on in Edmonton, he'd dig in and want to know everything. I couldn't let that happen. I couldn't.

"You're dead," she said gently. "You don't need to try to impress him, or me, or anyone else. You just need to go away. You've been here too long already. Maybe with Jim—"

"James," I said. "He said he wants to be called James."

"All right," she said, and sighed. "Talk to James. You don't have to answer his questions if you don't want to. Maybe you can say goodbye to him or something. Or at least tell him you're sorry—"

"I got nothing to be sorry about!" I yelled.

"You told me you made him leave his parents," she said. "You gotta feel sorry about that."

"You never met his parents," I said shortly. "I did the kid a favour."

"All right, so maybe not that," she continued. "But there were things. Things you did. Things you got him to do. You gotta feel sorry about some of that. Right?"

"I left him everything I owned," I muttered, "and he's making a real go of it, now. So it doesn't look like I hurt him. I don't think I have to apologize for that."

She sighed and shook her head. "So nothing you did made his life worse?"

For a second, I thought about him, in university. How I talked him into working for me one summer—and that summer turned into the fall, and then the winter, and for a while he tried to keep up with his studies until I finally convinced him to quit.

"You can always go back," I'd told him that cold November day. "When you get tired of hanging around with me."

He didn't go back, though. He'd stayed with me, through thick and thin. Even when I didn't let him know exactly what we were doing, and why. Even when we went for days without speaking to each other, near the end.

"I didn't make him do anything he didn't want to do," I said. "I got nothing to apologize for."

She stared at me for a long, cold moment. "All right," she finally said. "If that's what you think."

"That's what I think," I snapped. Then we sat in a silence that grew more uncomfortable by the moment.

"So, you going to tell me about this date last night?" I finally asked when I couldn't stand the quiet any longer. "Or do I have to guess?"

"You can't keep quiet for even five minutes, can you?" she replied. "If you must know, we went to the movies."

"Doesn't sound too exciting," I said, but inside, I was envious. I hadn't been to a movie in an age.

"It was nice," Crystal said.

"So, who's the guy?"

"His name is Roger, and he's just a guy. A nice guy who took me on a nice date."

"Is that right?" I said.

"That's right," she replied. "But before that, I went to Rita number three's apartment. One last time."

Rita number three. The last Rita in the phone book. The one Crystal hadn't been able to catch at home to this point.

"And?"

"What do you think?" she said. "Nobody answered the door. Again."

She scratched under the kerchief she was wearing and then adjusted it so it wasn't sitting quite so lopsided on her head. "I wish this wasn't part of the schtick," she muttered. "It's way too hot."

"So take it off," I said. "Nobody will care."

"I can't," she replied. "They expect the full Roma experience at the shop, and once I'm done here, I have to go there. But man, it's over a hundred degrees already."

She gave the kerchief one more tug, then stopped and looked at me. "You said that James was a good private eye, right?"

"Yeah," I said. "He is."

"So, what about this?" Crystal asked. "I'll ask him to look for Rita, like you want. You won't have to answer any of his questions, but please, can't we let him look for her? If he finds her, you won't have to stay here anymore. You can say your goodbyes, and then, well, you can go somewhere else. Doesn't that sound good?"

I thought about what she was suggesting.

"I guess," I finally said. "But you gotta stop him from asking any more questions about—well—anything else, because I'm not going to answer them. Do you think you can do that, at least?"

She sighed. "I'll do my best." She looked at her watch. "I just hope they get back quick. It's almost time for me to open up the shop."

Personally, I hoped that he and Marie got so lost they wouldn't ever find their way back, but all I did was nod.

If we both stuck to the plan, no one would have to get hurt. Especially me.

MARIE:
WHAT IS YOUR MAJOR
MALFUNCTION, JAMES?

JAMES WAS FAST when he was angry. By the time I got to the top of the stairs, he was standing by the algae-infested pool, glaring.

"James?" I called. I ran down the steps—well, I ran down a few of the steps until the heat sapped every bit of energy I had and I slowed down to just above a crawl. I walked up to the pool, then grimaced and put my hand over my mouth and nose. The pool smelled worse than it looked, if that was possible.

Of course, he didn't turn around.

"Jesus," I muttered, and grabbed him by the arm. "James, talk to me."

He finally turned and glared at me.

"What the hell are you doing?" I asked. I pulled my shirt away from my stomach and wished I wasn't sweating like an old man quite so much. "It's got to be over forty degrees out here, and the sun is frying me already. You trying to die?"

He shrugged. "It's not that bad," he said. "If you stick to the shade."

I looked around for the shade, but it was nonexistent, of course.

"We have to go back to Crystal's," I said. "And help your uncle move on. That's the game plan. You know that."

"What kind of game plan is that?" he asked. "I need to understand what he was doing working for Ambrose Welch. You can get that, can't you?"

"That guy is dangerous," I said.

"I know he's dangerous," James snapped. "And Uncle Jimmy was working for him. I have to understand what was going on. I have to. Don't I?"

"I guess so," I said, but I was pretty sure my tone didn't sound like I meant it.

"I have to know," he repeated. "And I'm going to make Uncle Jimmy tell me."

"You mean, *I'm* going to make him tell you," I said. "Isn't that what you mean?"

"Fine," he snapped. "So, you have to do the deed. Isn't this what you do?"

"James, you know as well as I do that I'm not supposed to be asking him questions like, 'Why the hell were you working with Ambrose Welch?' That won't help him move on, and that's the primary objective here, right?"

He glared at me. "So what, you're finally going to do what your mother told you?" he asked, fairly nastily, I thought.

My mother had the same gift as me, and before she died, she did everything in her power to teach me the right way to move on the spirits of the dead. As far as she was concerned, the way they died didn't matter. However, I tended to disagree. It seemed that how they died was just as important as how they lived.

"My mother doesn't have anything to do with this," I said. "That last ghost I dealt with convinced me that digging around in the past does no good at all."

"She was a little girl, and people wanted to know what happened to her," he snapped. "What was wrong with answering those questions?"

"Because it didn't help her move on!" I cried. "You know that. All she had to do was figure out what was holding her there. And it had nothing to do with her death. I'm guessing your uncle is the same. So, why can't we just leave the rest of it alone?"

He glared at me, his face stone.

"That might be enough for you," he said. "But it's not enough for me. He says he was a legitimate businessman back in Edmonton. Well, let him prove it, because nothing I've seen so far says that." He shook his head. "As far as I can tell, he was deep into Ambrose Welch's world, and that means he was dirty. If that's the truth, I want him to tell me that, to my face."

"You want him to break your heart?" I asked.

"He's already done that," he muttered. "I just want him to tell me the truth."

"All right," I sighed. "I'll get you the truth. If I can."

"Good," he said.

"Fine," I said. Which meant absolutely nothing was fine.

"Fine," he replied and I could tell by the look on his face that it meant exactly the same thing when he said it.

He headed back to Crystal's apartment at a trot, and damn him, I had to run to keep up. The only saving grace to any of this horrible situation was that we were going to get out of the merciless sun. At the very least, I could keep from burning to a crisp while James was having his heart torn out by his uncle.

Yeah. This was going to be great. I could hardly wait.

BACK IN CRYSTAL'S apartment, it looked like she was alone. And upset.

"I have to leave for the shop soon," she said. "And he has—demands."

"Demands?" I asked.

"Yeah," Crystal said. "I'm sorry."

I glanced at James, just to make sure he wasn't going to bolt again. "What are they?"

"He doesn't want to talk about Edmonton," she said.

"In other words, he isn't going to answer any of my questions," James snapped.

"That's about it," Crystal said. "There's a woman he's worried about. A Rita Sullivan. He wants to know where she is. That's she's all right. But that's all. I'm sorry."

"Well, he didn't say he wouldn't talk to me," I said. "Did he?"

"No," Crystal said. "He didn't."

"Where is he?" I asked.

"Back in his old hiding spot," she replied, pointing at the bathroom door. "He's all yours."

"I'll get him," I said to James. "I'll convince him to come out and talk to you. All right?"

"Yeah, whatever," James said, and walked into the living room

39

as I went up to the bathroom door and knocked twice.

"I'm coming in," I said, and opened the door.

Jimmy was standing in the bathtub with his back to me. "Did Crystal tell you I'm not talking to you about Ambrose Welch?" he muttered.

"She told us," I said. "She also said you're trying to find someone named Rita Sullivan."

"That's what I told her," Jimmy said.

"But nothing about Ambrose Welch," I continued. "Or Edmonton."

"That's right," he said.

"Why nothing about Edmonton?" I asked. "You spent most of your life there. And you were working for Ambrose Welch, you said that. So why won't you tell James what he wants to know?"

I knew better than to ask those questions and half expected him to fade away to nothing, or worse, get angry and start yelling. But he did neither. Just sighed, and turned, staring at me.

"I might have skated close to the edge a couple of times, but nothing too far over with Welch," he said. "But James knows the way the game's played. I don't get what he's so worked up about."

"He's honest," I said. "He doesn't work that way."

"Well then, he's never going to make it," he said, and shook his head. "What are you doing here, really? Besides trying to dig up dirt on me?"

"We came here to help you tie up whatever loose ends are holding you here so you can move on to the next plane of existence," I said. "Besides, it sounds like Crystal is getting tired of having you as a house guest. It's like you're haunting her." I smiled. "Are you? Haunting her?"

"She's haunting me," Jimmy said gruffly. "I didn't even want her to call Jim—James."

"I got that," I said, "but he's here now, and you're going to have to deal with him. First though, I really want to talk to you about moving on. It's important."

"What is that?" Jimmy asked. "You've mentioned it a couple of times, but I don't know what that is."

He sounded relieved, and I was pretty sure that he was glad the conversation had turned to a direction other than the one where he'd have to explain what the hell he was doing working for one of the biggest baddest drug dealers in Edmonton.

"Happy to," I said.

I walked him through the basics. How he had to figure out what was holding him here. How I'd do my best to help him either fix the problem or just get over it enough to be able to leave the living plane and go on to whatever was next for him.

He asked the usual questions. How is he supposed to decide? Is there a Heaven and a Hell? Will it hurt? And I did everything I could to calm him and give him the information he needed to actually make the move.

To be honest, he almost fooled me. I thought he was buying into the whole idea of moving on and was actually considering the possibility.

But when I opened the bathroom door, Jimmy the Dead lost every bit of colour and light he'd gained while we were talking.

"I don't want to see James," he said. "He'll start interrogating me again, and I don't think I can take that."

"Don't worry," I said to him. "James won't ask you any questions you don't want to answer." I hoped I was telling the truth, because it didn't look like Jimmy the Dead could handle much more.

"You know, I don't remember a time when he ever questioned me on any of my business decisions. He'd always seemed to like letting me do the thinking for both of us. Now, here he is, questioning everything and acting like a big damned girl about all of it, to boot."

I bristled. "Just talk to him. Then, we'll find Rita, and you can move on. Please."

He sighed, deeply. "I'll try," he said.

"Good," I replied, and walked into the living room where James and Crystal were waiting for us.

"You were right," I said. "He wants us to find Rita before he'll get serious about moving on."

"Good luck with that," Crystal said. "I haven't been able to find her, but maybe you can." She looked at me hopefully. "Do you think you can?"

"I don't know," I said. "Maybe."

"Please try," she said, and ripped off the edge of a *Bride* magazine that was sitting on her coffee table. She scribbled on it and handed it to me.

"That's her address," she said. "Well, I think it's her address.

I've gone there a few times, but I can never catch her in."

"We'll check it out," I said. "And we'll get back as quickly as we can. Give us a few hours."

"What do you mean a few hours?" Crystal said, and frowned. "Aren't you taking him with you?"

That was the last thing I wanted to do at this point. Dead Uncle Jimmy and James were not getting along—the biggest understatement of my life—and I knew that if I tried to get James to help me find this Rita person with his uncle there, the delicate peace I'd fostered would blow up in my face.

"It would be better if he stayed with you," I said. "We shouldn't be long, and I'd like to be able to talk to him again."

She sighed and shrugged. "I'll take him to my shop."

"I'm not going there," Jimmy said. "I hate that place."

"We shouldn't be gone too long," I said. "With any luck, we'll bring Rita to the shop. To you. Then, you can say goodbye to her. Isn't that what you want?"

Personally, I didn't think it would work out that way, because it hardly ever did. And it looked like Jimmy didn't think so, either.

"Why does he look like that?" Crystal asked. "All dark like that?"

"I had a rough morning," Jimmy said. "And don't act like I can't hear you, because I can."

"Sorry," Crystal mouthed. Then James jumped in, with both feet.

"Is he actually giving you a hard time?" he growled, looking around like he was trying to find something to punch. "Seriously?"

"Huh," Crystal said, and looked at me. "Usually people don't want to fight with their dearly departed. They just want to talk. Don't they?"

"Usually," I said. "James, you said you were going to let me handle this."

"He always pulled this crap," James growled. "All his life."

He looked around like he was still trying to find something to punch. *Someone* to punch, and Jimmy took a big step back.

"Just find Rita," he said. "I'll go to the shop. Just find Rita. Please."

"He's going to do what we asked," I said to James. "Let's go find Rita for him, all right?"

"Sure," he said. "Why not? Uncle Jimmy always gets what he wants."

Crystal rolled her eyes at me. "Looks like we both have our hands full."

"Seems that way," I said, and shrugged.

James snorted derisively and turned away.

"He always was a pain in the ass," Jimmy the Dead said.

"Two peas in a pod," Crystal replied, and scribbled on the ripped cover of the magazine that held Rita's address. "Here's the address to my shop. Come there when you find her."

I nodded and grabbed James by the hand. "Time for us to go," I said. "Crystal has work—and you and I have a woman to find."

"Thank you," Crystal said. Jimmy said nothing. Just glared at us like we'd figured out a way to really wreck his afterlife.

I pulled James to the door. "Let's get out of here before she changes her mind," I whispered. "'Cause I'm not dragging your dead uncle all over this city if I can help it."

He nodded, and then, finally, we were away from the two of them. But we could hear them bickering as we walked through the door and out into the screaming hot sunlight.

"They sound like an old married couple," I said.

"Nobody in their right mind would marry my uncle," James said shortly. "Living or dead."

MARIE:
LOOKING FOR RITA

"I'M SORRY," JAMES said as soon as we got into the rental car. "I don't know why I let him get to me that way."

"Looks like a big pile of unfinished business," I snapped. "But James, you gotta back off a bit. You know?"

"I know," he said. "Do you think finding this Rita chick will maybe get him to open up about what he was into?"

"Maybe," I said. "But James, even if it doesn't, it looks like he needs to know she's all right. Can we give that to him, even if he doesn't tell you anything else?"

"I suppose," James said. "But doesn't it look like Jimmy likes hanging out with Crystal?"

"Yeah," I said. "It does. But I think Crystal would like her space back. So, let's find Rita and see if we can at least do that. All right?"

He nodded, so I was able to enjoy the scenery. Well, enjoy was a strong word, because it seemed that much of the city was normal. Just houses and businesses—once we got away from the Strip.

"Look at that," I said, pointing out the window of our rental car. "People actually live here. Full time. How much further?"

"We're almost there, I think," he replied, and shook his head. "This Rita chick does not live in a nice part of town."

He was right. The buildings we passed looked increasingly

more rundown, though it did look like there were some half-hearted attempts at gentrification.

"Kinda reminds me of where Jasmine lives," I said. "Sort of. Don't you think?"

Jasmine was my best friend in Edmonton, and she was looking after James's dog Millie while we were out of town. She also lived in a part of Edmonton that was fighting the gentrification war.

"I guess so," he said. The GPS indicated that we'd reached our destination, and James pulled to the side of Van Der Meere Street.

The buildings were all two or three storey affairs, packed cheek by jowl down the street. "Looks like she lives in that one," he said, and pointed to a badly scarred brown door set in an otherwise blank wall.

"Doesn't look very inviting," I muttered.

"It looks like the door to our office building," James replied. "Maybe a little better."

He was right.

I opened the door, and the hot wind blew through the car like I'd opened a vent to the most powerful furnace in the world. Insta-sweat started to crawl down my back, and I sighed.

"Let's get inside before I melt," I said, and got out. James chuckled tightly as he followed me, but I noticed that beads of sweat quickly formed on his forehead.

He walked to the door, and when he tried it, it opened easily enough. I crowded in after him, hoping that we'd be stepping into more air conditioning. No luck, though. The stale air in the entryway was almost as hot as it had been on the sidewalk, and it smelled of cooked cabbage.

James scanned the list of tenants and pressed the button marked "R. Sullivan."

I crossed my fingers, hoping she'd answer, invite us up, and that she'd have air conditioning while we quizzed her about why Jimmy wanted to find her, and what she'd been up to for the past year.

No luck, though. James frowned, and pressed the button again. Still nothing, so he scanned the tenant list until he found the button marked "Manager."

No answer, but James really leaned into the thing. After a few moments of solid buzzing, we heard a click, and a deep voice emanated from the small speaker. "Frigging stop that!"

"Sorry," James said, not looking sorry in the least. "We need to speak to the manager. It's important."

There was another long silence, and I was afraid he'd hung up on us. "What do you want?" he finally asked.

"I'm looking for Rita Sullivan," James said. "I was told she lives here."

"You're about a month and a half late," he said. "As far as I know, she skipped town."

James and I looked at each other. A month and a half. Then the speaker crackled back to life. "You're not here to pay her rent, are you?"

"How much does she owe?" James asked. I looked at him, surprised.

"Two months," the voice said. "Eleven hundred, all in. I'm just about ready to clear out her crap. So if you want to help her out, you better hurry."

"I could be convinced," James said. "But you have to let me into her apartment. You know, so I can make sure all her stuff is still here."

There was a small silence as we all thought about things. I was thinking about how nice it would be to have an extra eleven hundred bucks lying around that a person could waste on someone else's rent. Seemed like the manager was thinking pretty much the same thing, because the speaker scratched to life again.

"You got cash?" he asked.

"Yes," James said.

"Then something might be arranged," the manager said. "Come up to 224."

The buzzer sounded, and easy as that, we were let into the building where Rita Sullivan lived.

IF ANYTHING, THE building was hotter inside than it was out on the street. And the stinking air was still. Choking hot and still.

"Holy crap." I stumbled up the dirty carpet that covered the stairs, trying not to touch the handrail. "I can barely breathe."

"It isn't good," James said. "And any idea what that smell is?"

"Eggs?" I guessed, and shrugged. "Or cabbage. Sulphur?

Maybe this place opens on to a pit of Hell or something."

"Sounds about right," James said. He reached the door that would let us onto the second storey, and held it open for me.

"At least it doesn't smell quite as bad," I said, and walked through. "And I think it feels a little bit cooler."

"Maybe you have heat stroke," James said, very unhelpfully. "Where's Rita's apartment?"

"Should be at the other end," I said. "You're not actually going to pay her rent, are you?"

"If it gets us in the door," he said.

"That's a lot of money," I replied.

"I can handle it," he said.

"He's probably scamming us."

"Probably."

The door to her room looked like every other door on the long, dark brown painted hallway. I don't know what I was expecting. Maybe a floral wreath hanging from the thing or some other pathetic attempt to brighten the place up. But there was nothing.

James tried the door, but it was locked. "Where is the manager?"

Before I could answer, I heard sounds, like an overweight, out-of-shape locomotive chugging up the back stairs.

"He's on his way," I said, and pointed at the exit door leading to a stairwell. "If he makes it."

James chuffed laughter and shook his head. "It's going to take him forever," he muttered. "Think I should go help?"

I had a sudden vision of James carrying a fat, balding guy up the stairs like a firefighter, and tried to hold in my own laughter. "Think it would hurry this up? I really want air conditioning, like more than I can say."

"Just hold your water," a voice floated up from the stairs. "I'll be right there."

James's eyes got big, and when I tittered more laughter—nervous this time—he shook his head at me.

The guy's head finally showed. Grey hair, and his face was thin. Not thin in good shape, but thin like he'd been sick recently. Sweat ran down his sunken cheeks and pattered onto his grey tee shirt.

He rounded the stairwell and hit the last set of stairs, clutching the handrail for all he was worth. I was suddenly afraid that he wasn't going to make it, and glanced at James. Maybe he should carry him. Maybe it would be safer.

The manager finally made it to the top of the stairs and stopped. He was leaning against the wall by the stairwell door, trying to catch his breath so he could talk to us. Jesus, what was wrong with the guy?

He stepped through the door and glared at the two of us. "So, you going to pay Rita's rent?" he rasped.

He was painfully thin, like a skeleton wrapped in leathery skin. He wiped at the line of perspiration sitting at his hairline with a dirty white handkerchief, then tucked it into the front pocket of his jeans. I noticed his belt. The long flap of leather hanging down the front. Two holes had been well used, but now he was using a hole a few inches in. He'd lost a ton of weight, and recently.

"Are you all right?" I asked, without thinking.

James threw me a quick glare and stepped up to the man. "Yes," he said. "I'm willing to pay whatever she owes you."

The manager half-smiled and held out his hand. James blinked and then reached for his wallet. "You going to give me a receipt?" he asked.

"You want one?" the guy said. "'Cause that will cost you an extra two hundred."

"No," James said.

He pulled eleven one hundred dollar bills from his wallet and laid them on the manager's outstretched hand, and I flinched. No matter what James said, that was a lot of money. The manager closed his hand around the bills and tucked them into the front pocket of his jeans, with the dirty handkerchief.

"Good enough," he said. Then he stood and stared at us, like he was waiting for something.

"You going to let us in?" James finally asked.

The manager smirked. "My tenants like their privacy," he said. "Unless you're a cop. Are you? A cop?"

James's back tensed, but he kept his nice, gentle smile plastered on his face. "I'm not a cop," he said. "I'm just looking for Rita. That's all."

The manager looked him up and down. "You gotta tell me if you're a cop," he said. "It's the law."

"I am not a cop," James said again, but his oh-so-nice smile drifted south just a tch. "And I paid you. Open that door. Now."

The manager's smarmy smile did a little drifting of its own, and he reached into his back pocket and pulled out a ring of keys. Made a show of running through most of them, then slid one into the lock in the door, and unlocked it. Pushed the door open, and glared.

"Go ahead," he said. "Just don't wreck anything. I get the feeling that at the end of the month I'll be cleaning this place out for real, and I can't make money on broken shit."

James didn't answer. Just pushed past the guy into Rita's apartment. I followed him, only sneaking one glance at the manager as I walked through the door.

He caught my eye and the smarmy smile was back, full wattage. "I'd let *you* rent this apartment," he wheezed. "Think about it."

"Not a chance," I snapped, and closed the door in his face.

Rita's apartment was neat as a pin. Absolutely nothing out of place, as far as I could see. A dead plant sat forlornly by the window above the kitchen sink, but that was the only bit of disarray I could see in the whole place.

"It looks like she still lives here," I said.

James stood by the fridge, and pulled the door open so I could see inside it. "I don't think so," he said.

Any real food in that fridge had gone over to the bad side months before. The smell of rot hit me, and I waved at him. "Close it. That's disgusting."

He latched it closed and shrugged.

"So, she's been away for a while," I said. "What are we looking for?"

"Something that tells us where she's gone," he said.

I walked to the bathroom and glanced in. Another neat room, and I couldn't see anything missing. Her toothbrush sat in a small glass next to a half-rolled tube of toothpaste. The mirror above the sink housed a medicine cabinet, but when I opened it, it was empty.

"She might have taken some stuff," I said. "But I can't tell. Hairbrush and toothbrush are still here, but no medicine or makeup that I can see."

I walked to the alcove that served as her bedroom. Opened a drawer in the beaten-up dresser and looked inside. Socks and underwear, neatly folded. The next drawer held tee shirts, and the last one held two blankets. Everything folded. Neat.

"Nothing missing here," I said. I walked to the wardrobe against the far wall. Opened it, and looked at the mostly dark, mostly business clothing hanging neatly inside. Shoes lined the bottom. I shrugged, closed it, and glanced at the top of the wardrobe. Nothing up there.

"She didn't have much stuff," I said. "But I don't see a suitcase."

"Look under the bed," James said. He was going through her tiny book case, one book at a time. Of course.

I leaned over and glanced under the bed. "Suitcase is here," I said, and pushed it aside. "And something else."

I pulled a small cardboard box toward me.

"What is it?" James asked, and looked up from the book he'd apparently decided to read.

"I don't know." I pulled the box out from under the bed and shook it. There was definitely something inside, so I set it on the bed. Neatly made, of course, and the bedclothes were so tightly tucked I could have bounced a quarter on them.

I opened the box. Looked like papers and photos. A rental agreement was sitting on top, and I chuckled as I read it.

"He ripped you off," I said to James.

"Who?"

"The manager." I held up the paperwork. "She only pays four hundred fifty a month."

"Whatever," he said dismissively. "Find anything else?"

"Photos."

"Photos?" James said. "Actual photos?"

"Yeah," I said.

I pulled them out and glanced at the topmost one. A young woman with red hair and a sprinkling of freckles smiled out at whoever had taken the picture, and I wondered if I was looking at Rita. Flipped to the next photo. Looked like a graduation picture, with the same girl and a couple of other graduates smiling happily beside her.

"I think I found Rita," I said, and held up the photos. "She has red hair."

I glanced at the rest of the photos. Stopped at the one that I suspected were her parents. From Minnesota. The photo looked a lot like the painting *American Gothic*, to be honest. No smiling, like they hated the fact that their souls were in the process of being trapped in a photograph or something. Behind them was a classic red and white barn, and almost out of the shot, a black and white border collie watching the proceedings with a puzzled expression on its face.

I glanced at the back. Just the date. "1997," which really told me nothing.

There was one photo left in the box. Facedown, with "2017" and "The three musketeers" written across the back.

I flipped it, and good old Uncle Jimmy's face smiled out at me. He was sitting in a booth at a restaurant with two other people. Rita, and someone else.

"James," I said. "Look at this."

He didn't answer, and when I glanced at him, I saw he was sitting, still reading one of the stupid books.

"James," I said. "No reading. We're on holiday, for heaven's sake."

He looked up at me and blinked. "What?" he asked. "What?"

"Good grief," I said and walked over to him. Grabbed the book out his hand and looked at the cover. "Money Laundering for Criminal Investigators," I read, and then stared at him. "Really?"

He took the book back and pulled what looked like a pay stub from somewhere near the end of the book. "She was using this as a bookmark," he said. "Looks like she worked for a numbered company. The date reads August 13, 2017."

"Last year," I said.

"Yep." He turned to me. "What did you find?"

"A picture of Jimmy," I said, and held it out. "Looks like it was from last year. Maybe at a restaurant?"

He took the photograph and tucked it into the book with the cheque stub. "You find anything else?"

"Nothing," I said. "I don't think she's been here for a long time. And it doesn't look like she took anything when she left."

"That's bad," he said.

"I know," I replied. "What am I going to tell your Uncle Jimmy?"

"Looks like his girlfriend didn't plan on leaving," he muttered. "Or maybe she didn't have time to come back here before she left."

"Maybe because it was too dangerous for her," I said.

"Yeah," he replied. "Maybe. Did you find a computer anywhere?"

"No."

"What about a phone?"

"No. No phone. No keys, either."

He huffed a sigh. "Let's go."

He tucked the book under his arm, and I wiped down everything we'd touched with a cloth from the kitchen sink. "Just in case the actual police decide to find out what happened to her," I said. "We don't need to get pulled into an investigation, now do we?"

"We do not," James said. Then, when I was done, we left Rita's apartment and closed the door.

WE DIDN'T SEE the manager again as we walked out of the building and back into the painfully bright sunlight.

"So what do we do now?" I asked. "All we know for sure is Rita hasn't been back here in a long time, and I don't see how that is going to help Jimmy move on."

"We're going back to our room," he said. "I want to find out more about this numbered company Rita was working for."

Looks like we had a plan. However, I was afraid that James was more interested in finding out what Jimmy had been up to before he died than what he needed in order to move on.

At least he was focussed on Rita, for the moment. But I didn't know how long that would last. He had a real burr up his butt about his uncle, and I was pretty sure it wouldn't help Jimmy move on.

THE ELEVATOR AT the Dunes was crowded. James pushed the button for our floor, and we waited silently, watching everyone else in the elevator as they laughed and chatted about the fun they were having. Which did nothing to make my mood any better.

"I need another shower," I said, when we got to our room.

"Later." He grabbed his computer. "Time for a little research. Give me that pay stub I found in the book."

I handed him everything we'd found at Rita's apartment, and he pulled the stubs free and stared at it. "She didn't make much," he said.

"Can you tell what her job was?" I asked. He shook his head again.

"Maybe she was a server," I said. "Servers live off tips."

"Maybe," he said.

I thought back to my days as a barista in MacMurray, that had ended when I'd poured coffee on a customer who had dissed my dad. "I imagine tips are pretty good here."

"Probably," he said. He opened his computer. "Let's find out who she was working for," he said, and Googled "97762 Entertainment Corp". Then he was lost in the wonderful world of research.

There was nothing I could do, so I took a shower. Then I did my hair, and actually put on some makeup. Well, mascara, anyhow. I looked over my wardrobe choices and wished I'd brought something a little nicer to wear. And lighter. Even shorts and tee shirts weren't going to cut it here.

"Will you look at that," James said. "I finally figured out who was paying her through that numbered account, anyhow."

I didn't have to guess, because it was there, in black and white. "Victor Tupilo," I said. "Who's he?"

"He has something to do with the Dunes," he said. "Plus a bunch of other companies. Mostly numbered."

I frowned. "So did Rita work for the Dunes?"

"Maybe," he said. "For services rendered, whatever that was. Guess we have to figure that out, too."

"Think there's something back at Rita's?" I asked. "That would give us a clue what she did?"

"We searched her place," James said. "There was nothing."

"So how are we going to figure this out?"

"I think we need to make sure that she worked here," he said.

"Seriously?" I said. "How are we going to do that?"

"I'm not sure," he said. "We'll have to come up with a scheme."

"Our schemes never work, James," I said. "We should have checked her mailbox. There might have been something in there."

"That would mean dealing with the manager again," James replied. "I don't think I can afford another conversation with him."

I snorted laughter and looked at the pay stub once more. "This is dated last year," I said. "How long has it been since she was last in that apartment?"

"No clue," James said.

"If she hasn't been there for a year, why is she still paying the rent?"

"Maybe her rent was paid by automatic withdrawal or something," James said. "But why would she leave enough money to pay her rent for a year?"

"Another very good question," I said. "I have no idea."

"We need bank statements," he said.

"Or we need to find Rita." I grabbed the photograph we'd taken from Rita's apartment and stared at it, hard.

"Does this restaurant look familiar to you?" I asked. "I feel like I should know it."

"Looks like an IHOP," he said. "Doesn't it?"

"An IHOP," I replied, and laughed. "You're right."

I stared at the photograph again. At the three of them sitting around the booth, grinning. "They look happy."

"Yeah," James said, and touched his finger to his uncle's visage. "I barely recognize him. He never smiled."

"Wonder who the other guy is?" I asked.

"We should ask Jimmy," James said. "He'd know."

"True," I said. "But he hasn't been that forthcoming, now has he?"

"If he wants us to find Rita, he has to give us something to work with," James said. "Might as well be this. Let's go talk to him."

He pulled out his phone and called Crystal. "We're coming over," he said. "Let Jimmy know we have some information, but he's going to have to answer some questions, first."

I could hear her complaining as James disconnected.

"I don't think she was done talking," I said.

"It doesn't matter," he replied. "We need to get this finished." He grinned at me crookedly. "After all, you have your bucket list for Vegas, and if we don't finish with my uncle, you'll never get to it. Right?"

"Right," I said. "My bucket list."

"So, let's go talk to the old man," he said. "So he can clear up a few things for us."

JIMMY:
CRYSTAL'S PSYCHIC SHOP

THINGS GOT QUIET after James and Marie left. Crystal and I settled into an uneasy silence as she finished getting ready for work.

"Marie and James are going to find Rita and bring her to you," she finally said without looking at me. "So, you're coming with me. And no arguments. Understand?"

"I understand," I said, even though I would've rather stayed in her ratty apartment with her cats and the never-ending talk shows. Usually, I would have fought her on it. But these were not usual times.

We headed out to her place of business. Crystal's Psychic Shop and Ghost Tours. She unlocked the door and flipped the switch that turned on the two neon signs she'd splurged on. A purple hand blinked and wavered in one window, while a white Egyptian-styled eye glowed in the other.

"Don't go too far," she said, as she brewed her first pot of tea for the day.

"You're hilarious," I muttered.

"I try," she said, then the small silver bell situated over the door tinkled, and she ignored the hell out of me when a couple of middle-aged women walked through the door.

"You open for business?" one of them asked.

"Absolutely," Crystal replied. "What are you looking for? A

reading? Tarot cards?"

I had to give her that. Crystal did it all. Didn't matter what bit of BS her potential clients believed, Crystal could accommodate.

"You got any candles?" the woman with the cat eye glasses and oversized sunhat said. "We're really looking for candles."

"Janey, I've always thought that getting my palm read would be fun," the other woman said. "And we're on holidays. You know?"

"I thought you said you were looking for candles." Janey pulled her sunhat off and ruffled her short haircut until it stood at attention all over her head.

"I know what I said," the first woman said, "But Janey—a palm reading."

"Fine," Janey said. "Go for it."

Then I had to listen to Crystal prattle on about love signs and life lines and voices from beyond the grave—the usual.

I didn't know how she could stand it. If that had been my career choice, I would have slit my own throat, swear to God.

Mind you, my own career choice hadn't been the best, for the most part. Jimmy Lavall, private investigator barely paid the bills until I hooked up with Ambrose Welch.

I had Rory to thank for that. He had been screwing around with a local cop, and I'd caught him in the act, after the cop's husband hired me to find out what his wife was up to.

The cop's husband found out, in spades, and I imagine that ended their marriage. By the time somebody came to me, marriages were pretty much over. All that was left was the crying and dividing property.

That's what happened when I showed the cop's husband the photos of his wife with the other cop, anyhow. Rory. He'd cried like a baby, then thanked me, paid, and left.

They always thank you. I never could understand that. I knew that if I was ever in that situation, I wouldn't thank the bastard that pulled my life to shreds. I'd pay, for sure, because that's just how I am. But I wouldn't thank him.

Luckily, I never let myself get into that situation. I never seemed to have the time to find a gal who wanted to settle down. Not that I was looking for one, exactly.

There were plenty of women in my life. But none of them were the marrying kind.

It wasn't the same for my brother. James's father. Good old Lloyd Lavall. Straight shooter if I ever met one, and we didn't get along much at all.

He met Suzette while he was in college, and I didn't think it would last. But they got married, and had a kid, and life seemed pretty sweet for them.

I probably shouldn't have gotten so involved in their lives, but that kid—well, he filled a hole in my gut I hadn't realized was there.

James was a sweet kid. Smart and gentle. I always bugged him about being my namesake, even though he'd actually been named after his grandfather. My father.

James Senior died when Lloyd and I were young. That was probably why Lloyd had such a soft spot for him. He always talked about what a good guy he was. How he'd take him camping, or to ball games, or whatever, but that wasn't the way I remembered him.

I was older by nearly ten years, so I guess James Senior learned a lot about being a father by the time Lloyd came along. But I only remembered him yelling. And hitting. I was a bit of a hard case, right out of the womb, but him beating on me didn't help. So, as soon as I could, I got out.

I sometimes felt bad about leaving Lloyd in that house, but I think things calmed down after I left. That was what Lloyd said, anyhow.

By that time, I'd moved to Edmonton and set up my PI office—the first one, on the west end of town—and was doing a booming business. Didn't hurt that I knew some of the tougher customers in the Edmonton area. Those guys were always up for a little surveillance—or whatever—in order to get the upper hand on their competition. And I was happy to help them out. For a fee.

A couple of them used to call me "Anything for a buck Lavall," and I guess they were right. Mostly. But I tried hard to stay on the right side of the law, and most of the time, I was able to.

Jimmy—dammit, James—started to take a real interest in my business when he came to Edmonton for university. So, it seemed almost natural that he'd come to work for me, part-time.

At first it was just cleaning up the office, shit like that, but after a while, he started actually helping with the cases. And he was a natural. Really good.

I finally convinced him to stop going to university so he could work with me full time, and his father and mother never spoke to me again. It was all right, though. Like I said, I had lots on the go. I hardly even missed them.

I just started going to Las Vegas for the holidays. It was better for everyone, all the way around. James didn't have to make a choice about where he was going to go—who he was going to celebrate with. I just got out of the way and let him have his family time. But somehow, that soured, and after a while—about the time I started gambling at the Nugget—James convinced me to stay home for the holidays, so I could be with him.

"You can gamble anytime," he said. "The holidays are for family."

That only lasted a couple of years, thank God. I really wasn't one for the family get-togethers, and besides, James saw me every day at the job. That was when he started travelling. And I went back to Vegas.

Christmas in Vegas. There's nothing like it. Trust me on that.

MARIE:
WATCHING CRYSTAL WORK

THE CLOSER WE got to Crystal's shop, the more agitated James became until I finally asked, "Do you want me to go in and talk to your uncle by myself?"

"No," he said. "Let's get this over with."

Delightful.

We entered the shop, and a small silver bell jingled above us. Everyone in the store turned and looked, so I plastered a smile on my face and walked into the dimly lit, incense-choked room.

"Did you find Rita?" Jimmy asked.

Before I could answer, Crystal shook her head and jerked her thumb at the couple *ooh*ing and *aah*ing over a crystal display at the back of the room.

"For fuck's sake," Jimmy snapped. "They're here for ghosts, aren't they? Let's give 'em a real show."

"Not now," I snapped, and deliberately turned away from him. I walked over to a candle display as Crystal dealt with her customers. Finally, the store was empty, and we were able to talk.

"Sorry it took us so long to get back," I said to Crystal.

"It's all right," she replied. "The thing is, Jimmy doesn't like it here much. He'd rather be at home, watching TV."

"Damn straight," Jimmy said. "Anything's better than dealing with these tourists."

"So you've told me," Crystal said. "Repeatedly." She looked at me and shrugged. "Ghosts don't usually stick to me like he has. Usually, it's like I can see them out of the corner of my eye, sort of. They don't look that real, you know? They definitely don't talk to me like he does. And they never won't leave." She grinned. "Please tell me you've found Rita."

I was surprised. My experience with ghosts was exactly the opposite. Once they were with me, I had a heck of a time getting rid of them.

"All we know right now is, it doesn't look like Rita's been back to her apartment in a while," I said.

"So you got into her place," Jimmy said excitedly. "I knew Jim—James—could to it." Then my words sunk in, and he frowned. "What do you mean she hasn't been there in a while?"

"Just like I said," I said. "She hasn't been there in months. Maybe since you died."

"Oh," Jimmy said. He looked disappointed.

"We found this," I said, pulling the IHOP photo from the pocket of my shorts. "Have a look. Tell us who this guy is."

Jimmy frowned and took a tentative step toward me. Glanced at the photo, and his colour darkened. "I don't remember," he finally said. "He was a friend of Rita's, but she stopped hanging around with him when we became an item."

He stared at the photo like he wished he could burn it right in my hand, and I had the feeling he was lying.

"What did he say to you?" James asked.

"He doesn't remember," I said shortly.

"No surprise there," he said.

The silver bell tinkled, and a small cadre of middle-aged women in sensible sandals and coordinated shorts and tops walked into the shop.

"Do you do palm readings?" one of them asked.

Crystal's face transformed. "I most certainly do," she said, and turned to me.

"Can you wait, over there?" she said, waving at the wall where James was still staring glumly at the hand-carved dwarves, "I'll be right back."

I glanced at Jimmy, who was glaring at the women, and then walked to James. "We're not going to be able to have a meaningful conversation with him," I said. "Not with all this foot traffic. Maybe we should take him back to our hotel room."

"To the Dunes?" James said.

"Yeah," I said. "Well, maybe being there will help him with his rotten memory."

"I'm not going back to the Dunes," Jimmy said and took a step toward Crystal, who was glad-handing the women at the other side of the room.

"You are if I say so," I muttered, and walked up to him just as he reached out and grabbed Crystal by the arm.

I imagine it looked fairly funny—or terrifying—to the women in the colour coordinated short sets, as I walked up to Crystal, and into Jimmy.

It was neither funny or terrifying to me. It was just sad.

I could feel his anger, of course. But I could also feel his overwhelming sadness. And through it ran tendrils of fear.

"You're coming with me," I muttered to him, trying to avoid the shocked glances of the tourists. Then I locked eyes with Crystal and mouthed, "Release him. Now."

"I don't know how," she said aloud. Then she shook her head, like she was trying to clear it, and I stepped even closer to her, to surround Jimmy's spirit even more completely.

"We'll talk later. All right?"

"All right," she said. For a second I was afraid she was going to hug me, which would have mashed the three of us together and could have possibly given Jimmy a way to cling even tighter to her, but she didn't. She took a big step back and jerked her shoulder free from Jimmy's grasp.

"No!" Jimmy cried, but I clung to his aura and headed for the door.

"We'll talk later," I grunted to Crystal, and looked at James. "Time to go."

James opened the door and held it for me as I pushed Jimmy out into the hot white sunlight.

I could feel the eyes of the women on me as they watched me fight my way to the car. Jimmy was not being cooperative at all, but I did my best, and got him inside.

"Drive," I said to James. "We have to get him away from Crystal so he'll stay with me."

James put the car into gear and headed out into traffic, and I turned my attention back to Jimmy.

"If you let go now, I don't know where you'll end up," I said to

63

the ghost roiling around just under my skin. "And can you please calm down? You're making me seasick."

"Jesus," he cried. "Don't take me back to the Dunes."

"Jimmy, you have to move on," I said, trying to keep my voice sounding reasonable even though he was really starting to make me feel physically ill. "And the only way I know how to do that is by figuring out what's holding you here. You say it's Rita—and Rita worked at the Dunes. So, we have to go there so we can find her."

I felt him slow and then flatten as all hope oozed from him. "Fine," he said. "Makes sense. Can you let me go now?"

"Happy to," I said. "But keep a hand on me, all right? Like I said, I don't know where you'd go, and I don't need to lose you now."

"Fine," he said again. I relinquished control, a bit at a time, and he settled into the back seat of the car, one lone tendril still touching me, filling me with cold and sadness. An ache I didn't think I'd ever be able to get rid of.

"So, back to the Dunes?" James asked.

"To the Dunes," I said.

MARIE:
THE DUNES

THE CLOSER WE got to the Dunes, the harder Jimmy clung to me. By the time we pulled into the parking lot, he'd wrapped himself back around me like a panic-stricken python.

"I wish you wouldn't do this," he muttered. "Why can't we go— I don't know—anywhere else? I promise I'll stay out of your hair. You won't even know I'm here. Just . . . let's go."

"No," I said. "We have to find Rita, remember?"

"I remember," he said, but didn't loosen his grip even a little bit as we handed the keys to the valet and walked through the front door.

I turned to James. "So, what do we do first?"

"Let's make sure Victor Tupilo works here," he said, "And then we can find out about Rita."

He walked up to an information desk where a young woman sat. "Good morning," she said. "How can I help you today?" She smiled brightly. Even her eyes smiled, which was quite a feat as far as I was concerned.

"I need to speak to Victor Tupilo," James said.

Her face drained of all emotion. "Is there a problem?" she asked. "Maybe I can help you?"

"No," James said. "I need to talk to Victor Tupilo. Now."

"Can I have your name please?"

"James Lavall," James said. "Tell him I want to talk to him about my uncle. Jimmy Lavall. And Rita Sullivan."

"Oh no," Jimmy said. "Not him. Jesus, Marie, tell him to stay the hell away from that guy. He's dangerous."

65

I leaned toward James. "Jimmy says Victor's a bad guy," I whispered.

"Then he's exactly who we need to talk to," James said and turned back to the girl behind the desk, who looked like she was considering fainting. "Can we speak to him, please?"

"I'll see if he's available," the girl said. She picked up the receiver and pressed a button on the phone.

"Stop him!" Jimmy screeched, but his voice sounded weak and far away.

"Stay with me," I muttered. "We have to find out about Rita, remember?"

"Save yourself," he whispered like he was already a mile away from me, and when I looked at him, he had darkened to grey ash. Then, he disappeared.

"James," I said. "We have a problem."

"What now?" he asked.

"Jimmy's gone," I said.

"What?"

"He's gone. He disappeared."

"I can page him for you, if you'd like." It was the helpful girl behind the info desk, and I noticed that some of her colour had returned.

"I don't think it would help," I said. "But thanks anyhow."

"Will Mr. Tupilo see us?" James asked.

"He said to tell you that he's busy right now, but if you can wait, he'll be down shortly."

"Shortly?"

"It'll be about an hour." Her face tightened. "I can give you coupons. For a drink. Or maybe lunch. Would that help?"

"Sure," I said before James could wave off the freebies. "Lunch would be great."

She handed me a coupon and smile gratefully. "This gets you into the Dome of the Sea," she said. "For two."

"Thank you," I said, and stuck the coupon in my pocket. Then I grabbed James by the hand and pulled him away from the desk.

"Call Crystal and see if Jimmy went back to her," I said. "Because if he didn't, then he's probably still in this hotel."

"In the room where he died?" James asked, his voice flat.

"That's right," I replied. "Probably in the room where he died."

JIMMY:
TRAPPED IN 214. AGAIN.

I APPEARED IN the room where I'd died and fell to the floor. Lay on the rough carpet and watched the sun crawl across far the wall. If James and Marie didn't find me, I was stuck in this damnable room again until someone else who could see me—talk to me— came into the room the way Crystal had.

Nobody bought my bullshit. Nobody except for Crystal.

And Rita.

I'd met her a couple of months before we started the casino scheme at the Nugget. A small backwater casino that smelled of beer, blood, and desperation. She'd come in like she owned the joint, and then she walked over to me like we were meant to be together and invited me to join her for a drink.

"You look interesting," she said. "Can we talk?"

I was more than happy to have a beautiful woman sit with me and order me my vodkas, water back as I fed her my line. About how the casinos had cleaned me out repeatedly, over the years. How I'd probably be a millionaire twice over, if I'd just figured out a way to keep the house from winning every damned time.

It was just patter, but she listened to me, intently. A couple of times I tried to find out something—anything—about her, but she always managed to bring the conversation back to me. Where I was from. What I did. My family. My life. And damn it, I was thrilled to have someone who seemed genuinely interested in me, so I just kept talking. Until the sun came up. And then, when we went for breakfast. That was when I met Jackson, but by that time she had me, hook, line, and sinker. I would have done just about anything for that girl.

When she came up with the scheme, I was more than ready to go all in. Hell, maybe I was starting to buy my own "oh poor me," talk. Maybe I did believe, somewhere deep, that the casinos owed me after all those years. Maybe, even then, I saw it as a way to finally make Victor Tupilo and the Dunes pay—really pay—for what they'd done me.

Yeah. Oh poor me.

MARIE:
CHANGING ROOMS, AS YOU WILL

JAMES MADE A quick phone call to Crystal to find out if Jimmy had jumped back to her. "No luck," he said. "So he's probably still here. In Room 214. We'll have to get in there."

"How are you going to do that?" I asked.

"We'll change rooms," he said, and grabbed my hand, pulling me to the reception desk. I could see the blonde at the information desk we'd just left giving us the eye as we walked by her again. I grinned at her and shrugged, and she wanly smiled back, then turned the wattage up to full as someone else asked her for help.

The woman behind the reception desk had brown hair, but her smile was just as big and white, and she was just as tall and beautiful as the woman at the information desk.

"How can I help you?" she asked.

"We want to change rooms," James said, and placed the card keys to our old room before her on the desk. "I'd like Room 214, please."

"Is there anything wrong with the room you're in now?" she asked. She picked up the card keys like she was afraid she'd get a disease and put them aside.

"No," he said.

She waited for a beat, and her smile disappeared when he didn't say anything more. She turned to her computer and punched a few keys, and her eyes widened. "Did you say Room 214?"

"Yes," James said. "Is there a problem?"

"No problem," she said. "Can you give me just one moment, please?"

She picked up the receiver for the phone. Punched a couple of numbers, her smile stretched thin. When whoever she called answered, she pointedly turned away from us and spoke urgently into the phone. Then she listened for what felt like forever before muttering, "Thank you, sir," and turning back to us.

"Looks like you're in luck," she said. Her smile looked painful. "No problem at all."

It seemed to take forever for her to punch our information into the computer, and I thought James was going to lose it when she asked for his credit card, twice. But finally, we were done, and we had the new card keys in our hands.

"I'll have your suitcases moved down to 214," she said. "If you like."

"Good," James said, and turned away from her.

When we were out of earshot, I said, "She was just doing her job, you know."

"I know," James said, and shook his head. "I'm sorry. The last thing I wanted to do was end up in Uncle Jimmy's old room. But here we are."

I didn't blame him. After all, we were now going to be spending the next three days in the room where his uncle died. "There wasn't anything else we could have done," I said. "Let's go find Uncle Jimmy."

An old woman was wheeling a cleaning cart down the hallway on the second floor when we got out of the elevator. She pulled it aside and smiled apologetically at us both as we squeezed by. I bumped into James's broad back when he stopped abruptly.

"Hi," James said.

"Can I help you with something?" the woman asked without looking up. "You need extra towels?"

"No," he said and pulled the IHOP photograph we'd taken from Rita's apartment, from his pocket. "Do you recognize this woman?"

She took the photo from him with arthritic fingers and stared at it for a long moment, then looked up at James. "That's Rita

Sullivan," she said. "What do you want with her?"

"We're trying to find her," James said.

"She used to work here, in the back office," she said. "She was a nice girl. Remembered everyone's birthday. But she must've moved away because I haven't seen her here in quite some time."

"How long?" James asked.

The old woman frowned and tapped the photo on her chin. "It has to be about a year now." She pointed at Uncle Jimmy's face in the photograph and sneered. "Around the time that this one died. I had no idea she knew him. I would have warned her, if I'd known."

"Why?" James asked.

"Oh, he caused trouble here, years ago. I thought he was gone for good, but then he came back." She pointed at the door to our room. "He died, right there. Did you know that?"

"I know," James said.

Her face closed. "I shouldn't be talking to you about any of this."

"Just one last question," James said, and pointed at the last person in the photograph. "Do you have any idea who this guy is?"

She sighed impatiently. "I have to get to work," she said. "I don't want no trouble."

James pulled a ten dollar bill from his pocket and pressed it into her hand. "Do you know him?"

She folded the bill and tucked it into her apron pocket, and then looked at the photograph once more. "I've seen him at Broadacres Marketplace," she finally said. "He helped his mother work a table there sometimes. They sell handmade soap.

"Rita gave me a bar of that soap for my birthday a couple of years ago," she muttered. "That's probably how she knows him."

"Maybe," James said. "What's his name?"

"I don't know," she replied. "Jackson, or something. I usually deal with his mother. Wonderful woman. Makes good soap, and it's cheap. It's not often that you find something good that's cheap."

"His mother?" I pressed.

"Yeah," she replied. "She's some kind of hippie. I mean, living off handmade soap. Can you fathom that? No idea why she'd come to a town like this. You'd think she'd go to San Francisco or

71

someplace. But she ended up here."

"What's her name?" James asked, and smiled at her. "Do you remember?"

"Of course," she said. "Her first name's Daisy. It's easy to remember, because that's the name of the soap. I bought some myself after I used up what Rita had given me. I mean, you gotta support the little guy, am I right?"

"You're right," James said.

"It's good soap," she said again, like she thought that he didn't believe her. "I still use it."

"And you bought it at the Broadacres Market?" James asked.

"That's the only place you can get it," she said, and shrugged. "Like I said, she's a hippie. Doesn't believe in going big."

"Thank you," James said. He pulled another ten dollar bill from his pocket and offered it to her. "For your time."

"I won't turn that down," she replied, and folded the bill twice, tucking it into the pocket of her apron. Then she turned away from us and pushed her cart slowly down to the next doorway. One wheel squeaked as she pushed it, and I felt the hair on my arms stand on end. It sounded creepy as hell.

"Looks like we're going to Broadacres Market," James said.

"After we find Jimmy," I replied.

He sighed and nodded, and I followed him to Room 214. He pulled the keycard from his pocket and opened the door, but he didn't walk in.

"See if he's there," he said. "All right?"

I nodded and pushed past him. It was cold in the room, past air conditioner cold, and I shivered. "Feels like he's here, somewhere," I said. "But I don't see him."

The room was not big and flashy like our other room had been. Just two beds—queen-sized—with a desk on the opposite wall. A flat screen TV was attached to the wall above one end of it, and in the black screen I could see the reflection of a dull grey glow coming from beyond the furthest bed.

"He's here," I said.

Jimmy was lying on the carpeted floor, and he looked just about as bad as any ghost I've ever seen.

"What's going on, Jimmy?" I asked. I crouched down beside him, because it was obvious that he wouldn't—or couldn't—get off the floor.

"I don't know," he breathed. "I don't feel so good."

"Do you think you can get up?"

"I don't know." He pointed at James, who'd finally entered the room, but looked like he wished he was anywhere but. "What's he doing here? I got the feeling he didn't give a shit about me one way or the other. You know?"

"Oh no," I lied, and smiled so brightly it hurt. "He's glad you're safe. Aren't you, James?"

"Tell him to hurry up and pull himself together," James said, shortly. "We have things to do."

Thanks, James.

Jimmy snorted. "He doesn't give a shit about me."

Self-pity wafted out of him in huge waves, but I ignored it. Ghosts and self-pity go hand in hand, and it was like James said. We had things to do.

"You have to get up, Jimmy," I said. "We have some questions for you." Well, I did. James was wandering around the room like he was trying to figure out how to escape.

"Questions?" Jimmy asked, and struggled to rise. "I told you, I'm not answering any questions."

"These are about Rita," I said. "If you want us to find her, you have to be honest with us. With me."

He stared at me for a long moment, then nodded. "All right," he said. "Ask away."

"Did you know that she worked here?" I asked.

His face closed. "No," he said. "I didn't know that. She never told me."

"Well, what did she tell you?" I asked. "About herself? I mean, she didn't tell you where she lived. She didn't tell you where she worked. What did you two talk about?"

"We talked about—what we were going to do after."

"After what?"

Jimmy glanced at James and then at me. "After we moved in together."

I blinked. "You two were going to live together?"

"That's right." He sneered at me. "What, you figure an old guy shouldn't have a frigging life? I loved her, all right?"

"That's nice," I said, because I honestly couldn't think of anything else to say.

"It would have been great," Jimmy continued, staring past me.

"She's great, you know? I'd never met anybody like her before. We were going to go away together. Somewhere new. Start over, you know? A fresh start for both of us."

He glanced at James. "I wasn't going to come back to Edmonton," he said. "We were going to make the break. Clean. Just disappear, you know?"

I blinked. "Were you going to let James know that you weren't coming back?"

James turned and stared at me, but I concentrated on Jimmy. "Were you?"

"I would've," he said. "Once we were set up. I would have let him know."

"What did he say?" James asked.

"He said he was going to tell you," I said. "Eventually."

"Typical," James said, and turned away from both of us.

"It's not like we were on the best of terms, before I left," Jimmy said, the self-pity whine back in his voice big time. "I don't think he would have even missed me."

"You left him in the lurch, Jimmy," I said. "If you'd just disappeared, he wouldn't have been able to keep your business running. You would have screwed him, royally."

"He would have been all right," Jimmy said. "He would have landed on his feet. He always did. He's like a cat that way."

"You realize that was a real jerk move, don't you?" I snapped.

"I've done worse," Jimmy said, and shrugged. "Besides, I think he was about ready to jump ship himself." He glared at James. "Weren't you?"

"He said that he was pretty sure you were going to leave him," I said to James's stiff, angry back. "Is he right, James?"

James slumped, and sighed. "Yeah," he finally said. "He's right. I'd had about as much as I could handle. The Palais job was going to be my last. If he hadn't died . . . I would have been done."

"Are you serious?" I squeaked. "If you were ready to let it all go, why the heck did you keep the office open? Why didn't you just shut it all down. You had an out. Why didn't you take it?"

"Well, I met you during the Palais job, remember?" he said. "You made things a lot more interesting,"

"Women always do," Jimmy muttered.

"Shut up," I snapped, and turned back to James. "Are you trying to tell me that the only reason you kept the doors open was because of me?"

"You weren't the only reason," he said. "But yeah. You were in the mix."

I stared at him for a long moment, trying to figure out what the heck to say. "I thought you liked the work," I finally said. "I thought you wanted to keep it going, you know, for your uncle." I pointed at Jimmy. "You know. Your dead frigging uncle."

"I wanted to keep it going in spite of him," James said. "For you. Because you needed a job."

"I had a job," I replied, stiffly. "Remember? I quit that job because you asked me to. Begged me."

"I didn't beg," James snapped.

"Close enough," I replied. I turned to Jimmy. "First, I'm going to move you on . . ."

"And get me out of your life," Jimmy said, and laughed when he saw the look on my face.

All right, so this was definitely not the way this was supposed to go, but James's confession had shaken me to my core. I thought I knew him. Why hadn't he told me any of this?

I took a deep breath and tried to clear my mind. "Sorry," I said to Jimmy. "That wasn't fair, and it doesn't matter, in the grand scheme of things. You need to find out that Rita is all right. So, we'll do that for you. And then, I'll help you move on."

"That sounds pretty good," Jimmy said.

"I have a question for my uncle," James said, and I sighed.

"He doesn't want to answer your questions, James. He's already made that abundantly clear."

"I know," James replied. "But I want to know why he decided to come back to the Dunes that last night. He told me once he'd never come back to this hotel. So, why did he?"

Jimmy's eyes fluttered as he tried to find something that was not me to look at. He was going to lie.

"Don't lie," I said, and he had the good grace to look surprised.

"I missed the place," he finally said. "You know?"

"Are you sure that's the only reason?" I asked.

He shrugged. "I had a bit of trouble here, and I had to move on. But I did miss it."

My ears positively perked. "Trouble?" I asked.

"Trouble," he said. "I—had a drinking problem, back in the day, and I acted out." He shook his head. "Wasn't my finest hour."

"So you left?" I asked.

"I was asked to leave," he said. "Basically."

"How'd you get back in?"

"I made amends," he said. But he wouldn't look at me. "You know, all part of the program. Gotta work that program."

"So you came here for old time's sake?" I asked.

"Something like that," he said.

I turned to James, who wouldn't look at me. "He says he missed the place," I said. "That he had trouble here before, but made amends." I turned back to Jimmy. "What amends did you make?"

"Apologies and the like," he said shortly. "You know. The usual."

He'd regained some of his colour, and he managed to pull himself up to sitting. "I just want you to find Rita. That's all I need."

James walked up to my side and crouched beside me. "What is he telling you?" he asked.

"He's back to Rita," I said. "He wants us to find her."

"Then we'll do that," he said. "Let's go to Broadacres."

"Broadacres?" Jimmy asked. "Why would you go there?"

Before James could answer, there was a knock at the door, and the three of us turned and stared at it.

"Maybe it's the maid," I said. "She might have remembered something else about Rita."

Another knock, harder this time. "Porter," a male voice intoned.

"They're bringing our suitcases," I said. "From our other room."

James shrugged. "Guess we better let them in then."

Three men stood in the doorway to our room. Two of them held our suitcases and looked acutely uncomfortable. The third man was dressed in a suit that looked like it cost more than the car I drove. A lot more.

"Yes?" James asked.

"I'm Victor Tupilo," he said. "You wanted to speak to me, correct?"

Jimmy leapt up from the floor and looked around like he was trying to find a place to hide.

"Looks like our meeting came to us," James said.

Jimmy stopped running in small, frantic circles and stood in front of me, shaking his head frantically. "Don't let him in!" he cried. "Make James get rid of him."

"I don't think that's going to happen," I whispered. "Just relax. James will handle him."

"Nobody handles Victor," Jimmy said. He flopped back to the floor and groaned as Victor Tupilo filled the entrance.

He was big, and I could see a bulge at the armpit of his suit jacket that looked suspiciously like a gun to me. He remained silent as the porters hustled into the room, carefully placing our suitcases on the beds and then heading back out. James handed both of them a tip, and they nodded and then disappeared.

"So," Tupilo said when they were finally gone. "Julia said you wanted to speak to me?"

"We did," James said. "Good of you to come to us."

Tupilo flicked a smile in his direction and then glanced at his watch in a "I'm a very busy and important person" sort of way. "I wanted to see who had requested this particular room," he said. "Especially after you'd set up a meeting with me. So, tell me. What do you want to talk to me about?"

I watched James transform in front of my eyes. He looked like he grew six inches, and his eyes glued to Tupilo's face like a mongoose tracking a snake. "My uncle, Jimmy Lavall, died here last year," he said.

"I remember," Tupilo replied. "It was in this room, wasn't it?"

"You know that," Jimmy muttered. He was barely a grey smudge over by the window.

"Correct," James said.

"Strange way to celebrate the anniversary of his death," Tupilo said.

"Excuse me?" James said.

"By staying in the room where he died."

James's face darkened, and he shook his head. "Here's the deal," he said. "Uncle Jimmy knew Rita Sullivan."

"Don't tell him that!" Jimmy cried. "He doesn't need to know that!"

"Is that right?" Tupilo said. His voice was calm, but his eyes glanced around the room, just for a second, like he was looking for Rita. Or Jimmy.

I was suddenly sure he knew they knew each other.

"Uncle Jimmy had a will," James continued. "Rita Sullivan is named in it and she works here. We've been trying to get hold of her, but have had no luck. So, we decided to come down here and find her."

I looked at him, surprised. We hadn't come up with a reason to be looking for Rita, but that was a good one. Excellent, in fact.

"You're looking for Rita Sullivan because she's named in Jimmy Lavall's will," Tupilo said.

James nodded.

"Hmm," Tupilo said. "Shouldn't lawyers handle this kind of thing?"

James didn't bat an eye. "It's Vegas," he said. "The lawyers can't have all the fun, am I right?"

"All right," Tupilo said. "So you're down here to contact—what was her name again?"

"Rita Sullivan," James repeated.

"This is what I can do for you," Tupilo said. "I'll get Legal to check about this Rita person. They can contact her, and if she decides she wants to talk to you, Legal will let you know."

"But—" James started, but Tupilo shook his head and turned to the door.

"That's as much as I can do," he said.

"We need to find her now," James said. "It's important. For the will. Because if something happened to her—"

Tupilo stopped short. "Why would you think something happened to her?"

"We can't find her," James said. "And people don't just disappear. They always leave traces."

"Not necessarily," Tupilo said, then shook his head. "Legal will let you know. All right?"

"I guess," James said.

"If there's nothing else," Tupilo said, and turned to the door, the meeting evidently over as far as he was concerned. James stepped in front of him, blocking his way.

"So here's the deal," James said. "We're not just here for the will. We decided, since we were going to be here, that we'd get married. We're going to tie the knot. In Vegas." He turned to me. "Aren't we, Honey?"

"What?" I asked.

"What?" Victor Tupilo asked.

"What the hell?" Jimmy cried. "Why didn't you tell me you two were getting married?"

Because most of us didn't know, Jimmy. Most of us didn't know.

MARIE:
SO, WE'RE GETTING MARRIED, ARE WE?

JAMES'S WILD ANNOUNCEMENT silenced everyone in the room. I tried to think of something—anything—to say, but couldn't. James's eyes bored into mine, doing a wild "follow my lead" tango, so I rearranged my features into something resembling a smile, and nodded, frantically.

"That's what we're doing, all right," I said. "We're tying the knot."

Tupilo, turned back to us and smiled coldly. "Congratulations," he said.

"We were going to try to get into the Graceland Chapel," James said. "You know the one? Just down from Fremont Street? I called to see if we could get in this weekend, but they're all booked up. But Marie would love an Elvis wedding. Think you can help us with that?"

An Elvis wedding? Seriously?

I batted my eyes at Tupilo. "It's the wedding I've always dreamed of."

Tupilo stared at me, like he couldn't believe I'd want something like that. I didn't blame him. "I'll talk to my people," he said. "See if we can help you. You do understand, this is extremely short notice, though."

"Uncle Jimmy always said that you were the man to talk to if I ever wanted anything done in Vegas," James continued, his smarmy smile locked on. "I figured you'd be able to help us out."

Tupilo's face froze. "Your uncle talked to you about me?"

"Yes, he did," James replied.

"I never said a word to you about him," Jimmy whispered. "Don't tell him that."

Tupilo stared at James for a long, cold moment, then turned back to the door. "I'll see what I can do. I'll be in touch." And then he was gone, and we were alone.

"What the hell!" I yelled as the door clicked shut.

James clamped his hand over my mouth, hard. "Not now," he whispered. "He's still out in the hall. He'll hear you."

I reluctantly nodded, and he took his hand away. "Sorry, Sweetie," he said, his voice just a little too loud. "I know I should have let you tell him the big news. But hey, he might be able to get us into the Graceland Chapel. Maybe even have Elvis Presley officiate. And that's what you wanted, right?"

"What the hell is going on here?" Jimmy asked.

James stared at me so hard I felt like his eyes were trying to bore into my head. "Yes," I said. "That's what I wanted."

"So, let's go pick out that dress," he said, gesturing at the door. "You know, for the wedding."

"That would be nice," I said. My mouth was so dry, I could barely speak.

As I picked up my phone and tucked it in the pocket of my shorts, James opened his suitcase. Dug through his clothing and pulled out a pair of socks. Unrolled them, and extracted a small jewellery box.

"This isn't the way I wanted to do this," he whispered, and handed it to me. "But you better put it on." Then he smiled and for a second, it looked real.

I opened the box and stared at the ring with a huge—and I mean huge—diamond set in it. Stared at him as I removed it from the box and then slid it on the ring finger of my left hand. It was a little bit big and felt strange on my finger, like something that shouldn't have been there.

"How's that?" I asked.

"Is that real?" Jimmy asked. "It looks real." He half smiled. "You must be doing all right if you can afford that, kid."

James took my hand and stared at the ring. "Looks good," he said, and dropped my hand. "Let's go."

I felt Jimmy's spirit grab my shoulder and shook him off. "You're not coming with us," I whispered. "Stay here."

I had questions for James, and I figured he'd be more forthcoming without his uncle present.

"But that's not fair," Jimmy whined. "I hate this room. I died here, you know."

I closed my eyes and tried to think calm thoughts. I had enough on my plate, without having to deal with him, too.

"We'll be back soon enough," I muttered.

"I'm not staying," he said. "And you can't make me."

"If you can figure out how to get out of here by yourself, go for it," I snarled, finally at the end of my rope.

He pulled away from me and self-pity washed over his dead face. "There's no reason for you to be so mean," he said.

I wanted to scream that I had every reason in the world to be mean, but shook my head at him, then turned to James. "Let's get out of here."

He opened the door, and I honestly expected Victor Tupilo to be standing there with his ear pressed to the door, but the hallway was clear. I breathed a huge sigh of relief.

"Can we talk now?"

"Not yet," James said. "Let's get out of the hotel, first."

"All right," I said. "Where are we going?"

"We're going to Broadacres, of course," he said.

"Not to buy a wedding dress?" I asked, archly.

He had the good grace to look embarrassed. "I'll explain everything," he said. "But once we're clear of this place. All right?"

"All right," I said. But I had the feeling that there wouldn't be enough time in that drive for him to explain everything to me.

I was beginning to wonder if there was enough time in the world to ask all the questions that needed answers.

MARIE:
A LONG OVERDUE TALK

THE VALET BROUGHT the car around, and James held my door. All very gentlemanly, and I played along until we were both in the car.

"A wedding?" I cried. "Why the hell did you tell that man we were going to get married this weekend?"

He looked at me, his face blank. "I wanted him to take us seriously," he finally said. "Why? Do you think it was too much?"

"Way too much," I said. "Rita being in Jimmy's fake will was enough—and that was a good idea, just so you know."

"Thanks," he said. "It just came to me." He glanced at me. "But you think the wedding thing was too much?"

"Yes!" I yelled, then took a breath to calm down. "So, let's just roll that back, shall we?"

"All right," he said, but looked confused. "How are we going to do that, exactly?"

"Well, for one thing, we aren't going to mention it again. To anyone."

"All right," he said. "But what if Victor asks about it?"

"Lie to him," I snapped. "Tell him we already did it. Or hell, maybe we can tell him the truth. We decided it was a stupid idea and called it off."

He looked momentarily hurt. "I didn't think it was a stupid idea," he said. "But we could do that, I suppose."

"Good," I said. I looked down at the ring on my finger. It was really pretty, and I kind of wished I could keep it on.

He noticed, and smiled. "The ring's real. Just so you know."

"Real?"

"It was my mother's," he said.

I stared at the ring. The real ring that used to be his mother's.

"Why did you bring your mother's ring with you to Vegas?" I asked. "You weren't going to ask me to marry you, were you? Like for real?"

"Maybe," he said, and gripped the steering wheel, hard. "I mean, we're living together now. Isn't getting married the next logical step?"

I blinked. "This ruse with Victor wasn't your way of popping the question, was it?" I finally asked.

"No!" he cried. "It's like I said. I was just trying to figure out a way to keep talking to Victor, so I could figure out the connection between him and Uncle Jimmy. You had to have seen the look on his face. Something happened between those two. Don't you want to know what it was?"

"I guess," I said. "But how are you going to figure that out?"

"I'll do whatever it takes," he said.

I didn't know if I liked that response. James wasn't normally a "do whatever it takes" kind of a guy. "What does that mean, exactly?"

"Don't worry," he said. "I won't get into too much trouble. Unless you're with me." He grinned, and I reluctantly grinned back.

"So, what do you think?" he asked. "About the idea of getting married?"

I stared at the ring, and then at his worried face, and my heart started to pound. All right, so he'd handled it all very badly, but still. We were living together, in real life. Maybe getting married was the next logical step.

"Maybe," I said. "But let's talk about it when we get back to Edmonton. We have people there, you know. If we decided to do this, they'd probably like to be invited."

"All right," he said. But he looked disappointed.

"Did you want a Vegas wedding?" I asked, surprised. "I didn't think you even liked it here."

"It might be fun," he mumbled. "You know, with Elvis and

everything."

Huh.

"So," I said, and touched the ring on my finger. "You want me to keep wearing it?"

"Yeah," he said, and grinned. "It looks nice."

"All right," I said, and grinned back at him. "Looks like we're engaged."

"Yeah," he said. "It does look like that, now doesn't it? Let's get to Broadacres and find out what Uncle Jimmy is hiding."

WE DROVE NORTH on Las Vegas Boulevard and turned into the overrun parking lot of the Broadacres Market.

Now technically, it was a flea market, but it had a lot going on. We paid the entrance fee—a couple of bucks per person—and wandered through the crowded walkways between the vendors' tables, trying to follow the totally inadequate map we'd been given at the door.

We finally made it to the centre of the market and walked into a huge commercial tent where a band from Ecuador was warming up. It wasn't much cooler inside the tent, but at least we were out of the sun. We walked past a small table where a pretty young woman was selling CDs.

I reached out to pick one up, and her face wreathed in smiles. Then, James stayed my hand. "Not until we hear what they sound like," he whispered.

The young woman's smile wilted, and she turned her attention back to the cheap paperback romance she was reading. The band roared into life, and for a moment their enthusiasm hid the fact that the equipment barely worked and that the drummer appeared to be keeping time to a completely different song.

"Nope," James said, and we walked out of the huge tent and back out into the merciless sunlight.

"They sound better out here," I said.

"They'd sound even better from the parking lot," James said. He stopped and looked around. "Can you figure out where Daisy's Soaps is from here?"

"I don't know," I said. "This map makes no sense."

I tried turning the map to see if that helped, but it didn't. James snorted impatiently and took it from my hands, and peered at it hard for a few moments.

"It's this way," he finally said, and pointed.

He acted like he knew where he was going, so I followed him past tables loaded with fruit and vegetables.

"I thought this was a flea market," I said.

"Looks like they sell anything," he replied, and pointed at a table covered with what looked to be medieval broadswords, tucked between two tables loaded with cabbages and oranges.

"What a weird place," I muttered. I reached out and touched an orange, which propelled the old man sitting half asleep behind the table into action.

"They're fresh picked," he said. "Ripened on the tree. You won't find better oranges anywhere."

"They look nice," I said, and breathed in the orange's fragrance. It smelled wonderful. So much better than anything we ever got at home. "How much?"

"A dollar an orange," he said, and I pulled my wad of cash from my pocket and handed him two sweat-wilted ones.

"You should haggle," James said.

I ignored him, and took the small plastic bag with the two oranges and smiled at the old man. "Thank you," I said.

"You are welcome," he replied, and then settled back on his chair. He picked up the paperback he'd dropped, and I noticed it was the same romance that the girl selling CDs had been reading.

"Do you know where Daisy's Soaps is?" I asked him.

"That way," the old man said, gesturing with his thumb without looking up from his book.

I turned to James. "See?" I said. "Worth it."

"We'll see," he said, but headed in the direction the old man had pointed.

I smelled the soap before I saw the table. It was a combination of flowers, sage, and citrus. The clean smell cut through the air, leading us by our noses to Daisy's Soaps.

The sign hanging from the front of the table looked old, with seventies-style lettering that looked like it had been taken from a rock album of the day. I wondered if the woman standing behind the table had been making soap since she was a teenager. She was a vibrant sixty-year-old with long white hair and a ready smile.

"Can I help you?" she asked.

I smiled, and then I saw the ghost hanging around behind the display, staring at two women haggling over a bright pink headscarf in the next booth.

I turned to James.

"There's a ghost," I whispered. "In the booth. With Daisy."

"Where?"

"There," I said, and pointed behind Daisy, who was no longer smiling. "He's right there."

I pulled the photograph out of my purse, glanced down at it, and then back up at the ghost. "It's Jackson, or whatever his name is," I said.

The ghost looked up as I spoke his name. He looked frightened as he stared at me, then turned.

"He's going to run," I said.

James shook his head. "You follow him," he said, "and I'll deal with Daisy."

"Be nice," I muttered.

"I'll be the perfect gentleman," he replied with a crooked smile.

"You better be," I said, and cut between the soap table and the headscarf booth, to cut off Jackson the ghost before he made a run for it and we lost another lead.

JIMMY:
ROOM 214, HOW I HATE YOU

HERE I WAS, back in this frigging room where I died. And all alone. Again. I was beginning to think I'd never get out of here.

I glanced at the welter of suitcases and clothing James and Marie had left all over the far bed. Marie's stuff looked old and cheap, like she preferred to shop at the local Sally Ann.

"She'd look better in designer stuff," I muttered. "She's got the figure for it. I should tell James to get her some decent clothes."

I walked away from the suitcase and stared at the dead eye of the television. If only I'd thought to tell one of them to turn the thing on. At least I wouldn't have to be here, trapped, with only my own thoughts for company.

The door knob rattled, and I turned back to it, relief running through me like cool water. They'd decided to take me with them. I knew they wouldn't leave me here alone.

"What did you forget?" I asked as the door rattled again. "I swear, boy, you'd forget your head if it wasn't attached."

No answer, just another rattle, like he was having trouble getting the door open. Those stupid card keys were useless, for the most part. De-magged at the worst moments, and then you had to go all the way back down to the front desk to get another.

"A waste of time," I muttered. "And less secure than a regular key, as far as I'm concerned."

Now, that wasn't, strictly speaking, the truth, but even the hour I'd been by myself had been too long, and I didn't want to have to wait any longer.

I walked up to the door, and it rattled again.

"Just take me with you," I said, though the door. "I'll keep my mouth shut. The whole nine. I just—don't want to be by myself any longer."

I expected Marie to answer, but instead, I heard two unfamiliar male voices through the door.

"I thought you said you could do this," one of them said. "That it wasn't hard at all to get through these locks."

"All right, so maybe I was wrong," another voice said.

I frowned, as the door rattled again. Who the hell was on the other side of this door? I touched the door. Felt the resistance that had kept me locked up here for so long, but pushed against it. I had to find out who was on the other side of the door before they gave up. James and Marie needed to know.

I put both hands on the door and pushed. The resistance felt overwhelming, and I almost gave up. Shook my head, suddenly pissed with myself.

"That's what I always did," I muttered. "Gave up when the going got tough. Screw it. This time I don't."

I pushed against the door again and felt it give. Just a tch, but my hands did move into the door.

I redoubled my efforts, and my hands slipped into the door. I could feel the cold of the interior. It was uncomfortable, but I didn't stop this time. Just kept pushing until I was half in and half out the door.

Two men stood hunched over the lock in front of me. I didn't recognize either of them. They didn't pay me any mind, which didn't surprise me in the least. I redoubled my efforts, and pushed my way through the door and out into the hallway.

I'd gone through one of the men, and felt nothing but a thrum of excitement mixed with caution. I couldn't honestly tell whether the feeling had come from him or me. But I have to tell you, I was thrilled to have made it out of the room.

I felt myself thin, as though the pull of the room was attempting to grab me and pull me back, so I stepped down the hallway away from the horrible feeling. "Not a chance," I muttered. "I'm not going back there if I can help it."

The man I'd walked through straightened and looked around

as though he'd heard someone. "Why is it so cold?" he asked.

"It's not," the other man grunted, fighting once more with the lock, with no success. "It's just the air conditioning. They keep it like a freezer here."

"Are you going to be able to do this?" the first man said, gesturing at the door.

"I don't know," the second man said. He slapped the door and straightened. "We should try something a little more straightforward."

"Like what? Kick the door in?"

"Like let's just go talk to him," the second man said. "Play it straight."

"The last time he saw me, I was working for a drug dealing shit-heel in Edmonton," the first man said. "I don't think he'll want to have a conversation with me."

I blinked. What drug dealing shit-heel did he work for? And why would he be trying to get into James's room?

"Are you sure you're not going to be able to get into this room?" he asked.

"Doesn't look like it," the second man said. "Sorry, R."

"Well, we'll have to find another way," R said. He turned away from the door and the second man followed.

"My turn to follow you," I said, and trailed them down the hallway to the elevator. I stepped in after them, trying not to touch them as we descended to the ground floor and out into the reception area.

"Let's gamble," the second man said. "While we wait for him to come back."

I felt that old familiar need course through me and hoped they'd want to go to the poker tables, but of course, they wandered over to the penny machines like a couple of old women, and were soon caught up in the colour and lights and noise as the machine syphoned off their savings, one penny at a time.

I looked around the room to the poker tables, which were half full and buzzing. Took a step toward them, and then saw the table where I'd pulled my last big score. The same dealer was there, smiling out at the three men scattered around the table as he dealt cards to them, and I felt myself tighten and thin, as though I was stretching.

I didn't want to be there, but I couldn't stop myself. I walked over to the table, feeling thinner and more stretched by the moment, and stared at the dealer. Wondered if he'd had an inkling what I'd been up to, that last night at his table.

A tall thin man in a cheap Hawaiian shirt won his hand and crowed in delight as the dealer counted out his chips. The noise caught the attention of the manager, and he walked over. He quirked his eyebrows at the dealer, who shook his head, once. There was nothing wrong. Just a guy who actually won.

But the stretching feeling continued. I could feel it, like a band of iron across my forehead, and I wondered, just for a second, if I was having a stroke. Kicked myself, because Jesus, Mary and Joseph, I was dead and past all that, but the thinning strengthened even more, and when I looked down at my hands, they were dark grey smudges floating in front of me.

"What the hell?" I muttered. "What's going on?"

Then, I thought of Crystal. She was probably at work, telling fortunes or whatnot, and I wished with all my heart that I was with her. Away from this place, and with her. And then—

I was.

A blink of darkness, and I found myself standing in Crystal's small, tchotchke-filled store. She was chatting up a couple of blue hairs. Her face froze when I appeared, but she never missed a beat with the old women, and soon she'd wrapped the candles and other geegaws she'd convinced them to buy and shooed them out into the street. When she finished with them, she turned to me, and for a brief moment, she looked almost happy to see me.

"What are you doing back here?" she asked. "I thought you were going to stay with James and Marie."

I shrugged. "I'm not staying long. I just—"

Then I stopped, because I wasn't exactly sure how I'd made it there, and whether I could leave on my own. "They went to Broadacres," I said. "Said they were following a lead or whatnot. They said I had to stay in that damnable room again." I shuddered. "And I wasn't about to do that."

"So—what?" she asked. "You can move now?"

"To you, at least," I said, and shrugged.

"Well, damn," she muttered.

I opened my mouth, to tell her about the two men who'd tried to break into Marie and James's room, but stopped before I said a word. She didn't need to know about that. It wasn't her business.

"Did you know that they're planning on getting married while they're here?" I asked, instead. "Did they tell you?"

Crystal loved frigging weddings, and I guess I thought it was a way to keep her talking to me.

She blinked. "Married?" she asked. "They're getting married?"

"That's what they said," I said.

She pulled her cell phone from the pocket of the voluminous skirt she wore. "I'm calling them right now," she said.

I assumed she was going to demand they come get me, and felt hurt. "Fine," I said. "Whatever."

She dialled, but the instant James answered the phone, she didn't mention me at all. She started rattling on about them getting married, instead.

"You should have told me you two were tying the knot here," she said. "I can help you with all the planning and organizing, and you know, whatever."

She glanced in my direction and blinked, like she'd forgotten I was even there.

"Oh yeah, and Jimmy's back here with me," she said. "Looks like he's figured out how to move around on his own."

She tittered laughter, and nodded at whatever James replied to her. "I agree," she said. "One hundred percent. So, you're coming to get him after you finish at Broadacres?"

Her face crumpled as he spoke. "Oh," she said. "You're going to go find a wedding dress? Look, if Marie wants help, I know some places. You know, if you can't find anything suitable."

She listened for a moment longer and then nodded. "All right," she said. "That sounds good."

She set down her phone and looked over at me. "Looks like we're stuck together, for a while at least," she said. "Unless I can convince you to go someplace else?"

I thought about that room where I died and shook my head. "I'm not going anywhere," I said. "Unless you left the TV on for the cats? I could probably get back to your apartment, if I tried hard enough."

"Well, the cats would be happy to see you, I'm sure," she said shortly. "But you can stay here until James and Marie come to get you. And Jimmy? When they come to get you, you have to promise me you won't come back unless you're invited. Please?"

I imagined it had to do with the new boyfriend and grimaced. "All right," I said, and turned away from her.

There was no way in the world I was calling ahead for an invite, or anything else. If I needed to see her, I'd come to her, and there was nothing she could do about it.

Besides, I felt safe with her.

MARIE:
DAISY'S SOAP, AND DAISY'S SON

I FOLLOWED JACKSON as he slipped through the booths, behind all the people hawking their wares. I watched as each one of them looked up, expectant smiles on their faces, but their smiles dimmed as I did nothing more than walk past them. I kept my eyes on the ghost, who occasionally glanced at me with more and more fear showing on his face.

"Leave me alone," he finally yelled at me, waving his hands to make me go the hell away.

"I can't, Jackson," I said, much to the consternation of the young woman who had leaned forward expectantly, holding a candle out for me to smell.

"My name's not Jackson," the young woman said.

"I'm not talking to you," I said shortly.

Her face closed, and she turned away from me, walking right through Jackson to get to the back of her booth.

"What the hell do you want?" Jackson rasped. "Leave me alone."

"I just want to talk," I said.

The young woman looked at me, just for a second, then shook her head. "I'm not talking to you," she said. "Move along, crazy lady."

"Yeah," Jackson said. "Move along, crazy lady."

"We have to talk," I said again. "About Jimmy."

"I don't know any Jimmy either," the young woman said. "Jesus, lady, leave me alone." She looked around like she was trying to find someone to help her, like maybe a security guard, and I sighed.

"Come on, Jackson," I said. "Come out here and talk to me. Please."

Jackson didn't answer. Just sneered at me from behind the young woman. I could tell he wasn't going to move, so I turned back the way I'd come.

"All right," I said. "I guess I'm just going to have to talk to your mother."

The sneer on Jackson's face fell. "Leave her alone," he said. "She doesn't know anything—about anything."

"My mother?" the young woman squawked. "What does my mother have to do with anything?"

I'd had just about as much as I could stand. I walked away from the outraged young woman and the ghost and headed back the way I'd come.

"Leave my mom alone!" the ghost cried.

"Nope," I said. "Not unless you come out and talk to me. Right now."

I kept walking as he fussed and bothered at me from the other side of the booths, but at least he was following me. I hoped I'd be able to convince him that talking to me was his best option, but we were only two booths away before he finally broke and jumped through the booth and in front of me.

"What the hell do you want with me?" he snarled.

"I want to talk," I whispered. "About Jimmy."

"What has that asshole done now?" he asked.

"He's dead," I said. An old man carrying a large burlap carryall over his shoulder stared at me, so I smiled and turned away.

"Is there anywhere we can talk?" I whispered. "Away from the crowds?"

Jackson stared at me until I wanted to give him a slap, just to get his attention. "Please," I whispered. "It's important."

"All right," he said and walked past the booth. "Follow me."

I could see James's look of surprise and called, "I'll be back. Just give me a minute, all right?"

He nodded and turned back to Daisy. As we turned the corner and they both disappeared from my sight, I heard him laugh. It sounded so natural, and so easy, I wished I could go back and sit with the two of them, drinking tea and telling stories like two regular people. But I knew that I couldn't. I had a ghost to talk to.

So I followed Jackson.

Only a couple of people even looked in my direction as we walked through the back alley to an opening that let onto another aisle of tables running perpendicular to the aisle where Daisy's Soaps was housed.

"Where now?" I muttered.

Jackson looked right, and then left. "This way," he finally said.

"Where are you taking me?"

"The bathrooms."

"The bathrooms?" I scoffed. "You honestly think it's going to be quiet at the bathrooms?"

"Behind the bathrooms, yeah it is," Jackson replied. "Give me some credit, will you?"

He slid through a grandma who shuddered and stepped aside sharply, looking around like she wondered why the world had suddenly turned so cold.

"Watch where you're going," I said sharply. "We don't need to attract any undue attention."

"Well, quit talking to me, and we'll probably be just fine," he snapped. "You attract a lot more attention by talking to the open air than I do by walking through a couple of people."

"Fine," I snapped back, hating the fact that he was probably right, and determined to keep my mouth shut until we got to a place where we could actually chat.

Jackson led me down one aisle of tables, and then another, until I was absolutely turned around. I wished I'd grabbed the pathetic map we'd been given when we first arrived, but it was in James's pocket.

Finally, finally, we stepped onto a small patch of badly dehydrated grass next to two small buildings marked "Boy" and "Girl." Jackson walked past the buildings to a small patch of green behind them.

"We can talk here," he said.

The smell was overwhelming, which was probably why we were the only people back there. "It really stinks," I said. "You're lucky you can't smell it."

I walked over to a ramshackle picnic table and sat down.

Jackson sat across from me, his mouth set.

"All right," I said. "Tell me everything."

His mouth worked for a moment. "So Jimmy's dead," he finally said.

"A year ago," I said. "Almost to the day."

"Huh," he replied.

"When did you die?" I asked.

"This is pretty close to the first anniversary of my death, too," he said. "But time moves differently now. Or it feels like it does, anyhow."

"How did you die?" I asked. "Can you remember?"

"It was Rita," he mumbled. "At least I think it was Rita."

"You saw Rita before you died?" I asked, and then blinked. "Are you saying Rita did this to you? Killed you?"

He shrugged. "She was pretty pissed when she came over. I was afraid she'd wake Mom up. She was yelling. A lot."

"Yelling? What about?"

Jackson shrugged. "Oh, me and Jimmy did something she didn't like," he said. "She'd warned us against going to the Dunes, but Jimmy said it was ripe for the picking. That Rita was being overly cautious, and that we could make the system work at the Dunes, same way we'd worked all the other places we'd hit. And he was right. We made nearly ten grand that night, no sweat, no problem." He grinned, but it looked sickly on his grey face. "I don't know how she found out about it though. I didn't tell her, that's for sure."

"What are you talking about?" I asked.

"We had a system," he said. "Rita came up with it originally. She talked to me about it. Me and Jimmy both. She said if we did it just right, we could make enough to be able to retire, or whatever. Move somewhere better than this."

He pointed around him, at the colourful booths and all the rest of it. "I wanted to help Mom," he said, then shrugged. "Well, mostly I wanted to help Mom. I did like the idea of maybe being able to do a little travelling, I guess. Not having to work this stupid booth with her anymore." He laughed, again, but it honestly sounded more like a sob. "Maybe even get my own place, some day. And now I'm stuck with her, because she doesn't go anywhere else. Forever, it looks like. Guess I shouldn't have gone along with Jimmy. He can manage to find trouble, no two ways about it."

He was jumping all over the place in his conversation and starting to darken, which was a great big signal that I needed to calm him down so I could actually get some information from him.

I tried smiling at him, but when he flinched, I gave that up as a bad job.

"Tell me what the system was," I said, trying to keep my voice calm so I didn't scare him any more than he was already. "Tell me what Rita's plan was."

He rubbed his face, as though he was tired. Exhausted, probably, because he'd been carrying this for over a year.

Then he pulled his hands from his face and nodded at me. "All right," he said. "I'll tell you everything. But you have to promise you won't tell my mom." He shrugged. "She thought I'd finally got my shit together, before I died." He grinned, looking sheepish. "I told her I got a job," he said. "An actual pay-by-the-hour job. That was where she thought the money had come from. I don't want her knowing that I didn't."

I hid a smile and nodded. "I won't tell her a word."

"Good," he said. "I really love her, you know. And man, I've learned my lesson. Honest to God. If I could do it all over again, I'd go straight. Just be a regular Joe, like she wanted. No doubt about it."

He glanced at me hopefully. Like I could somehow bring him back to life and send him back in time or something, but I shook my head.

"Can't help you with any of that," I said.

He looked disappointed, then shrugged. "Ah, what the hell," he said. "It was worth a shot. What else do you want to know?"

"Tell me about Rita's system, and why you think that she killed you," I said. "For a start."

"I met Rita a couple of years ago," he said, staring down at the tabletop like he was reading tea leaves or something. "At a casino. One of the little ones, you know. Kinda quiet. She bought me a drink, and we ended up talking all night." He chuckled. "I told her things I've never told anybody." He smiled. "We were—making plans. I think she even loved me."

"So when did the three of you start working together?" I asked. "And who came up with the idea?"

"Rita did," he said. "She said she knew how we could make enough money to be together, forever. She introduced me to Jimmy, and he seemed all right." He smiled. "We all went to the IHOP after we did the first casino. That was nice."

"So," I said, trying to keep the impatience from my voice. "What was this plan you three came up with? And why the IHOP?"

Jackson laughed. "Everybody likes pancakes," he said. "Don't they?"

I shrugged, and he shook his head. "All right, so maybe it wasn't the pancakes," he said. "We went there because it was on the way back to Jimmy's car, and Rita said she was starving. She got the waffles with blueberries and whipped cream. Man, I could have sat for a year, watching her eat those."

"How many casinos did you rob?" I asked, trying to get him back on track. I didn't know how much longer James was going to want to sit with Daisy, but I was afraid if I let Jackson go too far down memory lane, we'd never get back to the point. Which was—what happened to Rita.

"We didn't rob them," Jackson said primly, his mouth pursed. "We had a system, and it worked."

"And what was that system?" I asked, hoping that he'd tell me something. Anything that would explain what had happened the night they'd both died.

"Heh," Jackson snorted. "We gamed the system." He winked at me. "We used technology." Then he shrugged. "To be honest, it was pretty low tech. We were playing poker. There was the three of us, you see. One was the player. One was the watcher. And one was in the car. The player wore a hearing device. He was connected to Rita, who was the one in the car. She was connected to the watcher. That first time, it was me." He smiled. "I did a good job," he said. "Good enough not to get us caught anyhow. We took just under ten grand that first night. Just to see if we could do it."

He snapped me a look, just to make sure he still had my attention. I nodded at him, to keep him going.

"I had a camera up my sleeve," he said, "And I sat at the edge of the table, so I could catch the facedown cards from the dealer. That was the key, you see. The player had to know what cards the dealer had gotten rid of with every hand. I did a good job. Caught

E.C. Bell

most of them, even that first night."

"How did the camera help Jimmy?" I asked.

"The images went to Rita, in the car. Jimmy had an earpiece, and Rita told him the cards that were gone. It worked like a charm. Then, when we hit our limit, Jimmy cashed out, and we were done. We kept the limit low, so we didn't attract any attention. No attention at all.

"It was a good system," he continued. "We did it three times a night, at three different casinos. Jimmy and me took turns being either the watcher or the player. We'd hit a grand total of fifteen casinos, up and down the Strip. Made over a million, all told." He grinned. "We even paid our taxes. Rita made sure of that."

I frowned. "How long did you work this system?"

"Two years," he said.

We sat and thought about things for a minute.

"Well, excuse me for saying this, but that's not really that much money," I finally said. "I mean, you were taking a big chance every time you ran your 'system'." I air quoted the word, and he glared at me. "Why didn't you go for more?"

"Rita said when you attract attention," Jackson said, "you get caught. Which was why going after the Dunes was a terrible mistake."

He glared out at nothing for a long moment, and I tried not to listen as a mother dragged her three squabbling children into the women's bathroom.

"Jimmy wouldn't listen," he continued when the noise finally disappeared. "'It'll be fine,' he said. 'She'll never find out,' he said." Jackson glared at the knife scarred table top. "Guess he was wrong about that, that son of a bitch."

Hmm.

"Why weren't you supposed to go to the Dunes?" I asked. "Was it because Rita worked there?"

He jerked in surprise. "Rita worked there?" he said. "I didn't know that."

It felt like he hadn't known much about her at all. Just like Jimmy.

"So she didn't tell you why you needed to stay away from the Dunes?" I prodded. "Just that it was one place to stay away from?"

"More or less," Jackson said. "Hey, there were lots of casinos

103

to hit here. We didn't need the Dunes."

"So why did you end up there?"

"It was Jimmy," he replied. "He was hot for the place, right off the jump. Rita said no but Jimmy never let up about it." He grinned sheepishly. "He finally wore me down."

"So you ran your con on the Dunes," I said.

"Yeah," Jackson replied. "But Rita wasn't involved. Jimmy said to leave her out of it. That we could handle everything ourselves and then tell her about it later. It worked well enough," he continued with a shrug, "but it was easier with Rita. Everything was easier with Rita."

"And then?"

"Then we split the take and I went home, like always. I don't know where Jimmy went."

"What happened after that?"

"Rita showed up at mom's place late that night. The sun was just about ready to come up, that's how late it was. She said she wanted to talk to me about what Jimmy and me had done. I tried to calm her down, but it did no good. No matter what I said, she got madder and madder. Then, she said we needed to have tea."

"Tea?" I asked.

"Yeah," he replied. "She said so we could calm down and talk things over like two adults, or whatever. I think it was more for her than for me, but hey, I drank that tea down double-quick, because I didn't want her to keep yelling."

"And then what happened?"

"I fell asleep," Jackson said. "And when I woke up, I was dead, and she was gone. I knew she was mad, but I didn't think she was that mad."

"So you're saying?" I prodded.

"I think Rita killed me," Jackson said.

We sat thinking our own thoughts for a moment. I didn't know what he was thinking about, but I was thinking that Jimmy had Rita wrong. Completely wrong.

"Do you think she killed Jimmy too?" he asked.

"I don't know," I said. "Maybe."

"Guess we shouldn't have broken her rule," he said, and shrugged. "You need anything more from me?"

I shook my head. He'd given me a lot to think about.

"Then, how about if we get back," he said. "I don't like to leave

Mom alone for this long."

I nodded, and we headed back to the Daisy's Soaps table.

JAMES WAS DRINKING tea that looked like twigs and bark and laughing uproariously at something Daisy had told him as we walked back to the booth.

Even that brief time away from her dead son had brightened her appreciably. She looked ten years younger, and almost happy.

"See?" I said to Jackson. "Your mother would be all right if you move on."

"Looks like she's making a run for your boyfriend," Jackson replied. "Better watch it. She was a catch, back in the day."

I glanced at the man in the scarf booth next door. He was glaring mightily at James, and I said, "I don't think I need to worry too much. And I think there are people who think your mother is still a catch."

"Roy?" Jackson said, and scoffed. "He's out of his league."

"Maybe," I said. "But don't you think your mother should make that decision?"

I walked up to the table covered in fragrant soap and waved at James to get his attention. "Time for us to go," I said.

James smiled, put the cup of tea down on the table, and jumped up as Daisy's face fell.

"Are you sure I can't talk to you into a cup of tea?" she asked. "We were chatting about your upcoming nuptials."

I stared at James, but all he did was smile back at me like he didn't have a care in the world.

"I didn't think we were telling everyone," I said. Hadn't we just talked about a Vegas wedding being a bad idea, and that we would drop it until we got home? What was James doing?

"I was just asking Daisy where would be the best place to get you a wedding dress," he said. "She mentioned the Las Vegas North Premium Outlets. I think we should go there, after we finish our tea."

"All right," I said, doing my best to keep a smile somewhere in the vicinity of my face.

James turned back to Daisy. "I'll let you know where the ceremony will be held," he said. "If you're free—"

"Oh, that would be wonderful, dear," Daisy said.

"But—" I spluttered.

James laughed. "I told you she'd react that way," he said. "She's such a private person. I think we should share our special day with everyone. Don't you?"

"I think that's a wonderful idea," Daisy said, then smiled at me. "Unless you'd rather it be just the two of you?"

"To be honest, I hadn't thought of who to invite," I said.

What the hell was up with him?

"We have to go," I said, again. "We have things to do."

"Wish I could finish my tea," James said, "but it looks like Marie's in a hurry."

"Maybe Roy would like some tea," I suggested, gesturing at the man who was still glowering at James from behind the rafts of fine linen scarves at the next booth.

"Roy?" Daisy said, and glanced at me.

"Jackson told me his name," I said gently.

She blinked. "What are you talking about?"

"Your son Jackson told me his name," I said. "Just now."

"My son is dead," Daisy said, her face sudden stone. "He's gone. Gone."

"He's not gone," I said, and stepped around the table so I could be closer to her. She took a step back, and shook her head like she hoped it would make me disappear.

"What's going on here?" she asked, and looked over at James. "What is she talking about?"

James smiled gently. "Marie can speak to the dead," he said. "Your son is here, with you. Now."

"He's been with you since he died," I said. "But I can help you—him—move on. This isn't good for either of you."

"But—" she started, then glared at James. "Why didn't you tell me that's why you were here?"

"Marie saw him and wanted to help," James said.

"And you were supposed to what?" she asked. "Keep me out of the way while she made my son disappear?"

"It isn't really like that," James said. "We heard about your soap and wanted to meet you. Your son—your son was a surprise to us both. But Marie can help. She can."

Daisy straightened and glared at both of us. "I think it's time for you to leave."

"All right, we will," I said. "But you have to know this. It's not good for you, having your dead son with you. You both need to move on. Him to the next plane of existence, and you, to the next phase of your life. You understand that, don't you?"

"I don't understand any of this," Daisy snapped, then looked around. "Is he still here? With me?"

"I am," Jackson said. "I'm right here with you, Mom." He reached across the table for his mother's arm. She shuddered as he touched her, and I watched her face age as he clambered through the table and to her side.

"He is," I said. "He's not ready to move on yet. But he will be, soon."

Daisy stared at me for a long moment, then fumbled in the pocket of her light sweater and pulled free a business card covered in cartoon daisies. "You contact me," she said. "So we can talk. Just promise me you won't make him disappear behind my back."

"I promise I won't," I said, and pocketed the card. Then, I looked at James. "You ready to go?"

"Yes." He turned to Daisy. "Thanks for the tea."

"Goodbye," she replied, stiffly. "It was wonderful talking to you."

"And you," James said. He linked his fingers in mine, and we walked away from the table full of soap, and down the lane to the exit, and back to the rental car.

As soon as we got to the car, I disengaged my fingers from his. "What the hell, James?" I asked.

"What?" He tried to look all innocent, and failed, completely. "I'm sorry," he said. "I know we agreed not to do the wedding thing, but I got two calls while you were talking to Jackson. One was from Tupilo's assistant. She found us a room at the Dunes, and Tupilo comped it."

I blinked. "What?"

"He gave us a room at the hotel to hold the wedding," James said. "For free."

"Didn't we decide to tell him we weren't doing this?" I asked.

"Well, yeah, but, Marie. He comped the room."

Jesus.

"And then Crystal called," he continued. "Uncle Jimmy was with her, and he told her about us getting married."

Jesus!

"I was trying to deal with Daisy, and Crystal was so excited, and well, it just seemed easier to keep going with idea of us getting married." He glanced over at me. "I'm sorry."

"James, this is not what we decided," I said.

"I know," he replied. "But it feels like it's kind of on rails now. People are buying it, Marie. I honestly think we'll be able to cosy up to Victor this way. I want to know what his connection to Uncle Jimmy is, and I think this will work." He glanced at me. "Besides, we can treat this like a practice run for our real wedding. You know, when we get back to Edmonton."

I looked at him for a long moment. "Is this really what you want?" I finally asked.

"Yeah," he said. "It is."

Well, looked like we were going to have a Vegas practice wedding. It was not on my bucket list, but it definitely looked like it was on James's.

What would it hurt, really? We could have a few laughs, and find out what Victor Tupilo was up to. Might even be fun. Maybe.

"All right," I said. "But it's just a lark. Right?"

"Right," he said, relief all over his face. "Absolutely. Now, did you get any information from Jackson?"

"Your uncle was running a scam on a bunch of the casinos here," I said. "With Jackson and Rita. And they'd been doing it for a while before he died."

"Well, well," James said.

"Wait until you hear this," I continued. "Jackson thinks that Rita killed him. She was really mad about them ripping off the Dunes."

James's face flattened in surprise. "He thinks Rita killed him?"

"Yeah," I said. "She came to his place—well, his mom's place. Yelled at him about him and Jimmy ripping off the Dunes, and then made him drink some tea. He said he fell asleep and woke up dead."

"Poor Daisy," James muttered.

"Oh." I hadn't thought about the fact that Daisy would have been the one who would have found the body. "Yeah. That would have been hard."

"So Jackson got killed because they went behind Rita's back and ripped off the Dunes?"

"Looks that way," I said.

"Did she kill Uncle Jimmy?"

"Maybe," I said. "Apparently she had rules, and they both broke them."

"So, we're looking for a woman who probably killed two guys for breaking a rule?" James asked. "A woman my dead uncle is still in love with?"

"Looks that way," I said. "Guess I'm going to have to tell him some hard truths when I see him next."

"And Victor Tupilo had nothing to do with Jimmy's death?" James continued.

"Doesn't look like it," I said.

"Well then, why is he doing us favours?" James said. "I mean the guy is comping us a room for our wedding. Why would he do that?"

"I have no idea," I said. "It's weird though, right?"

"Yeah, it is," James said. "Looks like we still have a mystery to solve."

"Two," I said. "We still have to find Rita for your uncle."

James shook his head. "My guess is Jimmy won't ever want to see Rita again after he finds out she killed him."

"Well, we'll talk with him," I said. "And make sure."

"Honestly, I just want him to move on," James said shortly. "I don't want him stuck here for all eternity, or whatever. But I don't think I have much more to say to him. We were done before he died. He just didn't know it. The Palais was going to be my last job for him."

"You said that already," I said gently.

"But then he died," he said. "And here we are."

He stared out the windshield for a long beat and then turned on the vehicle. I wondered how much more he hadn't told me about his uncle. What had happened that had made James even think about leaving him.

I needed to get him to talk to me about what had happened before he died, or James could potentially hold his uncle to him. Anger worked just as well as love. His anger could keep him from moving on. And I didn't want that, any more than I imagined James would.

But I definitely had questions for Jimmy. Lots and lots.

"Are we going to Jimmy?" I asked. "And tell him what we found out?"

"No," James replied. "Not yet."

"Well, where are we going?" I asked.

"We're going to buy you a wedding dress," he said, and grinned crookedly. "Of course."

STAGE TWO

THE DRESS

MARIE:
SHOPPING

WE DROVE TO the outlet mall Daisy had told James about, and I was instantly overwhelmed. There were a ton of stores that sold wedding dresses. And then there were stores that rented them. Rented everything, in fact.

We could have done the whole deal at a place called Rent a Wedding, but James said no.

"I want to help you find a dress. One that you can take home and use at our real wedding, in Edmonton."

So we tried to find a dress that looked like we were in it for the long haul.

It went badly. Even though he'd said he wanted to help, James didn't seem to care what the dress looked like. He shrugged his way through me parading around in fifteen of them, and then I hit the wall.

"You're really shitty at this, you know," I said. The poor little woman who was trying to help me find the perfect gown for my perfect day gasped and mumbled something about looking for another dress, maybe a mermaid style, and clomped back down the long aisles of wedding gowns, disappearing in all the white. I was pretty sure she wasn't coming back.

I stepped down off the raised platform and glared at James, who stared at me with that stupid "Who me?" look men get when they screw up and know it.

"Why won't you help?" I cried. I grabbed handfuls of the skirt of the gown I was wearing, and shook it at him. "This is your stupid idea! I'm supposed to be finding a frigging wedding dress. And you're supposed to be helping me. Why won't you?"

"They all look fine," he said. "I thought—well, I thought you'd just grab one, and we'd be done. You know?"

"Well, that's not the way this works," I said. "They don't all look fine. I look ridiculous in most of them, and pathetic in the rest." I sat down on the edge of the platform and suddenly felt like crying. "I wish Mom was here," I muttered. "She'd help me find something nice."

Now, that wasn't the truth. My mother's taste in everything had always run to the florid and unholy, and I hadn't let her pick out my clothes since I was seven years old. I wasn't sure why I'd even mentioned her name, but James blinked, and then stood and took my hands in his.

"I'm sorry," he said. "This must be hard."

Then I burst into tears, big wimp that I was, and James pulled me into his arms and comforted me. He was right. This was hard. Sometimes a girl needs her mother, even if the wedding is a sham.

"Should we stop?" he asked, into my hair.

"Yeah," I said. "I can't even think right now. I wish there was someone else who could help me with this. Like Jasmine. Heck, even Rhonda would be all right." I sniffed. "I know it's supposed to be a lark, but somehow it doesn't feel like it. You know?"

James smiled and snapped his fingers. "Crystal said she'd help," he said. "She's a girl. She probably has opinions about things like this."

I remembered all the *Bride* and *Wedding* magazines that I'd seen in Crystal's apartment. "She'd probably go for that," I muttered, and stood. "I'm going to get out of this thing. Call her and see if she's interested."

"Will do," James said.

I went back to the dressing room and took off the white nightmare the retail therapist had chosen for me. Pulled on my shorts and t-shirt and felt like myself again. Sort of. Wishing that Mom was here with me had surprised me, but I guess it shouldn't have.

I missed my mother.

I had another boo-hoo session in the dressing room and by the time I'd wiped the last of the mascara from my face, James had made a deal with Crystal. She'd meet us later that night, at the front entrance to the hotel.

"She said she'd be happy to help you," James said. "She said it would be fun."

I didn't think it was going to be fun, but I didn't say anything. At least he was trying.

"What are we going to do now?" I asked.

"First, I owe you a shopping spree. A real one, this time," he said.

So, he took me shopping. The outlet mall was huge and had nearly every designer brand in the world. Or that was how it seemed to me, anyhow.

At the end of it all, I'd bought three new dresses and a cute pair of sandals. I wore the pink dress with a really pretty floral pattern and the sandals out of the store, and for the first time since we'd arrived in Las Vegas, I didn't feel like I was going to melt in the heat.

And the best part? The prices were terrific, even with the conversion rate.

Shopping therapy. There's nothing like it.

JIMMY:
GOING HUNTING

CRYSTAL DIDN'T LOOK too happy when her cell phone chirped at her.

"Answer it," I said. "Maybe it's James."

Nobody had dropped into her shop for most of the day, which meant that Crystal had to deal with me almost exclusively for just about four hours. All right, so maybe I got a little cranky because I didn't want to be there any more than she wanted me there, but still, it wouldn't have hurt if she'd acted just a little bit human.

All she did was glare at me before she turned her back and answered the call.

"Where are you?" she snapped. "You told me you'd be back in two hours. Two. He's driving me crazy, and he keeps saying he has information for you, but he won't tell me what it is."

I was going to say something really cutting, but before I could open my mouth, she spoke again.

"Shopping?" she exclaimed. "You want me to go shopping with Marie?"

She listened for a while more, the fingernails of her left hand tapping impatiently on the table holding the cash register. She didn't say anything, but the tapping slowed, and then stopped.

"A wedding dress, huh," she finally said. "I can do that. When are you coming back?" She listened for a moment more and then nodded. "Sure, I'll meet you outside the Dunes then."

"Tell him I'm coming," I said.

"Jimmy has info for you," she said, "so he's coming with me."

Then she hung up.

"He's not that thrilled," she said. "He wanted to know why you couldn't just tell me." She stared at me. "Any reason you couldn't tell me so I could tell him?"

I thought about telling her the truth, which was that I didn't trust her to get the information right, then decided against saying that.

"I just want to make sure he's all right," I muttered. "You can understand that, can't you?"

"Yes," she said. "I understand. Don't get your knickers in a twist."

Now, that stung.

It didn't take her long to shut up the shop, but it felt like years to me. I needed to deliver the information about the two men who tried to break into James and Marie's hotel room earlier that day. Why couldn't she understand it was important, and that we had to hurry?

BOTH JAMES AND Marie were waiting by the fountain at the front entrance of the Dunes when we drove up.

Crystal jumped out of her van, all excited about the shopping expedition, but James stared right through her into the side window where I was floundering around, trying to push my way through the van wall which had suddenly turned into steel on me. Which it was, I guess, but still. Couldn't get out no matter how hard I tried.

"Is he here?" he asked.

"He is," Crystal said. "He says he has something to tell you, but I have no idea what it is. He wouldn't say a word to me."

"Help me get out," I said, but all Crystal did was glance at me before turning to Marie.

"You should have told me you were getting married," she said.

"Sorry," Marie replied. "I guess it slipped my mind."

"Slipped your mind?" Crystal scoffed. "Are you kidding me now?"

"Yeah," Marie said, and snorted humourless laughter.

"We're going to have fun," Crystal said. "I know a great place. You'll love it."

Marie glanced at her. "Thanks for this," she said. "James is pretty useless, to be honest."

"Most men are," Crystal replied. "Besides, it's bad luck for him to see you in your dress. Before the wedding. You know?"

"Yeah, I've heard," Marie said.

"Enough of the hen party," I snapped. "Get me out of here. I have news."

Marie opened the van door and touched me, giving me the strength to get out. "Do tell," she said.

I told her about the two men who'd tried to break into their hotel room while they were gone—that got everyone's attention pretty damned quick.

"One of them was named R, or something. They talked about working for a drug dealer in Edmonton. And that you met them before."

Marie turned to James and told him everything I'd said, and I watched his face whiten. "So, he knows who they are," I said. "What are you two involved in?"

"Nothing," Marie snapped, and turned back to James. "What is going on here?"

"I don't know," James said, "but I'm going to find out. You guys go shopping, and I'll look around. See what I can find."

Before I really thought it through, I said, "I'll help him."

Marie glanced at me, and I remembered I was dead and James couldn't see me. I was useless.

"Do you think that's the smartest thing to do?" she asked James. "They were breaking into our room, James."

"Yeah," he replied. "And I want to know why. I'll just snoop around a bit. See what I can learn."

He reached into his pocket and pulled out a credit card. "Put everything on this," he said. "Now go have fun."

Marie took the card, tentatively. "Are you sure about this?" she asked, waving the card at him.

"I am," he said, and smiled at her. "Find something nice."

"I'll keep the price down," she said, but still looked concerned. "Promise me you'll be careful."

"I will," he replied. He reached over and pecked her on the cheek. "Enjoy yourself."

Marie turned away from him and then grabbed Crystal. "Keep him here for a minute," she whispered, and then walked me a couple of steps away from the van.

Crystal didn't even bat an eye. "Hey, James," she said. "I have a question or two about colour schemes."

James looked confused, but she had his attention, and Marie

was able to talk to me without him noticing.

"I want you to stay with him," she said. "And find out what he's doing. And I want you to tell me everything. Understand?"

"Sure," I said. Besides, I wanted to know what was up, too.

"Good," she said. "Grab hold of him."

Before I could ask her what she meant, she ran up to James and threw her arms around him. His aura surrounded both of us, and I was able to connect to him as he hugged her back.

"We won't be gone long," she said to James. "And if you need anything—anything at all—you call me. All right?"

"Will do," he said, and grinned at her crookedly. "Now, you better check with Crystal, because I don't think green and pink are very good colours for a wedding."

Marie almost smiled, but not quite. "I'll handle everything," she said. "But remember . . ."

"Call if I have a problem," he said and smiled down into her worried face. "But you don't have to worry. I'll be fine."

"Hope so," Marie said. Then she snuck a glance at me, clinging to James's arm for all I was worth, and her look seemed to say "Stick with him like glue."

"I won't let him out of my sight," I said.

Marie and Crystal got into the van, waved, and then Crystal wheeled out of the parking lot and onto the street, narrowly missing a station wagon that was going in the opposite direction. There was much horn honking, and I was pretty sure I saw Crystal give the driver of the station wagon the finger.

"Good grief," James muttered. "Be careful."

Then, when Marie and Crystal were out of sight, James turned to the entry of the Dunes, unwittingly pulling me with him.

I could feel a strange sort of energy zinging through him. Excitement and something else. Something I couldn't quite put my finger on. Then it hit me.

He was going hunting.

Whatever he had planned, I was going to stick to him for all I was worth, no matter where he went. If the young idiot was going to get himself into trouble, he'd need help getting out of it.

Maybe I couldn't do anything on this plane anymore, but I could sure as shit keep track of him for his cute little fiancée. Yep, I could do that.

MARIE:
BUYING THE DRESS. FINALLY

CRYSTAL DROVE FAST, with a nonchalance that bordered on neglect, and frantic honking followed her everywhere the big white van went.

"Maybe you should slow down a bit," I said when she ran the third red light in a row.

"We have to hurry," she replied, veering through the traffic like she was involved in a police car chase or something. "We're close to closing time."

"Ah." I grabbed the dash and tried to keep from being thrown around too much. "Got it."

"So what was Jimmy talking about?" she asked. "He never told me anything about a drug dealer breaking into your hotel room."

"I think he said they knew a drug dealer," I replied. "And they never made it into our room."

"Well, that sounds scary," Crystal replied.

"James will handle it," I said shortly. "I'm not worried."

"You're braver than me," Crystal said and smiled at me. "I would have made a beeline to the police by now. If I were you."

If we were home, we might have done the same thing. But we weren't home, and James was acting like he was above the law, so . . .

"It's nothing to worry about," I said, and smiled. "So it looks like you have a real empire going on here. A shop, ghost tours, and you wrote a book?"

"Two," she said, and smiled back. "I wrote two. To be honest though, the only thing that really pays is the store. I'm lucky if the tours are half full, and the books?" She grimaced. "I don't think anyone reads anymore."

"But you're writing another one," I said. "Aren't you?"

"Hey, you do what you can," she replied. "Throw everything at the wall and see what sticks. And hey, maybe somebody will want to make a movie out of one of them." She grinned. "That's where the money is."

I shrugged and watched the traffic stream around us.

"So, how did you get in the business?" Crystal asked.

"My mom," I said shortly. "She taught me how to interact with the dead. How to move them on."

"Most times I can barely see them," Crystal said. "The ghosts, I mean. Jimmy's the first one who ever stuck."

"You're lucky," I said, and laughed. "That happens to me all the time."

"But it must be nice to be able to help them," Crystal said. "You know, so they can have closure."

"I guess," I said.

"And the families," she continued. "Helping them. That must feel good."

I shrugged. "I don't help them," I said. "I'm just there for the spirits of the dead."

"Hmm," she replied. A noncommittal sound, but I was pretty sure I heard judgment.

"I only deal with the dead," I said again. "The living have to work it out on their own. I mean, they have shrinks, right?" I laughed, but it sounded hollow. "They have the living to help them. The ghosts—they only have me."

"But what if the dead want to—I don't know—say goodbye or whatever," Crystal continued. "Like Jimmy. He's so focussed on that Rita chick. What do you do about them?"

"I try to get them what they need," I said. "If I can. If the living get some closure out of it, that's just a bonus. You know?"

"I guess I'm just used to working with the living," she said. "They're the ones who come to me."

"Except for Jimmy," I said.

"Yeah," she sighed. "Except for Jimmy. Do you think you're

going to be able to find Rita for him?"

"I don't know," I said. "She has either moved away, or changed her name. Or she's dead."

Crystal jerked and stared at me. "Do you really think she's dead?"

"Maybe," I said. "We got into her apartment, and all of her stuff was there. Like she'd left the place yesterday. But she hadn't been there in a long time. People don't usually walk away from everything like that."

"Sometimes, they do," Crystal said. "If their situation is bad enough."

"I guess," I replied.

"So, what do you think happened to her?"

"I don't know," I said.

If anything bad had happened to Rita, it had probably happened because of the game Jimmy and Jackson had fixed at the Dunes. But I had no evidence that anything had happened to her. All I knew for sure was Jackson thought she'd killed him for breaking the rules. Jimmy had died the same night and he'd broken Rita's rules too.

So, there was a good chance that she'd killed them both and then hit the road. But she'd taken nothing from her apartment. Nothing.

"That'll break Jimmy's heart," Crystal said. Then she frowned. "Unless they can get together in the afterlife. Can they do that?"

"The afterlife isn't really for getting together," I said.

"But if she's dead and he's dead, couldn't they both be together. Dead?" she pressed.

"I guess," I muttered. "But there's a possibility Rita might have had something to do with Jimmy's death, so—"

"Are you serious?" she gasped.

"It's what Jackson thinks," I replied. "He—worked with both of them, and he's dead. And Rita was the last one to see him alive."

"Wow," Crystal whispered. "I thought he just wanted to say goodbye to her. Maybe he wants revenge. What do you think?"

"I don't know," I said. I rather pointedly looked around. "How much further is the shop?"

"Oh," she said, and giggled self-consciously. "Sorry. We're almost there."

She pointed, and I tried not to dive under the dash when the van swooped toward a line of vehicles parked along the street.

"You'll like Alice," Crystal said and she parked the van." She'll help you find the perfect dress. You'll see."

"DRESSES FOR HEAVEN" was not a dress shop for tourists. It was a little hole in the wall on a grubby street full of little holes in the wall for people who barely made minimum wage.

"It looks better inside," Crystal said. "And Alice, the woman who runs it? She's really nice."

"Great," I said. Tried to make my voice at least sound neutral, but it was hard.

We got out of the van, and she ran ahead of me, waving through the window at whoever was inside. "Come on," she called to me. "She'll be so happy to meet you."

All my visions of this taking a grand total of fifteen minutes, no fuss no muss, disappeared in a disappointed puff of smoke. I followed Crystal through the door and into the shop.

It was cool inside. Not air conditioner cold, but cool like the veranda of an old lady's house while you were waiting for her to bring you lemonade.

Alice walked up to us and wrapped Crystal in a hug. I could smell lavender or some other old lady smell, but it smelled good, coming from her.

"Crystal, my girl," she said. "I thought you were working."

"I decided to take a couple of hours off," Crystal said. "I'm helping Marie find a dress. A wedding dress."

Alice looked at me over her cat's eye glasses with crystal clear eyes and an appraising smile. "So," she said. "You're Marie?"

"Yes, Ma'am," I said. "Glad to meet you."

"Just call me Alice," she replied. "Any friend of Crystal's is a friend of mine."

Maybe I was wrong about her age. She stood tall—well, as tall as someone five foot two could stand—and the muscles of her arms looked firmer than mine.

"All right," I said.

"And you're here for a wedding dress," she said.

"Yes." I looked around the shop, but didn't see a wedding dress anywhere. Lots of women's clothing, much of it dark, which made me think, again, of funerals.

"They're in the back," Crystal said. "Alice likes to keep them out of the sunlight."

"The lace discolours," Alice said.

Lace?

Alice must have read my face, because she laughed. "Don't worry," she said. "We'll find you something nice."

She turned on her heel and marched to a drape-covered door in the back of the small store. I turned to Crystal.

"Are you sure about this?" I whispered.

Crystal smiled and nodded. "She'll find the perfect dress for you," she said, and took me by the arm. "Trust me."

I didn't really see that happening. Not in this lifetime. But I let her lead me through the drape-covered door to the back of the store. It was like walking into another world.

As cramped and dark as the front of the store looked, the back was bright and clean. A small desk stood in one corner of the room. On it sat a computer and a neat stack of invoices. Next to it was a table with an old-fashioned sewing machine. Three dresses hung on a small rack next to it. Pins with bright heads stuck out of them, marking alterations. In the other corner was a small coffee station with a high-tech coffee machine sitting, pristine, like it had just been taken out of the packaging.

Still no wedding dresses, and no Alice either, but Crystal led me to the far wall and pushed back a section of curtain that covered the whole thing.

"They're back here," she said, and pulled me inside.

The light in the back was delicate, and I realized it was coming from small lights set on tables around the room and actual chandeliers hanging haphazardly from the ceiling. Next to the tables were chairs, and in the centre of the room was a small platform.

All around the outer edges of the room were racks of white gowns, carefully wrapped in plastic.

"I like to keep grubby fingers off them, when I can," Alice said. "Crystal, can you lock up the front for me? Marie and I need to have a chat, and I would rather we weren't interrupted."

Crystal nodded and headed for the front of the store. Glanced back at Alice and asked, "Want me to make some tea?"

"Sweet tea's in the fridge," Alice said, and then glanced at me. "Or would you prefer hot tea?"

"Sweet tea will be fine," I said. Crystal nodded and disappeared, and Alice turned her attention to me.

"We should get started," she said. "Put your bag down, and get up on the platform. I'll take some measurements."

"I'm size six," I said.

"I'll be the judge of that," Alice said.

All right. I put down my purse and put myself into the hands of the master.

She measured absolutely everything and wrote the numbers down in a small journal with sixties-style flowers emblazoned on the cover.

Crystal came back in with three glasses full of tea on a small tray. She set the tray down on a table and sat, watching the proceedings.

"Do you have a style preference?" Alice asked. "And what's your price range?"

I shrugged. "Cheap," I said. "And I want to stay cool. Other than that, I don't really care."

Crystal looked shocked. Alice shook her head and *tsked*. "Everybody has an opinion about their wedding dress."

"Honestly," I said. "I'm okay with just about anything."

All right, so that wasn't the truth because James and I hadn't been able to find anything even close to nice, but honestly? I didn't know.

"All right," Alice said. She slapped the small journal shut and set it by the tray of iced tea. "Let's get started, shall we?"

She walked to the back rack and ran her hands over the plastic-covered shoulders of the dresses. Finally stopped, and pulled one free.

"Let's start here," she said.

I could see the mounds of lace through the plastic, and could tell I was going to be taught a lesson.

"I don't think—" I started, but shut my mouth when Alice shook her head and handed me the dress.

"Through there," she said, handing me the dress and pointing at a small change area in the corner. "Put it on."

"You want some help?" Crystal asked.

The last thing I needed was someone helping me put a dress on. "No," I said. "I'll be fine."

She shrugged and picked up a glass of the iced tea. "Up to

you," she said. "Call if you get stuck."

The change room was small, and I started to sweat almost immediately. I opened the zipper of the plastic covering the wedding dress, and almost felt like I was going to drown in the skirt. There were layers and layers of material that slithered out of the plastic like a demented parachute. How frigging big was the thing?

I finally got all of the dress out of the plastic, and looked for the price tag. There wasn't one, and that made me sweat even more. She'd heard me say I wanted cheap, right? This didn't feel cheap.

I carefully hung it up by one shoulder and tried not to trip on the skirt as I quickly pulled the pretty pink dress I was wearing over my head and dropped it on the teeny chair next to my left leg.

"You doing all right?" Crystal called.

"Just fine," I said. "I'll just be a minute."

I thought for a second about pulling the dress over my head, but gave up that plan very quickly. Took the dress off the hook and it settled to the floor in white waves. I did my best not to step on any of it as I put one foot and then the other through the bodice. Then I pulled it up by the shoulders and put it on.

I'd tried on fifteen dresses with James, but not one of them had looked or felt anything like this one. Even with the back undone, it fit me like it had been made for me.

But it was heavy. Really heavy. And there were about a million little buttons running down the back. I did up the one at the top to keep the thing on, but couldn't manage any more of them by myself. The lace arms clung to me, making me sweat even more, and the huge skirt just kept getting bigger.

"I don't know about this," I said, and scrabbled at the one button I'd managed to close, so I could take the dress off.

"Come out," Alice said. "Let us see."

"It's really not my style," I said. I could feel sweat literally running down my back, and was afraid that Alice was going to have a "you sweat in it you buy it" policy.

"Come out," Alice commanded. "Now."

So, I did. I tried not to look at myself in the mirrors spread liberally around the room, but caught sight of myself in one of them and all I could think was, "I look like I'm drowning in this thing."

"You're not drowning," Alice said.

"Oh." Guess I'd spoken out loud.

"Get up on the platform." Then Alice frowned. "Do you have shoes on?"

"No," I said. "I didn't want to rip it. Heels and all that."

Alice gestured impatiently at the open door of the change room. "Get her shoes, will you, Crystal?" she said. "She needs the full effect."

"Will do," Crystal said, and retrieved my sandals. She placed them on the dais beside the incredibly huge skirt. "Want some help?" she asked again. Rather unhelpfully, I thought.

"No," I said. "I'm fine."

Then I almost flipped myself off the dais when I bent over to put on one of the sandals. Crystal snorted laughter and held out her hand. "Let me help," she said.

"All right," I said through gritted teeth. "Help me."

She slipped one sandal on my foot, and then the other one, easily. "You good?" she asked when she was done.

I nodded, and she took a step back. "Turn around," she said. "I'll do up a few more of the buttons. You know, so you can see how it looks when you're all pulled together."

I turned, and she quickly did up four more of the tiny buttons. I could feel the dress tighten to my form, and when she stepped back, I finally had the courage to look at myself.

"Oh wow," I gasped.

I looked like a frigging fairy princess. Even with my haphazard ponytail and no makeup, I looked like a fairy princess.

My mother would have loved that dress.

"No," Alice said shortly. "That won't do."

"But—" I started. Crystal shook her head, and I momentarily shut my mouth.

"She's always right," she said. "Don't fight her. Let me undo those buttons for you."

I turned and held the bodice to me as she opened the back of the dress. "I thought it looked kind of nice," I muttered as I stepped off the platform.

"It did," Crystal said. "But the dress overwhelmed you. Right, Alice?"

"Right," Alice said. She was back at the racks, rustling through the plastic-wrapped dresses. "Less will be more with you."

"What if I get my hair done and put on makeup?" I asked. I couldn't quite figure out why I was arguing for a dress that made me feel like I was drowning, but I was. Probably because my mother would have fought for that dress. Fought me for that dress.

"It's much too heavy for you," Alice said. "Let it go. We'll find the perfect one. Promise."

She pulled another dress free from the rack and held it out. "Mermaid style. Try this one."

Crystal took the dress from her and followed me to the change room.

"Just thought I'd tell you that the dress you have on is $6,000.00," she whispered.

"Oh my god," I gasped.

"Didn't James say money is no object?" she asked.

"It is an object," I said as I worked my way out of the far too expensive nightmare that the dress had suddenly become. "I don't care what James told you."

"All right," Crystal replied. "I'll tell Alice."

I could hear them whispering to each other as I hung the fairy princess dress back on the hanger. I wasn't even going to try to stuff it back into that plastic for fear of ripping it. Six thousand dollars. What the hell was James thinking, money was no object? This wasn't even a real wedding.

The ring James had given me snagged on the lace arm of the dress, and I spent frightening seconds disengaging it.

"Want the next one?" Crystal called from the other side of the door.

"I don't know," I said. I opened the door and handed her the fairy princess dress. "Maybe we can stop. Try another place. Not so expensive."

"I'm sorry about that," she said, and held out the second dress. "Just try this one on. It's not expensive. Really."

I looked down at the dress, and could see a bunch more lace. "How much?" I asked.

"$600," she said. "And Alice says there's wriggle room."

Still way too much to pay as far as I was concerned. "I don't think so," I said, and felt my throat tighten. Why had James set me up like that?

129

Tying the Knot

"Just try it on," Crystal said.

The dress I pulled from the plastic cocoon was a mermaid style, covered in lace and little crystals. No sleeves, thank goodness, and the back was open nearly to my waist.

I stepped into it and pulled it up over me. It clung to my hips and my waist, but when I tried to take a step, it caught me at the knees. I wouldn't be able to take a full step in that dress. I wasn't even sure how I'd manage the steps up onto the dais.

But it did look wonderful. The warm light in the room reflected off the crystals, making me shimmer in light. Almost like a ghost, I thought, but pushed that thought away.

I managed to get up on the dais without having to crawl, but it was a close thing, and I knew that this one was not it, either.

And it was heavy. Almost as heavy as the first dress, and even though it had no sleeves, I felt sweat popping out on my upper lip.

"What do you think?" Alice asked.

"It's pretty," Crystal said.

"It fits nice," I replied. "But—"

"It's still not right," Alice said. She frowned and stared at me for a moment, then snapped her fingers. "I think I have the perfect one," she said. "Give me a minute."

I flailed my way off the dais and back to the change room. The dress seemed to gain weight as I walked, and I was happy to remove it.

"She'll find you the right one," Crystal said, through the door. "Honestly, she will."

Crystal sounded nervous, so I plastered a smile on my face as I opened the door to the change room.

"I know she will," I said, as I handed the beaded dress to her. "This one was close."

"It looked nice," she said. "You have the figure for it."

Alice reappeared, with one more plastic-encased dress on a hanger. "This one's from a couple of seasons ago," she said. "But I couldn't convince myself to get rid of it. I knew it would be perfect for—someone. I just had to wait for her to walk through the door."

She handed the dress to Crystal, who handed it to me. I took the dress back into the change room with me.

This dress was different. It did not fill the room with miles of material, or glint like a ghost. And it wasn't heavy. Not at all.

I pulled away the plastic and looked at the dress on the hanger. It had no sleeves, which was good. There was lace on the bodice, but it was filmy, light. There didn't seem to be anywhere that the dress would be overly tight to my form.

"What style of dress is this?" I called through the change room door.

"The designer called it a sheath dress," Alice replied. "Though I find it has more flare to the skirt than others I have in the shop. It's extremely simple. A belt might fancy it up a bit, if you'd like."

"Let's see what it looks like without," I said, and stepped into the dress.

It did not encase my body in miles of material like either of the other ones. As I pulled it up over my hips and shrugged the bodice into place, it felt right.

Light, and whatever the material was, I could breathe in it.

"Can you help me with the buttons?" I called to Crystal.

"It's a zipper, not buttons—the buttons are fake—but I'd be happy to," she said, and opened the door. Then, she gasped, her hand to her mouth.

"What's wrong?" I asked, and looked down at the dress in horror. I'd done something to it. Wrecked it somehow. "Is it ripped? Did I rip it?"

"No," she said. "No, it looks perfect. Turn around."

I'd steadfastly ignored the mirror in the change room to that point, but glanced at myself as Crystal zipped me up. It fit me like it had been made for me. And I could breathe. No drowning in fabric. No overwhelm.

"All done," she said. "How does it feel?"

"Good," I said. "It feels good."

It felt better than that. It felt like nothing at all. Like I was wearing sunshine and rainbows or something. I'd never had a dress fit me like that before.

"Let's show Alice," she said, and held the door open for me. I stepped through, and Alice looked me up and down.

"Well," she said. "Well, well, well."

I grinned at her. "This one looks pretty good, doesn't it?"

"Up on the dais," she said. "I want to see how you move in it."

I stepped up, easily. "Doesn't even look like you'll have to hem it or anything," I said. "It's almost like—"

"It was made for you," Alice said. "I knew I was keeping it for a reason."

She made me twist and turn. Hold my arms above my head, and then out to the side. "Twirl," she finally said.

I almost laughed at her. "Why would I do that?"

"People usually dance at their weddings," Alice said. "Let's see how it moves."

I twirled, and the skirt whirled around me, light as dandelion fluff. Both Crystal and Alice clapped delightedly.

"What about the belt?" I asked. "Should I try that?"

"No," Alice said. "Most assuredly not. That dress fits you perfectly. And you need no more decoration. You and that dress work together. Perfectly."

I turned and really looked at myself, and felt my breath catch in my throat. "Holy crow," I whispered.

"Holy crow, indeed," Alice said.

Crystal laughed, a joyous sound. "I think you found your dress," she said.

"I think you're right," I said, then stopped. I hadn't asked the price. I felt my heart practically drop to my feet. It was going to be too much, and I was either going to let it go and regret it forever, or I was going to pay for it, and hate it a little bit because of all the wasted money.

Nothing is ever perfect.

"How much is it?" I asked.

"Like I said, it's from a couple of seasons ago. It shouldn't even be here, but I had the feeling I'd find the right person for it." She grinned. "Looks like I have."

"How much?" I repeated.

"One hundred and fifty," she said. "And I'll throw in a veil, if you want."

I stared at her for a long beat, sure I'd heard her wrong. "Did you say—?"

"One hundred and fifty," she repeated. "With a veil."

"Keep the veil," I said, and grinned. "I'll take it."

"Excellent," she replied. Then she turned to Crystal. "Good thing you brought her to me. We found her perfect dress."

"I knew you would," Crystal said. She turned to me. "Let me help you get out of it."

"Happy to," I said. "Thanks."

Crystal asked me if I wanted to go check out flowers for a bouquet. I said no.

"Time to get back to reality," I said.

"But you're getting married the day after tomorrow," she replied, confusion on her face. "Isn't the wedding supposed to be your reality?"

I blinked. She was right. I actually had a lot to do, to get ready for the wedding, even if it was just for practice.

"All right," I said reluctantly. "Let's look at flowers, but then I have to head back. All right?"

"All right," she said. But I had the feeling that choosing flowers wasn't the only thing on her mind. I also had the feeling that she was putting a lot more thought into my fake wedding than I was.

Alice raised her hand and waved. "Try to enjoy your wedding, Marie," she said. "You're going to look wonderful."

"Thanks," I said. Then I ran back and hugged her. "Thanks for everything."

"You're welcome, girl," she said. "Let Crystal help you with the rest. She lives for this stuff, but I get the feeling you don't." And she smiled.

"I will," I said.

Then Crystal and I left the small shop, and I went on the shopping trip of my life.

JIMMY:
LOOKING AFTER JAMES

JAMES HEADED STRAIGHT into the casino. He searched high and low, but didn't find who he was looking for. Namely, the two fools who tried to break into his room.

After he'd searched every inch of the casino, he walked back out to the reception area and grabbed a white courtesy phone.

"I'm looking for a Ric Svensen," he said. "Any chance he has a room here?"

I imagined by the look on his face he got told that they don't hand out that kind of information. "Can you connect me with his room?" he asked.

Another pause, while he stewed. Then, he was put through.

"This is James Lavall," he said. "I hear you're looking for me. Time for us to meet. I'll be in the Savoy Cafe. Meet me there."

He slammed down the phone and stalked toward the coffee shop. Took a table at the rear and sat with his back to the wall. Ordered a coffee, but didn't touch it. Just stared at the door.

I honestly didn't expect them to come. Not after they'd tried to break into James's room and all, but after half an hour, there they were.

"About time," James said. He didn't move. Just stared at the two men as they looked around the room the way he had when he'd first entered. They stopped when they saw him. Glanced at each other, and then Ric walked toward James's table with the other guy behind, obviously looking for any potential problems in amongst all the tourists and starving gamblers scattered throughout the coffee shop.

"Lavall," Ric said. "James Lavall. I hear you're looking for me."

"That's right," James said. He still hadn't moved, but I could feel him tense up, like he was ready to jump the guy if he made any kind of a move.

Ric waited for James to explain himself and quirked his eyebrow when he didn't.

"So, what do you want?" he finally asked.

The other guy had joined Ric, but kept his eyes on the tables around them. He really was expecting trouble.

"I know you," James said. "From Edmonton."

Ric's face flattened, and he stared at Jim for a long, cold moment. "Is that so?" he finally asked. "I think you might have me mixed up with somebody else. I've never been to Edmonton."

"Oh, you have," James replied. He still hadn't moved. He kind of reminded me of a big cat readying for the strike. "I recognized you the first day I got here, Ric. And then I heard that you and your buddy here tried to break into my room. So, I think it's time we have a talk. You know. Man to man."

Ric stared for a moment more, then his whole demeanour changed. He relaxed and laughed. "I thought you recognized me," he said. "Man, it's been a while. Mind if I sit?"

He grabbed the chair opposite James before James spoke, and sat. Signalled for the server.

"Two bourbons, neat," he said. "Make sure it's Blanton's and not any of that cheap crap. Got it?"

The server nodded and hurried away, and Ric turned his attention back to James.

"You going to tell me why you tried to break into my room?" James asked. "Or do I have to guess?"

Ric blinked. "I didn't try to—" he started, but James waved his words away.

"Somebody saw you," he said. "And told me. Now, tell me what the hell is going on."

"All right, I'll tell you," Ric said. He leaned back in his chair and smiled, all teeth. "I just wanted to find out what you were doing down here. That's all."

"You could have asked me," James said.

"Nah," Ric replied. "I don't think you would have told me the truth. After all, we didn't meet under the best of circumstances, now did we?"

"No," James said. "We did not."

"You do get that it was just business," Ric said. "In Edmonton. I mean you came at us, right? About Brown Eddie. We were just protecting our interests."

"Eddie Hansen was killed," James said, his voice like ice. "Remember?"

"Oh yeah," Ric said. "Right. Poor bastard."

James shifted forward and stared at Ric. "Isn't Ambrose Welch in jail for that?"

"Yeah, well, you can always trust the cops to screw up an investigation," Ric said. He picked up his drink and swallowed it. "That hit the spot," he said. "Want one?"

"No," James said. "Tell me what you want with me. Right now."

Ric sighed and looked around the room. Glanced at his partner, who was still standing guard, and then smiled at James.

"Here's the deal, Lavall," he said. "Your uncle had business dealings down here. He talked about it to Ambrose all the time. He said he'd be able to hook him up, but then, well, you know, he died. So, we thought—" He shook his head. "Check that. *I* thought maybe you could help us out."

"He's lying," I said, staring at James and wishing with all my heart that I had a way to actually communicate with him. "I didn't have any connections here, James. You gotta believe me."

Now, maybe I'd talked to Ambrose about making connections a time or two, but that was all it was. Talk. He'd never taken me seriously. He hadn't.

James's face didn't change, but he did pick up the coffee and take a sip. "Was that why you tried to break into my room?" he asked. "Did you think you'd get on my good side that way?"

"Ah hell, Lavall, I was just trying to figure out who you know here. That's all," Ric said. "You know the way the game's played."

"Yeah," James said. "I do."

He set down his cup and leaned forward. "Why would you think I'd help you make a connection?"

"Family's family," Ric replied. "And you worked for Jimmy for a long time. You'd know who he knew down here. I mean, why else would you come down here?"

"To reconnect with the dead," I muttered. "And to find out what I was doing. Which was not connecting with anyone here so I could help a drug dealer do business."

But James couldn't hear me, and even if he could have, I doubt he would have believed me.

"And who is it you think my uncle knew?" James asked.

Ric's eyes shifted. "Victor Tupilo," he said. "And we know you've already contacted him."

James looked at Ric for a long, long moment. "How do you know I talked to Victor Tupilo?" he finally asked.

Ric looked around, like he was checking the other tables. The other guy, who was still standing, stiffened like a dog who smelled a threat.

"You weren't quiet about it, Lavall," Ric finally said. "Word gets around. We just want to know what you two talked about."

James stared at him for another long moment, and then he relaxed and picked up his coffee cup.

"We were just talking about Marie and me getting married here," he said. "That's all."

"You're marrying the chick who took out Ambrose's eye?" Ric said, and laughed disbelievingly. "Seriously?"

That bit of information took me aback. Marie didn't look the type, but looks could definitely be deceiving.

"Yeah," James said, and his smile was cold. "What do you want with Mr. Tupilo, anyhow?"

Ric blinked, picked up the other drink he'd ordered for his friend, and slammed it. Put down the glass, and sighed. "Ambrose thinks that Victor Tupilo would be a good connection," he finally said.

"For drugs?" James asked.

Ric shook his head. "No," he said. "We got all those connections worked out. It's the money," he said. "We need some help with all the money. Word is, Victor Tupilo knows how to get that done. So, we thought that since Jimmy knew him, you might be able to help us with a connect." He shook his head. "But if that ain't going to happen, hey, whatever."

He made a move to rise, but James waved him back into the seat.

"I didn't say I couldn't connect you." he said. "Just relax. I mean, it's like you said. This is all just business. Right?"

"Right," Ric said, but he didn't sound convinced.

James called the server over and ordered three more drinks. "So, let's talk about business. What I can do for you, and what you can do for me."

"James, what the hell are you doing?" I muttered, as Ric grabbed one of the glasses and James took another.

"All right," Ric said. "Let's talk. I want you to get us an introduction with Victor. That's all we need. Just an introduction. Now, what do you think that's worth to you?"

James knocked the drink back and placed the glass on the table. "Well," he said. "I wouldn't mind an introduction when I get back home. You know. With Ambrose Welch. After all, my uncle did business with him. No reason why I couldn't do the same. Is there?"

Ric shrugged. "It probably could be arranged," he said. "Though I don't know how receptive he'll be when he finds out you are marrying the woman who put his eye out." He laughed roughly. "He doesn't forget stuff like that very easily."

"Hey, the girl was scared," James said offhandedly. He pointed at the third drink on the table and, when Ric shook his head, picked it up and drank it. "And we didn't know who we were dealing with. You know? Things will be different now."

"Even with her?" Ric said.

"She won't be a part of this," James said. "This will be between you and me."

"Hmm," Ric said, and shrugged. "You sure about that?"

"I got her under control," James said. "No worries. Now, about me talking to Ambrose Welch. We'll be back in Edmonton in three days. Think you can set something up for me then?"

Ric shrugged again. "Depends on what happens here," he said. "Are you going to be able to get me a meeting with Victor?"

"I can do that," James said. "At the wedding."

Ric laughed, roughly. "You're really getting married down here?"

"Yeah," James said. "It's one of Marie's dreams. You know, that big Vegas wedding." He leaned forward. "Consider yourselves invited. If you want."

"And you'll set up a meeting," Ric said.

"Absolutely," James replied.

"Sounds good," Ric said. He picked up the almost empty glass, drained the last drops from it, and set it back down. "Hey," he said. "Since we're going to be working together, how about if we help you get ready for your nuptials?"

"Get ready?" James asked. He signalled to the server, who hustled over three more drinks. "What do you have in mind?"

"It doesn't look to me like you have anyone standing up for you down here," Ric said, looking rather pointedly around the cafe. "So maybe we can give you a hand. You know, do all that stuff a best man would do."

James blinked and I realized he was honestly taken aback. However, I understood completely. He'd just told them he would introduce them to Victor Tupilo, so they were going to make sure that they didn't lose sight of him before he did that very thing.

I could tell the moment he made the same connection, and he smiled and nodded. "Sounds good," he said. "We could have a few laughs."

"Great," Ric said. The server walked up with the drinks and he scooped one from the tray. "Here's to you," he said, and held the drink high. "Now let's go have a few laughs before you tie the knot."

"Sounds good," James said. "No strippers though. Marie would definitely not approve."

Ric laughed. "We'll see what you say after we get a few drinks in you." He threw some bills on the table and rose. "Let's get out of here."

I clung to James as he followed the two men out of the cafe and out to the parking lot. I had no idea where these two were taking him but I needed to be there, to at least bear witness.

Marie needed to know everything because I didn't think that James was going to tell her much. But he'd just stepped into a scorpion's nest. I didn't understand why he was doing it but I was determined to find out.

MARIE:
THE RED DRESS

CRYSTAL AND I bought everything. And I mean everything. Apparently, a person even needs new underwear for a wedding. The back of Crystal's van was full of boxes and bags, and I wondered if I should have picked up a suitcase to get it all home.

"You coming to the hotel with me?" I asked.

Crystal smiled, but shook her head. "I'll just drop you off. I have work. A ghost tour." She smiled. "Hey, you want to come?"

The last thing in the world I wanted to do was follow her around looking at places where there could be ghosts, but I didn't tell her that. She'd really me out and I didn't want to hurt her feelings.

"Maybe some other time," I said. "All right?"

"No problem," she said. "I run them nearly every night. All you have to do is ask." She stopped in front of the Dunes, and I jumped out.

"Thanks for everything," I said. "I'm going to get something to eat. It feels like we've been at this for days already. I'm starving." I looked at her and realized she was probably as hungry as I was. "Want to get something to eat before you take off?"

Crystal shook her head. "I have to get back to the shop. You know, you're probably the only bride in the history of the world who wasn't on some kind of diet."

My stomach growled, and I shrugged. "Gotta feed the

machine," I said.

"Well, you go rest, and I'll get back to work," she said. "But I'll see you tomorrow, right? So we can get the rest of the stuff?"

The rest? What more could there be? "Yeah," I said. "I'll see you tomorrow."

It took three porters to get everything up to our room. James wasn't there, so I texted him.

I'm back. Crystal's a slave driver and I'm starving. Where are you?

He texted back promptly, like he'd been waiting for me to contact him.

We're at the Dome of the Sea. Come down as soon as you can. I have news. And wear the red dress. Please.

I stared at the bag- and box-covered bed. Under all that wedding stuff, somewhere, were the dresses I'd purchased earlier in the day. I personally thought the dress I was wearing was good enough, but groaned and pulled myself upright.

"He wants to see me in the red dress," I muttered. "Good enough. But there had better be a fantastic meal waiting for me."

I WALKED INTO the Dome of the Sea restaurant and gasped. Las Vegas is overwhelming, and garish and big and over the top. But that restaurant—it was like walking into old-time Vegas. The one you see in the movies.

The darkness surrounded me like a cocoon. The tables dotted the room, the candles on each turning the white cloth tablecloths into golden water flowers floating in a dark blue sea. A young woman floated among the tables, playing a harp. It took me a minute to see the tracks she and the harp used, and for that moment, she looked like a beautiful sea creature serenading the few people sitting at the tables.

I glanced at my phone. It was 7:00 p.m. No wonder I was starving.

A beautiful woman in a tight black dress sashayed up to me. "Do you have a reservation?" she asked.

"I'm supposed to be meeting someone," I said. "Mind if I find him myself?"

"Just one person?" she asked, and pointed to a table in a far corner where an overweight middle-aged man sat, alone.

"No," I said. "There are more than one."

She shrugged and nodded, then turned away from me. I carefully took the three steps down to the main floor and looked around the room.

There were four occupied tables. Three with couples, and one with three people. Looked like all men. I took a step toward that table, when a jolt of cold hit me so hard, I felt gooseflesh form on my arms.

"We gotta talk," Jimmy said in my ear. "Go the bathroom. Back, and to your left. Now."

I sighed, and turned. Jimmy had run ahead of me, without saying anything more. I felt a jolt of concern. His light was faded, but ran through with red. He was afraid and angry.

I followed him to the restrooms, and made certain that it was empty. "All right, Jimmy," I said. "We're alone. What's up?"

"You gotta stop him," Jimmy said frantically. "He's going to work with the son of bitch when he gets back to Edmonton. He's going to work with a fucking drug dealer!"

"What are you talking about?" I asked. I tried to catch his eye, to make him at least slow down, but he just kept flying—literally flying—around the mirror-covered room, and to my eyes, it was like a black and red laser light show in that bathroom.

"Stop," I said when I finally couldn't stand it anymore. "You're giving me a headache."

"You gotta stop him," he said again. "You gotta save him!"

"Tell me what you're talking about," I said, again, and I finally caught his eye. He slowed and then stopped in front of me.

"Do you remember a guy named Ric?" he asked. "From Edmonton?"

I shuddered. That was the guy we'd seen when we first arrived at the Dunes. The one who worked for Ambrose Welch. "Yeah, I remember him."

"Well, he's having a sit down with Jim—James."

I stared at him. "Are you sure?" I finally asked.

"What the hell is wrong with you, girl?" he replied, red emanating from him like a flood of lava. "You asked me to watch him. To find out what he's doing. Well, this is what he's doing. And he welcomed the guy with open frigging arms. What the hell trouble did you two get into after I died? How the hell does he even know either of you?"

"A ghost," I muttered. "It was another damned ghost."

He laughed, a guttural moan. "Maybe you should stay away from ghosts. They seem to get you in all sorts of trouble."

"Really?" I said, sarcasm dripping from my words. "Well, thank you. I never would have thought of that on my own."

Jimmy looked down at his hands, which were still spraying red and black light around the room. "Oh," he said. "Yeah. Right."

"So, tell me what you know," I said, trying for businesslike because I knew that sarcastic would get me nowhere.

He looked around like he wished he could just disappear, and I was afraid he would before he gave me enough information to understand what the hell I was about to walk into.

"Think calm thoughts or something," I said. "You're just giving me information, Jimmy."

"You don't look like *you're* thinking calm thoughts," he replied.

"Cut me some slack," I snapped. "I'm doing the best I can. Just tell me what Ric does for Welch."

"Sounds like he's a lieutenant. Keeps everybody organized and on track. He also makes trips out of town to set up sales." He shrugged. "At least, that's what he told James."

"And you never met this guy, while you were working for Welch?"

"No," he said. "But I wasn't privy to too much. Welch kept everyone compartmentalized. I did land deals for him. That was all." He looked at me. "You believe me, don't you?"

I didn't know what to believe, to be honest.

"All right," I said, ignoring his question. "So James is having lunch with Welch's lieutenant. Why?"

"It looks to me like he's planning on being James's best man," Jimmy said.

"What?"

"Best man. You know. For your wedding."

I frowned and shook my head. "What the hell is going on here?"

"I'm not sure," Jimmy said. "But James is acting like this is all a great idea. And he keeps talking about working with them when you get back to Edmonton." He sighed, a dry sound that made gooseflesh raise on my arms. "At first, I thought he was hunting, but now I'm not sure what he's doing. All I know is, he's stepping into a pile of shit, Marie. I didn't think he was capable of anything

E.C. Bell

like this."

"Neither did I," I muttered, and stared past Jimmy's worried face to my reflection—just as worried—in the mirror. "But I guess I better find out what's going on. Right now. But you have to do me a favour. Just keep your cool. Because I have to keep mine. You understand?"

"Yes," he said, and the colour of his aura lessened appreciably. The room didn't look like a laser light show anymore, anyhow.

"Good," I said. "Now lead me to their table."

"Will do," Jimmy said, and disappeared through the bathroom door. I took one last look in the mirror, and tried to make my features look less like I was expecting a fight, and more like I was happy to see my fiancé. Then I followed Jimmy out the door and into the restaurant.

I followed his aura to the back of the restaurant to a booth. James was sitting on one edge of the booth and two men sat opposite him. I recognized Ric, but not the other guy.

"James," I said. "What's going on?"

He turned and smiled at me. A big smarmy smile that made me wonder if he'd been drinking.

"Sweetie," he said, and grabbed me by the arm. "Look who I found."

I glanced at Ric and felt a flicker of fear cross my face before I could stop it. "What do you want?" I asked.

"Aww, Marie," Ric said. "Relax. Neutral territory and all that. You know?"

"No," I said. "I don't know."

James gripped my arm even tighter and pulled me to him. I sat beside him and stared at Ric. "You going to tell me what's going on here?" I asked.

Ric looked at James. "You going to explain it to her, or am I?"

"Go ahead," James said. He grabbed his drink and downed it as Ric turned back to me.

"So," he said. "There was a misunderstanding in Edmonton." He looked at James. "Right?"

"Right," James said. "Absolutely."

"It was lucky we ended up here at the same time, so we could clear all this up," he said. "Don't you think?"

"I guess," I said. James said nothing, and I could hear Jimmy stewing around behind me.

145

"Yeah, it works out great," he continued. "Here we are, on neutral territory. We can develop a bit of a rapport. Get to know each other, so we can work together in the future."

"Work together?" I looked at James, hard. "What's he talking about?"

"You don't have to worry your pretty little head about business, Sweetie," James said. His smile tightened ever so slightly, and he pulled me even closer. So close I could smell the bourbon, and the fear. No, it wasn't fear. It was something else I couldn't place. "It just means that financially, life is going to get a lot better for us when we go home. Isn't that good?"

"Yeah," I said.

The table fell silent as a server came up with four plates of food and deposited them, one in front of each of us.

"You ordered for me," I said, and his hand tightened even more. He was going to leave bruises. I was sure of it. "Thanks, Sweet Meat." I flashed him a smarmy smile of my own. "I'm starving."

I grabbed my napkin and placed it in my lap. "So you told them about us getting married, huh?"

"Absolutely," James said. "Ric's going to help me get it all set up. Isn't that great?"

I stared at Ric for a long moment, but he ignored me and dug into his meal like he didn't have a care in the world.

"He's going to be my best man, Marie," James said.

"Isn't that nice," I replied. My mouth was suddenly so dry I could feel my lips stick to my teeth, and I grabbed a glass of water, downing half of it in a go.

"I'll make sure James is shown a good time before the big day," Ric said. "You know—"

"Like a best man," I said. I put down the glass and picked up my fork, spearing a vegetable of some sort.

"It'll be great," James said. Too loud, and when I glanced at him, that frigging smile was still all over his face and he hadn't touched his food.

"I told you," Jimmy whispered again. "He's in. Deep."

"So, what are you going to do?" I asked. "Take him to the strippers or something?" I tittered laughter that sounded like my throat was closing involuntarily. Like I was choking to death.

"Oh no," Ric said. "We got better things to do than go to the

146

peelers." He glanced at James. "Don't we?"

"Absolutely," James said. "Absolutely."

I stabbed another vegetable I didn't recognize, thinking that if James said absolutely once more time, I was going to stab him.

"Make him stop," Jimmy whispered in my ear. "Get him out of here."

I glanced at James, who was laughing at everything the two men on the other side of the table said. They were talking about all the fun they could have in Vegas if I wasn't there.

"But you don't have to worry," Ric said to me. "We made sure he ordered the marriage certificate, and we'll get you down to pick it up, tomorrow. And we'll get him here in time for the ceremony. Promise."

"Oh," I said. A marriage certificate? "Oh good."

Looked like this practice wedding just jumped up to something a lot more real.

All three men laughed. It was that horrible "I can see her tits" laugh I'd endured most of my life, and all of a sudden, I couldn't take it anymore.

James and I needed to talk. Alone.

I placed my knife and fork on my mostly untouched plate and dropped the napkin over it. "Sorry, gentlemen, but James and I have things to do," I said.

"You do?" Ric said.

"We do?" James asked at the same time.

"Yes, we do." I batted my eyes at all of them, feeling sick. "There's so much to get ready. You know, for the big day. You can have him later," I said. "Promise."

"So, a little bit whipped," the guy I hadn't been introduced to said and mimicked a bullwhip sound.

James laughed and shook his head. "No, Ollie, nothing like that," he said. "She's right, though. We do have a couple of things we have to get ready. But we're on for tonight. Right?"

"You got it," Ric said. "Meet us down in the casino at ten, and we'll get the show on the road."

"Excellent," James said. He reached for his wallet but Ric shook his head.

"Don't worry about the meal," he said. "We got this."

"Thanks," James said, then turned to me. "Let's go."

"Absolutely," I said, and pushed my way out of the booth. I

could feel the eyes of the two men on me as I walked away from them, and it was all I could do not to scream "Keep your eyes to yourselves, you bastards!" but I said nothing. Just sashayed away like a good little fiancée, with James following me.

I glanced back at the table and could see Jimmy hovering over it, listening intently to the conversation the two men were having now that we were gone.

Good. We needed to know what was going on with those two.

"You better be ready to tell me absolutely everything," I whispered to James as we walked past the young woman playing the harp and through the door to the outside. "And I mean everything."

"Will do," James muttered. "But not here. Want some dinner? I noticed you didn't eat much with Ric."

I was going to say no, but he was right. I was starving. "Where can we go?"

"What about that restaurant you wanted to check out while you were here?" he asked. "It's just a block down that way." He pointed and then took my hand and pulled me away from the Dunes.

He was talking about Hell's Kitchen. Definitely on my bucket list.

"I'd love to go there," I said, "but we'd need to have made a reservation. Like a year in advance or whatever."

"No," he said. "Don't worry. We'll get in."

I shrugged and followed him. "I have questions," I said. "And you have to answer them, James. You get that, don't you?"

"Yeah," he said. "I understand. But first, tell me how shopping went. Have a good time?"

"It was all right," I said, impatiently. "Crystal has a good handle on everything we'll need. But what I don't get is why did you tell Ric?" I turned my head so I could see his face. "I mean, he helped you order our marriage license? Really?"

"That online application was a bit tricky," James mumbled. "He walked me through it."

"But why?" I asked. "Why is anybody helping you with a marriage license application? And, didn't we decide this was just for practice? Weren't we going to do it up legal at home?"

"Well, Ric asked me about it and then offered to help. What was I supposed to say?"

"How about I have it handled?" I said. "And why are you even talking to Ric? He's a frigging drug dealer, James. What are you doing?"

He sighed, and stared straight ahead for so long I was afraid he was going to try to lie to me about what was going on.

"At least tell me why you contacted Ric," I said.

"Didn't Jimmy tell you everything that went on as soon as you got back to the hotel?" James asked.

I blinked. "What do you mean?" I asked. Not very convincingly, I was sure.

"I know you put Jimmy on me when you left," he said, and laughed. "It's what I would have done."

"All right, so I did," I said. "But you can't blame me, can you?"

"No," he said. "Can't blame you at all. So, what did he tell you?"

"Not much, to be honest," I said. "And you holding hands with Ric really threw him over the edge."

"We'll deal with that later," James said. "First, I'm going to feed you, and then I'm going to work on finding out why Ric is here at the same time we are. I mean, didn't that seem just a bit coincidental? Just a bit?"

"It seemed *very* coincidental," I replied. "Are—are we in danger? Do you think Ric would do something to us here?"

"I don't think so," James said. "Honestly, I think he just wants to be introduced to Victor."

I blinked. "Why?"

"He seems to think that Victor and Ambrose Welch could set up something that would be profitable for both of them," he said. "And he thinks I can broker that."

"Can you?"

James shrugged. "Maybe. Tupilo wants something from me. Otherwise—"

"Otherwise, why would he have comped you that room," I finished for him.

"Exactly," James said. "So I might be able to make it all work to my advantage and set something up between the two of them."

"But why?" I asked. "Why are you doing this?"

"I have to find out what my uncle was involved in, Marie," James replied. "Here and in Edmonton. Ric started talking about a truce. Right off the bat. How there had been misunderstandings in Edmonton, and that it would be beneficial for all concerned if we learned how to work together like my uncle had."

"Work together?" I shook my head. "Please tell me you're not considering working with that frigging drug gang when we get back to Edmonton."

"It's not like that," James said. "Not really. I have to find out what Uncle Jimmy was doing. No BS. But as soon as we get home, I'll talk to Sylvia Worth about everything. It'll all be above board, I promise. I just might be able to bring that gang down once and for all."

"So, you're saying this is undercover?" I asked.

"Of course, it is," he replied, and stared at me. "Why? What did you think, that I decided to play for the other side? Just like my uncle?"

I couldn't answer him, because that was exactly what I'd thought. That he'd fallen down a terrible rabbit hole that neither of us would be able to get out of.

"Why don't you call Sylvia now?" I asked. "Just to bring her up to speed?"

"Because I don't have all my ducks in a row yet," he replied. Then he pointed at the Ramsay sign, and I realized we were at the restaurant. "Hope you're hungry."

"We won't be able to get in," I said. "I don't know why we're even here."

"I told Ric you wanted to go here," James said. "He set it up. We can show up, anytime we want." He smiled. "I told you I'd get you in."

I stared at the flames and then shook my head. The last thing in the world I wanted was to go to the restaurant if that man got us in.

"Let's just go for a burger," I said.

He frowned. "But I thought you wanted to go there," he said. "Isn't it on your list?"

"I guess," I replied. "But not right now. Honestly, I would rather figure out Jimmy's deal and move him on, as soon as possible. Maybe you don't care, but I do."

He was silent for a moment and then shrugged. "All right," he said. "You deal with Jimmy. While you're doing that, I'll keep working the Ric angle. Let's go back to the Dunes so I can get ready."

I stared at him like he'd suddenly lost his mind.

"Seriously?" I asked. "You're going to hang out with Ric tonight? Our first night here?"

"You can come with us, if you want," he said.

I thought about hanging around with those guys and shook my head. "No thanks."

"This is serious work," James said. "And if you don't get that, I'm sorry. But there's a connection, and I have to figure it out. If you don't want to help me, that's fine. I'll do it myself."

"Fine," I said. "I'll deal with Jimmy, and you deal with Ric."

"Fine," James said.

We walked back to the Dunes' parking lot, and he reached in his pocket and pulled out the car keys. "Take the car," he said.

I blinked. "You expect me to drive in this city all by myself?"

"Ric is taking me out for a night on the town," he said. "Remember?"

"But—"

"You can handle it," he said shortly, and walked to the entrance of the Dunes without looking back.

Jesus. Looked like I was on my own.

"So what now?" I muttered. I was still starving, and James was off playing with his drug dealer buddies. Since Jimmy was still watching them for me, I'd get all the information I needed, which meant I was on my own. What could I do?

"Call Crystal, I guess," I muttered. "She'll help me move Jimmy on. And if that means finding Rita, she'll help me with that, too."

Screw James. I'd do this myself.

JIMMY:
DON'T TAKE ME SHOPPING
FOR THE LOVE OF GOD

"I DON'T THINK that chick is too happy with Lavall," Ric said as the three of us watched James and Marie leave the restaurant. Ollie laughed and shrugged.

"She's his problem, not ours," he said. "Let's go to the peelers until Lavall gets back. Hell, we might be able to convince him to dump the little bitch and find himself a real woman."

Ric didn't respond. Just watched Marie and James disappear out into the Las Vegas night. "Do you think he's going to play ball?" he finally asked.

"For his sake, he better," Ollie said. "Now that the connection to Colombia is secure, Welch definitely needs a way to take care of all the money. Tupilo will be able to work with the casinos in Edmonton and get them set up. Won't he?"

"He should," Ric said. "The word is, he set everything up here. I hear the casino makes more laundering drug money than it ever did with legitimate gambling."

"And if Tupilo agrees to work with us, right off the jump?" Ollie said. "Will we still need James Lavall and his little fiancée?"

"It all depends on what else he can do for us," Ric said. "Once we get home."

Ric pushed himself away from the table and stood. "No

peelers," he said. "Let's go play poker before Lavall gets back. What do you say?"

"Sounds good," Ollie said. "Maybe my luck will change."

Ric laughed. "Don't you know the house always wins?"

"Not always," Ollie replied. "Let me prove it to you."

I was going to follow them back to the poker tables, I really was. Felt the pull of the tables and everything, but as I watched them leave, I thought of Crystal.

And then, I was with her.

Crystal was not happy to see me.

"Aren't you supposed to be with Marie and James?" she said when I appeared at her shop.

"They've got business," I muttered. "I thought I'd hang with you for a bit. So sue me."

She picked up her phone and stared at it for a long moment, then sighed and put it down on the counter by the cash register. "Did Marie say she'd call when they're done?"

I thought about my rather abrupt disappearance, but shrugged. She'd figure out where I'd gone. "She probably will," I said.

I wasn't actually sure she'd bother with either Crystal or me. James looked like he was deep in something, and I didn't think she'd be able to talk him into letting it go to deal with me. Business first, just like I taught him. But I was really afraid of the business he was stepping into.

"I'll give her an hour," Crystal said, "and then I'm calling her. I've got a ghost tour tonight and I have to prep for that."

"I'm not going," I said. "Those are the most depressing things in the world. Have I ever told you that?"

"Repeatedly," she said, then pointedly turned away from me and set to dusting shelves of crystals.

"Well, they are," I said. "There are no ghosts at any of the places you use on your tour. You do understand that, don't you?"

"So you've told me," she said, without looking at me. "Repeatedly."

"Just saying," I muttered. "Maybe you want to find a place or two with an actual ghost. You know, just to change things up."

"The last time I found a place with a ghost, I was stuck with him," she snapped, glaring over her shoulder at me. "So, I'll take the places with no ghosts, thank you very much."

That brought the conversation to an abrupt halt. Then a couple of girls—no older than sixteen—waltzed in and wanted information on everything—and I mean everything—in the little shop, so I was on my own.

Crystal wasted nearly an hour tried to sell them her wares, but I could tell those girls weren't interested in buying. They were bored. Nothing more. So when they finally left, she was angry enough to spit nails.

"I'm done," she said, flipping the "Open" side over to "Closed" and locking the door.

I was going to ask her where we were going next, because I hoped I'd still be able to talk her into taking me back to her apartment while she worked her ghost tour. At least I could watch some TV. But before I could speak, her phone chimed.

It was Marie, on her way to the shop. Apparently, she'd decided to go on the ghost tour.

"Excellent!" Crystal said. "Jimmy showed up a while ago, so we can all go together."

She listened and then shook her head at me. "She's pissed," she whispered. "You were supposed to watch the drug dealers for her."

"Tough," I snapped.

She shrugged, then frowned as Marie spoke again. "You want what?" she asked. "A tee shirt and shorts? Why?"

She listened for a moment more and then laughed. "No problem," she said. "If you don't care what the tee shirt says."

"So, she's coming here," I said. "Is James with her?"

"James apparently opted to stay at the hotel," she said. "But Marie wants to speak to you."

"Great," I muttered.

Crystal ignored me and bustled around the shop, riffling through the various tee shirts she had hanging on racks. She pulled a multi-coloured shirt with a kitten on the front. "What about this?" she asked.

"What about it?" I said. "Looks like something a six-year-old would wear."

Crystal frowned and stared at it. "You're probably right," she said, and put it back, pulling out a black tee with constellations strewn across the front. "What about that?"

"Black isn't the best in this weather," I said.

155

"True," she said. Frowned and stepped back, staring at the rack of shirts.

"What about that one?" I said, pointing to a light blue shirt with "Crystals are life" etched across the front. "Looks like it would fit her."

Crystal pulled it free and shrugged. "It'll be good enough," she said. "And now, shorts."

She turned to the rack of shorts, mostly tie-dyed light cotton, and pulled a pair free. "This will have to do," she said.

"Why does she want clothing from here?" I asked.

Crystal bristled. "There's nothing wrong with these clothes," she said.

"I didn't say there was," I said. "Just wondered why she'd want to change here, is all."

"I don't know," she said. "But I'm happy to make a sale, whatever her reason."

She dropped the clothing on the counter by the cash register, and jumped when the door rattled.

"Open the door!" Marie called, and then hammered on the door with an open hand.

"Will do," Crystal called, and ran to the locked door. Opened it, and let Marie inside. She locked it, then turned to Marie.

"Oh," she said. "I understand."

"You understand what?" Marie asked.

"Why you need a change of clothes," Crystal said. "That's a bit—evening wear—isn't it?"

"James asked me to wear it," Marie muttered. "I didn't have time to change."

"Try these," Crystal said, scooping up the clothing on the counter and holding it out to Marie. "Change room is over there."

"Thanks," Marie said. She glanced at the tee shirt and shook her head. "Crystals?" she said. "Really?"

"It's on sale," Crystal replied, defensively. "Besides, this is not a clothing shop. You're lucky I've got anything here at all."

"True," Marie replied, and smiled. "This will work just fine, I'm sure. Then, can we go for something to eat? I am starving."

"What about the meal with Jim and his buddies?" I said. "Looked like you had plenty to eat."

She glanced at me. "It wasn't really an 'eat food' kind of a meeting," she said shortly. "And you know that."

She had me there.

"Why didn't you stick around after James and I left?" she asked. "I thought you were going to tail them all night."

"I don't know what happened," I said. "I thought I was going to, too. But then they walked away, and I thought of Crystal, and, well. Here I am."

"Huh," she said, then opened the drapes that covered the entrance the change room. "Let me get my clothes changed, then we can talk about next steps."

She came out of the change room looking like a hippie, and it took everything for me to keep from laughing out loud.

"You look great," Crystal said. She grabbed a bag and handed it to Marie. "For your dress."

"Thanks," Marie said, ramming the red dress into the plastic bag festooned with crystals and mushrooms. "What do I owe you?"

"Don't worry about it," Crystal said.

"But I thought you said—" I started, but Crystal stopped me with a look.

"We're good," she said.

"Thanks," Marie said, and pointed at me. "I'm going to take you back to the hotel. I want you to keep following James."

I shook my head. "I'm done with that," I said. "I just want to find Rita. That's all."

"You are a one note tune, aren't you?" Crystal said.

"I don't care," I said stubbornly. "Marie, you told me you'd help me find Rita. So do it already."

"Jimmy," Marie said. "We're doing everything we can to find her, but I don't think she's in town anymore, and I don't think you should bother trying to find her anyhow."

"Why?" I asked.

"I think she did something to Jackson. You remember Jackson? The other guy in the IHOP picture?"

I closed my eyes, then nodded. "I remember," I said. "What do you mean, Rita did something to him?"

"He's dead, Jimmy. And he thinks Rita did it. Hell, she might have done the same to you. I mean, it was weird that you both died on the same night. Wasn't it? And Rita was with you both before you died," Marie continued. "Sounds suspicious, right?"

"It does," Crystal said. She turned to me. "Are you sure you want to find her?"

"Yes!" I yelled. "She didn't do anything to Jackson! He was a drug addict, for God's sake! He's probably lucky he lived as long as he did! It was just a coincidence."

"Come on, Jimmy," Marie said. "You can't be that naive."

"Hard to take you serious, dressed like that," I snapped. "Freakin' hippie."

"Whatever," she said, and turned back to Crystal. "Look, I told Jackson I'd help him move on. Maybe he has a little more information about Rita. Want to help?"

"Help you move on a ghost?" Crystal said. "Hell, yes!" Then she stopped. "When?"

"Tomorrow?" Marie asked.

"Sounds good," Crystal said. "But if I help you, you have to promise I'm invited to the wedding. Deal?"

Marie stared at Crystal for a long moment, her face like stone. "Sure," she finally said. "If you want."

"I've put a lot of time into this wedding," Crystal said. "Of course, I want!"

She sounded happy—genuinely happy—so I didn't mention the fact that I could see Marie wasn't half as thrilled as Crystal was. Looked to me like there were problems in love land, past the fact that Marie had asked me to follow her fiancée to find out what the hell he was up to while she was gone.

If that wedding actually happened, I didn't give them a month. There had to be some trust, didn't there?

Then I thought of Rita, and what Marie had said about Jackson. She thought Rita had killed him. Had killed us both, but that couldn't be the truth. She wasn't that kind of girl. Was she?

Was she?

"So now we get ready for the ghost tour," Crystal said. "This is going to be so much fun!"

"Yeah," I muttered. "A laugh riot. Are you sure you can't take me back to your apartment before that?"

"Lighten up, Jimmy," Crystal said. "They're not that bad."

"They are," I mumbled. "They really are."

Then I thought about Crystal's cats. How nice it would be to just hang around and watch television with them and—

Then I was.

MARIE:
GOING ON THE GHOST TOUR

JIMMY DISAPPEARED, AND Crystal and I looked at each other in surprise. "He's getting really good at that, isn't he?" Crystal said.

"He is," I said. "I wonder if he went back to the hotel."

"He wasn't too keen on going back there," Crystal said. "He's probably at my place."

"You think?" I asked.

"More than likely," she said. "We'll get him later. It's almost time. I have to get ready."

She lit several electronic candles, setting the mood, and then unlocked the door. Moments later, the bell chimed and the first of her clients walked in.

"We're here for the tour," a man in his sixties said, and then pointed at the woman standing next to him, like it was her fault he was there. "She wanted this. One of the things on her bucket list."

Crystal smiled. "Did you bring your receipt?" she asked.

The woman nodded eagerly and dug a sheet of paper out of her purse and handed it to Crystal. Crystal opened it and glanced down at the names.

"Mr. and Mrs. Riding," she said. "So happy to meet you. You're the first here. Just have a look around the shop while we wait for the others."

Mrs. Riding grinned and headed off for the overfull shelves, but Mr. Riding scowled and looked pointedly at his watch. "We got a show at ten," he said. "We're going to be done by that time. Right?"

"Absolutely," Crystal replied. "You won't miss your show."

The bell jingled again, and Crystal turned to the next batch of tourists, welcoming them all like they were long-lost friends. Soon the shop had thirteen tourists, plus Crystal and me.

"Looks like we're all here," Crystal said. "If you'll all follow me, we'll head out back to the van, and the ghost tour can begin."

"About time," Mr. Riding said, but followed his wife obediently enough.

Soon we were all packed into the van, and Crystal pulled an old-fashioned hand mike from a holder by the steering wheel.

"Welcome to Crystal's ghost tours," she said. "I'm Crystal and I'll be your tour guide for an evening of chills and thrills. Everybody buckled up? We don't want to have an accident and have one of you end up on our tour, now do we?"

Tittered laughter all around, and a few seat belts clicked closed as Crystal backed the van from the parking spot and headed down the alleyway to the street.

"The first stop on our tour is the Oasis Motel," she said. "Any of you heard of it?"

A few people put their hands up, and I could have joined them because it was one of the places I'd read about and decided I would never go because it looked like there was probably at least one ghost there. Maybe more.

"Why'd you pick this place?" I whispered.

"Because it's creepy," Crystal whispered, and smiled. "Besides, it was easy to talk the owner into letting us into that room. I just cut him in on the take."

She stopped the van in the courtyard, and everyone disembarked, huddling in groups of three or four. Everyone was quiet as though they half expected to be attacked by a ghost at any moment.

Crystal rattled through the background of the place. Who had died, how, and how long ago. She shared tiny bios for the dead and I was surprised that I knew one of the names. David Strickland. Before he died, he was an actor and had played the part of a reporter in the TV show *Suddenly Susan*.

"And now," Crystal whispered. "We are going to enter the

160

room where they died. You ready?"

There were a couple of enthusiastic calls but most of the people on the tour were quiet. They shuffled up with decrepit stairs to the door to Room 20 and waited quietly as Crystal worked the lock and opened the door.

"You first?" she said, and laughed when, to a person, everyone shook their heads and pushed back, bumping into the people behind them in their effort to get away from the door to the death room.

Crystal entered the room, then called the rest of us in. I followed her, and after a moment, the rest herded into the room.

It smelled and I put my hand to my nose. It didn't smell like death. It just smelled like a badly cleaned motel room, but I was willing to bet that a lot had happened in that room over the years. And not just deaths, either.

It looked tidy enough, but the smell of must and rot made it hard to concentrate on the two beds, the small table, and the bureau. On the far wall was the door to the bathroom, and I was not interested at all in going into that room, but when Crystal gestured, a couple pushed open the door and peered inside.

I was surprised to see that it was Mr. Riding. He turned back into the room and shook his head. "I don't see anything," he said.

"That could be because both men died in the main room," Crystal said. She pointed at the bed closest to her and a young woman with blue hair gasped. "There," she said. "That's where one of them was found."

The questions started then, but the smell in the room was giving me a headache so I slipped out into the hallway. I left the door open so I could listen to Crystal's answers and was pretty impressed with the way she handled everything.

There were no ghosts there, though. None that I could see, anyhow. So, I drifted down the stairs and stood by the van, waiting for the production to be over.

I looked over at the sludge-filled swimming pool and realized there were no lights on in any of the rooms. No wonder the owner was willing to let Crystal drag people through one of their rooms. It didn't look like anyone had stayed there in a long time.

Soon, Crystal clattered down the stairs followed by her tour. Everyone was more relaxed and were chattering quietly amongst themselves as Crystal unlocked the van and let everyone in.

"Off to our next stop," she said into the old-fashioned microphone. "The Stratosphere Tower. The site of at least five suicides and the focus of a lot of paranormal activity!" She put the van in reverse and carefully backed out of the Oasis Motel. She didn't speak to me until we were on the road.

"So, what did you think?" she asked.

"You sure know your stuff," I replied. "Did you move those ghosts on before you brought in the tourists?"

"No," she replied, and looked back at the people sitting in the van. They weren't paying any attention to us, so she spoke again, even more softly than before. "I picked places with no ghosts hanging around. It's just so much easier. Ghosts are so unpredictable. You know?"

"I do know," I replied. "And it makes sense to me. But don't people complain?"

"Oh no," she said, and smiled. "Usually at least one of them claims they can see something. So, it all works out, without the unpredictability."

"I understand," I said.

We hit three more places—one of them an open field where a school used to stand. One of the tourists gasped and pointed at the fenced in area and swore she saw something moving in the weeds.

Mrs. Riding stared at the spot where the tourist pointed, then swore she saw something, too.

"Can you see it?" she asked her husband, breathlessly.

"I don't see anything," he replied. But he was looking at his watch, not the weed-infested field, and then he turned to Crystal.

"We're almost out of time, young lady," he said. "We going to head back to your shop soon?"

"Yes," Crystal said. "We're heading back right now."

There were groans of disappointment from a couple of the tourists, but generally, they'd had just about as much of the ghost realm as they wanted. I suspected they were like the Ridings and had other events they wanted to get to.

"So, time to go?" I asked.

"Time to go," she said. She hustled everyone back to the van, and soon we were on our way to her shop.

Generally, the night sky was almost impossible to see, but to the east, I glimpsed a series of bright lights pulsating against the sky. I pointed.

"What's that?" I asked Crystal.

I expected her to say that it was a hotel's light show, or whatever, but she shuddered, and shook her head and whispered, "I'll tell you later."

A number of the tourists hustled into the shop as soon as Crystal opened the back door. First in was Mr. Riding, and he scooped up a couple of books on the paranormal and a baseball cap with "Better off with ghosts" on it.

Mrs. Riding took him by the arm. "Time to go, Terence," she said. "We're going to miss the show if we don't hurry."

"What show are you going to?" I asked.

"We're going to one of the Cirque de Soliel shows," she replied. "If I can drag him out of here."

"Which one?" I asked.

"Michael Jackson's ONE," she said. "I can hardly wait."

"Have fun," I said, trying to keep a smile on my face. That was the show I'd been hoping I could see. Lucky Mrs. Riding.

She nodded and finally managed to pull her husband through the doorway. The bell jingled as the door shut, and then, finally, we were alone.

As Crystal locked the door to the shop, I glanced to the east. I could still see the pulsating lights and pointed. "Your clients are gone now," I said. "So tell me, what are those lights? Is that ghost activity?"

"Yeah," Crystal said. Her voice sounded strained. "I think so. I haven't checked it out, though. I have enough trouble with the ghosts I run into in town."

"Any idea why there would be so many ghosts gathered in one place?" I asked. "Was it a plane crash or something?"

"I don't think so," Crystal said. "Maybe they are just— gathering." She looked at me. "Do they do that? Gather in one place?"

I remembered the ball diamond back home. Ghosts had gathered there, from all over the province.

"It can happen," I said. "But they need a good reason. Like a connection to the place. What's out that way?"

"Nothing," she said. "As far as I know, there's nothing out there but sand and ravines."

I looked at the pulsating lights and wondered why they'd be

gathering so far out of town. For just a second, I thought that it might be interesting to go there. To find out what the lights were, but shook off the thought. I was on vacation. I didn't need that.

"So what are you going to do now?" I asked.

"Actually, I have a date," Crystal said, "Any chance you can take Jimmy off my hands for the night?"

"He's not ready to move on," I said.

"That's not what I asked," Crystal said.

She was right, but still I shook my head.

"Let him hang around at your place," I said. "Please. He'll just bug me about finding Rita, and I'm not going to be able to do anything tonight." I shook my head. "It's all about Rita for him."

"And just think. She might have killed him," Crystal said. "This is going to be so hard on him."

"It is," I said shortly. "But he's going to have to get over it."

Crystal frowned. "Why are you like that?" she asked. "Jimmy. All the rest of the dead. They're hurting. Can't you be a little nice?"

That stopped me. She was right. I wasn't being nice to any of the people I was dealing with here. Living or dead.

"Can I tell you something?" I said. "In confidence?"

"Sure," she said.

"I don't much like Jimmy," I said. "I suppose I should try to empathize more, but he makes it very hard. You know?"

"He's an acquired taste," Crystal said. Then she grinned. "He can stay with me tonight. You go have an evening with James. Enjoy the nightlife, or whatever. Then, tomorrow, you come with newfound empathy, and you can show me how to move on Jackson and maybe even Jimmy. All right?"

"All right," I said. "Thanks."

"You're welcome," she replied.

JIMMY:
THINKING ABOUT GOING HOME

THE CATS WERE watching a frigging talk show when I got there, which bored the piss out of me.

"Come on," I said to Rambo, the big tom who always sat next to the remote like he owned the thing. "Just smack it with your paw or something. Change the damned channel. Please."

He didn't even look in my direction. Just stretched out, rubbing his back against the remote like he was taunting me. Son of a bitch. I hated that cat.

"Screw you," I said and headed into the kitchen, just for a change of pace.

I wondered if Marie was going to come to Crystal's to try to talk me into going back to the hotel.

"She'll want me to follow James again," I muttered, pacing the five steps from the fridge to the stove and back again. "And maybe I should. He's getting himself in deep with Ric. And that's bad."

Why did I feel like him doing that was somehow my problem? Like I needed to save him from himself?

"Because I needed someone to do that for me," I muttered.

And, as I waited for Crystal and Marie, I thought about going back home. Back to Edmonton. Back to my old life, so I could help James.

All right, so it wouldn't be my old life. Not exactly. For one thing, I was dead. And for another thing, I'd turned my back on everything—and everyone—there. James wasn't even speaking to me. Didn't seem to give a crap what happened to me. Only Marie seemed to care.

"She's all right," I muttered to the clean sink and the equally clean counter of Crystal's little kitchen. "She seems smart. Smart enough for my nephew, anyhow. I have to think that she has a lot to do with him even keeping my business open. He never showed much interest in it—at least not in the last couple of years, that's true, but hell, I wasn't showing that much interest that last year, now was I? I had the deal with Welch, but it wasn't bringing in that much new business. And it was driving away all my old clients, so, from the outside, it was a bad deal. Hell, it *was* a bad deal." I punched at the fridge, but my fist went right through. "Why the hell did I let Rory talk me into it?"

I stared at the pristine front of Crystal's fridge and tried to remember how that had even happened.

Rory had caught me tailing him. I'd been hired to find out if he was screwing around with the cop's wife—what the hell was her name? Sylvia, or something. She was a looker, whatever her name. But Rory caught me sitting outside his place, with my camera no less. Such a rookie mistake, but there I was. Caught. And by a cop, too.

I figured I'd take a pounding for my trouble, but he was pretty prosaic about the whole thing. Didn't even tell Sylvia what was going on. Just told me that he'd heard of me, and if I wanted more work, he had some for me. If I could keep my mouth shut.

Which, of course, I could. Then he talked me into working with Ambrose Welch, and the rest, as they say, was history.

That deal? That was one of the big reasons I had wanted out of Edmonton. I thought it was going to be just for a little while. That I'd do whatever Rory—and Ambrose Welch—told me to do, and I'd get paid well, and it would eventually end.

But it didn't end. Not even after Rory died. Man, I was so deep in Ambrose Welch's business by that time, I don't think I could have gotten out if I wanted to.

That was why Vegas—and Rita—felt like such a good deal. I could walk away from Edmonton and everything I'd screwed up there. There was no connection to these two pieces of my life. Felt like a dream, right up until the night I died.

I shuddered and then shook off the malaise and walked back

into the living room. Plopped down in the midst of all the cats, and waited for Crystal and Marie to come back.

No matter what Marie said, I wasn't ready to move on. I had to find Rita, so I could finally know the truth. I had to find out what Victor Tupilo wanted from James. He never, ever, gave anything away for free. He wouldn't be helping them out unless he figured there was a big return in it for him. I couldn't see what return James and Marie could bring him, but I was pretty sure that whatever it was, it would bring trouble to those two. And I was afraid it was connected to me. I had to figure out what was up.

And then, I had to convince Marie to take me back to Edmonton, so I could help James get out of the hole he was digging for himself. I knew where all the skeletons were buried, after all. And, that was where I belonged.

I had to make her understand that.

MARIE:
YOU WERE DOING WHAT, JAMES?

AFTER I DROPPED Crystal off at her apartment, I drove back to the Dunes and left the vehicle with the valet. Got a lot of funny looks from the inhabitants as I walked through the entrance, because I'd forgotten to change out of my "go on a ghost tour" garb and back into my dress.

Whatever. I headed up to our room, but James was not there. *Where are you?* I texted. *Please call me.*

His phone call came three long minutes later, and I imagined him staring at his phone, counting off the minutes, just to prove to his friends that I wasn't pushing him around.

"Hey, Marie!" he yelled. "What's up?"

The noise around him made it almost impossible for me to hear him. It sounded like he was standing in the middle of a race track. "Where are you?" I asked.

"I'm at Speedvegas," he said.

"Speed what?"

"Speedvegas," he repeated. I could hear male laughter all around him now and felt my anger grow.

"What the hell is Speedvegas?" I asked.

"A race track," he replied. "We're racing cars, Marie."

I blinked at the phone, believing for a second that I was hearing him wrong. "What kind of cars?" I finally asked.

"We're doing the Battle of the Legends Package," he said. The roaring of car engines made it impossible for me to hear him for a second. Then he came back. "A Lamborghini," he said. "I drove a Lamborghini."

"Well, good for you," I replied. I mean, what else was I going to say? "You having fun?"

"I am," he said. "But I'm getting information, too."

I almost smiled at that. Almost.

"They get their drugs from some cartel in El Salvador," he said. "And guess what? It comes in by sub."

I frowned, figuring I'd heard him wrong. "What?"

"Gimme a sec," he said, and then the sound of the men and the cars receded. "You're not going to believe this, Marie," he said. "But the drug cartel has an actual submarine. It's how they get the drugs up the coast to Canada. They used to use boats, but the U.S. Coastguard kept catching them. So they decided subs were the way to go and started making them." He chuckled. "Pretty ingenious," he said. "They make submarines."

"Are you serious?"

"Hey, I can only go by what they tell me," he said. "But it sounds like it's the truth."

"When are you going to be back?"

"A couple more hours," he said. The sound of the high-powered vehicles grew. "I'll tell you all about it when I get back to the hotel," he yelled. "Hey, I gotta go. My turn to drive the Porsche!"

Then he was gone, and I was left in our empty hotel room, staring at the pile of stuff Crystal and I had purchased, strewn across one of the beds.

I grabbed James's computer and typed in "Speedvegas." The Battle of the Legends package cost a grand. Fifteen laps in really expensive cars.

"Good grief," I muttered.

I shut the computer and headed for the shower, more than ready to wash the day off me, and finally get something decent to eat.

I WAS GOING to do things up right for myself and go back to the Dome of the Sea restaurant, because I still had a coupon for a meal, but the restaurant was full.

"You could come back in a couple of hours," the beautiful

hostess said, her perfect smile at the ready. "If you want."

"That's all right," I muttered, and headed out into the reception area. The casino—with its cafe—beckoned, so I stepped into the noise and light and forced gaiety of the cafe and ordered a burger and fries. Not quite the fancy meal I was hoping for, but whatever. It filled the hole in my gut.

I people-watched as I ate the burger, until I saw Victor Tupilo out on the floor, chatting up the clientele. Seeing him wrecked my appetite, so I signed my bill, walked away from half my meal and out into the casino.

"Do you want to play?" A guy in a suit appeared by me as if by magic. "I'll find you an open table, if you'd like."

"No, it's all right," I said, and turned away from him. The smell of smoke and desperation overwhelmed me, and I thought about going outside but the heat of the day hadn't yet dissipated and I was not in the mood for more sweat and another shower.

So I went back to our room and turned on the television. Hey, it was time for *Jeopardy*. Didn't want to miss that, did I?

I FELL ASLEEP, and my dreams were jumbled and frightening. All thunder and lightning, in a dark grove of trees. I was looking for my mother because I had a question for her. An important question that I couldn't quite remember. All I knew was I had to talk to her before I saw Jimmy the Dead again. But I couldn't find her in the shadowy trees, even though I was sure she was just beyond my line of sight, in the black orchard.

I wondered what kind of fruit trees surrounded me, but couldn't tell in the dark. There was another clap of thunder, and I awoke, covered in sweat and not quite sure where I was for a second.

I heard a noise in the bathroom and sprang into action. Well, I scrabbled off the bed and floundered to the closed door, looking around for something—anything—with which to protect myself.

I could hear water running, then flinched when I realized it was someone peeing. James, back from his adventures with fast cars and drug dealers.

As I turned to walk back to the bed, the door opened and James stumbled out of the bathroom, still working at closing his pants.

"Wash your hands," I snapped.

"You're awake," he replied.

"Yeah," I said. "Now wash your hands."

"Right." He walked back to the sink and splashed some water on them, and walked back out. Grinned and then flicked water at me.

"Don't you hate it when you pee on your hands?" he said, then laughed like a loon and pushed past me to the bed I'd just left. He flopped down on it and sighed, like he was ready to go to sleep.

"How much did you have to drink?" I asked.

"A lot," he said. "I had a lot to drink." He waved at me, and I realized he was trying to gesture me over to the bed.

"You're out of your mind if you think I'm going to go to bed with you, James Lavall," I said. "We have to talk about what's happening with your uncle. Remember your uncle?"

He mumbled something and managed to grab an edge of the blanket, so I had to move fast before he covered himself and actually went to sleep. I leaped over to the bed, grabbed his hand, and tried to pull him upright.

He laughed and pulled me down onto the bed with him. Bourbon wafted off of him in thick waves as he clumsily groped me.

"Cut me some slack." I slapped his hands away and rolled off the bed.

"Oh, come on," he said. "Let's have a little fun. After all, we're in Vegas." He pulled the blanket over his face, and I was sure he'd gone to sleep, but he spoke again. Mushily, like he was already nearly unconscious.

"Ric took me to a place called Battlefield Vegas," he said.

"What's that?"

"A shooting range," he replied. "We did the *Swat Experience.*" He laughed. "You should have seen the guns. I think half of them are illegal. I don't know how they get away with this stuff down here."

"Second amendment or something," I said. "You went to a shooting range?"

"Yeah," he said. "It was fun. We should do it sometime."

"So, you went shooting guns and driving fast, expensive cars," I said.

"Yeah," he replied. Then he grinned at me. "I figured that would be better than going to a strip club."

I waited for him to ask me what I'd done while he was out playing with guns and cars, and then realized that his breathing had deepened.

"Are you asleep?" I said, loud.

"Nope," he mumbled.

I gritted my teeth, but tried to remain calm. "Don't you want to hear about your uncle?"

"Sure," he said, and tried to sit upright. "Tell me."

I sat on the edge of the bed and told him about Jimmy disappearing. "I think he's at Crystal's," I said. "Because the only other place he goes is here."

James stared at me blankly.

"So?" I asked. "What do you think?"

He said nothing. Just stared at me. Then, he snored. The son of a bitch had fallen asleep with his eyes open and I guessed he hadn't heard one word I'd said. I reached over and punched him on the arm, hard.

"Wake up!" I cried.

"Ow." He rubbed the spot on his arm where I'd punched him. "That hurt."

"So, what about your uncle?" I asked. "What do you think we should do?"

"Sounds like you had some fun," he muttered. "Didn't you?"

"Did you even listen to me?" I yelled. "I went on a ghost tour! And hung around with ghosts the whole day. It was not fun, James. I was working, while you were out driving fast cars and drinking way too much. Does that seem fair to you?"

"I was working too," he mumbled. "You get that, right?"

"Jesus," I muttered, and jumped up from the bed.

"Come with us tomorrow," he said. "We got the whole day planned." He grinned. "You should come."

"What about Jimmy?" I asked. "And Jackson? And Crystal?"

"They can wait a day. Can't they?"

"Crystal helped me pick up all that stuff for the stupid wedding," I said. "The least we can do is move your uncle on for her."

James frowned and struggled to open his eyes. "Stupid wedding?" he said. "You think this wedding is stupid?"

"Yes, I do!" I cried.

"I don't think you should call it stupid," he said, a hurt tone worming its way into his drunken voice. "A wedding is a sacred bond—"

"Can you hear yourself?" I yelled. "It's supposed to be a practice wedding! Nothing about it is supposed to be real. And now you've ordered a marriage license. What the hell are you doing, James?"

"Ric has to think we're really doing this," he muttered. "This is important, Marie. More important than even my dead uncle."

"But—" I started, but he waved me to silence.

"We're going to get the license tomorrow," he said. "Just remember that."

Before I could answer him, he turned and pulled the blankets up over his head, and then he was asleep.

"So, your uncle isn't important anymore," I muttered. "Well, maybe this stupid wedding isn't important to me."

I pushed all the boxes and bags off of the other bed, and threw myself down on it. I was tired, and angry, and couldn't believe that the first vacation I'd had in forever was turning to crap before my very eyes.

It took me a long time to go back to sleep.

JIMMY:
TALKING TO CRYSTAL

CRYSTAL ROLLED IN at 3:30, alone.

"I thought Marie would be with you," I said.

"She wanted to get back to James," Crystal replied. She pushed the kittens from the couch and sat down beside me. "Let's you and me have a talk, Jimmy."

"What about?" I asked.

"About how you're going to help Marie, so you can move on," Crystal said.

"I'm helping," I said, and heard her snort derisively. "Well, I'm trying to help," I continued. "But it's hard, you know?"

"You're not helping, Jimmy. And you know you're not."

I opened my mouth to respond, but shut it when I saw the look on her face. She wasn't about to take my guff. So I shrugged.

"I'm helping as much as I want to," I said.

"Well, you have to do more," Crystal replied. "She's only got a couple more days here, and then she'll be gone. I can't help you the way she can. As a matter of fact, I'm starting to think that maybe I'm holding you here." She reached down and patted one of the kittens, who looked up at her and purred adoringly.

"And that isn't fair to you," she continued. "So promise me you'll work with her tomorrow. Really work with her. Please."

I was going to make some smart-ass comment, but shut my mouth. Maybe she was right. "Your time on earth is done," she said. "So please. Let Marie help you."

I looked at her for a long moment, then nodded. "Sure," I said. "I'll play ball."

"Good," she said, and then she went to bed, and the cats and I were back to watching late night television.

I felt all right. I'd only lied to her a little bit, because she was wrong about one thing. My time on earth was not done. James was digging a deep hole for himself, and I was the only one who could help him get out. I was sure of it.

After I found Rita.

MARIE:
JACKSON, I HARDLY KNEW YA

48 hours . . .

I WOKE UP and glanced at the old-fashioned clock radio on the bedside table. It read 11:00 a.m., and I figured it had to be wrong. I grabbed my cell, but it said the same time.

"What the hell?" I muttered. "What's going on?"

I looked at the other bed, but it was empty.

That kind of freaked me out, and I threw back the bedclothes. Heard paper rustle, and found the note that James had evidently placed on me as I slept.

Marie, it read. *Didn't want to wake you, but remember we have a date at the courthouse. Keys are on the table. Call me and tell me what time you'll be there.*

Oh, and Babe, R and I have some real fun planned. Hope you'll join.

Dune buggies, Marie!

James

P.S. Daisy called. She said something's going on with Jackson. Maybe you want to check that out.

I stared at the note and then growled as I crumpled it up and threw it in the garbage.

I tried to calm down as I brushed my teeth. Then I called James.

"I'm on my way," I said. "If this is what you really want."

"It is," he said. "It really is."

I hung up the phone, ignored the hell out of my gut which told me I was making a mistake, and scooped up the car keys. Time to sign on the dotted line. For James.

WELL, THAT COULD *have gone better*, I thought as I got back into the car two infuriating hours later.

I'd met James. Signed the application, and smiled my way through the questions, and when we were finally done, tried to convince James to stay with me for the rest of the day. Alone.

"No can do," he said. "Ric and I have the day planned. It's going to be great. We're going out to the dunes. To drive dune buggies." He grinned. "Dune buggies. You'd like to do that, wouldn't you?"

"We don't have time for stupid dune buggy rides," I snapped, then took in a great big deep breath and tried to get back on an even keel.

"James, Daisy is having real trouble with her dead son," I said. "And have you forgotten about your uncle? Your dead uncle who I'm supposed to move on?"

"I haven't forgotten," James said. "But he's not ready to move on, is he?"

"Well, no," I said.

"And there really isn't anything I can do about Jackson," he continued. "Is there?"

"Daisy likes you a lot more than she likes me," I said. "Remember?"

"Oh, Daisy likes you fine," James replied. "You go there, find out what's up with the ghost, and I'll keep pumping Ric for information." He glanced around like he was afraid someone was listening in on our conversation.

"He told me the name of the Salvadoran cartel Ambrose is dealing with," he whispered. "It's Mara Salvatrucha. They are working with Ambrose through an international support arm called La Familia," He grinned. "The Family. Get it?"

"Yeah," I said, my mouth suddenly dry as the desert. Why was Ric telling him all this?

"He said La Familia is set up in BC and Edmonton," he continued. "So, the drugs come from El Salvador, up the coast to BC, and then into Edmonton."

"Are these the guys who use a submarine to move the drugs up the coast?" I asked.

"Yep," he said. "The very same. This is big, Marie. Huge." He grinned. "We're going to bring down an international drug ring," he whispered. "Isn't that cool?"

"Cool," I whispered.

"So, you can see why I can't help you with my uncle," he continued. "Or with anything else right now. This is so important." He stared into my eyes. "You get that, right?"

"Yeah," I said. "I guess so."

"Are you sure I can't talk you into coming with us?" he asked. "We're going to have some fun."

"No," I said, and took a step away from him. "I have to deal with your uncle. And Jackson. You go have fun with your drug dealer buddies, and I'll see you later."

"Cool," he said. Then he pulled me into his arms and swung me around him. "We're really doing this, Marie," he said. "Do you realize that by tomorrow night, we'll be man and wife?"

"Yeah," I said. "I get that. Can you put me down?"

"Sure," he said, and set me back on the sidewalk. Pecked me on the cheek, like I was an old maiden aunt. "Call me if you change your mind about the dune buggies."

"Will do," I said, and turned away from him. I headed back to the car and got in. Shook with rage for five full minutes, and then called Crystal.

"Hey," I said, trying to make my voice sound all bright and cheery. "You still up for helping me with Jackson? Apparently, he's having a meltdown. Want to come along? Good chance you'll be able to watch me move him on."

Crystal didn't sound quite as enthusiastic as she had the night before.

"I'm doing inventory," she said. "And I can't really walk away from it." She was silent for a moment, then sighed. "Jimmy's here too. He's helping."

"Oh," I said. "Oh, all right then."

There was another short silence as we both thought about things. "What about this?" Crystal said. "You help me with inventory, and I'll go with you to talk to the ghost."

I sighed. It was day two of my big holiday, and it looked like the high points were going to be doing inventory at Crystal's shop and talking to an upset ghost.

Well, at least I wouldn't be spending the day alone.

"Sounds good," I said.

"Really?" Crystal's voice sounded relieved. "That would be great! I'm almost done, really. Shouldn't take more than a couple of hours."

"Great," I said, and closed my eyes.

Great.

MARIE:
DOING INVENTORY. REALLY.

ON MY WAY to Crystal's shop, I called Daisy. I half expected her to tell me to go to hell. That she would only deal with James, but I didn't have any of that trouble at all.

She was nearly beside herself, and started to cry. "Things are flying around the house," she sobbed. "Around the house. It has to be Jackson. He's upset. You have to talk to him, as soon as possible. Please."

I promised I'd be there as soon as I could and then set the GPS for Crystal's shop.

"Fun," I muttered. "How am I going to handle so much fun."

HONESTLY, IT LOOKED like a bomb had gone off inside Crystal's shop when I arrived. Crystal waved me over to a huge pile of tee shirts lying in the middle of the floor, and then gave me a quick hug.

"Thanks for this," she said. "It's going to be so great, getting some help. Usually, I'm alone."

"Are you sure this is only going to take a couple of hours?" I asked, as she scooped up a handful of tee shirts and started counting them. "Daisy needs us ASAP."

"It shouldn't even take that," she said. Then she looked at the tee shirts and frowned. "Where was I?" she asked.

"No idea," I said.

"Oh well," she said, and started counting them all over again.

Jimmy wandered in from the back and looked around. "James isn't with you?" he asked.

"No," I said. "He had—things to do."

"Hmm," was all Jimmy said, but I could tell by the look on his face he wanted to say more.

"Whatever," I said. "Let's just get this over with, shall we? Like I said, Daisy needs us."

He darkened, and for a second, I was afraid he was going to disappear on me again, which was the last thing I wanted, because I hoped if I could get the two ghosts in the same room, they would be able to talk each other into moving on. That would help everyone.

Especially me.

"Daisy is Jackson's mom," I said. "So that means you're going to come to Daisy's and you're going to help me."

"And how am I going to help?" Jimmy said. "Jackson and I just worked a couple of deals. That's all. We're not friends by any stretch of the imagination."

"Well, you're all I've got," I snapped. "So suck it up."

Crystal had finally finished counting the tee shirts. "Come on, Jimmy," she said gently. "You said you'd try. Remember? We talked about it last night."

"I guess," Jimmy said. "If you want me to."

"I do," Crystal replied. "It'll be best for everyone."

I rolled my eyes. "Jimmy, this guy knows Rita too," I said. "Don't you want to know what he knows?"

"I guess," he said again. But he didn't sound enthusiastic.

"So let's get this inventory counted," I said. "And we can go."

I'm guessing I sounded just about as enthusiastic as Jimmy had, because Crystal pointedly turned away from the both of us and started counting skirts.

Great.

Two hours later, I pulled the car into the half-hidden driveway that led to Daisy's cabin. The two lines of trees on either side of the lane touched the sides of the vehicle, scraping the windows and the paint. I hoped that there was no damage, because James would be paying through the nose for that.

"What a cute little house," Crystal exclaimed.

I looked and she was right. It looked like a little house in the woods you'd find described in a fairy tale, and I hoped that we wouldn't meet any witches or whatever when we finally went inside.

Daisy was hunched over a flower bed by the front door. She straightened, briefly grabbing her back to stretch, before she turned and smiled at us.

"Welcome," she said as we got out of the vehicle. "Thank you for coming so quickly."

"She doesn't really look that happy to see you," Jimmy said, snidely.

I ignored him as Daisy turned to Crystal. "You must be a friend of Marie's," she said, and walked toward her, pulling her gardening gloves from her hand and holding it out invitingly. "I'm glad to meet you."

"My name's Crystal," Crystal said. She shook Daisy's hand enthusiastically, and then looked around at the garden that surrounded the little house. "This looks wonderful," she said, and took a deep appreciative sniff. "And it smells even better."

"I use all of these plants in my soaps," Daisy said. "They have to be all-natural. Otherwise, I wouldn't sell much, now would I?"

Crystal laughed, enchanted, and I realized if I didn't stop the conversation we'd be stuck on soap forever.

"You said Jackson's causing problems," I said, to get us all back on track. "Maybe we should talk to him."

"Oh," Daisy said. She turned away from her beloved garden, her face fell, and I felt like dirt. "All right, but after, we are going to have tea, aren't we?"

"We will," Crystal said, with a quick glance at me. "We absolutely will."

"You could probably take a lesson in etiquette from Crystal," Jimmy said. Crystal tittered nervous laughter and then linked arms with Daisy and headed to the house. I was left to bring up the rear.

Jimmy laughed and I glared at him.

"How about if you just keep your trap shut?" I muttered. "The main reason I'm here is for you, you know. So you can find out what Jackson knows about Rita."

That got his attention, and his laughter subsided. "Yeah," he finally said. "Sorry. You're right. We should talk to Jackson."

We walked through the open door and followed Crystal and Daisy into the old-fashioned kitchen at the back of the cabin. There was no sign of Jackson but all the kitchen chairs were stacked neatly on top of the table.

"He keeps doing that," Daisy said. "I wish he'd stop."

I heard a crash somewhere in the back of the house and frowned. "Is that Jackson too?" I asked.

"Probably," Daisy said.

"How long has he been doing this?" I asked.

"He's been at it, off and on, since you came to the market," Daisy said. "I thought it would be nice, having him with me again. But this is exhausting."

Ahh.

"Please talk to him," she said. "Find out why he's so upset."

"I'll help you with the chairs first," I said, but Crystal shook her head.

"I'll do this," she said. "You go find Jackson."

I looked at Daisy, who was busy making tea. "Do you know where he is?"

"Not exactly," Daisy replied. "But it's usually quite cold in his old bedroom."

"And where is that?" I asked.

"I found him!" Jimmy called. "He's back here."

"Back there," Daisy said at the same time. She pointed at a hallway that led off the kitchen. "Thank you," I said, and left her and Crystal to move the chairs and, probably, bond.

Jimmy was standing by a closed door. Hovering. "I think he's in there," he said.

"Why didn't you go in and make sure?" I asked.

He shook his head, and I pushed past him to open the door, gooseflesh rising on my arm where I touched his chill.

"Well, look who's here," Jackson said, from within. "It took you long enough. Mom's been losing her shit since you called."

He was standing over by a window at the back of the room, the only spot that wasn't taken up with rough-hewn tables and piles of drying herbs and flowers. A smashed pot was lying on the floor next to the window sill.

"This used to be my bedroom," he said. "She sort of took this space over after I died. I guess she didn't like the mess in the front room." He pointed at three boxes piled in the corner next to him, and one of them tipped over, spilling its contents on the floor. "This is my stuff," he said. "All that's left."

"I'm sorry," I said, because I really didn't know what else to say.

"Hey, it's not your fault," he replied. He looked past me and frowned. "Who's with you?"

I turned, but Jimmy was no longer visible in the entrance to Jackson's bedroom. Just a faint light touching the walls let me know he'd stuck around at all.

"It's Jimmy," I said. "He wants to talk to you."

"Just ask him the questions," Jimmy called from somewhere down the hallway. "I'll stay out here."

"Get in here now," I snapped and turned back to Jackson. "You'll talk to him. Right?"

"I guess I have to," Jackson mumbled.

Jimmy walked through the door and saw Jackson by the window. He stopped like he'd been poleaxed and then pushed through the tables piled high with the herbs and flowers. Their auras mingled for a moment, until Jackson shook his head and turned away.

"Don't," Jimmy said. He suddenly sounded desperate. "Don't run away. I need to know what happened. To you. To Rita."

"Don't you think I want to know the same thing?" Jackson asked. "The last time I saw her was after the Dunes. She called me. Said she had to meet me. That it was important we talk." He shook his head. "I thought she'd finally decided to dump you."

"She wouldn't have done that," Jimmy said, but the tone in his voice made me think he wasn't that sure anymore.

"She came out here," Jackson said. "I didn't even know she knew where we lived."

"I was probably already dead by that time," Jimmy muttered.

"How'd you die?" Jackson asked.

"Heart attack, they said," Jimmy muttered. "You?"

"Same," Jackson said. "It nearly killed my mother, me dying here like that."

"And it happened after Rita came out here?" Jimmy asked.

"Yeah," Jackson said, and sighed. "She did this to both of us, didn't she?"

Jimmy didn't answer. Didn't need to. That was too much of coincidence, even for him.

"She was really mad about the Dunes job, Jimmy. She kept saying we'd screwed things up for her." Jackson shook his head. "You have any idea what she meant by that?"

"None," Jimmy said. "Hell, it was just one small score. I don't get it."

His voice was low, and his light had guttered so much that I could barely see him.

"You okay?" I asked.

"I'm fine," he said, which was a lie, but I let it go. He was getting a big dose of reality, and it looked like he wasn't handling it that well.

Jackson, on the other hand, looked better. Brighter than the last time I'd seen him, and I realized that his aura was beginning to look clear. Then I saw the first light bee under his almost transparent skin. It was white, and it wormed its way up his neck, and popped free just under his chin.

"How about you, Jackson?" I asked. "You all right?"

"Yeah," he said, and sighed. Turned back to the window and looked out at the rows of flowers waving in the hot breeze just outside his room. "I'm good."

He flicked his hand at the light bee as it bumbled its way to the window and then out. Then he frowned and turned to me.

"What the hell is that?" he asked.

"It's your essence," I said, as gently as I could. "Leaving."

He blinked, and then laughed. "Are you trying to tell me that the only reason I stuck around this long was to talk to that old codger one more time?"

"I resent that remark," Jimmy said, but smiled, gaining a little light, a little colour. "We did have some laughs though, didn't we?"

"We did," Jackson said. "You going to find out what happened to Rita?"

"If I can," Jimmy said. "Don't you want to stick around and find out how it all ends?"

"No," Jackson said, and sighed. "I'm tired, Jimmy. You, me, Rita. Trying to make enough to get away from this place, and barely breaking even most times. Those schemes—that's all I did. I don't think I was ever going to leave Vegas. I just wanted one more score. Just so I could say I got it. And the Dunes was a good one, wasn't it, Jimmy?"

"It was the best," Jimmy said. "We almost made it."

Jackson frowned and shook his head. "No," he said. "We didn't."

He slumped to the floor beside the window, and a half dozen more light bees worked free. He flinched when the red and black ones broke through his skin, but there weren't that many. Not really. Most of them were white, or close to white.

"Mom's going to be all right without me," he said. "Isn't she?'

"Yes," I said.

"Say goodbye to her for me, will you?" he asked. "Tell her I did my best."

"I will," Jimmy said, and then looked at me. "I mean you will. Right?"

"I will," I said. I pushed past the fragrant debris in the room and knelt beside him. "Is there anything else holding you here?" I whispered.

Jackson sighed and stared into Jimmy's eyes. "She didn't love either of us," he whispered to him. "I don't think she could."

"But—" Jimmy started, but Jackson turned away from him and looked out the window.

"I always loved the smell of those frigging flowers," he said. "That smell told me I was home."

Then he let go, and the light bees flooded from him, through the window and out into the garden. And then, he was gone.

"Jesus," Jimmy said. "Is that what's going to happen to me?"

"If you're lucky," I said, then shook my head. Those words weren't helpful. "I can help you, if you want."

"I'm not ready for that yet," he said, then frowned and stared at me. "Are you all right? You look like you're ready to toss your cookies."

"I just need a drink of water," I replied. "I'm sorry he didn't give you what you were looking for."

Jimmy stared at the spot where Jackson had been and pursed his lips. "I still have to find Rita," he finally said. "No matter what she did."

"Why?" I asked.

"Because I want to hear from her lips that she didn't love me," he said. "It's important. You get that, don't you?"

"I don't know how to find Rita," I said. "Honestly, Jimmy. I have no idea."

"But I might," Jimmy said, and his aura darkened until he was just a sooty smudge in the herb- and flower-filled room.

"And how would you do that?" I said, trying to keep him with me, because I seriously did not want to have to travel all over Las Vegas tracking him down again. Not when we were this close to actually figuring out where Rita might be. Getting the answers he said he needed, so he could move on just like Jackson had.

"I think she might be dead," he said, and sighed.

I blinked. "Why would you think she's dead?"

"Because," he said. "You can't find her. And she told us to stay away from the Dunes, and we didn't. I'm guessing that Victor figured out our scam and made her pay." He closed his eyes as though he was trying to gather his strength. "But I bet Victor knows where she is," he said, then sighed, and disappeared.

Dammit.

"What's going on?" Daisy asked when I walked back into the kitchen. Her voice was sharp, like she'd hit the end of her rope. I wondered if she'd felt Jackson leave and thought it was probably possible. They'd been together for a year and I'd been surprised that Jackson hadn't wanted to say goodbye to her before he moved on.

Just Jimmy.

"I'm sorry, Daisy," I said. "Jackson is gone."

Daisy wailed and put her hands to her face. Crystal reached over the table and touched Daisy on the arm. Daisy gasped and pushed away from her, but Crystal didn't give up. She murmured something comforting and touched her arm again.

"It's for the best," I said. "It wasn't good for you, having him here. You both need to move on. Him to the next plane of existence, and you, to the next phase of your life. You do understand that, don't you?"

"I didn't want him to go," she wailed. "I just wanted him to stop throwing stuff around. He was a comfort to me, Marie."

"He was not a comfort," I said as gently as I could. "He was a ghost. And he needed to move on."

I could see my cup of tea sitting on the table and wanted more than anything to gulp it down, but I had to deal with Jackson's increasingly distraught mother first.

"What did you do to him?" Daisy asked. "You must have done something, to make him leave me like that."

"I didn't do anything," I said. "He was ready when I got here. He moved on to the next plane of existence, basically on his own."

I closed my eyes, waiting for the slap I was certain was going to come. But it didn't happen, and when I warily opened them, Daisy had fallen back into Crystal's arms, sobbing like her heart was breaking. Which it probably was.

"I'm sorry," I said. Then I sat down and grabbed the tea cup, slurping back the lukewarm liquid like it was the nectar of the gods.

"Why didn't she stop him?" Daisy asked Crystal. She refused to look in my direction, like I'd disappeared with her son.

"I don't think she could've," Crystal said, with a quick glance at me. "When it's time, it's time. Right, Marie?"

"Right," I said. "I'm sorry, Daisy, but this really is better for you. You'll see."

"I'm alone," Daisy muttered, still to Crystal. Apparently, I was persona non grata in her eyes. "What am I going to do?"

"You're going to live your life," I started, but Crystal shook her head at me, and I shut my mouth.

"I'll come visit you," Crystal said. "As often as you like."

"I'd like that," Daisy whispered.

"So would I," Crystal replied. She held Daisy until her sobs subsided, then rose. "We have to go," she said gently. "But I'll touch base with you later. Would that be all right?"

"Yes," Daisy said. She pulled her voluminous hand bag from the back of her kitchen chair and scrabbled through it until she came up with a business card. I recognized the daisy pattern on it from the card she'd given to me, the day before.

"You can call me anytime," she said. "I'd love to have you over."

She ignored me pointedly, and I sighed. No love here. Not for me.

"We should get going," I said, and Crystal nodded.

She hugged Daisy one more time, and then the two of us walked out of the little cabin. She dropped her head when she heard Daisy begin sobbing again, but I took her by the arm and pulled her toward the truck.

"Call her later," I said. "She has to work through what just happened."

"But what if she doesn't?" Crystal asked. "What if she hurts

189

herself? She's afraid of being alone, Marie."

"If she kills herself, then you can help her move on," I said. "But you can't stop her if she's determined. However, I think that having her son finally gone will actually help her. She'll be better, I can almost guarantee it."

Now honestly, I didn't know whether she was going to be all right or not. I didn't go back to the living, to check up on them, after I moved on their ghosts. It had never occurred to me that they might need help to adjust, and the thought of it exhausted me. But Crystal nodded, and tucked the business card into her back pocket.

Then she looked around and frowned. "Where's Jimmy?"

"He disappeared when Jackson moved on," I said. "I have no idea where he is."

"He's probably at my place," Crystal said. "He likes the cats." Then she glanced at me. "If he hasn't moved on."

"Oh, he hasn't moved on," I said. "He's still hung up on finding Rita."

Crystal frowned. "Back to Rita, is he?"

"Yes," I said. "But he believes Victor Tupilo knows something. We should find him. But I need water, first."

"Water?" Crystal asked. "Why?"

I was going to explain, but simply shook my head. "It's just a thing that happens after I help a ghost," I said. I put the keys into the ignition and started the car. "So, watch for a convenience store. Please."

"Will do," Crystal replied.

Then we took off, and soon Daisy was alone. Alone for the first time in over a year.

JIMMY:
BACK TO THE CATS. WHAT A RELIEF

ALL RIGHT, SO I'd talked pretty big in front of Marie about going to find Tupilo to find out what had happened to Rita, but all I felt was relief when I popped back into Crystal's apartment. The cats were watching TV, and they barely gave me a look as I flopped to the floor like a rag doll.

"Oh come on, you sons of bitches," I muttered, flailing around like a newly caught fish. "I know you know I'm here. Act like it."

Nothing from any of them. They all just sat on the couch and watched the antics of the humans on the screen like they were there for their entertainment.

I couldn't believe how drained I felt. Jackson's suggestion—that Rita never loved either of us—had hit me hard.

She'd acted like she loved me. Even that last night. Well, she'd had sex with me, anyhow. That had to mean something. Right?

"And then she killed me," I muttered, pushing through the closest cat, who didn't pay me any mind at all. "Jackson was right. She killed me. Killed me."

I stared at the TV and tried to think. I'd been thinking of nothing but finding Rita for so long. Finding her, and making certain she was safe.

And she'd killed me.

Something shifted in my chest, like the love I had for her had disappeared, and something else—something dark and angry—

191

took over the spot where it had been.

She hadn't loved me. She'd used me, just like she'd used Jackson. And when we didn't do things exactly her way, she'd killed us both.

For ripping off the Dunes.

"Oh damn," I muttered. "I should find out what happened at the Dunes. What Rita did. And what Tupilo had done to her."

But I didn't move. Maybe it would be better to stay here, with Crystal and her cats. Just watch TV and forget about everything else.

Forget about Tupilo. Forget about Rita. Forget about everything.

Screw it all.

MARIE:
FUN AND GAMES IN LAS VEGAS. RIGHT.

I TOOK CRYSTAL back to her apartment and found Jimmy sitting on the couch watching a Star Trek rerun with all the cats.

"You okay?" I asked. He grunted something and shrugged, and I felt for him. I really did. Jackson had laid a lot on him before he moved on, and I figured it was going to be difficult for him to deal. Besides, I was too tired to do much more than pat his aura before going into the kitchen where Crystal was pulling food out of her fridge.

"You hungry?" she asked.

"Definitely," I said. "But I need more water first."

I grabbed a bottle from the fridge and downed it, then sat at the kitchen table and pulled out my phone. Called James to give him an update but slammed it off when it went right to voicemail.

"He's out having fun and I'm dealing with ghosts," I muttered. "It just isn't fair."

"Well, maybe we can do something fun," Crystal said as she broke four eggs into a frying pan and scrambled them.

"Like what?" I asked. The eggs smelled good. They really did.

"Oh, I don't know," Crystal said. She pulled out two plates, split the eggs between them, then put one plate in front of me and sat at the other end of the table with her plate. "What would you like to do?"

I frantically tried to think of something—anything—I wanted

to do, but all I could think was how good the eggs tasted, so I shovelled the food into my mouth and shrugged.

"Well, there's something *I* want to do," Crystal said. "Before your wedding."

Oh yeah. The wedding.

"What would you like to do?" I asked.

"I'd like to get my nails done," she said. "Maybe we could do that?"

I pushed more egg into my mouth because I didn't want to answer her.

"Oh, come on!" she said. "It'll only take a couple of hours. After that you can find James and go out for a night on the town with him. With beautiful nails!"

"And if you don't want to find him," Jimmy said. "We can probably come up with a couple more things to do."

He'd wandered in from the living room and stood behind Crystal's chair. His colour was better. He almost looked whole, which surprised me a bit. He'd taken a lot of hits lately.

"He's right," Crystal said. "We can be fun, if we try. Right, Jimmy?"

"Right," he said. "We can be fun."

Yeah, I thought. Right.

But honestly? James was off playing with dune buggies with his new friends, and I didn't want to spend another day alone.

So I said, "All right," and after we finished the scrambled eggs and cleaned her kitchen, we headed off to find fun in Las Vegas. Starting with a manicure.

Yay.

THE STRANGE THING was, I actually had a good time.

We went for mani-pedis because what the hell, and Jimmy played the clown through the whole thing, screwing with the manicure tools and lacquer until we were both laughing like loons and the young women doing our nails thought we'd lost our minds.

"She's getting married tomorrow," Crystal said, like that explained everything, and both girls shrugged and smiled. Then we were finished, our nails resplendent, and we headed out to check out the "Welcome to Fabulous Las Vegas" sign.

Crystal took pictures of me with the sign and I actually looked happy in a couple of them. But when we were finished there, she got into a fight with Jimmy about where we should go next.

He wanted to show me a famous mob hangout I'd never heard of, and she wanted to take me on the monorail. Things got increasingly loud until Crystal finally held up her hand to stop the yelling and looked at me.

"What do you want to do?" she asked.

"Honestly," I said. "I want to ride the big roller coaster. The one at New York New York."

At least I'd be able to say I rode the roller coaster. At least I could say that.

"A roller coaster ride?" Jimmy snorted and shook his head. "You have no idea what you're passing up. You're going to miss the best corn-fed strip loin steak in the state. Maybe the whole country. Plus, mobster memorabilia. Really."

Corn fed steak? Really?

"Maybe later," Crystal said. "Marie wants the roller coaster, so that's what she gets."

"I guess," Jimmy said, but he didn't sound convinced.

"Don't you want to see Lady Liberty?" Crystal asked. Him, not me, I noticed. "And what about the Brooklyn Bridge?"

"If I wanted New York I'd go to New York," Jimmy said, then glared at me. "Nothing about me being dead and past all that."

"Okay, Jimmy," I replied. "I won't say a word. If you go with me on the roller coaster."

Crystal snickered when Jimmy looked at me like I'd stabbed him in the heart. "No fucking way," he said. "Want to give me a heart attack or something?"

We all laughed way too long and way too hard but Crystal said she'd go with me so, in the end, it was all right.

It really was.

WE RODE THE roller coaster, twice. Then we went to the Fremont Street Experience which wasn't on my bucket list but was definitely bucket list adjacent. We drove by the old mob hangout but didn't have to stop there because it looked like it had burnt to the ground.

"When the hell did that happen?" Jimmy moaned.

"No clue," I said, fairly unhelpfully. "Where to now?"

"Hate to tell you, but I gotta go home," Crystal said

apologetically. "It's three in the morning and I do have to open the shop tomorrow. For a while at least."

"You're right," I said. "It's late. James is probably wondering where I am."

They were both good and didn't mention the fact that he hadn't tried to contact me, even once.

I dropped them off at Crystal's apartment complex and then texted James.

Where are you? I typed. *It's getting late and I'm worried.*

I looked at the text, hated the fact that it sounded so needy, and deleted it.

"I'll go back to the hotel," I muttered to myself. "And he'll be there, waiting for me."

But he wasn't at the hotel, so the text I actually sent him was much terser.

Call me, I texted. *Right frigging now.*

Instead of phoning me, he sent me a text.

Playing poker with the boys. I'll be late.

"Late?" I muttered. It was already nearly 4:30 in the morning. How much later could he be?

I turned on the TV and watched an old-time black and white movie with Rock Hudson and Doris Day, and fell asleep just before the sun came up.

Alone. Again.

JIMMY:
I HAVE TO DO BETTER

24 hours . . .

I WOKE UP early and watched the sun creep over the living room and all the sleeping cats. The TV was droning quietly to itself, some infomercial about how to grow hair, and I wished it was off. I didn't need the diversion. I needed to finally do what was right.

I was crapping out, the way I always had. I had to do something, and I was pretty sure that Victor Tupilo was the key.

I thought of him, with his thousand-dollar suits and his manicured nails, sitting in his office, overseeing everything that happened at the Dunes. He'd been at that hotel as long as I'd been going there, and I wondered how he'd kept himself looking so good.

"Sure wasn't good living," I muttered. "I wonder what he did that I didn't."

Then, I was there. With Victor. And I finally figured out that little mystery.

He was in the gym, working out.

I didn't think anyone used the gym in the hotel, but there he was, running on a treadmill, sweat running down his back, as a young, pretty girl on the video screen yelled for him to work harder. Harder!

He was the only one in the gym but I could see his men

197

guarding the door. I was about ready to leave because nothing bored me more than exercise, when one of his men walked into the gym, holding out a cell phone.

"Sorry, sir," he said. "I think you'll want to take this call."

Victor snarled but shut down the machine. He mopped his face and then took the cell.

"What?" he said. He listened for a moment, then sighed. Noisily. "Can't you handle anything?" he asked, angrily. "You do understand that I'm in the gym. The gym!"

I almost laughed when the guy waiting for the phone flinched away like he was afraid that he'd explode, even though I got it. Victor could make things happen to people. He had that ability.

Victor listened a moment more, then grimaced. "So you caught him cheating?" he finally said. "How much has he won?"

A short answer, and Victor laughed. "That much," he said. "Gotta be a college student. They think they're invincible. Think he's connected?" Then he frowned. "What do you mean, you don't think so? Check him out and get back to me. 'Cause if he's not connected to the mob, he's off to the dunes."

Then he shook his head. "Check that," he continued. "We'll have to let the cops deal with him." He snorted impatiently. "That's right. Call the cops if he's not connected. Get to it."

He tossed the phone to the thug waiting in front of the workout machine. "Who the hell is that guy?" he asked impatiently. "He's an idiot."

"He's Jennifer's nephew," the thug said. "You remember? She asked you to get him on somewhere. He wants to be a cop."

"He's just about stupid enough for that job," Victor muttered. "Get down there and help him take care of the cheat. And you make sure the cheat doesn't get so much as a hangnail. We can't afford any trouble."

"It's been a year," the thug murmured. "Are they still watching you?"

"Yes!" Victor yelled, then mopped his face with the towel once more. "That bitch caused me a world of trouble when she stole that money," he said. "So yes, the cartels are still watching this hotel. And me."

"Too bad you had her offed," the thug said, and then took a step back when Victor glared at him.

"Yes," Victor said, his voice like ice. "In retrospect it would have been better to have handed her over to the people she'd actually stolen from, so they could figure out what she'd done with the money, but I'm not willing to lose their business, or piss them off further until I can prove to them that we are doing everything on the up and up. Are you?"

"No, sir," the thug said, shaking his head vigorously.

"Well then," Victor continued. "I think our little cheat needs to spend some time with the cops, don't you?"

"Yes, sir," the thug said. "Right away, sir."

He backed away to the door, practically bowing and scraping as he went, and then disappeared.

Victor watched him go and then turned his attention back to his exercise machine.

"I swear to God," he said as he turned the machine back on, and the pretty video girl pushed him to get his heart rate up. "If I could kill that bitch again, I would. She nearly ruined me."

I was willing to bet that he was talking about Rita. I should have felt a thrill, knowing that I'd finally figured out what had happened to her, and where she probably was, but I didn't.

I turned to leave, but Victor's next words froze me in place.

"I'm willing to bet that James Lavall and Marie Jenner know where the money is," he said. "So maybe it's time to let Carlos know. As a gesture of good faith." And then he laughed. "And I can keep my reputation intact."

MARIE:
APPARENTLY, IT'S MY WEDDING DAY

THE PHONE ON the table beside my bed rang, and I nearly knocked the receiver to the floor as I scrabbled around trying to grab it. My mouth was dry and my eyes felt like they were glued shut.

"What?" I growled when I finally got the receiver up to my ear.

"This is Victor Tupilo," Victor said. "The Twilight Room is ready for your inspection."

"The what?" I mumbled.

"The Twilight Room," he said again. He sounded impatient. "For the wedding. Follow?"

I pulled myself up to sitting. "James is handling all the arrangements," I said. "Call him."

"He's not answering," Victor said. "When would you like to see the room?"

I thought for a moment and decided I was going to throw this particular task right back at James, wherever he was. This was his deal, anyhow.

"I'll get hold of James," I said. "He'll be inspecting the room."

"Any idea on time?" Victor said. "We're jammed today."

"Nope," I said. I knew I sounded caustic but I just couldn't care. "I'll make sure he gets back to you."

I hung up before he was able to answer, then picked up my cell and texted James.

You have to inspect the room this morning, I texted. *Call*

Victor. Now.

I waited, but he didn't respond. So, I called him, but it went to voicemail immediately. The SOB still had his phone off.

"Call Victor Tupilo," I snapped. "He wants you to inspect the room for the stupid wedding. This morning, if you're not having too much fun, that is." I put all the nasty I could into the word stupid and then disconnected.

I was a little disconcerted that he'd shut his phone off for so long. He didn't normally do things like that. But then, these were not normal times, were they? He was probably still playing poker or something.

I paced the small room, counting off the minutes, unsure what to do. He wouldn't just shut off his phone, would he? I mean, he was out partying with a drug dealer. He'd know I would be worried if I couldn't get hold of him. Wouldn't he?

"Maybe he just doesn't give a crap anymore," I muttered, pulling the last dress I'd bought from the plastic bag lying on the floor with all the other crap we'd purchased over the past couple of days. It was wrinkled, but I didn't care. If he didn't answer my text or my voicemail, I was going to go and find him. Somehow.

My cell chirped, and I scooped it up. James's name was on the display, and I breathed a sigh of relief. "James?" I said. "Where are you? Are you all right?"

Wherever he was, it was loud. "Good morning, Babe," he yelled over the noise. "Can you handle checking out the room on your own? I'm not going to be able to make it back for a couple of hours."

"A few hours," Ric's voice intoned. "We're going to be out for a few hours."

"A few hours," James said.

"I heard," I replied. Now that I was no longer worried about him, I was back to being pissed. "Where are you?"

There was a short silence while James thought. I could hear people laughing and screaming and cheering, and I knew, before he said a word, where he was.

"You're at the roller coaster, aren't you?" I said.

"Yeah," he replied, then laughed uncomfortably. "It's not as much fun as I thought it would be."

"Yes, it is," I muttered, then shook my head. Whatever. Looked like I was going to have to deal with the stupid room on top of everything else.

"I'll talk to you later," I said. As I pulled the phone from my ear, I was pretty sure I heard him say, "See you at the ceremony."

"Good grief," I muttered, and called Crystal.

"Hey," I said. "Can you help me out with something? I really don't want to handle it myself."

"What is it?" she asked. I could hear voices in the background. "I've got customers."

"Oh," I said. "That's right. You're at the shop. Sorry to bother you."

"No, it's all right," she said. "What do you need?"

"I have to check out the room, for the wedding," I said. "You know? And I was hoping you'd come and check it out with me. I really have no clue about this kind of stuff, and I could use some help."

"I'd love to," she said. "Just give me a minute to kick everyone out, and then I'm there."

"Are you sure?" I said.

"Absolutely," she replied. "One question, though. Have you seen Jimmy?"

I looked around the room, half expecting him to staring at me, but I was alone. "He's not here," I said.

"Oh." I could almost hear her frown. "I wonder where he went?"

"We'll find him," I said. "After we check out the room. All right?"

"All right," she said. Then she disconnected, and I was alone in the dishevelled room. I realized that the wedding dress she'd helped me pick out was lying on the floor with everything else, and felt a pang of dismay.

"She'd kill me for treating it like that," I muttered, then stopped. When had I gotten to the place where I cared what Crystal thought.

"Hell, why not?" I said to the empty room. "At least she answers when I call."

I contacted Victor to let him know we'd be down to check out the room in an hour. He seemed a bit put off that it would take that long but I just didn't give a crap anymore.

"We'll be there in an hour," I snapped and disconnected before he could answer.

I'd had just about enough from men. They could just shut their mouths and let me be.

I tore off the dress James had helped me pick out and dropped it on the floor. I kicked it to the back of the closet, next to the wedding dress in its plastic wrap.

"I need a shower," I said. "And then I'm wearing my regular clothes. I really can't care anymore."

I have to admit, that felt like the best shower of my life.

I STARTED SWEATING as soon as Crystal and I walked into the Twilight Room, an hour later.

"Oh my," Crystal said, as we walked through the big double doors and into the banquet room. "Doesn't this look beautiful?"

It looked pretty heavily decorated, to me. There were rows of chairs, wrapped in white, all pointing to the front of the room where a low stage was festooned with garlands of white flowers and huge white bows. Down the aisle a white carpet ran between the two banks of chairs, with daisies stuck to the innermost chairs.

"Everything's white," I said.

"We talked about that," Crystal said. "Remember? And look! It works!"

She walked into the room with a big smile on her face, and did a quick spin, as though she was trying to take in everything all at once. "Don't you think it works?"

"I suppose," I said, and then shrugged. "It looks fine."

"Fine?" Crystal said. "Just fine? Marie, this is supposed to be where you are getting married. You have to love it." She stared at me with a worried expression on her face. "We talked about everything being white," she said. "You said that you were all right with it. Right?"

To be honest, if felt like we'd taken that shopping trip for decorations about a month ago, and I honestly couldn't remember what I'd said to her, but I turned and smiled, full wattage, at her anyhow.

"You're right," I said. "This looks good. Honestly. Looks just the way I thought it would."

"I'm glad," a male voice intoned behind us. "I'd hate to have to tell the staff to start over again."

We both turned. Victor Tupilo stood at the back of the room, and behind him was Jimmy. What was he doing here, I wondered.

Crystal turned up her smile to ten and held out her hand. "Mr. Tupilo," she said. "I'm so pleased to see you again."

Victor's face froze for a couple of long beats, but he took Crystal's hand and shook it perfunctorily. "I didn't realize you two knew each other," he said. "How's the book coming?"

"Very well," Crystal replied. "Just have a bit more research to do, but it's all coming together nicely."

Victor blinked, slowly. "I take it you didn't find any ghosts in the Dunes," he said.

Jimmy laughed, but he was the only one who made a sound. Crystal glanced at me, and I shrugged. Before she could answer him, Jimmy said, "Keep your mouth shut about me," and Crystal blinked her eyes furiously for a second before finally answering him.

"No ghosts here," she said.

Jimmy laughed again, as Victor pulled a handkerchief from his pocket and dabbed at his forehead, delicately.

"We'll have to do something about the air conditioning before this evening," he said. "It's a tad warm here, isn't it?"

It actually felt cold, but I suspected that had to do with Jimmy, who was floating around Victor, staring at him like he could read his soul.

"Ask him about Rita," he said. Crystal gasped and stared first at Jimmy and then at me.

"Have you been able to find out anything about Rita Sullivan?" I asked. "James really wants to find her. You know, for the will and all that."

Victor blinked at me, and mopped his face again. "I'm sorry," he said. "I'm not comfortable talking about her in front of—"

He pointed at Crystal.

"Would you mind giving us a minute?" I asked her. "It's just some business. You know, before we get to all the wedding fun."

"Absolutely," she said, and the smile she threw in Victor's direction was so bright, I was amazed he wasn't blinded by it. "I'll just be over there," she said, pointing at the stage. "Checking out the flowers and whatnot."

"Thanks," I said. When she'd stepped out of hearing, I looked at Victor. "All right, we're alone," I said. "Please tell me you've found Rita Sullivan."

"I'm sorry," he said. "I just discovered that Legal has been looking for her, for months. Unfortunately, it looks like she left town a short while after Jimmy Lavall died."

"Why was Legal looking for her for that long?" I asked.

"She worked as a bookkeeper here," Victor said. "And we found—irregularities." His voice was cold as ice. "Then, she missed her next shift. It is very suspicious."

"What kind of irregularities?" I asked. I remembered the book James had been reading, when we'd gone to Rita's apartment, and wondered if money laundering had anything to do with the irregularities.

"Nothing for you to worry about," Victor said. "But when Legal finds her, I'll make sure they let her know about the will."

"He's lying," Jimmy said. "That son of a bitch is lying. She's already dead. He killed her."

What?

I glanced at Jimmy's cold, furious face. "I'll tell you everything," he said. "As soon as we get away from this son of a bitch."

I nodded, then focussed on Victor.

"I'm sorry to hear that," I said. "We'd like to get everything cleared up. For the will. You know."

"I understand," Victor said. "And I wish we could help you more."

"I'm sure you are," I said.

He stared at me for a moment, then pointed at the room. "Are you ready to check the room for your big night?"

"Yes," I said. "But before we start, can I ask you one more question?"

"Certainly," he said.

"Why did you give us this room?" I asked. "For the wedding? It was nice of you, no doubt about it, but I couldn't help wondering why."

He stared at me for a long, frozen moment. "I did it for Jimmy," he finally said. "Lavall and I had a long relationship, and since he died here, the least I could do for his family was comp you the room for your nuptials. However, if you'd like to pay for it—"

"No, no," I said quickly. "We're thrilled, and Jimmy would

have appreciated it, I'm sure."

Jimmy darkened to a smudge. "He's lying about everything," he said.

I was pretty sure he was right, but we still had to check out the room. I gestured for Crystal to join us. We followed him around the room, and Crystal was more than happy to ooh and aah about everything, so I didn't have to bother.

Jimmy floated beside me like a shadow. "You're not buying that 'Legal's looking for Rita' crap, are you?" he asked.

"No," I whispered back.

"Well, I know where she is," he said. "She did something to cross him, and he got rid of her."

"What do you mean?" I asked, loud enough for Victor to glance at me. Luckily Crystal could see that Jimmy was in some distress, and grabbed Victor by the arm, pulling him over to a huge bouquet of white roses and baby's breath.

"Where did these flowers come from?" she asked, smiling at him brightly.

"From a local florist," he replied. "Why?"

"I know for a fact that it matters to Marie where the flowers came from," she said. "Originally, you know? She wouldn't want the floral equivalent of blood diamonds at her wedding, now would you, Marie?"

She glanced at me, and I nodded, doing my best to look like Bridezilla. Victor looked like he wanted to toss her out on her ear, but soon he was on his cell, talking to someone about the flowers, and I was able to turn my attention back to Jimmy.

"Victor Tupilo makes problems disappear for the hotel," he said. "I think Rita ripped off the hotel and turned into a big problem for Victor. My guess is, she was dumped with the rest of his problems. Out in the dunes. Probably with a bullet to the back of her head."

I could hear the Victor's voice getting louder as Crystal harassed him about where the chair covers had come from. "No," he yelled. "They were not made in China!"

"Where?" I asked.

"East," he said. "Get this done and I'll show you."

"Thanks," I whispered, then turned to Crystal, and the nearly apoplectic Victor. "I think this looks great," I said. "Crystal, we have to leave. Now."

Crystal didn't miss a beat. She grabbed the Victor by the hand and shook it enthusiastically. "We'll be back tonight at 9:30. Right, Marie?"

"Absolutely," I said.

"He killed her," Jimmy muttered, and took a straggling step toward Victor. "I want to make him pay for that."

"Let's go," I said, and walked through Jimmy, just to get his attention.

"He has to pay!" he howled, and I could feel him change from sorrow so deep I felt like I could drown in it to rage. Complete and utter rage. He pushed through me, almost knocking me down as he headed for Victor.

"Not now," Crystal muttered, and stepped in his way. She stopped him long enough for me to pull myself together and step back into him. I hung on, tight, and pulled him out of the room with me.

As soon as the big double doors slammed shut, I yelled, "Stop it!"

"But he has to pay!" Jimmy cried.

"Of course, he does," I said. "But there's nothing you can do right now. We need to find Rita. Find proof. Then we'll go to the cops. The cops can make him pay. All right?"

His frantic whirling slowed, then stopped. "All right," he finally said.

"You'll show us where he has the bodies buried?" I asked.

"Yes," he said.

"Good," I said. "Let's go."

Finally, finally we were going to get Rita and Jimmy together. It was too bad they were both dead, but there was nothing I could do about that.

I walked a few steps down the hallway then stopped when I realized that Crystal hadn't followed. I turned, and she was still standing by the doors, shaking her head.

"Come on," I urged. "We can find Rita right now, if we hurry."

"I don't want to go East," she said. "That's where all those lights are. I told you that."

I stared at her for a second and then shrugged. "Whatever," I said. "Jimmy knows where she is so we're going. Jimmy and Rita can talk, Jimmy can move on, and then I can come back here." I sighed. "For the wedding, or whatever. Stay. You're off the hook.

All right?"

"Why don't we do this later?" she said, and sighed. "I don't want to deal with any more ghosts. I just want to enjoy your wedding."

"Crystal, we're leaving tomorrow," I said, impatiently. "We've run out of time. If we don't go now—right now—Jimmy will still be with you when I leave. You get that, don't you?"

Crystal glanced at me. "Do you really think you can do this by yourself?"

"Honestly, I don't know," I replied. "But you're off the hook, like I said. Just go home. I'll be fine."

She stared down at her hands with the brand-new manicure and then sighed. "All right," she said. "I'll come with you. But please tell me I get to help you get ready for your wedding after. All right?"

"If you want to," I said.

"I'd be honoured," she replied.

Jimmy snorted derisively, but I think she meant it.

"All right, let's go," I said. "Let's go find Rita."

JIMMY:
SHE'S GOING TO BE MAD

BACK IN THE day, Victor used the sand dunes behind the Dunes Hotel as a spot to get rid of bodies that needed to disappear. What I heard was, they were buried, more or less, and the coyotes were expected to do their part, so that it would soon be impossible to either identify or figure out cause of death for the poor unfortunate that got in his way.

But then, the inevitable expansion happened, and the old dumping spots were no longer convenient. However, the landfill was already in operation by that time, and so, when Victor wanted to have problems disappear, that was where they went.

This meant money had to grease palms, but trust me, there was so much garbage leaving that hotel every damned day that the occasional body was hardly a problem. Drivers were paid off, and bodies disappeared. But everybody still called where the bodies were dumped, the dunes.

Now Victor had never actually talked about it to me when I was alive. Even when I was closer to the inner circle, I wasn't privy to much at all. But I'd heard stories, and when I got myself barred from the Dunes, I was sure I was going to find out where the bodies were buried, first-hand.

But for some reason, he didn't. All he'd done was tell me to get out of his hotel as his favourite tough guy grabbed my hand and broke three of my fingers, just to make sure I was paying attention. "And don't come back," he said. "You understand?"

"Yes," I'd gasped. The pain from my broken fingers was overwhelming, but I hung on his every word like my life depended on it. Which it did.

I was deposited just outside the North Las Vegas border, and the tough guy pointed at the sand just off the highway. I could see a ravine in the distance.

"You come back to the Dunes, and that's where you'll end up," he said. "You got that?"

"I got it," I'd said, and then watched him drive back to civilization. It took me a couple of hours to get a ride back into town, and I maxed my credit card getting my fingers fixed. And I never went back to the Dunes resort again. Not until the night I died.

"WHERE ARE WE going?" Marie asked me as we walked away from the Twilight Room. "Can we walk?"

I chuckled, stopping when I felt Crystal give me a look. "No," I said. "We can't walk."

"How far is it?" Marie asked.

"Just a few miles out of town," I said. "Not that far."

Then I walked ahead of them to Marie's rental car, so I didn't have to answer any more of their questions.

All I knew for sure was Marie wasn't going to be happy. We were going to end up at the biggest landfill in the U.S.

MARIE:
WHERE THE HELL ARE WE?

IT TOOK US nearly an hour to get to the entrance to the landfill for Las Vegas. It was huge, and stinky, and the garbage trucks never stopped rolling down the side road to the valley where the dump proper was, throwing up choking dust.

"Are you kidding me?" I barked when I realized where he'd brought us. "The dump?"

"It's harder to hide a body in the desert than it used to be," Jimmy said. "Eventually, they're found. And then the police investigation starts." He pointed past the trucks and the dust, to the entrance.

"This is where she'll be," he said.

I watched the big trucks roll past us, barely stopping at the entrance. There wasn't a break. "How big is this place?" I asked.

"They have twenty-two hundred acres," he said, and shrugged. "They got space for two hundred years' worth of garbage. That's what I heard, anyhow."

"Oh my God," Crystal cried, and put her hand over her mouth and nose. "I can't believe how much this stinks."

"It's a dump," I replied. "What did you expect?"

The sun was still high in the sky, so we weren't going to be able to use the light of the dead to guide us. Not yet. I wondered if it would have been better to have come here later, when the sun was down. The heat was stultifying. This was going to be horrible.

"Well, how are we going to do this?" Crystal asked. She looked wan and pressed her scarf even more securely to her mouth and nose.

"You're not going to get sick are you?" I asked.

"No," she replied. She threw the door of the truck open and got out. "Let's go talk to whoever is in charge," she said.

I scrambled out of the vehicle and barely caught her before she entered the building to the left of the entrance to the landfill.

It smelled bad inside, but at least it was cooler. Crystal walked up to the counter and smiled at the Santa Claus-wanna-be sitting at a desk, off to the right.

"How can I help you?" he asked, without looking up from his magazine.

"We need to get in there," Crystal said. "We—we lost something, and we think it got thrown away. Accidentally."

He looked up from his magazine for a long moment, then sighed. "Honey," he said. "It's real hard to find anything in here."

"I—I know," Crystal said, and leaned further over the counter. I imagined she was turning on the charm, but didn't know if it was going to work. She jerked her thumb over her shoulder and I jumped when I realized she was pointing at me.

"She's getting married," she said. "And somebody threw her mother's wedding veil away. We just have to look for it. Please, mister."

"A veil?" Wannabe Santa said, shaking his head. "You want to look for a wedding veil out there?"

"We do," I said, and tried turning on the charm myself. I was pretty sure I didn't do it as well as Crystal, but at least he didn't laugh in my face. "My mother's dead," I said. "It's the only thing I have that was hers. I have to try to find it, at least."

He hmmed and hawed for a few minutes, giving us a hard time for not going to our local pickup spot, then demanded to see ID. "If you don't live here you don't belong here," he said. "You understand that, don't you?"

Crystal smiled for all she was worth and pulled her ID from her pocket. He looked it over like he thought it was fake, and for a second I was sure he was going to bite it. Finally, he handed it back to Crystal.

"All right, so you do live here," he said. "I thought maybe you were tourists. You'd be surprised how many people we get who want to dig through the garbage." He shook his head. "I thought everyone came to this town for the shows."

"I understand," Crystal said. "But I live here, and I really want to look for that veil."

Santa stared at her for a long moment and then let out a long sigh. "I'm sorry, miss," he said. "I can't let you in there. It's dangerous, and honest to god, you won't find what you're looking for. You gotta trust me on this."

"Oh, come on," Crystal said, still working the charm even though I could tell we were done as far as the old fat man across the counter was concerned. "We'll stay out of the way of the trucks. I promise."

"It isn't just the trucks," he said, shaking his head. "There's a lot more equipment here, and all of it is dangerous. The company would be liable if anything happened to you. You're not getting in."

"But—" Crystal started, ready to get mad. I grabbed her arm and pulled her away from the counter as he sat back down and picked up the magazine he'd been reading.

"That's all right," I said. "I understand."

"But, Marie," Crystal said, trying to pull her arm from my grip. "We have to get in there."

"It's all right," I said again, and gave her a warning glance. "We'll figure out something else."

"All right," she said. I could tell she wasn't convinced, so I made certain I pulled her out of the air-conditioned office and back into the hot stinking air outside. I waved at the wannabe Santa, just in case he was still watching, and headed back to the truck.

"We can't just give this up," she said. "Jimmy needs to find Rita. We need to find Rita."

Then she frowned and looked inside the truck, which was empty. "Where's Jimmy?"

"I imagine he's in there, somewhere," I said, pointing past the building we'd just left to the clouds of shit hawks floating above the edge of a ravine. We couldn't see where the trucks were dumping the garbage, but I figured those birds could.

"We'll follow the birds," I said. "They'll take us where we need to go."

"But. But," she stuttered. "We're not allowed in."

"Oh we're going in," I replied. "Wannabe Santa just doesn't know it yet."

I walked past the car, to the fence that surrounded the entrance to the dump.

"What are we doing?" Crystal asked.

"Looking for a way in," I replied.

We were soon out of sight of the entrance, and it didn't take too long to find a spot where the fence didn't quite touch the ground. I pushed my way under. I only caught my jeans once, but flinched when I heard them rip.

Finally, though, I was through, and I stood, gesturing for Crystal to follow me.

She was in the long skirt and puffy white blouse she wore at her shop, and she looked at me like I was out of my mind. "I'm not doing that," she said.

"Suit yourself," I replied. "Wait in the car."

Then I made a big show of fishing the keys out of my jeans pocket. "Oh dear," I said. "Looks like you'll have to wait for me in the heat."

"Good God. You're worse than Jimmy," she said, but she scootched under the fence, and was soon standing beside me. "Are you happy? I'm covered with—well, I don't know what I'm covered with."

"You look fine," I said, even though she really did have something horrible across the butt of her skirt.

I looked out over the huge—and I mean huge—ravine with machines and trucks and garbage absolutely everywhere. The shit hawks screamed and wheeled above us, mocking us.

"What the hell," Crystal breathed. "We'll never find them in that."

"Come on," I said. "We're in. Let's go see if Rita is here."

"Jesus," Crystal said, but she did follow me as I skittered down the garbage strewn road by the fence, and into the Las Vegas landfill.

JIMMY:
I'LL FIND RITA MYSELF

I WATCHED MARIE and Crystal march purposefully into the office building, but I was certain they weren't going to get much further. Didn't matter, though. They'd gotten me close, so all I had to do was get out of the truck and go find Rita, wherever she was.

For a second, I was afraid I'd pop back to Crystal's apartment, or worse, Room 214, but then I steeled myself. I needed to stay. I needed to find her. Needed to find out what had happened. To her, and to me.

I stepped out of the truck and looked over at the road where the river of garbage trucks flowed, and for a second, I was in awe. Garbage without end. Appropriate for this town, I thought and then wondered where the hell that thought had come from.

"I never even thought about where the garbage went, before," I muttered. "It was all about the glitz and glamour. The unbelievably beautiful women, all ready to grant me my every wish. The chance to win, at everything. Something I thought I could only find here."

I felt a twinge of sadness, but shut it down. I was dead. That crap didn't matter anymore. I just had to find Rita, so I could get the answers I needed. Then I would be finished.

"I'll be finished," I muttered, surprised I'd even thought that. What had happened to going back to Edmonton and helping James? Staying with Crystal and her cats? I wasn't sure, anymore.

I scrambled down into the ditch by the road that led to the landfill, happy that my feet didn't get caught in the short scrub brush and garbage that lined the road. Then I thought about how much easier it would be if I could float above it all, and suddenly, I was.

It surprised me, and I fell back to earth. Collected my thoughts, tried it again, and found myself floating above everything, higher and higher, until my only companions were the gulls screeching and floating above the ocean of garbage below.

For a second, I wondered how high I could float. If I could leave all of this behind. Rita, and James, and even Marie and Crystal. Just float away and never come back down to earth.

Then, I saw a faint, small, light and let myself settle a little lower, to find out what it was.

A cat wandered in the debris, then sat down to preen. The light was coming from it, and I gasped when I realized that I was looking at a ghost.

"Poor thing," I muttered. "Somebody threw you away."

It didn't actually look that worried, or upset. Just preened, and then stretched out above the garbage that surrounded it, and went to sleep. Its light changed colour, and I wondered if it was dreaming.

A dead cat dreaming. What a thought.

Another cat wandered over and joined the first. This one was in rough shape, and I figured that it had probably been roadkill. The light from the roadkill cat was darker, angrier, but it seemed to calm when the first cat woke and walked over to flop down beside it, resuming its nap.

A dog trotted by, but there was no light emanating from it, so I figured it was probably alive. I watched it disappear behind a pile of discoloured mattresses, and then I looked around for more light.

Jesus, it was everywhere. There were dead things everywhere in the ocean of garbage, and I wondered if I had bitten off more than I could chew.

"Go up, a bit," I said to myself. "See if that helps."

I rose, and the height actually did help. The light from the cats and dogs and other dead animals who had been dumped here were weaker and lighter than some of the other lights I could see. And many of them were further east, in an older part of the dump. No animals there, as far as I could tell. Just the human garbage.

So, I headed over to where the humans had congregated. Half of me hoped that Rita wasn't here, with them, but the other half—the darker, angrier half—wanted her to be.

There were dozens of human ghosts sitting and staring out at nothing. Some were bright, but many of them were dim, and I wondered how long they'd been there.

"I'm lucky I didn't end up here," I said, and then frowned. Why the hell hadn't I ended up here after I'd died? If there had ever been a problematic death at the Dunes, it was mine. Why had they left me for the cops to find? Why had they let my body go home? What had been so different about me?

I closed my eyes and shook my head to shake loose the thoughts I was having. It didn't matter why they hadn't dumped me here. All that mattered was finding Rita.

Most of the ghosts were women and a lot of them were young. The most disposable of the disposable. Many of them had horrible wounds that would never heal, and I wondered, just for a moment, about the people who could have inflicted all this damage and then dumped them. Wondered if they thought about them. Felt bad at what they'd done.

"Nope," I said. "They would only feel bad if they got caught."

I looked up at the edge of the ravine, where the gulls wheeled and screeched, and saw that the sun was much closer to the edge of the world. Soon, it would disappear, and all I'd be able to see would be the river of garbage trucks way off at the other end of the landfill, and the lights of the dead.

I headed down and landed by a group of ghosts. They barely looked at me. Just stared out at nothing, their light dim, their eyes exhausted.

"Does anyone know if a Rita Sullivan is here?" I asked, feeling a little foolish. "I'm looking for her."

One of the ghosts, dressed like a five-dollar hooker with fifteen stab wounds in her red sequin-covered torso, slowly turned to me. "Who you looking for, honey?" she asked. "Maybe I can help."

I blinked. "How old are you—were you?" I asked.

"Thirteen," she said. "But I can be any age you want." She

smiled, and blood drooled down her chin. I saw that half her teeth were missing. "You looking for a good time?"

"I'm looking for Rita," I said. "I'm sorry."

The thirteen-year-old dead hooker rolled her eyes and turned away from me, pointedly.

"Does anyone know if Rita's here?" I asked. "Anyone?"

"I might," said another hooker, this one with her throat gaping open below her pasty face. "What's in it for me?"

"Nothing," I said.

"Fuck off then," she said, and glared.

Then I thought of Marie. Maybe she could help this girl.

"Wait here," I said, and floated up until I could see the whole landfill. Just off the road, I noticed two figures working their way through the edges of the dump. They were heading in my direction, sort of, and no light emanated from either of them.

"I'll be right back," I said.

"Whatever," the ghost with the slit throat said. "What the fuck ever, old man."

That brought me up short. I hadn't ever thought of myself as old. Then I looked down, and saw myself the way she saw me. A wifebeater undershirt, tight white underwear, and black socks. A paunch where my six-pack used to be, and my hands looked gnarled. Old. Jesus. She was right. I was old.

I turned away from her and floated toward Marie and Crystal. Marie could help them. And she'd be able to convince them to tell us where Rita was.

I hoped.

MARIE:
GHOSTS, GHOSTS EVERYWHERE
... OF COURSE

"I DON'T KNOW if I'll be able to do this," Crystal said. "My god, I can't believe the smells down here."

She was right. It was pretty horrible down in the ravine proper. Above, the wind moved the air around some so we weren't trapped in the scent of death but down in the ravine the wind barely moved at all. Which meant we were trapped in it.

I heard her gag and resisted the urge to cover my ears when she threw up. It was probably better for her to get it all out of her system but the sound of puking bothered me more than the smells.

I walked away from her to put some distance between her noise and my gag reflex. After a few fairly horrible minutes, the gagging noises slowed and then stopped.

"You okay?" I called, without turning around.

"Yeah," she said. She didn't sound good but at least she'd stopped the horrible noise. "Yeah, I'm all right. Any idea where Jimmy is?"

I scanned what I could see of the landfill but did not see Jimmy. There were small odd lights here and there but no sight of him anywhere.

"We'll keep looking," I said. "He'll show up."

If he was still there.

Crystal ran up behind me and then her hand grabbed mine. Her fingers felt hot, needy, but I didn't pull away.

"How're you feeling now?" I asked.

"Better," she said. "Sort of."

She pointed to the east. To the older end of the landfill. "Can you see those lights?" she asked. "At the other end of the ravine?"

I gasped. There were lights everywhere, scattered over the old garbage like grotesque Christmas lights. "Jesus," I muttered. "Looks like there are hundreds of them."

"Do you think Jimmy's with them?" Crystal asked. "Looking for Rita?"

"Probably," I said. I tightened my grip on her small, hot hand and pulled her with me. "Let's go find out."

"This is going to take forever," she muttered. "What about the ceremony?"

"Ceremony?" I asked. "What ceremony?"

Then I remembered I was getting married just before she gasped like I'd spit on Baby Jesus or something. "We've got time," I said. "Don't worry about it."

"All right," she said, but she didn't sound all right. She sounded horrified.

I wondered how much more horrified she'd be when we got to the other end of the landfill and she realized just how many people had been dumped here over the years.

Almost as horrified as me, I guessed.

The one thing I'd wanted to do in Vegas was stay away from the dead, and now here I was walking into a bunch of them.

"Hell of a holiday," I muttered.

"What?" Crystal asked.

"Nothing," I said. "Forget it."

The shit hawks above us swirled and screamed as though something was disturbing them, and then, suddenly, Jimmy appeared before us, floating in the air like a bedraggled half-dressed angel.

Crystal gasped as he slowly settled in the garbage before us. "Where were you?" she asked. "And when did you learn to fly?"

"I was over there," he said, pointing somewhere over his shoulder. "I found someone who says she knows where Rita is."

"And the flying?" Crystal asked.

"It just came to me," Jimmy said and shrugged. "You going to follow me or what?"

"We're right behind you," I said. "Don't be a smart arse."

He chuckled and turned. He stayed on the ground but sped over the garbage like it wasn't even there. Crystal and I had to work a lot harder to go half as fast, and we were covered in filth and sweat by the time we made it to the top of the hill where he'd stopped.

There were ghosts everywhere. Most of them were young when they died and so badly hurt my heart ached for them all.

"She knows something," Jimmy said, pointing at a pretty-faced ghost with a slashed throat.

"And I'll tell you, for a price," the girl said.

"I can't pay you," I said as gently as I could. "Because—"

"I'm dead," the ghost said impatiently. "I know. But business is business."

"Maybe you can move her on," Jimmy said. "You know, like you said you were going to do for me."

"What's that?" the girl asked, looking directly at us for the first time. Her colour, which hung around her in muddy waves, brightened briefly, then settled back as I explained what moving on was and how I could help her.

I had the feeling I was seeing hope rise up and then die, and it truly made me want to weep. Crystal sniffled behind me, and I realized she'd noticed the same thing.

"Help her," she said. "Please."

"I'll try," I said, then looked at the girl. "Does this sound like something you'd like to do?"

"I don't know," she said. "I've been here so long. I can't imagine being anywhere else, to be honest."

"How long have you been here?" I asked.

"I died in 1983," she said. "Giving a blowjob to a psycho in the back seat of a Chevy Nova on June 6, 1983." She shook her head. "I found this place a few months later. So, I been here a while."

"And why did you come here?" I asked. "Usually ghosts stay where they die. Why—"

"It was the lights," she said, and smiled again. She had a lovely smile. "I knew they were the lights of my kind, so I followed them here. And when I got here, I realized that my body was here." She pointed at the filthy ground beneath her. "Right here. So, I stayed."

"So, your body holds you here?"

"No," she said. "Being with my kind holds me here. 'Cause I have to tell you, I sure am sick of the living. Why would I go back?"

I did not have an answer for her and looked down at my hands to calm myself. The feeling of sorrow was so prevalent in this place that all I wanted to do was throw myself to the garbage-covered ground and cry my eyes out but I couldn't do that. I needed to stay strong.

"There are a couple of things you can do, if you'd like to move on," I said. "And I can help you. If you want, you can start over again on this world. If you'd like, you could do your life over."

She looked at me and laughed. "Not a chance," she said. "I'm not doing this over again. I want off this rock."

I looked at her pretty face and her slit throat and decided that she didn't need to do the "think of your life" thing. She'd been brutalized in this world and if she wanted off I would do my best to help her find her equivalent of heaven.

"Then think of the best place in the world," I said. "The absolute best."

"Like Broadacres?" the girl mumbled. "I went there once. Damn, I loved that place."

I stared at her. "Are you talking about the flea market?" I asked.

"Yeah," she said, and smiled. The first real smile I'd seen on her face. "The music is wonderful, and you can get anything you want to eat. You know? Like real food. I had such a good time there." She sniffled. "Best time of my life."

My god.

"All right," I said. "Think of that place. Going there. Being there."

"Like heaven?" she said.

"Sure," I said. "If you like."

Her face closed, and I knew she was going to say something like "I don't deserve to go there," and all I wanted to do was cry because she was talking about a glorified flea market but I shook my head before she could say a word.

"You deserve heaven," I said. "Just think of it and let this place go. Let this life and death go. Let it go."

"Wait," Jimmy said. "Wait! I need to know where Rita is! Tell me where she is. Now!"

The ghost blinked and then pointed over her shoulder. "She's in the old part," she whispered. "She found a dumpster she likes to stay in. She says the lights hurt her eyes."

Jimmy whirled around and ran in the direction the girl had pointed.

"Go with him," I said to Crystal. "I have to help—" Then I frowned at the ghost. "What's your name?"

"Birth name or chosen?" the girl asked.

Something about the way she said "birth name" made me think that it was the last name she ever wanted to be associated with. "Chosen's fine," I said.

"Angel Whitfield," she said.

"All right, Angel Whitfield," I said. "Think of heaven."

The muddy colour of her aura lightened, and brightened. She put her head back and stared up at the sky. "It's pretty, isn't it?" she whispered.

I glanced up and saw that the sun was going down. The sunset was pink and gold, and she was right. It was pretty.

The first light bee popped out of her aura. It was pink, like the sunset, and I took that as a good sign. Another followed, and then another.

"This isn't going to hurt too much, is it?" she asked, and closed her eyes.

"No," I said. "It won't hurt at all."

"Finally," she muttered. And then, all at once, she disappeared in a flurry of light. Pink and gold, with just one big fat black light bee bumbling its way into the sky.

She was gone. Finally gone from this godawful place.

I stood on legs that wobbled and found a broomstick lying on the ground next to me. I picked it up, wrapped a white plastic bag around one end, poked the other end in the ground, and took a step back. I was happy to see that it stood, all on its own. With any luck it would stay upright until Crystal could bring someone here to find Angel's body, if anything was left, and take it out of this place.

Another girl, this one in a red sequinned tube top who had been horribly brutalized before she'd died, touched my hand. The spot was so cold, I shuddered, and then looked down at her.

"Would you do that for me, too?" she asked. "I don't got nothing to trade but I really don't want to stay here if Angel's gone. You know?"

"I do," I said. I looked over at the next hill of garbage, and in the settling twilight, I could see Jimmy's light. Crystal's white shirt marked her as she stumbled up the hill. I still had time. Time for one more.

The girl in the tube top didn't take any time at all to move on. She just wanted to know where Angel had gone. I told her, and her face brightened.

"Perfect," she said. Then she opened her eyes and smiled at me. "My name's Bethany," she said. "Bethany Miller."

Before I could say another word, she blew apart in a red and yellow light show.

"Goodbye, Bethany," I whispered, and put my head down, suddenly exhausted.

"Marie?" Jimmy was calling my name, and I looked over at the next hill. He was waving his arms excitedly.

"What?" I called.

"We found her," he said. "Rita. We found her."

I closed my eyes and sighed. "Coming," I said, and pushed myself upright.

I had more work to do.

JIMMY:
RITA, IN A DUMPSTER,
WITH A DEAD CAT

"RITA!" I CALLED, flying over the hills of garbage to a burned-out dumpster lying on its side at the top of one hill. The open end of the dumpster looked out over the edge of the ravine, and when I flew over it and landed, Rita was sitting, watching the sun go down.

In her lap was the ghost of a cat. She petted the animal and it arched its back against her aura. I could hear it purring.

Even with the bullet hole over her right eye she looked beautiful. "Rita?" I said. "It's me. Jimmy."

She didn't respond but I thought I saw a small flare in her aura, and the cat quit purring.

I walked up to her. Stood between her and the sunset. "Rita," I said. "Talk to me, girl. I know I caused you trouble, but please. Talk to me."

Still nothing, but the cat growled and then thrashed in Rita's hands. I realized she was strangling the animal. Killing it again.

"Make her stop," a small voice from the other side of the dumpster whispered. "Please, mister. Make her stop hurting my cat."

"Rita," I said, kneeling down so we were at eye level and she couldn't avoid me. "Don't do that. Please. You're better than that."

She looked past me, but released the aura of the cat. It dashed away from her and disappeared around the edge of the burnt-out dumpster.

Crystal came flying around the other side of the dumpster, sweating and puffing like she couldn't get her breath. She skidded to a stop when she saw the ghost of the woman sitting, immobile, in the burnt-out dumpster. "Is this Rita?" she asked me.

"Yes," I said. "But she won't talk."

It was like my words kicked a switch in Rita's brain. She blinked, and then turned and stared at Crystal. "You're not dead," she said. "But you can see me."

"I can," Crystal said. "I'm here with Jimmy." She gestured at me, but Rita's eyes didn't waver. Just stared at Crystal's face with an intensity I'd never seen before.

"What do you want?" Rita asked. She looked around, and I realized she was looking for the ghost of the cat. It was like she did not remember that moments before she'd tried to strangle the thing.

"We wanted to—find out how you were," Crystal said, then shook her head. "I mean, Jimmy wanted to find you. He has things to say to you about what happened. Don't you, Jimmy?"

Before I could say a word, Rita sneered, her eyes skidding past me to the rapidly setting sun. "I have nothing to say to him. After all, it's his fault I'm here."

She glanced at me and her aura darkened. So, she could see me. She just wasn't talking to me.

"Come on," I whispered. "Please, girl, I need to talk to you. Explain—"

"Explain what?" she asked, finally looking into my eyes. It was like looking into the mouth of a tomb. "Explain why you couldn't follow my simple instructions? Just stay away from the Dunes, I said. That's all you had to do."

"I know," I whispered. "And I'm sorry—"

"You're sorry?" she barked. "You're sorry? Trust me, I'm the one who's sorry. I swear, Jimmy, you had the worst timing I'd ever seen in my life. All you had to do was wait two days. Hell, one would have been enough. But no, you decided to scam the Dunes the day I ripped them off."

"What?"

"You incredible idiot," she cried. "I was working the longest con of my life and all you had to do was wait one more day. But no, not you. You managed to screw the whole thing up for me. Didn't you? Didn't you!" She screamed the words at me, and I stumbled away from her rage.

"What did I do?" I asked. I was pretty sure I already knew, but I wanted to hear the words from her mouth.

"I took four point three million dollars from the Dunes," she said. "Four point three million absolutely untraceable dollars. I'd finally convinced Victor Tupilo to trust me enough to handle the bank transfers. All the bank transfers—and I'd figured out how to syphon the money from his offshore account to mine. One big move and it all went perfectly. Perfectly. I was set for the rest of my life. Nobody would have looked at the books until the end of the month, because he trusted me!" She screamed the words at me, spittle flying.

"But then you and Jackson did what you did—and you had to rub my face in it. You took that room at the Dunes, and you made me come down there and deal with you."

"Kill me, you mean," I said.

"Well, what did you expect?" she asked. "You knew better than to break the rules, Jimmy. And you screwed everything up." She snivelled. "All I needed was one more day, but they found your body and you led them right to me. To me!"

I frowned. "What do you mean, I led them right to you?" I asked. "How would they know about you and me?"

"Because of the security video!" she screamed. "They found your body, and then Victor saw me leaving your room on the tape. If you hadn't forced me to go there and deal with you, he never would have known." She groaned. "I just needed one more day," she said. "Just to get the key."

"What key?" I asked.

"To the safety deposit box," she said. "At my bank."

"Is that where the money is?"

"No, you idiot," Rita spat. "It holds all the information for my offshore account. Where I transferred all the money." She sighed. "All I wanted to do was buy an island and live like a queen."

"I thought that was our dream," I muttered.

She looked at me and smirked. "Did you really think I was going to run away with you? Really? You and Jackson were diversions. Nothing more. Trust me, if you hadn't screwed me over, you never would have seen me again."

"But he wasn't the one who screwed you over," Crystal said. "Was he?"

Rita glared at her. "Yes, he was," she said. "He knew the rules."

"Maybe he did," Crystal continued. "But you were the one who killed him that night. And you were the one who got caught on camera. Weren't you?"

Rita stood and took a threatening step toward Crystal. "Take that back," she said. "He broke the rules. He did. Not me. Him."

Her colours had darkened, and red lightning bolts shot through her slender frame. She was angry. Seriously angry, and if I didn't do something she was going to go after Crystal. I didn't know if she could physically hurt her but I wasn't willing to take the chance.

"You're right, Rita," I said, stepping between her and Crystal. "This was all my fault. I'm sorry."

"Are you?" she asked, her eyes a thunderstorm in her grey face. "Really?"

"Really," I said. "But I might have a way to make it up to you. If you want."

She frowned at me, but the lightning in her eyes had lessened a little. I had her attention. Now I just had to keep it while Crystal got away.

"There's another woman here," I said. "Someone who might be able to help you. So you don't have to live like this anymore."

Rita looked at me and then laughed. "I'm not living," she said. "You get that, don't you?"

"I get that," I said. "But I think Marie could take you away from this place. Maybe to somewhere nice. What do you say?"

I was just spitballing, trying to keep Rita's attention on me and away from Crystal, who was still standing behind us like she was frozen. But I did have Rita's attention.

"So where is this Marie chick?" she asked. "The one who's going to get me to Heaven?"

Heaven felt like a stretch to me, considering she was a murderer, but I waved my arms over my head and called Marie's name.

Marie answered my call but she sounded tired. Exhausted. And I wondered if she'd have the strength to deal with Rita, who

E.C. Bell

was more like a monster than a woman.

Who had I been in love with?

Marie clambered up the hill to the dumpster.

"Is this her?" she asked me. "Rita?"

"Yeah," I said and my damned throat tightened. Monster or not, I'd loved her. "She needs your help."

"You want me to help you move on?" Marie asked.

"You can help me get to heaven," Rita said.

She looked at Rita. "Heaven?" she said. "You want to go to heaven?"

Rita smiled, turning the old charm up to a ten. "I hear you might be able to help me."

"Were you killed here?" Marie asked.

Rita snorted laughter. "No," she said. "I died in the Dunes, the morning after Mr. Tighty-Whities there."

Marie's forehead creased in a frown. "And you did that to him?" she asked. "You killed him?"

"Of course, I did," Rita said. "Both him and Jackson. My two partners, who went behind my back and messed up the best con I'd ever run."

"She ripped off the Dunes," I said. "She took money they were laundering through the casino. Drug money. Untraceable."

Rita looked out at the darkening skyline and howled. And, damn me, even though the sound frightened me, I admired her silhouette against the darkening sky. Her perfect—absolutely perfect—face. The face I'd fallen in love with. God, she was beautiful.

She turned and glared at me, the lightning back in her eyes. "All that money's mine," she said. "And you're going to help me get it."

She came up behind me, and suddenly I felt cold. Freezing. She touched me and, my god, I couldn't believe the anger and ugliness that wafted over me from her.

"Don't," I whispered, but I couldn't move fast enough to get away from her.

"It'll only take a minute," she said. "Just stand still and take it like a man, for God's sake."

She stepped into me and the cold immobilized me. I'd never felt that helpless in my life.

"All right," Marie said, somewhere behind us. "That's enough,

231

Rita. Let him go."

"Not going to happen," Rita said. "It's time for him to pay."

She wrapped her aura around me and I was frozen. I tried to call out but couldn't until I felt something touch my right arm.

"That's enough," Marie said again. She was standing beside both of us and had placed her hand on mine. "Get out of him, now."

She took another step forward and suddenly there were three of us in the space that before only I had occupied. Rita's cold rage began to recede, bit by bit.

"What are you doing?" she gasped, struggling to stay in control. Marie wasn't having any of it, though, and gave her a huge psychic shove.

"Get out of him!" she cried.

Rita fell to the garbage-strewn ground and screamed incoherently as I flailed around, trying to pull myself together.

"How did you do that?" I gasped.

"A trick my mother taught me," Marie replied. She sounded a little out of breath but that was all.

"You'll have to teach me that trick," Crystal said. She'd appeared at the side of the dumpster, and I wondered where the cat was.

"Help Jimmy while I take care of Rita," Marie said.

"Okay," Crystal said. She scrabbled over to me, settling by my head. She stared into my eyes, concern all over her face.

"Stay with me," she said. "All right?"

Whatever Rita—and Marie, I suppose—had done to me had really taken the wind out of my sails. All I wanted to do was lie down and sleep.

"Girl, I'd give you all the money in the world if you'd just take me back to your apartment," I said. "This—this is too much to bear."

Her eyes flicked over my face, like she was checking to see if I was kidding or not. Her face went pale so I guessed she realized I meant every word.

She glanced over at Marie, who had squatted by Rita's form and was whispering to her urgently. "She'll be done with Rita soon," she said. "Just stay with me until she's done. Please?"

"I'll try," I said. But the truth was I wanted to be off this mountain of garbage more than I could say. I could feel something—her apartment, Room 214 in the fucking Dunes, something—pulling at me. I closed my eyes and thought about just disappearing.

Everything I thought had been the truth was a lie. Rita hadn't loved me. Had never loved me. I wasn't even sure if she had the capacity to love me, or anyone. She'd used me.

I'd honestly figured that she would forgive me for going after the Dunes. After all, we were in love. Right? And that's what love's all about. Forgiving and forgetting.

But Rita hadn't done that.

"Just let me go," I muttered to Crystal.

"No," she said and placed her hand over the aura of my arm. I could feel her warmth, and sobbed, because in that spot I almost felt like I was alive again.

I clung to her warmth and she flinched. I think I was hurting her but I didn't know how to make it stop. I just wanted to feel warm again.

Or, I wanted to feel nothing. One or the other. Just not the cold. Not anymore.

MARIE:
RITA'S A SOCIOPATH. WHO KNEW?

ONCE I'D PULLED Rita away from Jimmy, she convulsed on the ground. There was something off about her colour and her light, and I suspected she was trying to fool me into letting her go, so she could get to Jimmy again.

Jesus.

"Stop that," I said. "I mean it, Rita. Stop it now. You're not fooling me."

Her flailing slowed and then stopped. She sat upright, pushed her hair away from her face, and sighed.

"That bit has worked on everyone since I got here. What makes you so smart?"

"I've known a few ghosts," I said.

"I bet you have," she replied. She stood and, out of habit, I supposed, brushed her dress clean. There was nothing but blood on it, of course, but she did it anyhow. "I suppose you want me to leave. Like everyone else here." She grinned. "They're all jealous. That's why they want me gone."

"I'll help you, but only if that's what you want," I replied.

"I am a bit tired of this place," she said, without turning around. She was staring out at the darkening landfill. "There are so many of us here."

"I can help you," I said, taking a tentative step toward her. "If that's what you really want."

She turned and glared at me. In the darkening light, the red and black etched through her aura like lightning. She was one scary-looking person, no doubt about it.

"How are you going to help me?" she asked.

"Well, we can talk," I said. "About where you would like to go next. If you're truly done with this place."

I looked around, at the garbage and the burned-out dumpster. Her kingdom, or what was left of it.

"I almost made it, you know," she said. "I almost made it out of this place." She looked around, distractedly. "Have you seen my cat? I can't just leave him here by himself."

"I haven't," I said.

"Marmalade is not her cat," a little voice echoed from behind the burned-out dumpster. "Make her go away. Please."

I stood and caught the eye of another ghost, so terribly burnt I could barely recognize her as having once been human. She was holding a cat in her heat-crippled hands, petting and petting.

"Who are you?" I asked.

"Don't listen to that little bitch," Rita said, behind me. "She stole my cat. I want him. Now."

"He's my cat," the charred ghost cried. "And that's my spot. Just go away, Rita. Please. Can't you leave me alone? Leave us alone?"

"No," Rita said and laughed. It was an ugly sound, and when she brushed past me to get to the burnt ghost, the rage I felt from her was complete.

"Stop it, Rita," I said, but she ignored me. I heard scrabbling behind me, and then Jimmy walked up to the burnt ghost. For a second I thought he was going to pull the cat from her crippled hands, but he stepped past her and stood in Rita's way.

"That's enough, Rita," he said. "Leave the girl alone."

"Why should I?" Rita snarled. "She has my fucking cat and I want him. Now!"

She grabbed Jimmy and gave him a big shove. I half expected him to fly down the garbage hill, but he didn't. He stood his ground and shook his head at Rita.

"That's enough," he said. "Quit hurting people."

I wasn't certain what Jimmy's end game was but he'd distracted Rita so I scrabbled over to the burnt girl with the cat. "Move," I said, pointing at Crystal who was watching like a terrified statue. "Go over there, by her. She'll protect you."

Now, I didn't know if Crystal could protect anyone but I needed to focus Rita's attention on Jimmy and me. If there was a chance of moving her on and getting everyone else out of danger, she had to focus on us.

The girl nodded and scrabbled behind the dumpster to Crystal. Rita's head didn't move in her direction at all. Jimmy definitely had her attention.

"What do you need?" I said to Rita. "What would help you move on from this plane?"

"Besides my cat, you mean?" she snarled.

"Besides the cat," I said. "What's holding you here?"

Rita's eyes swung in my direction. "I want my money," she said. "So I can go to heaven."

"What?" I asked.

Rita shook her head and looked tired. "Jesus. You're as stupid as Jimmy. I want my money," she repeated. "So I can get out of here and go to heaven."

I continued to stare at her because I honestly couldn't tell if she was kidding or not. "You think you need money to go to heaven?" I finally asked.

"Well, yes," she said. "I'll have expenses. Besides, I think I've earned that money. Don't you?"

I shook my head. "You won't have expenses," I said. "You won't have anything. Rita, you're dead. Beyond material needs."

"Well, if you think I'm staying in a dump like this when I've got over four million dollars waiting for me in an offshore account, you are out of your mind," she replied. "Jimmy said you could help me. So help me already."

"I can't do that, Rita," I said. "You are not of this world any longer. You don't need money. You don't need anything. You just need to make a decision and move on to the next plane of existence." I looked her in the eye. "Do you understand that?"

She frowned and glanced over at Jimmy. "I thought you said she'd help me," she snarled. "But she's not willing to do what I want."

"Just listen—" I started but Rita sneered and turned away from me.

"What I need is my money," she whispered. "After Victor pays for doing this to me."

She touched the bullet hole in her forehead and grimaced. "He made such a mess," she said.

Jimmy took a tentative step toward her, careful to keep just out of her reach. "Maybe you can't use the money you took, but what if I promise you, I'll make Victor Tupilo pay for killing you?" he asked.

"You?" Rita laughed and shook her head. "You're useless. You know that."

Jimmy shrivelled before her disgust. "What about Marie?" he said. "She could make sure he pays for what he did to you."

"Revenge isn't the answer," I snapped.

"But what if you—I don't know—went to the police?" Jimmy said. "After all, she's here. Her body's here, in the dump. You could help them find it and then they could make sure he pays." He half-smiled. "Justice, not revenge. You could do that, couldn't you?"

I glanced at Rita and her colour had calmed a bit. The black and red had run together, muddying both. She wasn't quite so frightening any more.

"What about that, Rita?" I asked. "I'll find a cop and tell him what happened to you." I gestured around, at all the lights I could see in the landfill, each one representing someone dead. "What happened to all of you."

"I don't care about the rest," she muttered. "I just want to make sure that son of a bitch pays dearly for what he did to me." She glanced at Jimmy. "Just like you did."

"Yeah," Jimmy said. "Just like me."

"So you admit that what you did was wrong?" Rita asked. "And you deserved what you got?"

"Yeah," Jimmy sighed. "I probably deserved everything I got."

Rita smiled and nodded. Then she looked over at me. "So," she said. "You going to find a good cop and make sure that son of a bitch pays for what he did to me?"

"I will," I said.

"Then, I guess it's time for me to go," she said.

I was surprised, because she sure hadn't seemed on the road to moving on, but her light lightened and brightened until she was almost clear. That in itself was odd. She'd done so much damage, she shouldn't have been clear. She should have been dark, and she should have been hurting. What was going on?

"How do I do this?" she asked me.

"Actually, that's up to you," I said. "What would you like to do? Start over? Go to the next plane? Your decision."

Rita looked at me and laughed. "You think I'm doing this again, you're nuts," she said. "The house always wins here. I am going to heaven, just like I said."

"All right," I said.

She was still clear, but I noticed that a number of black and red light bees were starting to form under her skin. No white. Not one. And that wasn't going to be good for her.

"First, it's important for you to recognize the things you've done that have hurt people," I said.

She looked at me and frowned. "I've never hurt anyone who didn't deserve it," she said.

"I understand," I said, as gently as I could. "But even if they deserved it, you need to acknowledge what you've done. The hurt you've caused."

"You mean, like Jimmy?" she said. "And Jackson?"

"Yes," I said. "Like them."

She laughed and lay back on the ground. "Jackson was collateral damage," she whispered. "And Jimmy? Jimmy deserved everything he got." She sighed. "They all deserved everything they got."

"Rita," I started, but she waved her hand at me dismissively. "I don't have to apologize for anything. I never did anything that wasn't warranted."

"Including stealing that little girl's cat?" I said, almost desperately. She had to recognize the wrong she'd done. She had to.

"She didn't know how to look after the thing," she whispered. "She was a terrible cat mother. I was better. Ultimately, it was for the best."

A big black light bee pushed its way through her skin and up into the darkening sky. She didn't flinch. Didn't act like she'd felt it at all.

Then another and another pushed their way out of her. Still she didn't flinch. I bent over her, but she looked past me like I wasn't there at all.

"Rita?" I said. "Can you hear me?"

"Sure," she said.

"Please, do the right thing," I said. "Just tell me what you regret. Then you'll be able to go to heaven—or whatever."

"Oh, I don't think I do," she said. "I think everything's going to be fine." She sighed out the last words and then grabbed me by the arm.

The cold from her touch made my arm and hand cramp, and I tried to pull away, but she wouldn't let me.

She wouldn't let me. And that was bad.

"I'm going to heaven," she said. "And there is nothing you can do to stop me. Got that?"

"I got it," I said.

She wasn't going to heaven. There was no way in the world—but the light bees poured out of her, even as she kept a tight grip on my arm. They were all black, but she didn't flinch. Not once.

"You tell the cops what that son of a bitch did to me, all right?" she said. "You promise me you'll bring him down."

"I will," I said.

"Good." And for the last time, she smiled at me. "Don't make me come back and make you pay, too."

"That's not the way this works," I started, but before I could finish, she disappeared in a flurry of black light bees.

All black. Every last one of them. And they burned me, wherever they touched me. They burned me, but they hadn't burnt her.

One of them floated toward Jimmy and landed on his arm. He flinched as it disappeared.

"Where did that go?" I asked. He looked at me like I'd lost my mind.

"What are you talking about?" he asked, confused.

"The light," I said. "That black light from Rita. It touched you. Didn't you feel it?"

"No," he said, and then looked around. "She's gone, isn't she?"

"It looks like it," I said. "Are you sure you didn't feel anything?"

Before he could answer, Crystal called, "Are you all right?" from the relative safety of the other side of the dumpster.

"Yeah," I grunted. "I think so."

"We have to go," Crystal said. "If we don't hurry, you're going to be late to your own wedding."

"That's right," I heard Jimmy sigh. "You're getting married."

I looked at him, and he stared at me for a long moment and then looked down at his grey hands. "There's only one thing holding me here," he said. "Really, just one thing."

"What's that?" I asked.

"I just want to see you two get married," he said. "So I know that Jim will finally be happy. Then I think I'll be ready to go. Promise."

"All right, Jimmy," I said. "Come to the wedding."

Crystal came up behind the two of us with the burnt girl and the dead cat in tow. "We have to go talk to the cops first," she said. "They have to know about all these people. Don't they?"

I stared at the burnt girl, and she nodded, her eyes glistening with her version of tears. "Please," she said. "Somebody has to know about us. We need—"

"Justice," I sighed. "You need justice."

"Justice will do," she said.

"Are you ready to move on?" I asked.

She shook her head and took Rita's place in front of the burnt-out dumpster. "Not yet," she said. "I won't be ready until I see all of us get justice here."

"I'll make sure that you do," Crystal said.

"That would be nice," the burnt girl replied. She looked down at the dead cat, which had curled up in her lap. "We all deserve a little justice, don't we, Marmalade?"

The cat purred.

AS THE THREE of us walked down the hill of garbage, I stumbled and nearly fell.

"Are you all right?" Crystal asked and grabbed me by the arm to keep me upright.

"I just need some water," I said. "Do you know where the cop shop is?"

"We need to go back into town," Crystal said. "Are you sure you're all right?"

"I will be once I get to the car," I replied.

We didn't sneak around the way we had when we broke into the dump, and a guy working on a huge bulldozer saw us and yelled, "What the hell are you doing?"

We didn't answer, just ran past the gate to the car as he stared at us, dumbfounded. I tripped again and cursed myself as Crystal grabbed me more securely by the arm and dragged me the last few feet.

"Want me to drive?" Crystal cried.

"No," I said. "I'll be fine."

But as we barrelled down the roadway back to the entrance and I worked at keeping the car on the road, I wondered if maybe I'd made a mistake.

"Water," I gasped. Crystal dug around in the back seat and found a half full bottle.

"Sorry," she said as she flipped off the top and handed it to me. "I don't know whose that is."

"Probably mine," I said. It was either mine or James's. I hoped. I downed the warm liquid in three huge swallows, and sighed, wishing that there was more.

Jimmy was uncharacteristically quiet in the back seat, and I wondered if he was all right. He'd been hit with a lot in a short period of time and probably needed support but I wasn't up to giving it because it was taking all my wherewithal to keep the vehicle on the road.

"Talk to him," I said to Crystal. "He seems—off."

"I don't blame him," Crystal said. "That Rita was something, wasn't she?"

"Something," I said. "I'm just not sure what."

Crystal shrugged. "I think Vegas attracts people like her."

"That's a depressing thought," I replied, and she shrugged again.

"It's just the truth," she said. "Thinking about anybody but yourself isn't really in the DNA of anyone who wants to make it here. At least, that's what I think."

She turned and looked at Jimmy. "How are you doing?"

Jimmy looked down at himself and chuckled. "I never realized just how out of shape I am," he said. "Or was, before I died. Wouldn't have hurt me to hit the gym, would it?"

Crystal blinked. "I guess not," she finally answered.

"How long until we get to the Dunes?" Jimmy asked.

"A while," Crystal said. "We're going to the cop shop first."

"Jesus, just forget that," Jimmy hissed. I could see his colour change. He was angry. "Go to the Dunes."

"No," I said as Crystal sucked wind. "We're going to the cop shop and telling them what we found, first. We promised Rita.

Remember?"

Jimmy was silent but his colour deepened to a violent red and then subsided. "All right," he said. "But after, we go to the Dunes. Right?"

"Of course," Crystal said. "Marie's wedding starts in—" She looked at her phone and gasped. "We only have two hours," she said. "We have to hurry."

"The wedding," Jimmy said. "Of course."

Crystal looked at him like he'd lost his mind. "Of course, the wedding," she said. "You said you wanted to see them get married, Jimmy. That's the reason you're still with us."

"Right," he said. "That's right."

And then he was silent once again.

Crystal glanced at me. "What's up with him?" she muttered.

"No clue," I said and really put my foot into it. "Let's just get to the cop shop. I need more water, desperately."

We drove toward Las Vegas as the sun set. It was pretty, but darkened as we drove toward it. Then, all there was left was the scream of neon.

JIMMY:
WHAT'S WRONG WITH ME?

THE BLACK LIGHT bee that landed on my arm when Rita disappeared burned me as it burrowed into my aura and under my skin. I could feel it spread, that blackness, that otherness, and I tried to tell Marie that something was wrong but I couldn't say a word.

Oh, I spoke. I heard my voice talking and talking but not one word was mine.

I tried to grab Marie so she could feel what I was feeling but I couldn't move my arm, either. But when Marie said we had to run, I ran. I don't think I could have stopped even if I'd wanted to.

Something had me. Was using me. Like a puppet.

MARIE:
THE LVMPD

"HERE," CRYSTAL SAID. "It's right here."

We stopped at the front entrance of the Las Vegas Metropolitan Police Department. The building was off-white, with lots of windows, and it didn't actually look like a cop shop to me.

"Are you sure?" I asked.

"Yep," she said.

We parked and got out. Jimmy didn't move. He looked like he was frozen in place, and Crystal glanced at me, then reached over the front seat and gently touched him. He jumped like he'd been burned and glared at her.

"Keep your hands to yourself," he said.

She blinked and pulled away from him. "Sorry," she said. "I thought you'd want to come in with us."

"Into another cop shop?" he said and snorted unpleasant laughter. "No thanks. Just hurry up and get your little mission done so we can get to the Dunes. All right?"

"All right," Crystal replied. "No need to get nasty, Jimmy."

"You do understand that you could do this later, don't you?" Jimmy continued. He held up his hand and looked at his nails. Shook his head and "tsked" like he couldn't believe how bad they looked.

"We can't," I said. "I'm leaving early tomorrow morning."

247

"Well, do you have to be involved with this?" he said, and pointed at Crystal. "Can't she do it? She knows where the bodies are, for heaven's sake. Let her handle something."

"No," I said, before Crystal even had time to respond. "We're in this together. Right, Crystal?"

"Right," she said. "Stay here if you want, Jimmy. We're doing this."

She slammed the car door shut and stormed across the parking lot.

"What the hell's wrong with you?" I snapped at Jimmy, then followed Crystal before he answered. But I thought I heard him laugh, and the sound of it brought gooseflesh up on my arms.

What *was* wrong with him?

I ran across the parking lot, catching Crystal at the front door. "You okay?" I asked.

"I wish he was gone," she muttered. "He's gotten so mean."

"I know," I said. "Hey, maybe he'll disappear before we get back."

"That's the dream," she said and smiled a bit as we pushed the doors open and entered the cop shop.

We walked up to the reception window and, after what felt like forever, a uniformed officer noticed us and sauntered over.

Crystal explained, as well as she was able, what we wanted them to know. As she spoke, the cop's eyes grew flat. He wasn't buying what she was trying to sell. He wasn't even writing down anything. Just stared at her with his flat, disinterested eyes.

She looked at me, desperation etched across her face. So I stepped up, hoping I could help the situation.

"Come on," I said. "Listen to her. Let us give a statement about what we saw out there."

"Fine," the cop said, and finally picked up his pen. "So, you're telling me you're both psychics. Do I have that right?"

"Right," Crystal said. She sounded relieved but the tone of his voice did nothing to make me feel any better.

"And you both think that there are bodies—human bodies—buried at the landfill," the cop continued. He did not write anything down.

"That's right. We saw them," she said, and shrugged. "Well, we saw a few. Mostly we saw their emanations."

"Hmm," the cop said. His face hardened, just a tad. "So what you're saying is you were at the landfill. Tonight."

"Yes," Crystal said, her voice edging over to impatience. "We told you that already."

"Hmm," the cop said again. He leaned back on his chair and called out to someone we could not see.

"Hey, Ryan," he said. "Didn't we get a call about someone trespassing at the dump?"

"Yep," Ryan drawled. We still couldn't see him. "We sure did."

"Which means," the cop at the reception desk said, "it looks like you two are in some trouble."

Ryan, who was still invisible to us, laughed, and the cop at the desk worked to keep his face impassive.

"So, you're saying you're going to arrest us," Crystal said. "For trespassing?"

"That would be up to you," the cop said. "All you have to do is walk out that door and we'll forget we saw you. Right, Ryan?"

"Right," Ryan said.

"Let's go," I said. "We're not going to get any help here."

"But what about the bodies?" Crystal cried. "Those women deserve to be found. Their stories deserve to be heard."

She looked like she was going to cry, and the cop behind the reception glass sighed, loudly.

"Convince your friend to go with you," he said to me. "We don't want to have to bring her in."

"Come on, Crystal," I said, and turned away from the glass. "They're not going to help."

"Well, if they aren't, who is?" Crystal cried.

"I don't know," I said. "We'll have to figure that out. But let's go."

The cops laughed as we left, and Crystal burst into tears when the big front doors finally eased shut and we could no longer hear them. I grabbed her by the arm and pulled her to the car.

"We'll tell James," I said. "He might know who we can tell."

But, to be honest, I didn't think James would help us either. He had his "work with the drug dealer" thing on the go, and the women we found, the ones who had been treated like so much garbage? He might not want to bother with them, either.

A tiny flame of anger caught in my chest, and I nurtured it as we slipped into the truck. I was sick of having to convince people that what I saw—what we saw—was real.

"I told you it wouldn't do any good," Jimmy said, snidely.

"Shut up," I barked. "Just shut your mouth."

"Touchy," Jimmy said but did what I asked and I knew why. It was because we were going where he wanted and doing what he wanted.

And I hated him for it. Almost as much as I was beginning to hate this city.

"Let's get this done," I said. "So I can get out of here."

Crystal didn't say anything. Just stared at me like I'd smacked her across the face. And Jimmy? That son of a bitch laughed.

JIMMY:
SERIOUSLY, WHAT THE HELL
IS WRONG WITH ME?

AS MARIE MANEUVERED down the streets of Vegas back to the Dunes, Crystal cried. And I laughed at her. That girl had done nothing but try to help me, and I laughed.

I couldn't stop myself, much as I wanted to. Even when I saw the look—the hateful, hateful look—Marie threw my way, I couldn't stop.

I was out of control. I could feel it. I was in real trouble and couldn't even tell anyone.

So I laughed at Crystal and I laughed at Marie. And I laughed at myself. At my pathetic attempt to make amends. Or take revenge. Or whatever the hell I'd been trying to do.

I'd wasted my one chance to make things right, and all I could do was laugh.

Pathetic.

But then, I always had been.

MARIE:
SO ... LET'S GET MARRIED, SHALL WE?

WE PULLED UP to the Dunes but I didn't have the strength to get out of the car. I couldn't remember ever feeling that tired in my life.

"Are you all right?" Crystal asked for what felt like the fortieth time.

"I just need a drink of water," I said.

"And a shower," Crystal said. "Because you're getting married in—" She glanced at her phone and gasped. "You're late," she said, "You have to hurry."

A valet tapped on the side window. I rolled it down.

"Want me to park it for you?" he said, and then took a giant step back. "Something die in there?" he gasped.

"We were at the dump," I said shortly and pushed the door open.

Crystal grabbed me by the arm. "Let me use your car," she said. "I have to get my dress."

A lone thought wormed its way into my head through the exhaustion. "I've got a dress you can use," I said. "I haven't even worn it yet."

"Are you sure?" she said.

"Yeah," I replied. "You'll look great."

"Thanks," Crystal said and jumped out of the car. Jimmy slithered through the side of the vehicle and stood beside her, and then they both walked toward the front entrance of the Dunes.

"You going to get out?" the valet asked.

"Absolutely," I said, even though all I wanted to do was curl up and sleep for the next ten years or so.

"You want I should get this cleaned?" the valet asked. "I'd be willing to do that, for a small fee."

"Don't worry about it," I said. "It's a rental."

I pulled myself out of the vehicle, headed for the door after Crystal and Jimmy, and walked into the air-conditioned splendour that was the Dunes.

As soon as I was inside, I turned on my phone so I could text James. I watched in dismay as thirty-five texts appeared. All from James and, I suspected, most of them panic-stricken.

I'm here, I texted. *I have to get dressed, and then I'll be down.*

I didn't wait for him to answer. Just dropped the phone back into my pocket and headed to the elevators where Jimmy and Crystal were waiting. Everyone stepped away from us, so we rode up to the second floor alone. We didn't speak to each other. Just kept our eyes on the numbers as they lit.

The elevator door opened, and we walked out and to the door of Room 214. Jimmy shuddered as I flashed the key card and the green light lit.

"I don't want to go back in there," he said. "Not ever again, if I can help it."

"Well don't, then," I said. "Go down to the Twilight Room. We'll be down as soon as we wash the stink of the landfill off."

"All right," he said and disappeared.

I looked at Crystal. "Jimmy still seems off to me," I said. "Does he seem off to you?"

Crystal shrugged. "I think that learning the truth about Rita really shook him up," she said. "But being able to come to the wedding should help. If you're actually going to go through with it."

I blinked at her in confusion. "What do you mean?" I asked. "I'm here. I'm going. Heck, I'm even lending you a dress."

"Yeah," she said. "But honestly, Marie? You act like you'd rather be anywhere but here."

I sighed as another wave of exhaustion rolled over me. "I'll explain everything," I said, and opened the door.

The room looked like a bomb had gone off in it. Crystal looked at the mess, and then bent over to pick up the tie-dyed tee shirt she'd given me before we'd gone on the ghost tour. "Feels like you wore this months ago, doesn't it?" she said.

"Yeah." I grabbed a bottle of water sitting on the desk and spun the lid off. Watched it roll over the carpet and stop when it hit Crystal's foot. Then I drank, deeply, and when I got to the bottom, I almost felt human again. Almost.

"So, you ready to tell me what's going on?" Crystal asked. She pushed a small mountain of clothing off the bed, and it cascaded to the floor. She sat on the cleared edge and looked at me coolly. "I'd really like to know."

"There's nothing going on with me," I said. "Let me find that dress for you."

Before she could answer, I dove for the closet and dug around to find the last dress James had bought for me. The one I'd abandoned.

It was a little wrinkled, but I figured it would be all right.

"Here," I said. "It's cute. You'll look great in it."

She looked it over and half smiled. "It's blue," she said. "Something borrowed. Something blue. Except it's supposed to be for you." She set the dress on the bed and walked over to me. "What's going on?" she asked. "You act like you don't want to be here. Don't—don't you want to get married?"

I stared at her for a long moment, and then, damn it, felt tears prick my eyes. "I—I don't even know," I whispered. "I thought I did, but it's going so fast, and James is being so strange—"

She frowned. "How so?"

"He's hanging around with those guys . . . Did I tell you they're drug dealers? Drug dealers! He's hanging around with drug dealers, and I feel like I don't even know him anymore!"

Crystal's eyes popped. "Drug dealers?"

"Yeah," I said. "Actual honest-to-God drug dealers. From Edmonton. He says he's trying to—I don't know—infiltrate their organization or something, but those guys are dangerous." Tears dripped down my dirty face, and I snivelled. "And he went on the roller coaster without me."

"Let's put a pin in that just for a minute and concentrate on the drug dealers," Crystal said. "Are you in danger?"

"I don't think so," I said. "It looks like he's got that situation under control for the moment, but I don't know what'll happen when we go home." I snivelled again, and wiped my nose on my dirty hand. "The good thing is, we know people, at home. People who can help, if things get dicey."

"Boy, he really dropped you in it, didn't he?" Crystal asked as she reached for the box of tissues on the table beside the bed and handed them to me. "Prick."

I pulled a tissue from the box. "And then there's Jimmy. Man, James won't deal with him at all."

"I kinda noticed that," Crystal said. "Is he always like this? A prick?"

I laughed and shook my head. "No," I said. "This is new."

"So, what do you want to do?"

"Do?" I asked. "What do you mean, what do I want to do? I'm getting married. Apparently."

"You don't have to, you know," she said. "You and I can walk out of this room right now. Go back to my place, make tacos, and hang around with the cats." She grinned. "Sorry. I'm hungry."

"We could, couldn't we?" I said. "We could leave."

I honestly thought I'd feel relief at the thought of running away, but I didn't. I looked at the wedding dress, still in its plastic cocoon, and thought about James waiting for me in that room full of people. All right, so most of them were strangers, but still. He'd be there. And then we'd be going home, and I wanted to go home with him. Live with him.

I wanted to happily ever after with him.

"I'm not going to leave," I said. "But you're right. He's being a real prick."

"Did I tell you he asked me to invite people that you know to the wedding?" Crystal asked.

"No," I said. "You didn't tell me that."

"I invited Daisy and Alice," she said. "They were thrilled."

"Huh," I said.

"I know it doesn't make up for the roller coaster and Jimmy and the rest of this," she said. "But he did do that."

"I guess it's something," I muttered.

"But is it enough?" Crystal asked. "Seriously, Marie. Is it?"

I thought—really thought—about her question. "No," I finally said. "No, it isn't."

She blinked. "So, are we actually going to leave?" she asked. "I mean, I understand, and I know the cats would have a good time with you, but. It's a big thing. Isn't it?"

"Yes, it is," I replied. "And no, I'm not running away."

"What then?"

"I'm going to get dressed and I'm going to get married," I said. "I love the guy, Crystal. I really do."

Crystal stared at me for a long moment. "Are you sure?"

"Yeah," I said. "I'm sure."

"Well, I guess you can always divorce him if it doesn't work out," she said, and chuckled.

"True," I said. Then I pointed to the bathroom. "You get the shower first, because, girl, you smell worse than I do."

"I do, don't I?" she said and disappeared into the bathroom with the borrowed blue dress slung over her shoulder.

A QUICK TWENTY minutes later and I'd finished my shower and blown my hair dry. I pulled the wedding dress—the one Crystal had helped me pick out a million years before—off the hanger and out of its plastic cocoon. I stepped into it, tugged it over my hips, and settled the straps on my shoulders.

Crystal walked over to me, and without saying a word, zipped the dress so that it finally fit me as snugly as it had that first day I'd tried it on.

"How do I look?" I asked.

"Good," she said. "Want me to do your makeup?"

"No," I replied. "We gotta go."

I took one last look at myself and wished, just for a second, that I'd let Crystal help me with my makeup because I looked washed out. Wasted.

Whatever. It was time to finish what James and I had started.

I pulled my phone free and texted James.

I'm on my way. You better be there.

JIMMY:
WELL, LOOK AT THAT.
JAMES MADE A WEDDING.

As I WALKED away from Room 214, the blackness that had overwhelmed me at the dump receded. I felt more like myself. Like I was in control again.

Maybe what had happened to me had just been like a bad drug trip. Rita being my drug of choice. But she was gone now so I could enjoy the wedding with my family.

My family. Marie and James, Crystal and her cats. They were my family and I wanted what was best for all of them.

The big double doors to the Twilight Room stood open with white balloons on either side of them like outsized bouquets. An easel stood, holding a large poster announcing the marriage of Marie Jenner and James Lavall.

There was a photo of the two of them, both laughing. I realized they were standing in my old office. I also realized that was the first time I'd seen them both look happy.

People stood around the door, chatting. I recognized a couple of them as I pushed through the crowd. Many of them shivered and moved away from me like they could feel me in their space. I figured it was probably just my lack of heat that was forcing them to step aside but I didn't care. I was looking for Jim—James.

Across the room I saw him, standing off to one side. He was in a tux and actually looked pretty darned good, all things considered. I wondered where he'd gotten it.

I looked down at my complete lack of formal garb and wished that it was possible for me to wear clothes. To take part in this union. To stand by James and tell him how proud I was, how he'd turned into a real man.

But that wasn't going to happen. I was dead.

Ric, the one who had decided to be James's new best friend, stood off to one side of the low stage that had been set up at the far end of the room talking into his phone. When he finally hung up, he turned to James and whispered something, and then both of them headed to Victor, who was sitting in the first row of chairs like he was a guest of honour or something. He'd been invited to the wedding. Why would James have done that?

I had to hear what they were talking to Victor about, so I hustled up the aisle to the front. I slowed and then stopped when I saw James talking to Victor, who looked bored and a little angry.

"I wanted to introduce you to Ric Svensen," Jim said. "He's a friend from Edmonton. And my best man."

Victor looked at Ric for a long moment, then back at Jim.

"I didn't realize you had friends here," he said.

"We got lucky," Ric said. "We ran into each other down here, and then Lavall—James—told me he was getting married." He laughed. "Guess he was going to spring it on us when they got home."

"Yeah, that was lucky," Victor said. "What was your name?"

"Ric Svensen," Ric said. His smile slipped, just a little, but he held out his hand. "I work for Ambrose Welch in Edmonton, and I knew we had to meet when James told me he knew you. Do you know Ambrose?"

Victor looked around at the still empty seats. "I might have heard of him," he said, "let's talk after the nuptials," Victor said. He took Ric's hand and shook it once, perfunctorily, then let it drop.

"Good enough," Ric said, and turned to James. "You ready to do this thing?"

"As soon as Marie gets here," James said. His phone buzzed, and he jumped and nearly dropped it. "It's her," he said, relief running through his words. "She's here. She'll be right down."

"Good," Victor said.

James walked onto the stage and smiled out at the crowd clotted around the outside edges of the room. "Marie's on her way. If you could just take your seats, that would be great."

Ric stepped onto the stage and stood beside James. An officiant, dressed as old fat Elvis Presley, stood to their left, and the three of them looked past the crowd to the door, where Marie would soon enter.

Harp music twinkled over the crowd from somewhere, and off to one side I saw that they'd hired the girl who played the harp at the Dome of the Sea restaurant. Nice touch.

Victor pulled his phone from his inside front pocket and turned away from the stage as he answered it. I found myself standing beside him. Listening to his conversation like my life depended on it.

Not my life. Marie's life, because he was talking about her.

"Are you sure?" Victor said. "Absolutely sure? How would they have any idea about the landfill?"

He stepped further away from the stage, his shoulders hunched. "They said what?" he finally asked. "They said they were psychics? That they saw ghosts?"

He turned and stared out at the crowd of people, most of whom had already found seats. He glared at each face in turn, like he was looking for one in particular.

"Why did you let them leave?" Victor asked into the phone. Then laughed incredulously. "Did you really think that was going to stop them? One of them is writing a book, for Christ's sake."

Crystal. He was looking for Crystal, too.

He laughed harshly and bent over the phone. "Never mind," he hissed. "I'll handle them from this end. But you have disappointed me. Deeply."

He dropped his phone back into his pocket and turned to one of the men standing guard next to him. He whispered something I couldn't hear. The man turned and walked through the back entrance, into a hallway that connected the room to the inner workings of the hotel.

I knew I had to warn Crystal and Marie. They were walking into a trap.

Then the blackness I'd felt at the dump rushed over me in a wave and I couldn't move. Just stared at Victor and felt the anger build. He'd ruined my life. Ruined me. Killed me—

Then I stopped. What the hell was I thinking? He hadn't done anything to me. He'd killed Rita, or ordered her killed. He hadn't done anything to me.

I turned toward the now-closed entrance of the Twilight Room. I needed to warn Marie. I took one step toward the door, and then another, but it felt like I was walking through cement.

"What the hell?" I muttered as I fought the urge to turn back to Victor. "What's going on?"

I took another step toward the door, but that step was harder than the first. The cement was up to my knees now and the anger was blooming through my chest like a black rose opening its petals.

Black? What had made me think of a black rose? Why would I think like that at all? It sounded more like Rita, whispering in my head. In my chest.

Rita. It was Rita here with me. I could feel her working her way through me, filling me with her rage, with her unbelievable thirst for revenge, trying to make me turn away from the door that Marie would soon be walking through, and back to Victor.

And I could finally hear her voice whispering that I needed to do something. I needed to man up. Finally. Since I'd caused her death, I had to avenge it.

"No," I whispered. "No. I have to save the girls."

But she didn't care about any of that. Had never cared about any other person. Just wanted what she wanted, no questions asked. I could feel her cold black rage move through me, and I threw myself to the floor, clinging to it in an effort to keep her from using me to get close to Victor.

I tried to crawl down the aisle so I could warn them both but it was like I was frozen to the carpet. I couldn't move.

The door opened, and Crystal hustled into the room, looking a little embarrassed as everyone turned to look at her.

"Marie's here," she said and scurried to an empty seat. Then, the harp music swelled and Marie walked in. Everyone stood, and she stared at the full room and then at James standing on the low stage, waiting for her. And then she looked at me, spread-eagled on the aisle she was supposed to walk down. She frowned, and I yelled, "Victor knows about you and Crystal!" before Rita took control and dragged me down the aisle.

I fought as hard as I could but I couldn't stop her.

"I won't do anything to Victor!" I cried.

"I don't want Victor, you idiot." I heard her voice in my head and groaned. If not Victor, then who was she after?

"What's wrong, Jimmy?" Crystal asked, and I opened my eyes.

Rita had dragged me in front of her and she stared at me, pop-eyed. I tried to tell her to run, but I couldn't do anything as I watched my hand reach out and grab hers.

"Get what I want and I might let you live," I heard myself say, in Rita's voice. Then I felt the blackness focus in my arm and my hand. I screamed when I felt it push from me to Crystal, who slumped over like she'd passed out. But almost immediately her eyes opened, and she stared at me with a cold smile on her lips.

"Thanks for the ride, Jimmy," she said. "This one will help me get the key, and then I'm out of here and off to Heaven."

"Crystal?" I mumbled.

"Not anymore." She stood, jerkily, and pushed her way past the rest of the people in her aisle. And then the door opened and she was gone.

Jesus. Rita had used me to get to the Dunes and now she was using Crystal to find the key. What was I going to do?

STAGE THREE

THE WEDDING, THE WATER, THE WHOLE DAMNED THING

MARIE:
HE EVEN USED THE "WEDDING MARCH."
DAMN

CRYSTAL AND I walked up to the door of the Twilight room and stared at the bouquets of white balloons standing around it. They hadn't been there when I'd checked the room out that morning.

She pointed at the plaque announcing our wedding—an hour earlier than it was at this moment—and I could have killed James for using the picture he'd chosen. Sylvia Worth had taken that picture of us two weeks after we'd officially reopened Jimmy Lavall Detective Agency and my hair, pulled back in a haphazard ponytail, looked like crap.

But still, he'd made an announcement placard.

Crystal reached over and gave me a quick hug. "I'll see you soon," she said, as she opened the big double doors and disappeared inside.

I stood with my hand on the knob for a moment, trying to focus. For a tiny second, I wished my mom was in that room beyond that door. True, she would have given me royal hell for the dress I'd chosen. But still. It would have been nice.

I pulled the door open, and as harp music flooded over me, I looked down at my hands. I didn't have a bouquet. Was a little surprised Crystal hadn't thought of it either but we had been pretty busy.

"Let's do this thing," I muttered, my heart pounding. Then I stepped inside.

For a moment, there was complete silence in the packed room. Then the harpist started playing the "Wedding March" and everyone stood and stared at me.

Everyone but Jimmy, who was sprawled on the aisle I was supposed to walk down. I stared at him for a moment, trying to figure out what the hell was going on, when he crab-crawled his way through the crowd to Crystal, who was in the far corner of the last row of chairs. He grabbed her, and then I watched her aura turn from a nice light blue to midnight. What the hell was he doing to her?

Crystal finally pulled her hand free from Jimmy's and pushed her way down the aisle to the door. She passed me without a glance, which was weird in the extreme, and the door boomed shut behind her.

Why had she left? What had Jimmy said to her?

"Jimmy?" I called. "What the hell did you do?"

There were strange looks around the room, but I didn't care.

Jimmy scrambled through the people sitting in the chairs and finally made it to me. "It wasn't me," he gasped. "It's Rita. She invaded me somehow, and now she's taken Crystal. She's gone to get the key to her bank, so she can get the money she stole. We gotta stop her!"

I looked down at his distraught face and then up at all the other distraught faces around the room. Including James. "I can't go," I whispered. "The wedding."

Jimmy looked around and sighed. "Damn," he said. "I'm going to miss it." Then he pulled himself upright and oozed toward the door.

"I'll try to slow Rita down," he said. "But maybe you can hurry?"

"I'll do my best," I said.

I took a couple of steps down the aisle, but was stopped by a woman at the edge of the third row.

"Here," she said, and ripped free the bunch of daisies that had been taped to her chair as a decoration. She pushed them in my hand with a smile. I had no idea who she was, but she looked really happy to be involved. "Now go. He's waiting for you, you lucky duck."

"Thanks," I said to the woman. Then I headed down the aisle.

I looked out at the crowd and saw Daisy. Two rows over, I recognized Alice, the woman who had sold me the dress. They both smiled and waved at me, and I was pretty sure Daisy was crying. She touched a handkerchief to her face and I hoped they were happy tears.

I didn't recognize anyone else and wondered how James had had the time to meet so many people. Then I gave my head a shake because I'd met a bunch of people too, only most of them were dead hookers. They hadn't really been in the mood for a party, either.

I walked quickly down the aisle and stepped up onto the low stage, turning to James, who looked dumbstruck. "You look so beautiful," he said.

"We have to talk," I whispered to him.

His glanced out at the crowd. "Now?"

"We've got trouble, James," I replied.

"What kind of trouble?" he asked, and his eyes did that pinwheel thing they did sometimes, and I could tell he felt like everything was about to blow up in his face.

He turned to the officiant, and whispered, "Can you just give us a second more?"

"The clock's a-ticking," the officiant replied with a tight smile. "The bride was an hour late."

I looked at her, my own face tight. "I got here when I could," I said. Then I turned back to James. "We found Rita."

"Good," James said. "Does that mean Uncle Jimmy has moved on?"

"Not really," I said. "I thought that I'd moved Rita on, but somehow she figured out a way to hitch a ride with Jimmy to the hotel. Then she jumped from Jimmy to Crystal, and now she's making Crystal find a key."

"A key?" James asked, and then shook his head. "I don't care about the key."

"You might," I said. "Rita stole money from this hotel. From Victor—" I looked around me, and froze when I realized Victor was sitting in the front row, staring at both of us.

"Victor's here?" I whisper-screamed.

"I kind of had to invite him," James whispered back. "He did comp us the room."

"Right," I said. Then I took a step closer to James and whispered in his ear. "She stole the money from Victor," I mumbled. "And he killed her for it."

"So," James said. "He'll want that money back and if he thinks Crystal is involved at all, he could hurt her."

"He could kill her, James. We have to find her."

"I understand," James said, and turned to the officiant. "Let's get this show on the road."

The officiant's face tightened even further but she pulled herself together and began the ceremony.

"We are gathered here to witness and celebrate the union of Marie Celeste Jenner and James Patrick Lavall in marriage," she said, then started down a flowery verbal path that I could tell was going to take us forever.

"Get to the point," I growled.

The officiant's mouth gaped and she stared at me like I'd lost my mind. "What?" she asked.

"Get to the end," I said. "Man and wife. You know. That part."

The officiant glanced at James, who shrugged. "Whatever she wants," he said. "Do whatever she wants."

"Fine," the officiant said. "Did either of you write your own vows?"

"Well," James said. "Actually—"

I stared at him like he'd suddenly lost his mind, and he shrugged and looked embarrassed. "The regular vows will be fine," he said.

"All right," the officiant replied. "If you're absolutely certain that's what you want."

She spoke softly, and I almost laughed when I realized she was giving James an out. All he had to do was say help and that officiant would have fireman-carried him away from me and the certainty of a life of misery. But James nodded and smiled so she read the vows and we repeated them back as she requested.

James spoke the words with more passion than I'd believed possible. But I didn't have the emotional strength for any of that. I just wanted this over, so I could find out what Rita was doing to Crystal.

I mean, I had a lot on my plate.

The officiant got to the "you may kiss the bride" part and James pulled me into his arms.

"Thanks for this," he said, and then he kissed me. It was gentle but passionate and, for just that moment, I was able to put aside everything that had happened over the whole stupid holiday. Well, most of it, anyhow. And, just for that moment, when I kissed him back, it was real.

That was when he pulled away from me and turned to the crowd. "We're married!" he cried. "Time to party!"

The crowd erupted and rushed the low stage, which took me by surprise. Ric pulled me into his arms, kissed me briskly on both cheeks, and then held me in a hug that went on way too long.

"Good luck," he said, into my hair. "I think you got a good one here."

"Thanks," I said, and tried to pull away but he wouldn't let me go.

"You don't need to worry about anything," he said. "We'll make sure your life together is perfect."

This from a drug dealer was too much and I pushed away from him.

"Yeah," I said, acidly. "I'm sure. And now James and I need to leave."

He blinked and then laughed and pointed to the bar which was already three deep with all the strangers at my wedding.

"You gotta have at least one drink," he said. "So we can toast your life together. What would you like?"

I looked at James but all he did was shrug. "A shot," I said. "Tequila."

"Good enough," Ric said, and finally, he was gone. I ignored all the rest of the well-wishers around us and turned to James.

"We have to go," I whispered. "Now."

"Wait," he said, and then the most fake smile I'd ever seen covered his face. "Mr. Tupilo," he said. "Thanks again for coming to the ceremony."

I turned and stared into Victor Tupilo's dead cold eyes. "Yeah," I said. "And thanks for the room. It looks wonderful."

"I'm glad you like it," he said. "I'm sorry, but I'm going to have to leave. There's a disturbance down in the laundry room, and I need to take care of it."

"Sorry to hear that," James said.

"All part of running a hotel," Victor said. "Congratulations on your marriage."

He turned away and I grabbed James by the sleeve. "I bet money it's Rita," I said. "Which means Crystal is in real trouble. James, we gotta go."

I headed for the door, James in tow, but Ric stepped in my way, a shot glass in hand. "Ready to toast your new life together?" he asked.

"We gotta go," James said. "We have a friend in trouble."

Ric didn't miss a beat. Set the glass down on the stage and turned to James. "Need back up?" he asked.

"Maybe," James said, before I could speak.

"Good enough," Ric said and signalled to his friend, who had stepped in as bartender. "Ollie!" he called. "We got work."

"We don't need them," I said to James, but Ric spoke over my words.

"Where do you need to be?" he asked. "We'll make sure you get there."

"The laundry room," James said. He headed for the big double doors but Ric shook his head and pointed to the back of the room, behind the stage.

"That way's quicker," he said. "And you can get us up to speed before we get there."

"Victor's involved," James said and Ric started.

"Am I going to burn this relationship before it gets off the ground?" he asked.

"I don't know," James said. "Maybe."

"You're going to have some 'splainin' to do if that happens," Ric said.

"I understand," James said.

"You don't need to help," I said acidly. "We can handle this ourselves."

"I doubt that," Ric said. "Let's go."

We ran through the labyrinth that was the back halls of the hotel. James briefly explained who we were saving, and what the situation was and, I have to say, Ric took it all pretty much in stride.

"So you're saying that your little friend—"

"Crystal," I said. "Her name is Crystal."

"Crystal. Right. She's a psychic? Like you?"

"I'm not a psychic," I said.

"I saw you on TV," he replied. "You looked like a psychic to me."

Good grief! Had everyone seen that stupid TV show?

"And you're saying that Crystal's possessed by a ghost? Who's trying to find the key to a safe deposit box in a bank that holds all the information to an offshore account the ghost set up—"

"She set it up before she became a ghost," I snapped.

"Yeah yeah," Ric said. "I get that, I guess. But you're telling me she stole this money from Victor?"

"Yeah," I said, and Ric laughed.

"Maybe you're off the hook, Lavall," he said. "I'm thinking we don't need to work with anyone who loses their money to a frigging ghost, now do we?"

We ran through the kitchen, and the staff steadfastly ignored us.

"Where's the laundry room?" James asked.

"In there," Ollie said, and pointed down a hall to a closed door.

I was ready to burst inside, but Ric stopped me. "You and James get behind us," he said. "Ollie? You go low. I'll go high."

They both pulled guns from somewhere and James and I cowered behind them. Ollie kicked the door in, and the two thugs who were trying to overwhelm Crystal—and doing a bad job of it, I noticed—turned, saw the guns trained on them, and froze.

Jimmy, who was attempting to hold on to Crystal's arm, turned to us. "Rita's still in Crystal. You gotta do something, now."

"Let the girl go," Ric said to the thugs. "Right now."

The two guys let her go, keeping their hands up. "We weren't going to hurt her," one of them said.

"Whatever," Ric replied. "Get away from her."

They stepped away, and Crystal shook herself free from Jimmy.

"Crystal!" I called. "We're going to get you out of here!"

"It's not Crystal," Jimmy said. "I told you. It's Rita."

"All right, Jimmy," I said.

"Who are you talking to?" Ric asked.

"A ghost," I said tersely.

"My dead uncle," James added.

Ric blinked and shook his head. "You really can see ghosts, can't you?"

"Yep," I replied, then turned to Crystal. "Rita, let her go."

"Not until I get the damned key," Crystal said. She pushed past the security guys to a line of industrial dryers. She reached behind one, and pulled a small envelope free.

"I got it," she said. "I'm set. Let's get the hell out of here."

"Let her go, Rita!" Jimmy cried and flew to Crystal. He grabbed her arm, his aura a firestorm of red and black.

He caught Rita off guard and his attack pushed her nearly free of Crystal's body. I ran past James and lent my strength to his and, finally, Rita was out and Crystal was free.

"Good work," I said to Jimmy as Crystal slumped to the floor. "James, help her. I've got my hands full here."

James gathered Crystal in his arms. "You're safe," he said.

"I'm starting to hate ghosts," she muttered.

"I understand," James said. "I really do."

Rita howled like a wild animal and tried to tear herself free from Jimmy and me. "Let me go!" she screamed. "I need the key. I need that money!"

But Jimmy clung to her like a tick as she threw herself —and us—around the room.

"The money won't do you a bit of good now," I gasped. "You're dead, Rita. It's all over for you."

I felt her power lower just a little bit. At least we weren't bouncing off the walls anymore. "I'm right," I said. "And you have to know I'm right. Let it go, Rita."

"That money was my ticket out of here," Rita sobbed. She fought Jimmy and me, but I could feel her power wind down. "I was going to buy an island—"

"Not anymore," I said. "Rita, you're done. It's time for you to let go."

She stared at me for a long moment, then I saw her aura flare. "What about Victor?" she said. "He has to pay for what he did to me. Doesn't he?"

"No," I said, firmly. "Stop it, Rita. No revenge. No bringing Victor down. No nothing, Rita. You're dead. You gotta move on. Now."

"I don't want to!" she cried. "You can't make me! You can't make me do anything!"

But her voice had weakened so much I could barely hear her. And she wasn't fighting either of us anymore.

She fell to the floor of the laundry room and stared up at

nothing, whispering, "You can't make me do anything," over and over as she faded and faded and then, finally, blew apart in an explosion of grey.

I watched carefully to make sure it wasn't another trick but the faded grey light bees that poured from her simply hung in the air and then puffed away, one by one, like ashes from a long dead flame.

"Is she gone?" Crystal asked.

"I think so," Jimmy said. He fell to the floor, looking completely depleted.

"She is," I said, feeling pretty depleted myself. "Man, I could stand a drink of water."

"What the hell is going on here?" one of the security guys exclaimed, and that brought everyone's attention back to the task at hand, which was getting Crystal out of that room and somewhere safe.

Ollie found duct tape in a tool kit tucked under the laundry table and quickly bound the two security guys. "That should hold them," he said. "Long enough for us to get out of this hotel."

Ric nodded and then turned to James. "I can get Crystal to safety," he said. "If you want."

"Sure," James said, but I pulled myself up from the floor and faced them both.

"No!" I cried. "You are not counting on a frigging drug dealer to save my friend!"

"I'm your friend?" Crystal asked.

"Of course, you are," I said. "And I need to make sure you get out of here, safely."

"Don't forget her cats," Jimmy said.

"Right," I said. "Your cats too."

"She has cats?" Ric asked.

"Twelve of them," James replied.

"That's a lot of cats," Ric said. I ignored the hell out of him and turned back to Crystal.

"Can you get up?" I asked. "We have to get you out of here."

She nodded. I helped her stand, and then we both staggered to the door. The men brought up the rear, and then we were back out in the labyrinth of hallways, making good our escape.

James took Crystal by the other arm. "Marie," he said. "Ric could help. You know?"

"No, I don't know," I said. "Why the hell would you even trust this guy, James?"

"I got connections," Ric said, before James could speak. "I know a guy on the force. He'll believe you. Well, he'll believe me. We can get Crystal into protective custody—"

"I'm not going to jail," Crystal said. "Absolutely and positively not going to jail."

"Her cats," James said. "Remember?"

"All right, then he'll get you into a safe house," Ric continued. "Would that work?"

"How do you know a cop?" I asked stiffly. "Especially one who could pull strings like this?"

"Like I said," Ric said, just as stiffly. "I got connections."

"Why are you going to do this for me?" Crystal asked. "You don't even know me."

"You're Marie's friend," Ric said. "And she's married to Lavall, who is my friend. Friends look out for each other. Right?"

"Yeah," Crystal said. "They do."

"Besides," he continued. "You're a civilian. Not part of any of this. Not like me and James. You didn't do anything wrong. So, we'll get you out of it."

Crystal nodded and turned to me. "I think I'll go with him," she said. "Somewhere safe." She handed me the envelope Rita had forced her to find. "Do something with this," she said, and then laughed. "Consider it a wedding present."

"Pretend it's from both of us," Jimmy said and smiled when Crystal laughed. "I'm going to miss your laugh," he said.

"You—you could stay with us for a while longer, if you want," Crystal said. "You don't have to move on right away, do you?"

"Well, you are definitely singing a different tune," Jimmy replied. He looked genuinely surprised. "I thought you wanted to get rid of me so you could date. You know, living men."

Crystal shrugged. "I won't be dating for a while," she said. "And the cats will miss you."

Jimmy shook his head. "No can do," he said. "I have to get home."

"Home?" I asked.

"Home," Jimmy said. "Somebody's got to watch out for our guy here." He hitched his thumb in James's direction.

"So, you're coming back to Edmonton to keep an eye on

James?" I said, looking at James.

James shook his head and sighed. "I don't need to you watch out for me, Uncle Jimmy," he said.

"Could've fooled me," Jimmy replied.

"Can we discuss this later?" I asked, rather frantically. "We've got to get Crystal out of here, and then we should probably do some running away ourselves. Shouldn't we?"

"We should," James said. Then he handed the envelope to Ric. "Tell your cop friend about the money, too," he said. "Right, Marie?"

I was going to say no. Not because I thought we should keep the money, because I didn't. I thought we should take the key home to Sylvia Worth and let her deal with it, because I was pretty sure that Ric would use that key to get in good with Victor. After all, wasn't that the reason he was in Vegas? To connect with Victor Tupilo?

But maybe if Victor had the key, he'd leave Crystal alone.

"Please keep my friend safe," I said and then pulled Crystal into a hug. "Sorry I helped blow up your life."

"Oh, it's all right," Crystal replied. "I was kind of thinking of getting out of the ghost business anyhow. They really are a lot to take, aren't they?"

"True words, sister," I said, and let her go.

She turned to Jimmy. "I'm going to miss you, old man," she said.

"And I'll miss you," he said. "Thank you for helping me. Really. Thanks for everything."

"You're welcome," she said and I could tell she was starting to choke up. She turned to Ric. "Let's go," she said. "Before I make a fool of myself."

He nodded and then glanced at James. "Are you two going to be all right alone?" he asked. "Maybe Ollie should go with you."

James shook his head. "Our flight leaves tomorrow. We're going to pack and then go the airport right now," he said. "We'll be safe there."

"That's one hell of a honeymoon," Ric said, and then he and Ollie walked down the hallway with Crystal. Soon they turned a corner and disappeared.

We were on our own.

JIMMY:
1 WOULDA TAKEN THE MONEY

THAT ENVELOPE JAMES had handed over without a second thought held a key that could have given him and Marie access to millions—literally millions—of dollars.

I would have taken the money. And I probably would have blown it on wine, women, and song, or whatever, and found myself back here, in Vegas, trying to figure out another get-rich-quick scheme to keep me going for a few more years. Or months. Hell, probably for a few more days. When I had money, I liked to spend it.

But James wasn't like me. He wasn't about to take money that didn't belong to him. I guessed he didn't need it, and then I wondered what he did need.

Did he need me? Maybe not. But something was pushing me to stay with the two of them, so I decided I would. Until that something told me I no longer needed to.

But not until then.

I silently followed James and Marie to Room 214, for the last time, and stopped stock still, as surprised as Marie and James, when the door opened and we caught two more of Victor's security thugs rifling through their belongings.

"What the heck are you doing?" James asked.

"We're looking for the will, of course," Victor said as he walked out of the bathroom.

Marie gasped and grabbed James by the arm. "Run," she whispered.

"Not so fast," Victor said and before either Marie or James could move, the security thugs were on them and had dragged them in front of Victor.

"Close the door," he said. "We don't want to be disturbed."

"Let them go!" I yelled, which did nothing at all. "Dammit," I muttered. "I should have convinced Rita to teach me that possession trick. Then I'd make you stop."

"What do you want?" James asked. He'd tried to get away from the thug holding him and had taken a good smack to the side of the head for his trouble.

"The will," Victor said, again. "Remember that? You said that Rita had been written into Jimmy's will. Well, I want to see it. Prove to me that's why you're here. Right now."

"We didn't bring it with us," James started and Victor snorted derisively.

"I don't believe you," he said. "You know what I think? I think you're after the money Rita stole from me. Rita had to have hidden it somewhere. So I had this room taken apart after Jimmy's body was removed, because I thought that maybe Rita'd hidden it here. But I found nothing.

"I was just about ready to write it all off, but then you two showed up. And you rented this room. The room where your uncle died. I realized then that your uncle must've figured out a way to get information about the money to you, and that you were finally here to collect it.

"Then, the psychic came back, and I realized that he must have told her about the money. That was the only reason she'd be in the laundry room. Right? She was looking for the money Rita hid. Right?" He glared at both of us.

"I finally figured it out, didn't I?" he asked.

"I have no idea what you're talking about," James said. "We came here about the will and to get married. Nothing more."

"Oh, quit lying to me," Victor snapped. "My men will be here soon with whatever little miss psychic was looking for. Then, all your lies will be out in the open."

"What are you going to do with us?" Marie asked, her voice shaking. I was surprised. I didn't think anything would scare her.

"I'm giving you a nice little wedding present," Victor said. "A honeymoon, if you will. Do you like the ocean?"

"Not really," she said.

"Well, in a few hours, you're going to be on it," Victor said. "And then, you're going to be under it." He sighed and shook his head. "I wish I could finish you off right here, myself, but I can't. Too many eyes watching this hotel since that money disappeared, so I can't take a chance on having your deaths linked here. But at sea? Nothing will tie you to this place, even if your bodies are found."

"You can't get away with this," Marie cried and struggled to get free. The thug that held her tightened his grip, then glanced at Victor.

"Do it," Victor said, and the thug plunged a hypodermic needle into Marie's arm. She squealed and tried to pull away, but it was too late.

"Help me, James," she gasped, and then her eyes closed and she slumped down. But before she could hit the floor, Victor's henchman scooped her up.

"What did you do to her?" James gasped. He tried to pull free but the guy holding his arm jammed a revolver into his ribs. James roared, but stopped. All he could do was stare helplessly at Marie.

"Relax," Victor said. "I told you I wasn't going to kill you here. I just gave her a little something to calm her down." He glanced at his man. "Let's get them out of here and into the limo. Then you can go find the little psychic. She can go with them."

He looked at James and smiled, coldly. "You're all friends, right?" he said. "You won't mind a third person with you on your honeymoon, will you?"

"You son of a bitch," I cried. "Let them go!"

They grabbed James and pulled him out into the hallway. The gun in his ribs kept him docile, and he got onto the elevator with them. I followed and soon we were all down in the bowels of the hotel.

I felt completely useless as I followed them to a back door that led outside to the row of garbage bins, with a stretch limo waiting beside them. The thug dropped Marie rather unceremoniously into the back seat of the limo and then pushed James in after her.

"There will be a third," he said to the driver. "And then you're taking them to the yacht. Without any screw-ups. Mr. Tupilo is counting on you."

"Will do," the driver said. The thug with the gun got in the front seat beside him, and then turned and trained the gun on James.

"Don't do anything stupid," he said. "Or I'll kill her."

I threw myself into the limo, thinking that maybe, just maybe there was something I'd be able to do to help them. Because it was my fault they were even here. I had to do something to help. Something.

But all I could do was cower on the far seat and watch as James pulled Marie into his arms, trying to waken her. He couldn't, of course. Whatever the thug had given to her had really taken her out of the equation.

Then the driver closed the window between the front and back seat, and we were truly trapped.

A few long minutes later, the thug hustled back out the door and knocked on the driver's window. He looked furious, and I figured they'd just found the mess in the laundry room.

"Just go," he said, and the driver nodded and put the car into gear.

I watched Marie flop around in James's arms as the limo wheeled out of the parking lot of the Dunes and headed west, toward California, and the ocean.

Holy crap. We were well and truly screwed.

MARIE:
THE HONEYMOON,
FOR WHAT IT'S WORTH

1 1/2 hours . . .

I WOKE UP with a fierce headache, and the sickening feeling of rocking back and forth. I grabbed my head.

"What the hell?" I grunted and scrabbled around trying to gain something like control.

"You were drugged," James said. The room was so dark I couldn't see him. "Just keep lying down."

By the sound of his voice, he was standing somewhere at the other end of the room.

"What are you doing?" I asked.

"Trying to get us out of here," he said. "There's a bottle of water beside you on the bed. Drink it. It would be better if you got your head together, because we gotta figure a way to get off this yacht."

"We're on a yacht?" I asked, quite uselessly.

"Yes," James said.

A light pushed through the door and coalesced at the foot of the bed. It was Jimmy.

"You made it," I said.

"Yeah," he said. "And you're finally awake. I was starting to

283

think that you were going to miss all the fun."

James glanced at me. "So my uncle is here, too. Guess he didn't want to miss the fun."

"Tell him I think I've found a way off the boat," Jimmy said.

"He says he can get us out of here," I said to James, then turned back to Jimmy. "What did you find?"

"I was up in the engine room," Jimmy said, "and one of Victor's men was there, arguing with the captain, or whatever. He wants to dump you now because he's mucho seasick and just wants to get back to shore. The captain, or whoever he was talking to, said he didn't want to hear any of that but that we aren't in international waters yet."

"Great," I muttered, and told James what Jimmy had said, and then, I could hear metal grating on metal. "What are you doing, James?"

"I'm trying to get this door open," he snapped. "So we can get out of here."

He pulled at the door and when it didn't move, cursed.

"I thought he was good with that kind of thing," Jimmy said.

"So did I," I said, and gently lay my head back down on the pillow. It was really spinning. "What's taking you so long?"

"Just give me a second," James grunted, and then I heard a dry click. I lifted my head, and could see a sliver of light on the far wall. I could see James, too, with his hand on the door.

"See?" he said.

"You're my hero," I replied.

"I try," he said. "Do you think you can move?"

"I think so," I said. "Once my head stops spinning, that is."

"Well, drink the water," he said, as I pulled myself off the bed. "You know you need it."

I picked up the water bottle, spun off the top, and downed half of it in three big swallows. My head instantly started to clear.

"Looks like the next room's clear," James said. "Time to go."

I looked down at the wedding dress I was still wearing. "I sure would like to change," I said. "Any chance they brought our stuff with us?"

"There's nothing here," he said. "You're stuck with the dress."

"Great," I muttered, and walked over to him. "Jimmy should go ahead," I said. "He'll be able to warn us if anyone's coming, or whatever."

"I can do that," Jimmy said. He pushed past James and through the door.

"What did the guys who kidnapped us say to you?" I asked. "I mean, they must've said something. Doesn't it take four hours to get from Vegas to the ocean?"

"Four and a half hours," James said mournfully. "And no, they didn't say a thing."

"So what? They dragged us onto this scow without saying a word?"

James snorted unamused laughter. "This is definitely not a scow."

"Whatever," I said again.

"Are you two coming?" Jimmy called from outside the door. "Time's wasting, you know."

"He says we should hurry up," I said.

"I don't care what he says," James replied, but he did push the door open a tiny bit more. He glanced up and down what I could now see was a hallway of some sort.

"Looks empty," I said, rather unhelpfully. "Just like Jimmy said."

"Ask him how many crew are on board," he said. "And where they are."

"Five," Jimmy said. "That I saw. Can we hurry up, please?"

"He says five," I said to James.

"So, a skeleton crew," James said. "Good. If we can get outside, we should be able to get overboard without anybody seeing us."

I blinked. "How close to shore are we?"

"If we haven't crossed into international waters, then less than twelve miles," he replied, without looking at me. "I think."

I stared at his back like he'd lost his mind. "Twelve miles?"

"Less than that," he said.

"How much less?"

"I don't know," he said.

"So, you've decided we're going to swim twelve miles back to shore?" I said. "Twelve miles."

"Yeah," he replied. "That's the plan." Then he frowned. "Why? Can't you swim?"

I tried to remember the last time I'd actually swum and shuddered. Thirteen. I'd been thirteen and a couple of goons on the beach where my family was spending the day had decided that I was cute enough to accost.

They got me to the end of the pier before I made them all pay for touching me. But that wasn't really swimming, because I never left the pier. Only they had.

"It's been a while," I said.

"It's like riding a bike," he replied. "You'll remember when we're in the water."

"What are you two doing?" Jimmy yelled. "We gotta go. Now."

James slid open the door, and the section of the boat we entered was a hallway. It was also empty. James reached for my hand and pulled me behind him out of the cabin.

"Which way?" he whispered.

I looked for Jimmy, who was at the end of the hallway. He gestured at me and I nodded.

"Left," I whispered. "He says go left."

Then the two of us crept down the hallway like a couple of rats trapped on a boat. All we had to do was get to the side and throw ourselves overboard so we could drown in the ocean like rats, or whatever.

God, this was a bad plan.

But I followed him because I couldn't think of anything better.

ALL RIGHT, SO James was correct. This was not a scow. We crept through one room after another of perfection. Like money really was no object. Jimmy walked ahead of us, looking around corners and then gesturing us forward.

Once he froze and called for us to stop. We threw ourselves to the floor and waited as we listened to someone on the outer walkway, heading to the front of the boat. My heart was pounding so hard I was sure whoever it was would hear it, but soon we were again alone.

"Come on!" Jimmy yelled. I touched James, who jumped a foot into the air and then glared at me.

"Jimmy says it's safe," I whispered. "Let's go."

We crawled through a cabin that was nicer than any room I'd ever been in, in my whole life, and stopped at a set of doors Jimmy had disappeared through moments before. James reached up and opened the door closest to us, then stuck his head out and checked that we were indeed still alone.

"Let's go," he muttered, and we finally made it out on the back deck of the boat.

I couldn't believe it. We were two stories above the frigging water.

James pointed to a set of stairs that arched down over the water. "Looks like we go this way," he said, but before either of us could move, Jimmy waved at me.

He was standing by a ladder. "Use this," he said, and then disappeared over the ledge of the balcony on which we were standing.

"Over there," I muttered, pointing to the ladder.

"That's better," James said. "We won't be so easily seen." He took me by the hand and pulled me along the wall to the ladder, then gestured for me to go first.

I only stepped on the hem of my stupid dress twice before we finally made it to the lower deck.

"Look," I said, and pointed at a small boat sitting on the back end of the yacht. "Can we use that?"

"Maybe," James said, and crawled over to have a look.

"Forget it," Jimmy said. "You need a key to start the stupid thing, and I couldn't find one anywhere."

Honestly, I wanted to cry. I hoped that James would have better luck than his dead uncle, but soon he crawled back to me.

"Sorry," he said. "I can't figure out how to start the thing. But I did find this."

He held up a chunky-looking plastic gun, and I stared at it. "What kind of a gun is that?" I finally asked.

"It's a flare gun," he said. "It was in the boat."

"Are you going to fire it now?" I asked.

"No," he said. "All we would do was attract the crew's attention, and that wouldn't help much. No, first we have to get away from the boat. Then, I'll fire the flare gun, and with any luck somebody will see us."

"That doesn't sound like much of a plan," I said, extremely unhelpfully.

"Well, it's all I've got," he said. "Unless you want to stay on the boat and take your chances with Victor's men."

"No," I said.

"So, we jump," he said.

I shuddered and looked out over the water, and then I stopped and pointed at something floating behind us.

"What is that?" I asked.

"What?" James stared out at the dark choppy water, and then shook his head. "I don't see anything," he said. "Are you ready to jump?"

"I'm sure there's something down there," I said. "Something big. In the water. Hey, maybe we can swim to it and use it to get away from these guys without actually drowning. You know?"

"Maybe," he said. "If there was anything there, but I don't think there is." Then he jerked his head to the right and gasped as a hatch slapped open on the yacht.

"Quiet!" Jimmy yelled at the same moment. "Somebody's coming!"

Victor's thug ran across the pristine white deck next to us and leaned out over the rail, staring into the dark, rippling water.

"I told you there was something there," I whispered.

"Be quiet," James whispered back.

Feedback screeched over the choppy water. "Ahoy!" a voice called. "Ahoy, *Lucky Me*. Release James Lavall, immediately."

That was when I saw that the guy on the deck had a gun in his hand and he was taking aim at whatever I'd almost seen in the in the water. "Get away from this ship!" he cried. "Do you want me to call the coast guard?"

"You're not going to do that," the voice over the megaphone snapped. "Release James Lavall and his wife, and you'll be free to go."

"Are you fucking kidding?" the thug called back. "Lavall and his bitch aren't going anywhere. Do you know who this vessel belongs to?"

"Yeah," the disembodied voice said. "We do. Do you know who owns *this* vessel? Release them. Now."

"Not a chance," the thug said and fired into the dark.

I heard the bullet ping off something metal, and finally saw what looked like a platform on the water behind the yacht. A small figure appeared on the platform and fumbled with a metallic tube as he struggled to keep his footing, because the water was getting choppier by the second.

"What the hell is that?" I asked.

"It looks like a submarine," Jimmy whispered behind me. "Doesn't it?"

"Is that a submarine?" I asked James, but I spoke too loudly, and the thug on the deck of the yacht turned and saw us.

"What the fuck?" he gasped, and aimed the gun at us. "You move and I'll kill you. I don't care who these fuckers are, you are not getting off this boatuntil I throw you off myself ."

The small figure on the platform knelt on one knee and set the tube on his shoulder. "Last chance," the megaphoned voice called, echoing over the water. "Or we're blowing that piece of shit out of the water."

Jimmy pointed. "That's a rocket launcher."

"What?" I gasped.

"You both better jump," he said. "Because this idiot is taking on someone with a rocket launcher."

"Jesus," I gasped. And that was when James went into absolute superhero mode. He pulled the flare gun free, aimed at the thug, and fired the flare all in one fluid motion.

The thug screeched and got one shot off, missing absolutely everything, before the flare hit him. He screamed as it bounced to the deck, and then it was time for me to do *my* superhero thing.

I pushed James toward the edge of the boat, yelling, "We gotta go! Now!"

The thug kicked the flare aside and turned as we pelted for the edge. He raised the gun and cried "Stop!", but I couldn't have, even if I wanted.

And then we were over the rail, and we hit the water, hard.

I flailed around until James grabbed me by the hand. "Go under," he cried. "We have to get away from the boat. You understand?"

I nodded and dove. Felt the pull of the dress and went deeper than I'd planned when the first explosion hit the boat we'd just abandoned. The percussion hit me and drove me even further under the water, and I looked around for James. Couldn't see him, but above me and to the right, I could see that the back of the yacht was ablaze, and starting to list.

I kicked away from the fire, holding my breath. Better to drown trying to escape.

Then the second explosion hit us and I thought, Jesus. We're really going to drown. This sucks.

JIMMY:
THE NARCO SUB

JAMES AND MARIE jumped into the ocean just as the yacht exploded. I was afraid they'd been sucked into the vortex and felt relief when I saw them both bob up thirty feet or so from the burning yacht. James fought with the zipper of Marie's wedding dress in an effort to get her out of it. She kept going under, and he kept yanking her back to the surface.

"Just hang on," he gasped. "Hang on to me."

All right, so zippers can be difficult, especially if they were wet, but I couldn't believe he was having so much trouble. Finally, he yanked a small object from the top of the zipper, and then pulled the dress apart.

Marie fought, which didn't help James's job any. She managed to pull them both underwater as James frantically tore the straps that had her arms pinned.

The dress finally floated away, and Marie kicked herself free as James pulled her back up to the surface. They broke the water, gasping and choking, and then clung to each other as Marie got herself under control.

"Just lie back," James wheezed. "Float for a minute. Until you get your breath back."

She sobbed, but complied, clinging to his hand like it was a lifeline. Which it was.

"I don't want to die out here," she whispered. "Please don't let me die."

"You aren't going to die," James replied. He reached over and pulled a strand of hair from her face, and then leaned back so he was floating too. Both of them bobbing in the water, like just two more pieces of flotsam from the burning yacht.

I looked for the submarine that had destroyed the yacht but there was so much burning debris on the surface of the water I couldn't see a thing. So, I went under the surface, just as the yacht settled further under the water, and then, finally, sank into the depths.

I watched the hulk of what had been a pretty darned nice yacht, as it slid further and further under the water, heading for the ocean floor.

I saw something in the dark water past the conflagration on the water's surface. I pushed myself toward the dark mass, shuddering when another explosion from the yacht threw everything in the water into a turmoil.

Brief lights flared and died around me, and I realized, with a start, that I was seeing fish die. The lights were their spirits leaving their bodies. They flared a brief white light and then disappeared. It almost made me laugh, it really did. Frigging fish were more well-adjusted than me?

I swam past the dead fish and the collection of still burning debris to the relatively clear water beyond, and watched the submarine surface.

It was big. Nearly one hundred feet long at my guess, but it looked like it had been fiberglassed together in someone's back alley garage. All right, maybe not someone's back alley, because that would have been a hell of a big garage. But still.

I wondered who made it. And who was driving it. And why they'd done what they'd done. And then I wondered if they would be able to save James and Marie.

I floated up to the two of them. "Tell James the sub is still here," I said. "Just past the wreck."

Marie turned, a wave splashed over her, and she gasped and choked, nearly losing her grip on James.

When she finally got herself more or less under control, she told James what I had told her.

"Maybe they'll save us," she said. "Because Jesus, James, we're going to drown if we don't do something."

That was when the sub started moving through the burning debris toward us, and the small figure pulled out a large spotlight. He ran the light over the debris-filled choppy water, finally stopping on James and Marie.

He called down to someone inside the sub, and it slowed and turned to the spot where Marie and James were frantically waving. Finally, it stopped a few yards from the two of them, and the man threw a rope.

"Hang on!" he cried, and when James and Marie did so, he pulled them to the deck of the sub, and then up so that they were finally beside him.

"Are you James Lavall?" the man asked. His accent was so thick, I could barely understand him, but James nodded. "Good," the man said. "Ric said you might be in some trouble out here. Glad we could help."

"Thanks," James said, looking thunderstruck. Then he turned to Marie and pulled her into his arms.

"Are you all right?" he asked.

"As soon as I get some clothes on, I'll be fine," she said.

James gasped and pulled his shirt off, wrapping Marie in it. Then the two of them clambered beside the man with the spotlight, and down the hatch. With one last look around, the man who had just saved them closed the hatch, and the submarine began to submerge.

I wasn't going to miss my ride, so I pushed my way through the side of the sub and went to look for Marie and James as the sub headed north, up the coast, away from the debris that was all that remained of the yacht.

We'd just been saved by Ric's narco sub. What kind of juice did James's new best friend have, anyhow?

MARIE:
GIVE ME SOME CLOTHES. NOW!

WHOEVER THE GUY on the deck of the submarine was, he was strong. He hauled James out of the water like he weighed nothing at all and then reached for me. Dropped me on the hull beside James, and then gestured for both of us to follow him.

James grabbed me by the arm and hauled me to the tube of metal that led into the sub. "Go," he said.

I looked into the tube and was relieved to see a ladder leading down into darkness. I slithered down the ladder, with James right behind me. The man who had saved us pushed us out of the way as soon as we landed on the lower deck, and scrambled back up the ladder. I heard the clang of a hatch closing, and then the man slid back down beside us.

"I got them both," he yelled. "Let's go!"

Everything lurched, and I stumbled forward, nearly falling into the guy's arms. Now, I was glad to be out of the water, really I was, but all I had on was James's soaking wet shirt, which really hid nothing at all, and he was ogling me.

"Get me a blanket or something!" I yelled, pushing out of his arms and covering myself as best I could. "Now!"

The man who had pulled us from the sea chuckled and then took off his sweater and handed it to me.

"Thanks," I said, and pulled it around me. It smelled like tobacco and sweat, but at least it covered me. More or less.

"You're welcome," he replied.

"And thanks for saving us," James said. "We would have drowned out there."

His words made my heart jump. "I thought you said we could just swim to the shore," I said. "Isn't that what you told me?"

"Well, what was I supposed to say?" he snapped. "Just give up, because we're going to die? You were freaking out. I had to calm you down so we stood any kind of a fighting chance."

"All right," I said, and pulled the smelly sweater around myself a little closer. "Fair point."

"Ric let us know you were in trouble," the man said. "We picked you up as a favour to him."

I blinked. "How did he know where we were?" I asked.

The man chuckled. "He used GPS through a pet tracker," he said. "You Americans and your pets."

"We're Canadian," I mumbled.

"Oh," James said at the same time. "So that's what it was."

"What are you talking about?" I asked.

"When we were in the water, and I was trying to get your dress off you," James said. "There was something attached to the top of the zipper. Looked like a key fob. That must've been it. I wonder when he attached that to your dress."

"When he hugged me," I said with a head shake. "After the wedding ceremony. I knew he'd hung on way too long."

"Well, I'm glad he did," James said. "Otherwise we'd still be on that yacht."

"Or dead," I said, and shuddered. "And now we're here," I continued, and looked around. "Where are we exactly?"

"Narco sub," Jimmy said, He appeared through the far wall next to the entrance to the conning tower. "Looks like they've got tons—and I mean tons—of cocaine on this thing."

"A narco what?" I gasped, and then shut my mouth when the man who'd so kindly pulled us out of the water glared at me like he was thinking that throwing me back would be a very good idea.

James quickly pulled me into his arms. "What's up?" he whispered into my hair.

"It's Jimmy," I whispered back.

"Oh," James said, and looked over at the man who'd saved us. "Where are you taking us?"

"We'll be meeting a fishing boat off the Canadian coast," he said. "They'll take you to shore, and then Ric will contact you."

I blinked. "Won't that take days?" I asked. "People are expecting us home tomorrow." I shut my eyes for a moment. "Today," I said. "They'll be expecting us home today."

"I can't do anything about that," the man said. "I have a cabin you can use. You'll be comfortable enough."

I was going to say something more—probably something stupid, because that seemed to be all that came out of my mouth lately—but James touched me on the arm and shook his head.

"That sounds good," he said.

"I'll try to find you some clothes," he said to me as he herded us before him down a narrow hallway that seemed to go on forever. "And some food, if you're hungry."

"Thank you," was all I said, finally taking a cue from James.

We followed him to a small door, and when he opened it, we entered. I wasn't surprised at all when I heard the door being locked behind us.

Jimmy floated into the cabin—which was actually nothing more than two bunk beds attached to the wall—and looked around. "The yacht was nicer," he finally said.

"At least it doesn't look like these guys are going to kill us," I replied, acidly. James glanced at me, but I just shook my head and then walked over to the lower bunk.

"I need to lie down," I said. "My head hurts really bad."

"Probably all the salt water," both of them said at exactly the same time.

"Whatever," I replied, and wrapped myself in the rough blanket folded on the end of the bunk.

I'd had enough. I just wanted the headache to go away, and this ongoing nightmare to stop.

I dropped onto the bunk, which was lumpy and hard, of course, and closed my eyes. I don't think anyone was more surprised than me, when I instantly fell asleep.

I WOKE UP alone in the cabin. A tee shirt and pair of dungarees hung over the bunk I was occupying and a bottle of water sat on the pillow next to my head.

I drank the water and then pulled on the clothes. Too big, but I made do. Then, I checked the door, and was surprised when it opened.

I heard men talking and laughing in the direction we'd come when we'd first been brought on board.

I looked for Jimmy, hoping he'd be able to give me some idea what was going on, but he wasn't around, so I padded down the hallway to the open area of the sub. James was sitting at a fold-out table with the two men who had rescued us. The table was covered with the remains of a meal, and James looked more relaxed than he had the whole time we were on holidays in Vegas.

"Marie?" he called from the table, and turned. "You found the clothes. Good. You hungry?"

"Yes," I said. "I am."

And I was. God help me, I ate with more appetite than I had even once in Sin City.

JIMMY:
FIVE DAYS IS A LONG TIME

WE WERE ON that sub for five days. I thought that Marie would lose her mind, because she didn't seem to be so good with just hanging around, but she didn't have a problem after she convinced the captain of the narco sub to contact Ric to let her sister know she was still alive.

I could tell James was surprised. Not that she'd talked Ivan into anything—that girl quickly had both him and the other crewman, Alejandro, wrapped around her little finger—but that she'd decided to contact her sister.

"Rhonda?" he'd asked. "Really? I thought you would have wanted to let Jasmine know. She is looking after Millie, after all."

"Hey," Marie said, with her patented eye roll. "Millie is your dog."

It didn't surprise me, though. Those girls had lost their mother not so long ago. Marie would have wanted to make sure not to cause her sister any more anguish.

That was what my brother Lloyd had done, when James's mother, Suzette, died. Even though he hadn't spoken to me since the day James dropped out of college, Lloyd called me to let me know what had happened, so I could tell James. Because by that time, James wasn't speaking to either of his parents.

That was my fault. I got that. But hell, I'd given James a decent life and a decent livelihood. At least I thought I had, until we were both sick to death of each other, and had each made plans to leave and never come back.

Looked like I taught him better than I thought.

Marie was willing to listen to me so I talked her ear off, because suddenly, I wanted to unload. I was tired. Tired past death of the weight of my history, and as long as she was willing to listen, I was willing to tell her everything.

I told her about the work I did for Ambrose Welch. And I told her about Rory.

"He was a cop, I think," I said. "You should look him up. He'll tell you everything."

She'd frowned at the name, like she knew it, but all she said was that she'd try to find him.

Then I told her about stealing James away from his parents, and how I felt sick all the time, because all I seemed to do was hurt the people who should have meant something to me.

"That was why I was going to leave," I said. "Rita had given me the out I needed, because I couldn't stand thinking about what he could have become, if I'd left him alone."

"You should tell him that," Marie said.

"I don't know how," I replied.

"Think about it. He needs to know."

We sat in silence for a few moments more, and then she turned to me. "Jimmy, you gotta tell me one thing. Why did you pick the Dunes? You stayed away from that place for a lot of years. Why did you go back?"

I stared at her for a long moment and then sighed. I'd lied to everybody about the Dunes. Told big stories about how important I'd been there, how connected I'd been. I'd told James those stories when he was growing up. Hell, I'd even told Ambrose Welch a story or two. But most of it had been horse shit to cover up the truth. Which was that the best I'd ever managed to do was get myself invited to a party or two with the inner circle, but then I'd screwed even that up, and got my ass kicked out.

I glanced at Marie, and almost gave her the same line, then let it go. What the hell. Might as well tell the truth. Finally.

"I got myself banned from the Dunes ten years ago," I muttered. "I wasn't ever supposed to go back to that place again."

Marie blinked. "Ten years?" she asked. "What did you do? Run a scam? Try to rip them off?"

"No," I muttered. "Nothing that *Ocean's Eleven*."

She looked at me blankly.

"The movie," I said. "You know. That movie about ripping off the casinos."

"Oh," she replied, and shrugged. "I've never seen it."

"Oh, well, all right then," I said. "I didn't try to rip them off, or run a scam on them. Not then. No, I did something really stupid, and it cost me, big time."

"What was it?" Marie asked. I could hear the impatience in her voice.

"I bedded one of Victor's partners' wives," I said. "Trina. No wait. Tina." I shrugged. "Something like that. Anyhow, her husband took a real exception to that, and Victor decided to teach me a lesson."

"Are you serious?" Marie asked. "What the hell were you thinking?"

"I was thinking that Tina—or Trina, or whatever—looked pretty fine," I said, and shrugged. "Last party I got invited to."

"I wouldn't doubt it," Marie said. "So, why did you go back?"

"What they did to me screwed me over big time in Vegas," I said. "I was basically blackballed everywhere. All I could do was gamble. Like a fucking tourist. I wanted to teach them all a lesson."

"So it was revenge."

"Yeah," I said. "Pathetic, huh?"

"Yeah," Marie said. "It was kind of pathetic."

"And it got Rita killed," I replied. "So it was way worse than pathetic."

"Rita got herself killed," Marie said. "Remember that. She ripped them off, and she got caught. That had nothing to do with you."

"That's not exactly true," I replied. "If I hadn't done what I had done she would have been long gone before they'd found out that she'd ripped them off."

"Maybe," she said. "But she put herself in harm's way. Remember, she killed you."

"Which I deserved," I whispered.

"No," she said. "You didn't deserve that. Nobody deserves that."

"At least Crystal's all right," I said, then started. "She is all right, isn't she?"

"I sure hope so," Marie said. "Ric said he'd get her somewhere safe, anyhow. But it looks like she's going to have to start her life all over again."

"From square one," I said, and Marie nodded.

"Yeah," she finally said. "I can have that effect on people and their lives."

"But you're going to be good for James," I said. "Right? You two won't have to restart your lives because of this. Will you?"

"No," she said, and then shrugged. "I hope not."

"Good," I said. "That's good."

I looked down at my hands and saw that my colour was much lighter than it had ever been. And I felt light, too. Like all I was made of was air. "What's going on?" I asked.

"Jimmy," Marie said, and stood. "You're going to move on. Looks like it's going to happen soon. All you have to do is—"

I shook my head and stood. "Nope," I said. "I'm not moving on now."

"But Jimmy," Marie said. "It's almost time. Don't fight it."

"No," I said again. "Not yet. I won't be moving on yet. I've got one more thing to do. Just one more."

"What is still holding you here?" she asked.

"I want to get back home," I replied. "I've got one more thing to show James. At home."

Marie looked at me and sighed. "This isn't good for you, Jimmy. You gotta know that."

"Maybe not," I said. "But that's how things are going to be."

I turned away from her and pushed my way through the wall of the cabin and through to the space where the cocaine was stored. It was quiet there. No life anywhere. A place where I could focus and pull myself back together.

I just had to get back to the office. I had to show James everything. I just hoped he'd understand, and forgive me.

But even if he didn't, I had to show him. I owed him that, at least.

MARIE:
THE HONEYMOON, I GUESS

WE HIT BAD weather off the coast of Haida Gwaii, and it took us a day and a half longer than it should have to meet the fishing boat and then get dropped off at Hooper Point on the BC coast.

Two guys in a Crown Vic picked us up at the dock at midnight on the seventh day, and drove us home. They quit talking to us after I made a joke about them driving an old-time cop car.

"Ric will be in touch," the driver said when they dropped us off at our office back in Edmonton.

They'd offered to take us to the apartment, but Jimmy was adamant that we go to the office first. I convinced James that it was the right thing to do, because Jimmy was barely hanging on to this plane. He needed to do whatever it was that was still holding him before he lost so much strength he wouldn't make it.

James wasn't thrilled, until he realized that Jimmy had something he wanted to show him. Something important.

We stood on the sidewalk and stared at each other, hardly able to believe that we were finally back in Edmonton. Finally safe.

Jimmy looked around and shook his head. "I never thought I'd see this town again," he muttered. "Doesn't look much different, does it?"

He'd lightened even further. Was almost clear, in fact. "Jimmy," I said to him. "We have to get upstairs, to the office. I think you better hurry."

303

When we got up the stairs, I grabbed the extra key from the top of the door jamb and flailed with the lock until James finally took it from my hand and opened the door. Then he picked me up in his arms and carried me over the threshold of the office.

"Hey, we're newlyweds," he said. "I'm supposed to do this, aren't I?"

"I guess," I said. "Now put me down."

We looked around the reception area but Jimmy wasn't there.

"Jimmy?" I called. "Where are you?"

"I'm here," he said. "In my—in James's office."

As James opened the door to his office, light poured over both of us. Jimmy was sitting by the first file cabinet and he was almost blinding because of the number of light bees just below his skin, pushing to get out.

"It's here," he mumbled, pointing at the bottom drawer. "It's right here."

"What are you looking for?" I asked, and opened the drawer. "A contract?"

"No," he said, and pointed. "Below that."

I closed the drawer and looked at the bottom of the cabinet. And then I saw it. Small bits of the grey paint had been chipped away at one edge. Like someone had hidden something behind it.

I tried to open it, but had no luck.

"Use this," James said, and handed me a letter opener from his desk. It worked perfectly, and soon I had the bottom of the cabinet open.

"They're in there," Jimmy said, and sighed. "They're all in there."

I slipped my index finger into the small opening and felt paper. Hooked it, and managed to slip it out.

"It's a letter," I said, then started. "It's addressed to Lloyd and Suzette Lavall. Your parents."

James plucked the envelope from my hand and stared at it. "What is this, Jimmy?" he asked.

"I wanted to let them know you were all right," Jimmy muttered. "I didn't have the courage to mail them after the first one came back 'Return to Sender'. But I wrote them, every month."

"Why did you do that?" I asked.

"Because I stole their only kid," he said.

I told James what his uncle had said and he shook his head. "You didn't steal me," he said. "You just offered me a job. I'm the one who left home."

"No," Jimmy breathed. "I wanted what Lloyd had. The life, the son." He shook his head. "I stole you, boy. And I can never be forgiven for that."

I watched as his light bees darkened and whirled, a kaleidoscope of guilt.

"Forgive him," I whispered to James. "Forgive him so he can move on."

James stared at the letter in his hand and then looked at me. "He just gave me a job," he said again. "The rest of it? That was all on me. I could have gone back anytime. But I wanted to stay here. With him. Jimmy, you did the best you could."

"And it was shit," Jimmy mumbled. "But thanks for that, boy."

The first light bee burst through his skin, and he slid down until he was lying flat on the carpet. "Tell Jim I like what he did with the place," he whispered. "It looks real nice."

JIMMY:
MOVING ON

I CONFESSED MY last big sin and slipped to the floor. I was so tired.

Marie was hovering over me, and I tried to push her away. Didn't work, of course, but I tried. "Gimme another minute," I whispered. "Just one more minute."

"I can't," she said and put her hand on my chest. "It's time for you to move on."

"You'll be good together," I sighed. I felt a warmth pushing its way through my skin and watched a little blob of light bumble its way from me to the wall and then disappear. "If you don't let someone like me mess it up."

"I won't," she said.

"Good," I said. "I wish I could help James with Ambrose Welch, but I can't. Maybe you can though. You need to talk to Rory. Think you can find him?"

Marie's face worked. "He's dead, Jimmy. I moved him on, months ago. He's gone."

If I had a heart it would have sunk through my shoes. "Well shit," I said. "He was my only connection to the cops."

"Maybe not," Marie said. "He was haunting Sylvia Worth. The cop he was having the affair with. She asked me to move him on, so I did. Maybe he told her something."

"Could be," I said. "Pillow talk and all that."

"I'll find out," she said. "As soon as we get home."

307

It wasn't perfect, but at least it was something. "Good," I said. "That's real good."

"We'll be all right, Jimmy," Marie said. "Heck, we both deserve a happily ever after. Don't we?"

"You do," I said, my voice whisper thin. "Absolutely."

I felt a rush and watched in wonder as the lights flew from me everywhere.

My last thought was, *this is almost as beautiful as the Vegas skyline.*

Almost.

MARIE:
LIFE AFTER UNCLE JIMMY

"HE'S GONE," I said to James, who was still staring at the letter in his hand. "He wanted us to get hold of Rory. So he could help us deal with Ambrose Welch."

"Who's Rory?" James asked, then looked at me. "You look like you need a glass of water."

"Rory was a cop," I said. "And he was also Sylvia Worth's boyfriend. He died and I moved him on. Remember?"

"Oh. Right." Then he frowned. "So Uncle Jimmy was working with the police?"

"Or Rory was a dirty cop and they were both working for Ambrose Welch," I said. "I honestly don't know."

James snorted soft laughter. "Trust Uncle Jimmy to leave us with one more mystery," he said. "I guess we could ask Sylvia." Then he shook his head. "How can we ask her something like that?"

"I don't have a clue," I said.

"Neither do I," he muttered, then stood. "I'll get you some water."

He disappeared through the office door, and I lay back on the carpet and stared at the ceiling. I was frigging exhausted and wished he'd hurry with the water.

Then I heard the outer door to the office open and struggled to sit up.

"Who's out there?" I yelled. James didn't answer, so I pulled myself to my feet and strode through the door.

James was staring at Ric, frozen, with my glass of water in his hand. I walked over to him, took the water, and downed it. Then I hooked my arm around James's waist and smiled at Ric.

"Thanks for saving us," I said. "That was real James Bond of you, getting us out of that jam with an actual submarine."

"Yeah, well, what can I say?" he said. "I knew it was on its way to Canada with our shipment, so I figured what the hell." He grinned. "But now you owe me big time."

"I guess we do," I said.

He walked over and dropped a small package on my desk. "Here's a burner phone for you to use," he said. "And I saved your ID. Victor had your room cleared by the time we got back, but Ollie went through the garbage and found it." He grinned. "You owe him, too."

"Is Crystal safe?" I asked.

"Safe as houses," Ric said. Then he turned to James. "You all right, Lavall?"

"I'm good," James mumbled. But he didn't look good. He looked sick.

"Glad to hear it," Ric said. "Because the honeymoon's over. You go to work tomorrow."

"Tomorrow?" James asked.

"Yep," Ric said. "Tomorrow." He looked over at me, and then pointed at the old-fashioned answering machine on my desk. "Looks like you got some messages. You should check them."

"I will," I said. "Thanks."

"You want a ride to your place?" he asked. "I'll take you there, if you want."

"No," James said. "We're good."

"You're sure?" Ric asked again.

"Absolutely," I said.

"All right," he said. "If you're sure."

He finally walked to the door, and was gone. I tottered to the door and listened as he rattled down the stairs, then turned to James.

"Jesus," I said. "We owe drug dealers. What are we going to do?"

"Looks like I'm going to work," James said.

"What have you gotten yourself into?" I muttered.

"A big mess, probably," he said. "But I'm definitely in. With a little more information, we'll be able to bring everything down. We're talking an international drug ring, Marie. Remember that."

"If you say so," I said, and pushed a button on the answering machine. Ric was right. There were a bunch of messages, but we only listened to one.

"Hi, you two." Sylvia Worth's voice sounded tired, but then she always sounded tired. "I know you're coming home tomorrow, but I just wanted to warn you that Ambrose Welch has been released. I don't even know if there's going to be a trial. So you might want to watch your backs. Well, at least you, Marie. I've heard he's still pretty pissed about the eye."

There was a short pause, and I turned and stared at James, horrified.

"Anyhow," Sylvia's voice continued, "That's all the bad news I've got. Hope you had a good holiday. I frigging love Vegas, you lucky dogs. Call me. We'll do coffee and you can tell me all about it."

I dropped into the desk chair, feeling sick, and fumbled with the machine, finally managing to shut it off.

"Well, that explains why I start work tomorrow, doesn't it?" James's voice sounded cold, and when I looked at him, I honestly couldn't read his face. "Now it begins."

"What begins?" I asked.

"The end game," he said. "We're going to bring this to an end."

The End

ABOUT THE AUTHOR

E.C. (Eileen) Bell's debut paranormal mystery, *Seeing the Light* (2014) won the BPAA award for Best Speculative Fiction Book of the Year, and was shortlisted for the Bony Blithe Award for Light Mystery. The rest of the books in the series have all been shortlisted for awards (look at her go!), with the fourth in the series, *Dying on Second* (2017) winning the Bony Blithe Award for Light Mystery.

When she's not writing, she's living a fine life in her round house with her husband and their two dogs. (Only one of the dogs has made it into her books so far, so don't tell the other one, OK? She doesn't want to hurt his feelings.)

Want to know more? Check out her website: www.eileenbell.com